OUT OF TIME

"When I heard about that elf ship," Escargot stated, "I knew there was trouble ahead. There was only one reason for the ship to be upriver—they was looking for the watch. And they found it, too, the hard way. This watch freezes everything. Just stops things dead. Lets a chap do what he will, if he has that watch.

"Then one day I ran into Miles the Magician. He said that the watch tells time. I said that every watch does that, if it ain't broken. He said that with any other watch, it's *you* who tells time by it. With this, it's the watch that *tells* the time. Do you follow me?"

Jonathan supposed so, and nodded.

"You don't think they had time before they had a watch to tell it, do you? Well, that was the watch. And there's one man who should run it and a dwarf who shouldn't but does. Lucky for us he ain't had it very long. If you understand the watch, you can run it ahead and you can run it back and you can stop it from running at all. When I first used it, it didn't seem to have no effect farther than about ten feet. When I sold it, I could slow the whole show down and stop it for twenty-five feet around.

"But Selznak—there's no telling what tricks he's been up to with the thing!"

By James P. Blaylock
Published by Ballantine Books:

THE ELFIN SHIP

THE DISAPPEARING DWARF

THE ELFIN SHIP

James P. Blaylock

A Del Rey Book

BALLANTINE BOOKS • NEW YORK

A Del Rey Book
Published by Ballantine Books

Copyright © 1982 by James P. Blaylock

All rights reserved under International and Pan-American Copyright Conventions. Published in the United States by Ballantine Books, a division of Random House, Inc., New York, and simultaneously in Canada by Random House of Canada Limited, Toronto.

Library of Congress Catalog Card Number: 82-3998

ISBN 0-345-29491-2

Printed in Canada

First Edition: August 1982
Sixth Printing: February 1988

Cover art by Darrell K. Sweet

TO VIKI

Contents

"And beyond the Wild Wood again?" he asked: *"Where it's all blue and dim, and one sees what may be hills or perhaps they mayn't, and something like the smoke of towns, or is it only cloud-drift?"*

"Beyond the Wild Wood comes the Wide World," said the Rat. *"And that's something that doesn't matter, either to you or me. I've never been there, and I'm never going, nor you either, if you've got any sense at all."*

Kenneth Grahame
The Wind in the Willows

Chapter 1

Gilroy Bastable and the Airship

❈

SUMMER had somehow passed along into autumn, as it will, and with October came a good bit of rain. And rain, isn't at all bad—as long, that is, as you're not caught out in it. The blue skies and white bits of clouds had gone south like geese some weeks back and rolling gray masses had taken their place overhead.

A deep rumble, something between the bellow of a giant and the echoing crack of a rock sailing into a canyon, could be heard away up the valley. It appeared from the village as if the green slopes of the mountains merged there where the River Oriel finally fell away into the sea, but that was only because it was so far away. The river, as broad by then as the sky itself, had worked away at the mountains for an age, and although you couldn't tell it from Twombly Town, the valley opened up beyond the mountains into green rolling hills which continued to roll smack into the sea.

So the leaves were falling slowly in the cool breezes, and of those left on the trees few were green. Most were brown and red and gold, and when they piled up on the ground and were rained on, they smelled awfully good, although it was a sort of lonesome, musty smell.

Great gray clouds and ominous rumbles of thunder usually meant that rain wasn't a long way off. As Jonathan Bing sat in his old wicker chair which had pretty much gone to bits in the weather, he thought of all of this business about the changing seasons. He could smell the musty odor of the forest which wasn't more than a stone's throw off to his left, and he could see three lone boats on the dark river below the village all pulling along toward shore and shelter. The first drops splashed down heavily, as if warning that here was a serious rain; they were followed by a steadily thickening curtain of drops until the shingled roof above his head rattled merrily.

Jonathan nodded in approval, patted his dog, and took a long swallow of the hot punch he'd prepared against this very eventuality. Something about the simple fact that there were people on the river, soaked, no doubt, to their toes, made his punch taste punchier and his woolen coat feel more snug than it might have. High time, he thought, to light his pipe. And so he did, afterward puffing away on the thing as if the rising smoke would form a misty barrier against the wind and rain.

His old dog, Ahab, named after the seventh king of The-Land-Beyond-the-River, was a fat sort of a dog. He didn't, in fact, look doggish at all. His head seemed much too big for his body and was round as a plate. His eyes, which appeared a trifle piglike, were set off on either side a bit too much—as if Ahab had been caught facing a stiff wind and had had his face pushed about. He was enormously fat and was white with speckles of odd shades of gray and brown all over, and he had short little legs. His legs moved wonderfully fast, and he could have run rings around any rat in the village bakery. He was, however, on moderately good terms with rats and so probably wouldn't run rings around them anyway. Jonathan used to joke that he had come upon Ahab playing at cards with three or four rats and a crow in the barn once, just to indicate Ahab's good nature.

He and Ahab had lived in the village for a long time, as had almost everyone else there. Jonathan made cheeses. He was known about town as the Master Cheeser, or simply Cheeser which wasn't at all strange.

Beyond his house, about halfway up to the dense line of green at the edge of the forest, were the cheesehouses: one was a smokehouse and the other simply a house for curing cheeses. If Jonathan needed a smoked cheese he'd say, "I'm going to the smokehouse." If he wanted something else, a nice cheddar or a carroway seed cheese, he'd say, "I'm going for a cheese," and let it go at that.

During the months of October and November Jonathan prepared great circular white cheeses made of goat's milk and raisins and walnuts and the essences of ripe fruit which he kept secret. The custom was to slice one of these amazing cheeses up on Christmas Eve and eat it with fruitcakes and sherried trifles and roly-poly puddings and, most importantly, honeycakes. In mid November, Jonathan loaded a boat with raisin cheeses and floated down the river to Willowood Station where he sold them to traders who sailed away west to sell them in turn to the field dwarfs along the coast.

These dwarfs, anxiously awaiting their cheeses, prepared honeycakes in huge quantities, some for themselves, some for the elves that lived above in the Elfin Highlands, and some to trade for the round raisin cheeses which had come downriver from Twombly Town. Honeycakes, made with pecans and cinnamon and, of course, honey and a dozen strange grains and spices and good sorts of things that the people upriver in Jonathan's village knew nothing about, were as much a part of the holiday feast as were raisin cheeses.

Jonathan had contemplated, one afternoon over his pipe, trading the secret of his raisin cheeses for the secret of the honeycakes thereby making the November trading unnecessary. But the good thing about thinking over a pipe is that it takes some time to puff and tamp and light and puff, puff, puff again, giving time to get through a problem from back to front. This idea of trading secret recipes, Jonathan decided, was a bad one. It would no doubt ruin more than it would accomplish. And besides, there was a certain feeling of pride, not a bad pride at all, in being the only person responsible for something as wonderful as raison cheeses.

But it was getting on into autumn, and it was a gray rainy day for the people of the valley. Jonathan drained his mug of punch and tapped out his pipe against the bottom of his shoe. It was time, decidedly time, to be about cooking supper. As far as he was concerned, all the rain in the sky could fall and he wouldn't care. He'd rather enjoy it because there was no place he had to go and nothing he had to do but eat a good meal, read a bit, and go to sleep. Nothing is better than having absolutely nothing to do when it's raining outside. Part of you might say, "Weed the garden," or "Slap a coat of paint on the cheesehouse," and another part of you can reply, "I can't. It's raining outside fit to shout," and then all of you can go back to doing nothing.

Jonathan stood up, walked just to the edge of the porch—just to where the raindrops ended—and stood for a moment watching the smoke tumble up out of a dozen chimneys scattered about the hillside and down toward the center of town. Padding along beside him, Ahab straightened up, rolled his eyes, and growled deep in his throat as if he'd heard a suspicious but undefinable noise.

Now Ahab never growled, especially down deep in his throat, unless something was genuinely amiss—such as someone crawling in through the window of the cheesehouse or if a bear had come prowling out of the forest. So Jonathan Bing looked lively. He craned his neck to peer around the corner of the house but saw nothing. To be on the safe side, he whispered, "At him, boy!" to Ahab who simply with his peculiar looks could frighten almost anything save, perhaps, a bear. But Ahab, after sticking his nose out into the storm, lay down and pretended to sleep, opening one eye now and again to see if Jonathan was taken in.

As he stood there listening, a low humming sound gradually became audible from way off in the gray sky. It was a drone like a bee might make who was busy at a flower, and it was a lonely and sad sound. Jonathan had the feeling for a moment that he was a young boy standing alone on just such a rainy afternoon in a grassy clearing in the woods. He didn't *think* of that—he just felt it all over and it made his heart race and his stomach seem empty. It was then, when he remembered the rain and the woods, that he recognized the sound.

He put one hand over his brow to shade his eyes— (simply out of habit, of course, since there was no sun)— then squinted for a moment before being able to make out the tiny dark blurred shape against the clouds. It was a flying machine, an elfin airship, launched from the mountaintops and whirring along miles above the valley, almost in the clouds themselves if that were possible.

Jonathan watched in wonder, this being the first flying machine he'd seen since that day in the meadow many years before. And even though it was just a tiny dark spot hovering in the sky, it was the most beautiful thing he'd seen—more beautiful than the emerald globe, big as your head, in the village museum or the view through the giant golden kaleidoscope that sat like a great cannon at the gates of the village for anyone in the world to look through. And just as it seemed as if the airship was drawing closer, just when he fancied he could see batlike wings jutting out from either side, the ship sailed silently into a cloud and was gone.

"To be able to see the inside of a cloud!" thought Jonathan. "Yoicks!" But he knew immediately that "Yoicks" didn't quite capture what he felt. He envisioned great lakes of crystal rainwater in there with rainbow-colored fishes swimming through them and elfin airships sailing overhead. Then it occurred to him that such fishes would, as often as not, swim right through the bottom of the clouds like the rain did and find themselves in a predicament. And after all, he'd never seen any rainbow-colored fish sailing out of the sky, so it was all fairly unlikely. But he'd like to see the inside of a cloud anyway, lakes and fishes or no.

He waited for a moment for the airship to reappear, and when it didn't, he took his mug and his book and wandered inside to cook up some sort of stew. "It's a funny day to be out sailing in the sky," Jonathan thought. "Not at all a pleasant day for that sort of thing. Something must be afoot." But the ways of the elves were always a mystery, and mysteries are almost always better left unsolved. After all, the fun of a mystery is that it is one.

The sun went down and it was a terribly dark night with thunder cracking and clouds whirling overhead caught in a frantic wind that couldn't seem to make up its mind which way to blow next. Jonathan piled the fireplace with oak logs, and, full from supper, slumped back in a great fat armchair and put his feet up onto a footstool. He looked at Ahab who was curled up before the hearth and considered the possibility of teaching him to smoke a pipe. But the idea, he quickly saw, wasn't a good one. Dogs might not go for pipes anyway, being dogs, and so the whole plan seemed a washout. He puffed away thinking about what a grand thing it was to be able to enjoy a good book and to be warm and dry and full of good food and have the finest fire and armchair in the village. "Better than being a thousand kings," he thought, but he didn't entirely know what he meant by it.

He'd dozed off after having barely begun *The Tale of the Goblin Wood*, by G. Smithers of Brompton Village, when someone began pounding away at his door, causing Ahab to leap about, awake but still embroiled in a strange dream involving toads. Jonathan swung open the door and there, shaking the water from his coat, stood Gilroy Bastable, Jonathan's nearest neighbor and mayor of Twombly Town.

He had a look about him that seemed to indicate annoyance, an attitude that was not surprising, for he was splashed with mud, and his hair, which grew mostly on the sides of his head, spiraled away in either direction like two curly mountain peaks turned sideways. He wore a heavy greatcoat and a pair of immense woolen gloves which smelled a bit gamey as wool does when it gets wet. Mayor Bastable, clearly, had been in the thick of the storm.

Jonathan waved him in and shut the door against the cold wind. First it was airships, then Gilroy Bastable, all out under peculiar circumstances. "H'lo there, Gilroy! Quite a night out, wouldn't you say? Could be described as a wet one if it came to descriptions, don't you think?"

Gilroy Bastable seemed to say something but his meaning was unclear, his teeth, somehow, got in the way. Ahab, having realized that there was no threat from toads, wandered over and laid his head on Bastable's boot, intending to sleep. He discovered, however, that the shoe was too wet and muddy to be altogether comfortable so he padded back to his spot before the fire.

"Filthy night out; that's what I call it. Full of mud holes and hurricanes. Blew my hat into the river. I saw it with my own eyes right here in my head. Hat sails off spinning like the widow's windmill, turns round the church steeple twice, then lands smack and was gone in the river. Brand new hat. Hideous night."

"Does make you feel a bit snug though when you're in out of it," said Jonathan.

"Snug!" the mayor shouted, mainly through his nose. "My hat's gone downriver!"

"Unfortunate. Very bad business indeed," said Jonathan, who was sympathetic. But it was as much his night as it was the mayor's and he was determined that nothing should spoil it. He hung Bastable's coat and muffler near the fire to dry, and with a good deal of struggling between the two of them they managed to pry his boots off and set them beneath the coat and muffler. Ahab awoke momentarily and, mistaking the lumps of boots for something else, considered eating them. But he thought better of it and nodded off again.

Bastable sat across from Jonathan's chair, calming down due to the effects of the fire. A good fire, as you know, is second only to hot punch in the way of soothing. Jonathan walked out to the kitchen and soon emerged with a platter and two steaming mugs. He set the works down next to the mayor and popped out and back in again with the most amazing cheese, all red and orange and yellow swirls and round like Ahab's head. Gilroy Bastable, already wading into the punch, was astounded.

"Aye!" he bubbled. "What's that! A cheese, I believe, or my hat's not downriver." He looked at it closely and poked an inquisitive finger at it as it lay there. Jonathan cut a slice or two, and the mayor, raising his mug and nodding his head, tied into it manfully. "Why, I'm a codfish!" he said through a mouthful of cheese, his manners having gone out the window due to the heartiness of the thing.

"There's a taste here I know. Port wine, I believe it is. Am I mistaken, or what?"

"No, sir," said Jonathan. "Port wine it is, and not your dog-faced port from Beezle's market either. I made this with Autumn Auburn from the delta."

"No!"

"Yes, sir," said Jonathan. "And with a little of this and a thimbleful of that, I think you'll agree, it's just the thing on a night such as this."

The mayor, finally, had to say that it was, and if all had gone along those lines much longer, he would have forgotten about his escaped hat and been convinced, as was Jonathan, that the storm outside was one of the finest he'd encountered.

He pushed down a last mouthful, however, and his eyes clouded over like the skies outside. The corners of his mouth turned down and stuck there, causing Jonathan to fear that part of his cheese had gone bad and that the mayor had wandered into it. Such was not the case though. Gilroy Bastable had suddenly remembered why he had braved the storm and lost his hat and slopped mud up and down his trouser legs and over his greatcoat. He had come with grim sorts of news.

"See here, Jonathan," he began in a tone so filled with authority that it woke Ahab from a deep sleep. "I haven't just come slogging over here for a lark, you know. No indeed."

"Oh?" said Jonathan, rather disappointed. He much preferred larks to serious business.

"No, sir! I've come about the traders."

"Which traders are these now?" asked Jonathan, not really concerned yet but being polite out of regard for the mayor, who seemed about to pop from the importance of his mission.

Old Bastable looked at Jonathan bug-eyed. "Why which traders do ye suppose, Master Cheeser? Do we have such a crowd of 'em that we can pick and choose which ones we'd wade knee-deep through a hurricane to chat about?"

Jonathan had to admit that the mayor was right although he could see no reason to bluster about it. "That would be the traders of Willowood then," he said, putting on a serious look. "Have they been caught dipping into the cargo again? Trading to the linkmen for brandy and hen's teeth?"

"Worse than that," replied old Bastable, leaning forward in his chair and squinting like a schoolteacher. "They've absconded—disappeared!"

"They've what!" cried Jonathan, interested finally in the mayor's story. "How?"

"Why walked away, I suppose. Or, more likely, sailed away downriver. Willowood is deserted. No one's there."

In truth, Jonathan was only a week or so away from his own annual journey from Hightower to the trading station at Willowood Village where the traders would give him a note for the Christmas cheese, transport it downriver to the edge of the sea, and return with honeycakes. He'd accomplish all of that, that is, if there *were* traders at Willowood. But why, one might ask, would anyone suppose otherwise? And it was just such a question which Jonathan posed to Gilroy Bastable.

"Because word's come up from Hightower," said Bastable. "They found the Willowood Station looted and smacked up. Deserted, it is, and the wharf is gone. Or at least half of it is—all off down the river. Whole place gone to smash. Now, Wurzle says it's pirates and Beezle says it's flood, and the bunch from Hightower say the traders went downriver to the sea just out of lunacy."

"Like lemmings," offered Jonathan.

"Just so," said Bastable. "And me, well I don't pretend to know, but they've gone, and that's sure."

"I don't like the sound of this," Jonathan said ominously. "Something's afoot. I saw an airship today."

"In a storm like this? Very odd, an airship in a storm like this."

"Just what I said myself. And then here you come, out in the rainy night like a duck."

Bastable was at a loss for words. He could see that, as he'd hoped, his news had startled Jonathan, but he wasn't sure of all this duck business. "See here," he began in a mildly questioning tone. "I'm not sure that ducks—"

But Jonathan cut him off short, although under normal circumstances he wouldn't consider doing so. "My cheeses!" he cried, and Ahab, noting the perilous tone in his master's voice was up and racing toward the kitchen at a gallop, toppling a chair, setting the rest of the ball of cheese into flight, and careening off a stout wooden bread-cupboard before becoming sensible again. He wandered back across the wooden floorboards of the kitchen and peered around the sideboard at the two men who sat astounded, gaping at him.

"The news has rather upset your hound, Jonathan," said Gilroy Bastable, retrieving the cheese and gouging out a hunk the size of his nose. "And well it should. Do you know, Jonathan, what the word about town is?"

"Not a bit," said the Cheeser.

"The cry goes round, my man, that you're a stout enough lad to sail downriver yourself, all the way to Seaside with your cheeses and back again with cakes and elfin gifts."

"Stout lad, is it!" shouted Jonathan, astounded at the suggestion and calculating the time it would take to make such a journey—weeks, surely. "It's a fool's idea; that's what it is."

"But the people will have no cakes!" protested Gilroy Bastable.

"Then let them eat bread," Jonathan almost replied before wisely reconsidering. It *would* be a sad holiday without honeycakes, not to mention elfin gifts for the children. But then again, the very idea of sailing down the Oriel through the dark hemlock forests to the sea frightened him.

Bastable could see that Jonathan was in a turmoil and knew that turmoils are bad things to go butting into, so he let the matter stand. "Well," he said, "*I'm* not one to make such statements, for a man has to do what he has to do. I think you'll agree to that."

Jonathan gurgled a reply and poked his forefinger into the cheese, stabbing little craters into its surface until it sat on its plate like a moon plucked from a miniature sky—half a moon, that is to say, for Gilroy Bastable had eaten the other half and, until he saw that Jonathan had fingered it so completely, he was prepared to shove down the remaining half.

"I say," said Gilroy, "you've gone and ruined the cheese."

"What? Me?" Jonathan said, lost in thought. "Oh, yes. I suppose I have. Poked it full of holes, haven't I?" He picked up the punctured lump of yellow, tore off a sizable hunk and rolled it toward Ahab who, it seemed, could smell it approaching even though he was again deeply lost in sleep, dreaming this time about finding a great treasure made of beef bones and ice cream, the two great passions of a dog's life. Somehow the ball of cheese became connected to the idea of ice cream in his dream, and Ahab scooped it up and, still asleep, mashed it about in his mouth for a moment before the odd flavor and weird texture of the cheese made him lurch awake, fearful that he'd been poisoned. There are few things more unpleasant than innocently eating or drinking one thing when you mistakenly suppose you've gotten hold of something else.

Once awake, however, Ahab forgot about the treasure dream and, being a cheeser's dog, quickly determined the nature of that which he ate. He swallowed heartily and, as his master and Gilroy Bastable were clumping toward the door, Ahab thought it a first-rate idea to have another go at the last chunk of wrecked cheese on the plate.

Outside, the wind was still blowing in fits and gusts that sailed right down the center of the valley between the mountains. The forest was a black line against the wild sky. When there was a break in the clouds, the moonlight would creep out across patches of the valley and, as if by enchantment, the dark fringe of the woods would cast wavering shadows along the hillsides. Rocks and bushes and clumps of raspberry vine that were familiar and friendly in the light of day soon became strange and forbidding night shapes, weirdly lit and twisted beneath the moon. Jonathan was glad it was Gilroy Bastable and not himself who had to trudge away through the nighttime. At least the rain had stopped. If the wind continued to howl, it would pursue the last of the clouds to the ocean by morning, and the day would dawn clear beneath a cool autumn sun.

The mayor assured Jonathan that this business about river travel would surely be brought up in the morning. The next day was market day, and a meeting was planned at the Guildhall to discuss the Willowood doings and the fate of the holiday celebrations.

After returning to his chair by the fire, Jonathan picked up *The Tale of the Goblin Wood* and tried to read. He pretended that the issue of sailing to sea was closed and that his unconcerned reading proved it. But he merely looked at words on the page and found that after working through a page or two, he hadn't any idea of what he had read. "A stout enough lad," he said aloud to himself, and Ahab, who was sitting in the chair opposite, naturally thought it was he who was being spoken to and was half afraid that Jonathan would scold him over the disappeared cheese.

"Stout lad is it? Surely," thought Jonathan, "I *am* the Master Cheeser, and I *do* have a fine little raft, and I am, I suppose, the man in the village best suited for an adventure such as this. Still, weeks of travel through the long miles of empty river . . ." The proposal, a bit much for the Cheeser, was best pondered by the light of day. Late at night sometimes, things seemed deeper and smokier than they were.

The hour finally arrived for Jonathan Bing to turn the lamp down, bolt the door, and crawl into bed. Ahab elected to spend the night on his pillow by the embers of the fire and was lost immediately in his dreams.

Chapter 2

A Good Month for Traveling

❈

A<small>HAB</small> awoke before Jonathan did because the fire had burned itself out, and the morning was frightfully cold. Jonathan was covered with blankets topped by a feather comforter that came up to his chin and covered his bed all the way to the floor. He wore his cloth nightcap and striped nightshirt and, all in all, he was as warm as a honeycake in a dwarf's oven. Ahab climbed onto the bed and began burrowing beneath the covers pretending to search for some lost object. Awaking with a shout at the sudden cold thing that had crept into his bed, Jonathan slid over far to one side and let Ahab have the other.

He couldn't fall asleep again, however, because of the ticking of his pocketwatch which lay nearby on the table. The harder he tried to ignore the noise, the louder it seemed to be. Then the bottom of his foot, which should have been feeling warm and content, began to itch and no mere scratching would suffice; it wanted to be up and about. But Jonathan was far too snug for any such foolishness. Then just when he'd managed to ignore the pocketwatch and the itch in his foot, Ahab set in to snore like a grizzly bear and began to flail his legs about. He was lost in a very active dream in which he seemed to be chasing a boatload of funny little men wearing tall hats along the banks of a river.

Jonathan, in a rage—not a wild rage, but one of those mild, morning rages—flew out of bed. Just as well, for the bells in the village struck seven times, and if he wished to be at the Guildhall by eight-thirty and have a load of cheeses with him to boot, he'd best make tracks.

His first duty each morning was to put the coffee on the stove. He ground a handful of dark, oily coffee beans, measured out a third of a cup of grounds, and threw them into the botton of a porcelain-coated coffee pot which he filled three-fourths to the top with cold water. Jonathan then set about boiling another pan of water for oatmeal porridge and slicing wheat bread for toast. Soon the coffee water started to bubble and steam, and when it was just set to boil, he took the pot off the stove to let the coffee steep. Its rich smell filled the kitchen, and there was nothing for it but that Jonathan should have a cup at once. As he was enjoying his toast and porridge and peach jam and sugared coffee, Ahab wandered in from the bedroom. Barely awake, he stretched deeply and stood by the table eyeing the slices of buttered toast. Jonathan tore off a piece, smeared a dab of jam on it, and tossed it to Ahab, who found the morsel very good indeed. Together, they decided on having another.

Breakfast finished, Jonathan trudged up the gravel path to the cheesehouse and pulled his wagon out from beneath its covering. With Ahab trotting alongside or resting now and again just inside the door, Jonathan carried out some two or three dozen cheeses of various shapes and sizes including a half dozen crocks of creamed cheese and three of the round swirly cheeses that he and the mayor had picked at the night before. Goat's milk cheeses covered with rock salt hung from the ceiling, and there were wedges of fancy cheeses made with onions and bacon and sardines. Before long he had the wagon loaded and was off down the hill toward town, marveling at the clear sky and the thin crusts of frost on the rooftops and on the deep, still river that sailed along below on its way to the sea. At some point during his reveries, his wagon shook and suddenly grew heavier. When he looked over his shoulder, Jonathan discovered that Ahab had crawled up onto the rear of the cart and fallen asleep among the cheeses.

The Guildhall was bustling with activity. A score of the sort who take everything very seriously were shouting and pounding their fists into open palms and clearing their throats to make everyone note that something important was being said. Old Beezle of Beezle's Dry Goods and General Merchandise was red-faced; his spectacles kept sliding away off the tip of his nose. He maintained, in a loud voice, that Willowood Station had been demolished by flood. He had, he said, scientific proof that the sorts of levees and piers built at Willowood could not have stood the onslaught of swollen rivers over the course of many seasons. If those present would just pay attention to the diagrams and charts he'd brought along, the whole matter would be clarified and the people of Twombly Town could set about fortifying their own banks against the same eventuality.

All in all, the villagers appeared to be uninterested in Mr. Beezle, mainly because he brought the same charts and diagrams to town meetings every time the rainy season began. His wonderful drawings of what looked like medieval fortifications were written all over with large numbers and words like "stress load" and "flow value" and "whirl schute"—words which sounded marvelous and important.

Old Wurzle, the researcher, was also carrying on. As Jonathan poked his head in through the door he could hear Professor Wurzle saying, "We've seen your piers and levees, Mr. Beezle. We've seen your piers and levees until they've given us the pip!" Even though the Professor's comments were made in a loud voice, Mr. Beezle didn't seem to hear them. Professor Wurzle, as a consequence, repeated the part about having gotten the pip and added, as a capper, that he was a "man of science" and that Mr. Beezle was a greengrocer. But, as far as Twombly Town and perhaps the whole valley was concerned, Professor Wurzle *was* fairly scientific. He had a laboratory filled with apparatus and with devices continually bubbling and whistling.

But the Professor's main accomplishment was that he was a historian. He knew the history of Twombly Town and of most of the families living there, and it was even rumored he had once climbed into the mountains in the east and lived with the Light Elves for a month or so. But that was thirty or forty years ago, and almost nobody remembered much about the incident anymore. What they did remember was that Wurzle, while researching the mysteries of Stooton Slough, a water lily-choked swamp far below Willowood Station, had come across the hulk of a very old and very beautiful sailing ship—rather like a sloop—mired in the rushes.

The figurehead and three masts with a few tattered bits of stiff and crusted canvas were visible above the stagnant water and pond lilies of the swamp. The figurehead itself was carved in the semblance of a frightful dragon with furled wings. In either eye was a great jewel, one a ruby and the other an emerald. The masts themselves were minutely carved with odd runes and hieroglyphs. Wurzle's intention was to cut off all that was above water and haul it back upriver to Twombly Town.

He realized, of course, that such a feat would require a barge and tools and ropes and the help of several men, so he returned to Willowood and found three traders and a raft. The four men set out, although it was late in the season, and hadn't floated halfway down to Stooton-on-River when a great storm overtook them and forced them ashore. For two days the men huddled in a cavern above the banks, the masts and sails of their own raft having been reduced to rubbish by the wind and rain. Finally two of the traders struck out overland for Willowood. When the storm cleared, Wurzle and the last trader, who had an enormous nose and the unlikely name of Flutesnoot, continued on Wurzle's raft which had somehow survived the storm, to see what they could see.

To poor Wurzle's dismay, the ruins of the mysterious sloop had gone to bits in the storm and there was nothing at all jutting up through the swamp lilies which floated purple and yellow on the surface of the water. The two men probed below the dark surface, but found nothing. Whereupon Mr. Flutesnoot, having come so far on a wild goose chase, began to complain.

First he grumbled that a man had to be a lunatic to journey out after enchanted sailing ships. Then he moaned that he supposed the money Wurzle offered wasn't half worth the trouble. He had, he said, eight little children, all wearing the same pair of shoes in shifts, and his wife had certain problems with her joints. Finally, he seemed to hint that it would be only fair that the Professor pay him the salary he'd promised the two deserters and, "Cut 'em out," as he put it.

Just about then, both men were wading in a shallows several hundred feet below the mouth of the slough when Wurzle saw the flash of green in among the rocks. He plunged in and, after dredging about for a moment, plucked up the emerald eye of the dragon. Two more days of searching and sifting through sand and pebbles, brought forth two strawberry-size rubies and a three-foot-long fragment of one of the carved masts lodged in a stand of rushes plus another curious elf device which was altogether unidentifiable. The Professor gave the two rubies to Mr. Flutesnoot, who returned to Willowood and, on the strength of his adventure, was promptly elected mayor.

Professor Wurzle brought the faceted emerald eye back to Twombly Town where he graciously contributed it to the museum. The section of mast he studied for several years, deciphering runes, puzzling out hieroglyphs. He finally determined that the carvings told the story of an entire nation of piratical elves living on some far distant Oceanic Isle, thousands of leagues from the coast of the field dwarfs. Why their sloop had sailed upriver and why it had been left deserted and how long ago all of this had come to pass were mysteries.

The meeting took up the better part of the morning. Almost everyone there had something powerfully important to say, or at least thought he did. Beezle had his say; Professor Wurzle had his; then Gilroy Bastable made it clear half a dozen times that *he* couldn't say one way or another but that everyone, as far as he could see, should do his duty. The high, open-timbered roof of the old Guildhall fairly shook with the tumult while Ahab slept outside, guarding the cheeses and dreaming about roaming through subterranean caverns in pursuit of gingerbread cookies.

Jonathan remained silent throughout even though broad hints were dropped here and there concerning the necessity of saving the holiday celebrations whether or not there were traders at Willowood Station. In fact, Jonathan had already made up his mind. The previous night while staring into the embers of his fire, he had chosen his course of action. Without question, adventure was on the horizon, gesturing to him like a forest nymph—his fate led downriver to the sea. He had heard stories of the fogbound coast and of the great fish and sea monsters that frolicked in seaweed gardens. Such tales held a certain appeal for him, although he, like most of the people of Twombly Town could be easily satisfied. Though they loved beyond anything to be told tales of travel to distant lands, they rarely, with the possible exception of Professor Wurzle, actually enjoyed the prospects of such travel.

Jonathan was filled with a sense of adventure though. By the time the meeting wound down he was just a bit puffed up with pride and when it was finally his turn to speak, he came near close to strutting up to the front of the hall. Amid a great deal of applause, he held one hand aloft and began a very pretty speech that, remarkable enough, said exactly what the people of Twombly Town wanted to hear—that theories about Willowood Station were all fine, but it was action, not theories, that was called for in this situation. Someone, he insisted, must sail south to complete the trading and return before Christmas or else the holidays would be a rather sorry lot. Without honeycakes the traditional Christmas feasts would suffer, and without elfin gifts, the children would be sad. If the feasting were poor and the children were sad, Jonathan said in a stout voice, then the Christmas holidays might as well be Willowood Station all smashed and gone down the river.

Jonathan's speech was inspired. The people of Twombly Town were, up until then, uncertain as to whether Jonathan would undertake the voyage or not. What with Gilroy Bastable's pessimistic account of his conversation with Jonathan the previous night, the outlook had been grim. Their response, therefore, was to shout hurrah and stomp about and lift Jonathan onto their shoulders and carry him up and down Main Street. Ahab looked on the scene in won-

der. Even Wurzle and Beezle seemed content in their way.
Beezle was happy that he'd had an opportunity to lay out
his diagrams and explain them, and Professor Wurzle was
happy for other reasons.

Jonathan spent the rest of the day at market, trading
cheeses for cabbages and hams and mushrooms and nets of
onions and garlic. His wagon, when he finally towed it
home, was as full as when he'd set out. For the return trip
Ahab wasn't allowed to ride on top of the load for fear that
he'd squish the produce. Besides, the way home was uphill,
and Jonathan had a hard enough time of it without having
to contend with the dog's additional weight. The wheels of
the wagon got mired in the mud twice so that by the time
he lurched up before his porch, Jonathan was as splashed
and muddied as Gilroy Bastable had been after his tussle
with the storm. But all in all it had been a very good day.
His decision to make the journey seemed almost as wise as
it had when he made his speech at the Guildhall.

Supper that night wasn't as good as it should have been,
as Jonathan was preoccupied and his mind wasn't on what
he was doing. His cornmeal muffins burned and tasted like
sour charcoal, and the lima beans in his ham-and-bean
soup refused to cook, and cracked rather than mushed
when he bit into them. About halfway through the evening,
Ahab began to walk in his sleep and strode stiff-legged
around the room three times, one eye open and one shut,
moaning fearfully. Coming on top of the ruined muffins
and hardened beans, Ahab's behavior was a bad omen indeed.

Jonathan didn't pretend not to know what was the matter. It was, of course, the journey he'd proposed in such a
strutting manner at the Guildhall. As the night became
blacker and the wind picked up and whistled through the
redwoods in the forest beyond his house, Jonathan developed an even greater liking for his home and fire than
usual. The spirit of adventure in him was being wrestled
down by the spirit of stay-at-home, and by eight o'clock in
the evening he was pacing up and down the room, first
planning the trip, then unplanning it. He could already feel
the cold night wind off the river and the wet socks that
were the curse of raftsmen everywhere. He could imagine

his disappointment when his eggs gave out and the fresh meat wasn't fresh any longer. Unless he stopped to hunt— a sport he wasn't inclined to—he would exist for the better part of the voyage on oatmeal porridge, jerked beef and hard biscuits. With luck, he would be able to pick wild blackberries on into the first of December, especially in the rainy hemlock forests closer to the sea. But as good as wild blackberries are, it doesn't take too many days before they aren't so good anymore. Jonathan's thoughts were bleak indeed, and the more he paced and thought, the less he wanted to go.

At one point he had the wild idea of piling all his valuables onto his cart, breaking a lot of windows in his house, and hanging a sign on the door that indicated he'd been robbed and carried away by pirates. The notion sounded very good at first, pirates being greatly talked of about town. He could simply sneak out under the cover of night and head upriver, maybe to Little Beddlington or to the City of the Five Monoliths. He could leave and never return, so as not to have to discuss his reasons with all the people who were so anxious that he risk *his* head on a fool's journey downriver. But as he paced and thought, several major gaps became visible in his plan. Pirates, probably, didn't hang placards about to advertise their affairs, nor did they, he supposed, allow their victims to do so. Besides, if he were to make a journey anyway, what matter if he went north or south, if he traveled by raft on the river or dragged his wagon along the highroad?

So Jonathan continued to pace, bemoaning his fate and blaming it, a bit unfairly perhaps, on the people of Twombly Town. His destiny which just that afternoon had beckoned like a wood nymph, now winked and leered like a soggy and bedraggled tramp.

A sharp rap on the window brought him up short. A tap on the window could mean very few things—either trouble of some sort was poking its nose in where it wasn't wanted, or Dooly, a thick but well-meaning lad, was doing the same. A flurry of giggles from outside the window seemed to indicate Dooly. In truth, Jonathan was partial to the young man who was dim-witted as a pine cone at times but who believed every wonderful and marvelous thing anyone told him, especially if it was an obvious lie. But he wasn't a bad sort, and he and Ahab seemed to have a mutual understanding. Dooly would talk to Ahab for hours, the dog cocking an eye every now and again and mumbling under his breath.

Jonathan opened the door, glad for any sort of company. Dooly strode in, shouting and gesturing and coatless even though it was a cold and windy night.

"Hey-ho! Cheeser!" cried Dooly, his eyes seeming to sail about in their sockets like spiraling leaves in a gust of wind. "So it's hey-ho and away we go, eh!"

"So they say, Dooly. So they say," replied Jonathan not nearly as enthusiastically.

"I had a grandfather once," said Dooly, pausing as if that were the end of the thought.

Jonathan waited for a moment, preparing for another of Dooly's lunatic stories. "We all had such things, Dooly. Every man-jack of us had."

"What I meant to say, sir, if you'll just pardon my tongue, as it is, sir, is that my grandpa took and sailed south, he did. And he found, sir, a great sort of cabinet, there at the seaside. It was one like you or I might keep our clothes in. And do you know, Cheeser, what was in this here cabinet?"

"No," said Jonathan.

"A great fat clown," said Dooly, "all made up with feathers and paint and diamonds and such and with a tail curled all up like a corkscrew. A magic pig, it was, says I, pretending to be a circus clown."

"Well that's marvelous, Dooly. Who was it told you such a story?"

"My ma," said Dooly, "just afore she told me about the devilfish that swallowed my uncle."

"Ah. So that's the case. Perhaps I'll see such a thing as an enchanted clown-pig. That would lend an air of what-do-you-call-it to the journey."

"So it would," Dooly nearly shouted. "Imagine such a thing as that! Imagine such a wonder!"

Just about then Ahab awoke and lumbered over to welcome Dooly; whereupon the two of them trotted off to the fireside to chat. Jonathan then resumed his pacing. He wanted very much to talk to someone about the journey, but there was only one person around, and he was already talking to the dog. It was a sad state of affairs.

He tried to buck himself up by thinking about the hero's welcome he'd get, sailing back into Twombly Town wharf with a raft piled high with honeycakes and candy and elfin gifts for the children; kaleidoscopes with lightning bugs inside and marbles that rolled themselves and glowed like living rainbows when the sun went down, and moon gardens encased in glass balls that sprouted and grew weird castles and caverns and tiny fish that you needed a special eyeglass to see. How glorious it would be to sail into Twombly Town a week before Christmas with the likes of that on your raft.

Jonathan almost convinced himself and actually began thinking of the provisions he'd need for the journey. But the more he thought the more tiresome it all seemed. When he began to think about storms and goblins and long river miles, he sank once again into a gloom.

"Cheeser!" came a voice from near the fire. Jonathan jumped, having forgotten that Dooly was present. "Shall we take Ahab along, Mister Cheeseman, when we go a-rafting?"

"I suppose *I* will," replied Jonathan. "*You,* however, aren't going rafting—at least not with me."

"Ah!" cried Dooly. "But do you suppose, Cheeser, that one would go a-rafting without such a dog as this?"

"No," said Jonathan, "I don't imagine he would."

"No, sir! He would not. My old grandfather never set out nor put his coat on without a dog such as this. A specimen he called it. Dogs was specimens to him. It was 'a fine specimen that' and 'a poor specimen this' to Grandpa."

"Your grandfather was a man who knew his dogs, Dooly; that's apparent."

"Bless me!" Dooly shouted, causing Ahab to leap to his feet and howl. "Did he know them? I should say, if you'll pardon me carrying on. His dog, Old Biscuit, if I remember, was the one as found the treasure near Bleakstone Hollow."

"Quite a treasure, was it?"

"Quite a treasure!" Dooly cried like an astounded parrot.

"Twas a whacking great iron pot, the kind the goblins cook men in for supper. And do you know, Master Bing, what such a thing was full of?"

"I haven't even a foggy idea."

"Red diamonds bigger'n a house. Zillions, there were, as made old Wurzle's emerald look like a green ant."

"All piled in this goblin pot, were they?"

"Like spring cherries!"

"That must have made your grandfather a rich man."

"Not a word of it. He come back to the farm to get his wheelbarrow, and by the time he got back up to the hollow, they were gone!"

"No!" said Jonathan.

"Oh yes, Mister Bing. And there was a powerful lot of stick candy there. Any flavor you want. Grandpa was always one for sweets, so this didn't bother him. He set in to load up his wheelbarrow, and you know what came up out of the bushes?"

"Uh-uh."

Dooly fell silent and peered about the house. Then, in a barely audible whisper, he said, "Goblins, fit for dinner and carryin' big knives and forks and with teeth comin' out all over, and Grandpa knew what it was—enchantment! And one great goblin with eyes like pinwheels come for Grandpa. He opened his mouth bigger'n that door over there, and do you know what was inside?"

Jonathan was on the verge of shaking his head when a half dozen sharp knocks on the door caught his attention. Dooly imagined the source of the noise to be the great whirling-eyed goblin with the unspeakable thing in its mouth. He cried out in terror, jumped up, made a dash for the window. Then he turned and leaped through the kitchen and ran out the rear door fearful of demons.

The visitor turned out to be Gilroy Bastable.

"Jonathan, Jonathan, Jonathan Bing!" cried old Bastable, hearty as a beef stew.

"Lo there, Gilroy."

"Here, Jonathan, I have banknotes amounting to a goodly sum and a sheet of paper listing every villager's share. We decided, if you'll agree, to work things the same as always. If things go bad, the city makes the notes good.

You aren't responsible, not in the business sense leastways. How's that?"

"That's just fine, Gilroy. Couldn't ask for more." In truth, Jonathan was being a bit short with people that night, not because he was mean or annoyed or anything, but because he was down in the dumps.

The mayor assumed that Jonathan was simply tired after a busy day and so did his best to be cheerful and rally round. He strode back and forth beaming like a satisfied toad. At every third or fourth stride he'd pause and cry, "It's a fine day, a great day, a wonderful day!" He smiled over his spectacles.

"Do you know," asked the mayor, pausing for a moment, "that the boys were for storming the hill here and riding you up and down on their shoulders again? And they'd have done it too. But I put the damper on it, Cheeser, because I know you're not one for that sort of celebratin'."

"Thank you, Gilroy. You're quite right."

"Well, Jonathan. We loaded provisions for you down at wharfside and got hold of the best raft in the parts. I know you have your own, Jonathan, but this one is a sight bigger. It has a new wheel on it that can be cranked by one man and can almost make headway upriver without sail. It's a wonder, Cheeser—a raft for a prince.

"We managed to lay in a store of beef—some salted and some dried—and barrels of candied fruit, salted vegetables, wheat flour, oats, and dill pickles. There's a keg of rum and a rack of port and all the pots and pans and cutlery you'll need. There's a cabin midway back big enough for an army that will double for a hold. Does all this fill the bill, Jonathan?"

"I should say, Gilroy. Will the cheeses stay dry in a storm?"

"Dry as a bug."

"And is this raft rigged like my own? Double masts and a square topsail and foresail and oversized jib?"

"All of that, Jonathan. Just like you said."

"And extra rope—two hundred feet of it—and canvas too."

"The canvas we've got; the rope we'll add tomorrow."

"Yes," said Jonathan, perked up again now that there was work to do.

"Can you sail morning after tomorrow? Wurzle says it would be wise. And of all of us, he probably knows best."

"I don't know," Jonathan hesitated, "That's sort of soon."

"The farther into fall, Cheeser, the more chance of storms and high water. You'll have plenty of help tomorrow and the work's half done already. Shall we say morning after tomorrow, then?"

"Yes," said Jonathan, "I suppose we shall."

Chapter 3

A Sandbar South of Twombly Town

❈

THE river lay out black and winding along the center of the valley. Shadowy cottonwoods and alders and dark beds of moss and oxalis climbed away up the sloping banks. A fall sun, huge through the morning mist, crept up over the rim of the White Mountains in the east, and the swirls and ripples of the river caught glints of light and sparkled.

Jonathan Bing and Ahab sat on a log below town where the river began to wind slowly around a great bend. Jonathan threw pebbles into a pool of slowly eddying water along the bank with his right hand. His chin rested on his left hand, and it seemed to Ahab that his master wasn't really enjoying his rock throwing. Every now and then a great frog, usually green and striped, came sailing past on a lily pad that had torn loose from a distant lilly pad jungle. Each one looked at Jonathan and Ahab with huge unblinking eyes as if he knew a terrible or wonderful secret which the two on the bank wished they knew but didn't. And the secret, if there was one, slipped away down the river as the frogs sailed their crafts around the swerve of the shore and into shadow.

The rising sun should have been a welcome sight to the

Cheeser, who had been sitting on the log for an hour or so and whose trousers had soaked up a good bit of the morning dew. It was the morning of the day of departure, and sun on such a day couldn't help but be welcome. The wind and rain of the past days were forgotten, Jonathan's raft was packed with cheeses and provisions and even empty casks which he would use for the storage of cakes and gifts on the return voyage.

And that's why the sun wasn't such a welcome sight. Now nothing was left but for Jonathan and Ahab to climb aboard and cast off. A crowd of villagers, up with the sun, already lined the docks where the raft was moored. Within the hour they'd be trudging homeward to hot biscuits and gravy and thick strips of bacon and cups of dark coffee. Jonathan didn't much want to think about that.

The sun meant, then, that he'd have to wander back down to the dock and set out, alone. He wasn't in a mood to pace and think as he had been on the night of Dooly's visit, nor was he tearing at his hair or gnashing his teeth or furrowing his brow as people in books might. Instead, he simply sat there like a lump and plopped stones in among the green forests of water plants.

A familiar voice hailed him from above. "Hallo there, Jonathan!" The tone was altogether too bluff for either the hour or the occasion. It had to be Gilroy Bastable come to fetch him. "Here you are then!" shouted Gilroy.

Jonathan waved up at him.

"Why it's daylight, man! Sun-up. Old Mr. Sun himself has come along to see to the launching, Bing my boy!" Gilroy Bastable came clumping down and sat on the log. Since his winter hat had gone downriver in the storm, he'd been forced to wear his summer hat, a very wide and wonderful hat. He scratched Ahab behind the ear, an odd thing since Gilroy Bastable generally held no concourse with dogs. But Ahab, I suppose, had become a sort of hero dog, and so perhaps it wasn't such an odd thing. Old Bastable cleared his throat about seven times, and sneezed calamitously. His hat jumped off his head because of the violence of the sneeze and, being round like a wheel, began to roll down toward the swirling waters. Gilroy Bastable, it turned out, moved wonderfully fast for a man of his age and size.

Ahab, however, was every bit as quick and leaped for the hat almost as soon as it pitched off. Both Ahab and Gilroy scoured along the bank for the space of thirty feet, Bastable with one hand pressed to the top of his head as if to hold down the very hat that he was chasing. The two of them caught up with the renegade hat right at the water's edge and lunged for it simultaneously. Ahab charged in between Gilroy Bastable's legs, whereupon the mayor, with a shout of surprise, tumbled head over heels toward his rolling hat which went twirling up into the air. Gilroy rolled to a stop in a clump of grass, and Ahab, in his wild rush, bounced into him. The spiraling hat settled onto Ahab's head and perched there. Sailing past on a bed of river grasses and lily pads, a group of wide-eyed frogs paused momentarily before the disheveled mayor, whose legs and arms splayed out in every direction, and the dog Ahab, who wore a hat that was clearly too small for him. Now it was the frogs' turn to wonder at the goings on. Jonathan stepped along and helped Gilroy Bastable to his feet then removed the hat from Ahab's head, dusting it once or twice for good measure. That done, the three set off up the path toward town.

Thirty or forty villagers along the dock caught sight of them when they rounded the millhouse and the great wheel which turned as methodically as the river ran. A shout went up, hands clapped, and old Beezle's grandson began tooting away, oompah oompah, on a caved in tuba. The sun was burning through the mists, and the raft looked like something a king would sail about in. All in all, the sight, was fairly spectacular. Jonathan waved at the townspeople, and Ahab began to prance about sideways like a crazed parade horse.

The villagers had apparently never seen the like, and they continued cheering mightily. Ahab capered across the green, first tilting his head this way and then that way and drawing the admiration of the townspeople. Jonathan thought of making a speech and tried to think of something really fine to say. But he was only sailing away for a few weeks, and there was, after all, no *real* danger involved. As someone had said, he *was* a stout enough lad for the journey. So, tramping across the dock, Jonathan helped Ahab aboard and with a final nod toward his neighbors, set about casting off.

A great shout from the direction of town brought cries of "Here comes the Professor!" and "Horray for old Wurzle!" Jonathan, pausing, could see that Professor Wurzle, dressed in a pair of very businesslike shorts and wearing a visored cap, was indeed hurrying along toward them. He drew up, puffing like a teakettle on the boil, threw a suitcase and bedroll over the low bulwark, and climbed aboard. His face was red as a rock cod and his spectacles were fogged over.

"*Whoosh?*" was all he could say. Between *whooshes* he managed to smile at the onlookers and nod seriously at an astounded Jonathan. He didn't stand around idle though— not Professor Wurzle. He liked to consider himself "an old hand" and that's what he told Jonathan. "I'm an old hand at this, Cheeser," he said with a sharp nod of his head. "An old hand," and with Ahab sniffing along behind him, the Professor puffed across to the port bow and, to the echo of a rousing cheer, untied the final mooring line and threw it back up onto the dock.

Jonathan was astounded. The intent of the Professor's actions was clear; his "old hand" attitude seemed to indicate that arguing or gasps of surprise were unnecessary. The Professor obviously was going along. Jonathan poled the raft across the calm waters of the tiny boat harbor. Both men waved slowly toward the wharf where Mayor Bastable stood with both hands atop the crown of his hat, and they drifted out into the leisurely current of the River Oriel.

Pushing the tiller hard to starboard, Jonathan veered out away from shore to deep midstream. They floated past the log on which Jonathan had rested that morning and rounded the long bend where the frogs had faded from view. Jonathan half expected to see all of them collected there along the bank in some great amphibian convention, but, of course, the bank was silent and green and empty of visible life aside from a pointy-nosed hedgehog down from the fringe of the woods for a drink. Once out on the river, the two finally relaxed, and Ahab, tired of keeping forever vigilant, fell asleep amid the cheese kegs and empty casks in the hold.

"Well, Master Cheeser," said the Professor, tamping a great wad of chocolaty smelling tobacco into his pipe. "Here we are, then! Stap me for a lubber if we're not!"

Jonathan, not used to such seawise talk, mistook his meaning, supposing him to have said blubber instead of lubber and feared, just for the moment, that the Professor was talking like a lunatic. Long curly strands of tobacco poked out of the bowl of Wurzle's pipe like the overhanging branches of a hemlock. The Professor stabbed away at them with his fingertip, but they insisted on springing up afresh. Finally he struck a long match and lit the bowl, the fragments burning away and dropping roundabout. "Yes indeed," he muttered shrewdly, "here we are."

"I should say," said Jonathan in response to the Professor's comments which were as truthful as anyone could wish. "I didn't know that you'd be coming along, Professor. Gilroy Bastable didn't mention a word of it."

"Oh," said the Professor, "Gilroy didn't know. He's not your man for research and scientific investigation. I suppose I should have told him, though. He might have laid in another barrel or two of salt beef. But I've brought my arms and money to buy supplies at Hightower when we get there, so I suppose it doesn't matter, really."

Jonathan again was puzzled at this mention of arms. Why had the Professor thought it necessary to mention having brought his arms? Had he a choice in the matter? Jonathan thought about the blubber business and gave the Professor what is commonly called the fish-eye.

The matter soon cleared itself up, however. There, tied to the Professor's bedroll was a weird-looking weapon. It was a sort of blunderbuss mixed up with an oboe and a tiny millwheel. To Jonathan it was a very formidable-looking thing. "You did come armed!" he shouted, pointing toward the oboe gun.

"So I said just a moment back. I don't suppose you've seen one of these before?"

"No indeed," replied Jonathan. "What sort of a thing is it? A very grand thing, for sure."

"Oh my yes." The Professor tamped his pipe slowly, looked at it once, then tamped it again. The pipe seemed to lend such an air of authority to him that Jonathan decided to light up one of his own. "Very old design, that," the Professor continued. "I found it when old Flutesnoot and I came upon the gems and the bit of mast from the pirate craft. There's a good lot of mechanical know-how in here, Cheeser. Mechanics is the glory of the sciences—the crowning bud of the cosmos. Don't you agree?"

Jonathan nodded. "I never stop saying so. Can't we load this gun up and have a go at it. Just shoot into the air. Looks complicated. What are those little arms at the side there with the spots on them? They look squidish."

"I suppose they do," Wurzle agreed, looking puzzled. "I hadn't much thought of squids when I acquainted myself with the design, but yes, I can see something of the squid in it. Actually, they're velocitudes—whirl-gatherers."

This meant nothing to Jonathan, but he decided to pretend it did. "Ah, yes," he said, "whirl-gatherers. Couldn't we just pop away at a rock once with it? I'd like to see the whirl-gatherers spin. And that crank affair, what's that?"

"A twist-about, I call it. Sort of a gyro, I believe, although I'm not sure."

"You're not sure?"

"Not entirely. I haven't actually utilized the thing yet. Some of the hieroglyphs on the mast itself seemed to refer to it, but they were difficult to understand. I believe I got the gist of it though. Mechanics, Master Cheeser, is a fundamental to the designer."

"Of course it is."

"And when one knows the laws of mechanics, Cheeser, one can make certain deductions, come to conclusions. Construct entire assemblies from imperfect knowledge by these deductions."

Jonathan peered wisely at Professor Wurzle and glanced at the gun. The more he looked at it, the more it resembled anything but a weapon. It was more like a great mechanical squid with a funnel mouth and a crank nose. Jonathan longed to wind the thing up and let it whirl about. What could be more awesome, he thought, than an elf weapon?

But the Professor seemed to have an aversion to popping away at rocks, so Jonathan let the matter slide. He'd likely have ample opportunity to see the thing work.

The morning was cool and a very slight breeze blew now

and again, rippling the water. But as morning slid away into afternoon, the sun grew hotter, and the breeze fell off. Jonathan began to wonder why he'd been so worried about the journey. He leaned back against the wall of the hold and watched the trees sailing slowly by along the banks. Here and there wide clumps of lilies spread out toward midstream. About lunchtime, they floated through a section of river where the lily pads with their huge eerie flowers of violet and pink and yellow were so thick they almost stretched from shore to shore.

In the occasional shallows, egrets strode back and forth on legs like stilts. Every now and again one would plunge his head below the surface of the water and come up with a fish in its beak. All in all, Jonathan decided, the river was something of a wonder. Had he not been so hungry, he would have dozed off to sleep and let the raft take its course. They would not reach Hightower until the next afternoon but one, and until docking at Hightower wharf, a mile or so below the old ruin of a tower, they had nothing to do but wait.

Jonathan tapped his pipe out against his shoe, thrust it into his trouser pocket, and gathered energy for the ten-step walk into the hold. He fancied a strip or two of jerked beef and a wedge of cheddar cheese. They had best eat a loaf of bread also, since the dozen loaves Jonathan had thought to bring wouldn't be worth much after a few days.

On the point of rising, Jonathan heard, or thought he heard, a phantom voice mumbling from somewhere far away. It was difficult to pinpoint exactly where the sound had come from, but it mumbled along in such low, whispering tones that it seemed the very voice of dread itself. Jonathan sat up very quickly and listened. The voice was still. He determined that somehow the breeze in the rushes had caused the sound, but it was a moment before he thought about being hungry again. Then just as he did, he heard the sound again. It was clearly a voice, somehow muffled. He woke Professor Wurzle, who sat up with a shout, reaching in haste for his awesome weapon. A moment passed before his eyes cleared and he saw that he was on the river adventuring to the sea. Jonathan winked six or eight times meaningfully and pressed his forefinger to his mouth.

Professor Wurzle was quick to catch on, and the two sat as still as a pair of croquet wickets for the space of a long minute. Just as the Professor began to open his mouth the mysterious sound came again, the MUMBLE MUMBLE MUMBLE that seemed to come from nowhere and yet everywhere, as if it were the spirit of the river or the voices of the lost frogs whispering their dire secrets. Wurzle squinted his eyes and stared away at the tip of Jonathan's nose for a moment before shoving his ear up against the wooden wall of the hold.

"It's the bloody dog!" he cried, leaping to his feet. "I swear it!"

Jonathan was unconvinced, knowing from long experience that Ahab—although he seemed to have the most wonderful sorts of dreams—couldn't speak. Both men jumped up at the same time and, though the voice had hushed, went creeping around either side of the hold and booted open the door which hung ajar. There on the floor, in among the kegs, lay the peaceful Ahab.

"Hello, old Ahab," said Jonathan.

Ahab stood up and, stretching, wandered over. "He looks completely innocent," Jonathan stated, giving the Professor a look.

"Of course he does, of course he does," the Professor replied. "It was a little joke of mine. Dogs speaking like men and such. Bit of a joke. Ha-ha! Eh? Rather funny, what?"

"Yes, sir," Jonathan agreed. "But we did hear the voice. You don't suppose, do you . . . No, I guess not. No," continued the Cheeser, "that wouldn't do."

"What?" cried the Professor, anxious to hear Jonathan's explanation and secretly hoping it would be as foolish as his own.

"Do you suppose that a dog might talk in his sleep?"

"Well," said the Professor, giving Jonathan a look in turn. "No, I don't suppose he could. At least I can't see how. I saw a dwarf up in Little Beddlington who had an ape which could shout a poem. But it had to be mesmerized first. Then it would rise up, straight as a mainmast and pipe out 'The Madman's Lament' just as you or I might. Now as a man of science, I never believed such a tale. And yet I'm sure, Cheeser, that in this world of ours, science doesn't hold the only key; it only unlocks one of the doors—and perhaps the side door at that." The Professor looked shrewdly at Jonathan, then philosophically lit his pipe. Jonathan, however, brought the subject back around to his sleep-talking dog theory.

"But I was thinking, Professor, that if a dog had a dream about a man, mightn't that man say a few words now and again, like men do? And so, if a dog were to talk in his sleep it mightn't all be dog talk; perhaps the people in his dreams might get a word in now and again."

"This ape up in Little Beddlington . . ." began the Professor. But before old Wurzle could get well into the story of the Beddlington Ape, Jonathan had bolted past the puffing Professor and out the cabin door. The raft had, somehow, worked its way over toward the starboard bank, thick with trees, and with a lurch and a scrape had run aground on a sandbar. Just like that. There they sat, in the middle of the quiet river with their bow run up a third of the length of the raft onto the sand.

The two struggled for an hour, vainly attempting to work the bow of the raft out into the deeper channel that ran along the edge of the bar. Too much of the raft was aground, however, for this maneuver to prove of much use. The long, stiff wooden poles could find nothing solid in the sandy river bottom to pry against, and simply gouged along through the sand and accomplished nothing.

The Professor, finally, paused and sat down on an empty cask. "I think I see it, Cheeser."

"Ah," said Jonathan, not knowing exactly what it was the Professor saw. "Do you now?"

"That I do. We can't, you'll agree, pole this craft off the bar. Not the two of us."

"I agree."

"And we can't sit and wait for the river to rise."

"True again. It may drop before it rises. And a rise would mean a storm, and we don't want to weather a storm while aground in midriver."

"Just so," said the Professor, "just so. As I see it, we're men of science."

"I believe you're right."

"And men of science use their heads, you'll agree again.

Now my head tells me that there are three ways to get off this bar. Muscle is the first, and that, apparently, doesn't work. That leaves us two options. One of those is to rig the mizzenmast and take advantage of the crosswind to help swing the stern out into deep water. With the current to help, we could then pole the bow free."

"That's a good plan, Professor, a good plan. But we'd be the better part of the day accomplishing the task. And who's to say that we wouldn't spin round and beach the whole larboard side?"

"And if we do, are we much the worse off?"

"No," said Jonathan, "I suppose not. But you mentioned a third option. What is that?"

"It would be possible to row across to the far shore in the coracle. Then by looping a line round one of the great alders, we could drag the raft free by use of a block and tackle."

Jonathan pondered for a moment. "I'm afraid it's too great a distance for such a thing. The weight of the wet rope alone would make it an impossible chore for one man to accomplish. And one of us would, of course, have to stay aboard the raft. And think of the pressure on a rope of that length once the raft is free in the current. We'd likely lose the rope, block and tackle, and all."

"Well we could cut the rope as soon as the raft was free. Clearly the one on the raft would have to tack upstream so as not to outdistance the coracle anyway. So those fears shouldn't much interfere with the scheme."

The two sat there puffing on their pipes during this interchange, and both realized at the same instant that the lunch they had considered eating an hour and a half before hadn't been eaten.

"Are you hungry, Professor?" asked Jonathan.

"Ravenous."

"Shall we eat then?"

"I suppose we shall."

As they rose and reached for the door of the hold, both men paused. From within, unmistakably, came the murmur of a voice, droning along as if engaged in earnest conversation. Jonathan, stealthily, bent an ear to the door and caught the words, "hairy thing" and "goblin" and "buckets of ice cream." He was sure of it. The door swung to, and both Jonathan and Professor Wurzle peeked in half expecting almost anything. What they saw was Ahab, round as a tub, hunched over a half-eaten dill pickle. The top of the pickle keg was ajar. The whole mystery was peculiar to the utmost.

The Professor was the first to speak. "It looks as if your beast has been having a go at the pickles."

"I should say."

"Abominably odd."

"Yes indeed. How could he have purloined a pickle? Even if he had been able to reach the top of the keg, he couldn't have popped the top loose."

"A good deduction, Cheeser," the Professor whispered. "Odd things are afoot." The two stealthily crept into the hold although it was clear from the outset that there was no one in the room aside from them and the dog Ahab. Kegs of odd sizes sat about, and ropes and sailcloth and buckets and various sorts of stores and tools lay heaped here and there. No mysterious whisperers were to be seen. It was all a puzzle.

Jonathan removed his cap and scratched the top of his head. Both men shrugged then said, almost simultaneously, "The kegs. The empty kegs!" There were a round dozen of the large kegs, and Jonathan, as if to surprise something that might be hiding within, tiptoed toward the closest and reached for the lid.

The Professor made a noise like an ape might make if his mouth were taped shut and gestured at Jonathan to wait. He rushed out and was back in a flash with the oboe gun, squid arm whirl-gatherers flapping roundabout. He squinted one eye and nodded to Jonathan to continue.

The Cheeser snatched the first lid up, then the second and third, but nothing save air lay within. He approached the fourth, reached for the lid as Professor Wurzle stood guard, and the lid, as if on command, popped off and clattered down onto the deck.

"Hey there, Mr. Bing Cheese!" cried Dooly, popping up out of the barrel like a jack-in-the-box and causing Jonathan to leap back onto a sack of beans.

Professor Wurzle, in the excitement, failed to recognize

poor Dooly who had, it seemed, stowed away in an empty keg. He twirled away on the crank device and the whirl-gatherers began flailing round, making little whistling noises until the oboe gun nearly sang a tune. Both Jonathan and Dooly stared silently in amazement for a moment at the dumbfounded Professor, who was immediately sorry that he'd started the thing up. The motion of the whirl-gatherers finally became so intense that the Professor was forced to drop the entire affair, and the weapon went whizzing round the hold like a giant rotating moth.

Dooly grabbed the fallen lid and dropped back down into his barrel, pulling the lid shut after him. Jonathan took refuge behind the bean sacks. The Professor, fearful of damaging the weapon, leaped after it and attempted to throw a burlap sack over it as it careened off the walls. The burlap, in the end, got caught up among the whirl-gatherers and fouled the entire machine which dropped clattering to the deck. Dooly peeped out, sweat prickling his brow.

"What is it, Professor?" asked Dooly. "Some sort of bird? Looks like a thing my grandpa had once to find treasures with."

"Well, Dooly!" the Professor gasped. "I don't suppose your grandfather had one of these. It's just a sort of a thing I use for this and that."

Dooly nodded.

"The question," said Jonathan, rising from the bean sacks, "is what are you doing here?"

"Aye, aye, Captain," cried Dooly, clambering out of his keg. "It's a jolly day to be a-roving, Cheeser, if I do say. And, Cheeser, you said once that you and me couldn't go a-rafting without we took a fine dog like Ahab along beside us. So there you are, and here I am, and there, with his pickle, as I, if you please, felt I had to give him, is the dog."

The answer, somehow, wasn't completely satisfactory, but Jonathan could see no profit in being upset. Of all the things the Cheeser disliked, being upset was the worst, and so usually, if he had the choice, he ignored anything that would provoke such a thing.

"Dooly," he said, taking a pickle from the barrel for himself, "Welcome aboard."

"Ahoy, Captain," said Dooly. "Shall I make up a lunch?"

"I believe you should."

"And did I tell you, Cheeser and Mr. Wurzle gentlemen, about the time my grandpa went in to fix *him* a lunch?"

"I don't suppose so, Dooly," Jonathan replied rather abruptly. "But . . ."

"About the great Toad King," said Dooly.

"But," continued Jonathan, "I imagine the Toad King and your grandfather can hold on until our own is served."

"Don't let me forget," said Dooly, lunging out through the door. Jonathan followed, leaving Professor Wurzle separating burlap from whirl-gatherers and puzzling over the odd behavior of his machine.

Chapter 4

Two Trolls Above Hightower

❧

At long last they completed lunch, and though their stomachs were well filled, they were no closer to being free of the sandbar. But then there's nothing like a full stomach, or so Jonathan had always thought, to make a fellow sleepy. Just a bit of a catnap is not at all a bad thing after lunch. "I say, Professor," said Jonathan. "What about a bit of a rest?"

"We've been taking a bit of a rest, my boy," replied the Professor, "all morning long."

"But you know, Professor, that afternoons are somehow the dullest part of the day, and a chap shouldn't fight against it. Where would we be if we denied human nature?"

"We'd likely be a ways further downriver before nightfall," said the Professor, "instead of stuck here."

"I suppose," said Jonathan, wondering whether, as captain, he couldn't order all hands to their bunks for a good two-hour lunch recovery period. He was never one to enjoy ordering people about, however, besides the Professor was very much right. So they began debating the various merits of the two plans. The addition of Dooly to the crew made

41

things a trifle more simple, and it was altogether possible that they could quite easily rig the mizzenmast and, with the extra muscle, pole the raft free. They began, in fact, to do just that.

Dooly managed first off to tangle a length of rope into a knotted mass and, almost at the same time, to drop a spread of canvas overboard into the river. The canvas immediately sank. Amid shouted apologies, Dooly, leaped overboard after it. The rush of water, cold as a herring, swept his feet out from under him. He sputtered and floundered and thrashed until his feet found the bottom and he realized that the water over the bar was no more than waist deep. He stood up shaking the water from his face.

"*Whew!*" he said to the Professor, Jonathan, and Ahab who all stood at the edge of the raft. "This is pretty wet!"

"A good deduction—worthy of a man of science," shouted the Professor, happy that Dooly was safe and almost as happy again that no one would have to leap in to save him. He'd always wondered what the proper method of saving a drowning person was—whether it was correct to remove one's shoes and shirt and unclasp one's pocketwatch, or whether merely to sail in without pause.

"Do you know what I saw, Mr. Wurzle, down beneath the sea?"

"I haven't an inkling," replied the Professor.

"My whole life. Right before my eyes."

"All of it?"

"If you please, sir. It just come past like a flash: candy bars, sandwiches, my new pair of shoes, my grandpa, everything. Just like a batch of flappin' birds it come past."

"I've heard of such things," said the Professor, "but I never hoped to meet anyone who'd seen it."

"Especially underwater," said Jonathan, leaning across to take the heavy, soaked canvas that Dooly had managed to retrieve.

"Aye!" shouted Dooly, flabbergasted as the idea of his life having gone past underwater. "I suppose so!" Then, without so much as taking a breath, Dooly's eyes widened into circles and his mouth fell open. "The Toad King!" he cried. "The Toad King himself!"

"Why don't you just hop on up here onto the deck,

Dooly, before you start in with the Toad King story. We've got weeks of travel ahead of us; plenty of time for kings of all natures, toads included." Jonathan bent over the rail to give Dooly a hand onto the raft, but Professor Wurzle cut him short by placing a cold hand on his arm. Dooly clearly wasn't listening to Jonathan either but was staring goggle-eyed at the shore.

There, between a pair of huge, twisted alders with inter-woven roots exposed on the riverside, stood a pair of awe-somely misshapen beasts. They were larger and fatter and more stooped than men and were hunched and scaly-looking. Their faces were lumpy and knobby, and they squinted through little slits of eyes. Each wore a skin gar-ment wrapped around his midsection, and each held a great gnarly club in his hand. All in all, they looked a bit on the stupid side. Ahab didn't like the look of them by half, and he went barking about the deck cutting capers every six or eight steps as if he were a tap dancer.

"Trolls," the Professor announced.

"I beg your pardon," said Jonathan, astounded at the sight of such things.

"I said trolls. Two trolls, and very ugly ones from the look of it."

"Hallo, Mr. Toad King!" shouted Dooly in a quavering voice. "You might remember my old grandpa."

One of the trolls wandered down to the riverside and stood with his feet buried in a cushion of moss. The branches of the old alder stirring now and again in the breeze nearly brushed his hair for him. With a long, pointed talon of a fingernail he picked at the few great teeth that he had. The second troll stepped along to join him, but slipped on the mossy bank and collapsed all of a heap and ended up sitting in the water, very much upset. The first troll emitted a noise like the creaking of a tree in a stiff wind which must have been some sort of troll laugh-ter because the fallen troll wasn't at all happy with it. He reached out with his club and pounded the second troll on the foot once, then again for good measure, and although the second troll seemed unpleased, he merely shuffled a few steps to the side and climbed in among the roots of the tree, brooding and rubbing his foot.

During this interchange, the Professor tiptoed away toward the hold, and Dooly still stood agog in the river. He winked at Jonathan once or twice and whispered, "This ain't the Toad King. He would have remembered old Grandpa if he was. Grandpa and the Toad King went to the Magic Isles once to find the Purple Pearl you heard me speak of once or twice. No, this ain't such a one as a Toad King, even though he'd fool the likes of us."

Jonathan merely nodded. He'd heard stories of trolls that, at the time, he'd rather not have heard. Most had to do with iron cauldrons like the one Dooly's grandpa found the stick candy in. In the old tales, trolls were fond of making pots of stew from men lost in the woods and from carefully selected stones. Jonathan had never been amused over the idea. He knew, as did everyone, that trolls were real and not just tales told to children on a stormy night. G. Smithers of Brompton Village had written a story entitled, "The Troll of Ilford Hollow," which, when he'd read it as a child, had frightened Jonathan so that he couldn't sleep through a night without dreams of dark, lurching things creeping in the deep woods. But he'd finally convinced himself that such fears were unreasonable and, when he'd grown up, the thought of anything making a meal of stones became rather laughable.

The two trolls waiting on the riverside, however, were anything but laughable. As Jonathan stood watching the trolls which were watching him, the one atop the roots reached down in among them, came up with a stone, and began to gnaw at it.

The Cheeser was off and running with Ahab at his heels. Poor Dooly thought he was abandoned there in the river and lost no time in clambering up the side of the raft back onto the deck. Almost as soon as he stood on board, however, Jonathan came leaping along with two of the long rafting poles and shouted, "Over we go, Dooly." He eased himself over and down into the cold river. It didn't take Dooly more than a moment to catch on, and he and Jonathan each wedged a pole in under the hull of the raft and pushed away for all they were worth. For the first time, the trolls on the bank began looking anxious. The one that had slipped into the river rose and paced back and forth heaving his club into the air now and again in a business-like way.

Jonathan shouted for the Professor, who had disappeared into the hold. Old Wurzle then appeared, armed to the teeth. With his jaw set and his eyes wearing a look of determination, he cranked away at the oboe weapon, menacing the trolls on shore.

"Grab a pole there, Professor," hollered Jonathan as he strained against the hull. The two in the water made a concentrated effort, and Jonathan leaned into it when he heard the scrape of gravel and sand against the bottom and the raft inch sideways toward freedom. Professor Wurzle laid the weapon atop a cask and, from on deck, wedged another pole into the gravel of the river bottom. As the three of them pushed together, the raft slid another foot out into the stream where it jammed once again on the bar. Strain as they might, the raft clung tightly.

Jonathan climbed back onto the deck as the two trolls, their differences settled, probed the water with inquisitive toes. Between the bank and the sandbar the river flowed swiftly, but the channel appeared to be shallow. The Professor shouted, "Here they come, the blighters!" as the trolls, seeking lunch, waded out toward them.

The sails on the mizzenmast were half furled, and Jonathan intended to rig the mast entirely, as the Professor had suggested, to take advantage of the wind. But it looked like a lost cause. The Professor, however, thought otherwise. Grasping his weapon for the second time that afternoon, he mounted the cask and finished cranking the thing up.

"Avast ye, trolls!" he shouted in a voice filled to the hatch covers with authority. "Cease!"

Although trolls, no doubt, spoke a language very different from that spoken by humans, they knew a fearful sight when they saw one. The whirl-gatherers rotated with increasing speed, and the trolls, as the Professor suggested, halted some twenty feet into the river.

Dooly, who was once more in the process of scaling the railing, dropped again bravely and hauled away single-handedly at his task.

The sails stretched taut, Jonathan joined Dooly in the river, and the crew made a final valiant effort to float the raft. The trolls, dull-witted though they were, were sharp enough to see their lunch about to escape downriver, and so, heedless of the Professor's whirring device, they came sloshing out toward the raft mouthing fearful things beneath their breath.

Professor Wurzle gave the gun a final crank, and, though he was at a loss to explain the workings of the wonderful device, he stood grimly as the arms flailed and the entire gun shot away in the direction of the stupefied trolls. Both turned, shrieking, and splashed for the shore. But they hadn't gotten more than a foot or two on their way before the oboe gun sailed whistling past overhead. They watched in mute wonder as it scoured across the slope of the shore and was lost momentarily in the trees. Miraculously, the weapon emerged again, careening unsteadily back out toward the river before it ran afoul of the lower branches of one of the alders and hung whirling till it played itself out.

The trolls scented victory now that the threat was over, and they surged riverward once more. But between the wind and the three poles, the raft inched free. Before the trolls were two-thirds of the way out and were almost chest-deep in the quick waters, the stern swung round into the current and began slipping away on its own. Jonathan climbed aboard as if his trousers were on fire and gave a hand to Dooly, who looked back at the approaching trolls. Dooly's foot slipped on the side of the raft, his hand slid out of Jonathan's, and he fell backward into the river as the raft broke free and sailed off.

Dooly suddenly found himself in a predicament. There was deep water before him in which he would surely drown and two trolls behind him who would gobble him up as Ahab had gobbled up the dill pickle. Dooly stood there waiting, afraid even to look over his shoulder at the two trolls lumbering toward their supper. He watched his companions gesturing wildly from the raft, but he didn't hear their cries, for his own voice drowned out all other sounds as he shouted, desperately, to his old grandpa for help. Even Dooly knew, however, that old Grandpa wouldn't be of much use at such a time as this.

The river, usually lazy, raced along with increased fervor between the sandbar and the far shore, but as the bar dropped away, the pace of the river slackened. Professor Wurzle, heaving on the tiller, brought the bow around toward shore. Clearly they had run up onto the bank at least a hundred yards below the stranded Dooly. Jonathan could see no profit in that.

He cast around for a weapon and seized upon a brass marlinspike that had been shoved in among the canvas and rope. It wasn't of much use as a club, but it was new and unblunted, and a troll might look askance at being struck with it. Wurzle couldn't understand a bit of what Jonathan shouted, but could only watch as the Cheeser vaulted the rail and plunged into the cold waters of the river.

He held the marlinspike in his teeth as he struck out for the sandbar which he lumbered into several yards before he expected it. Jonathan splashed along toward the hapless Dooly, shouting wild and unlikely things like, "You, there!" and "Hey, Mr. Troll!" hoping to call their attention away from Dooly, who still stood as if frozen a few scant feet before them. Both trolls had paused for a reason unknown to Jonathan and were twisting their heads about and scratching behind their ears with grimy talons.

Dooly had given up calling for his grandfather and had pushed a forefinger in either ear. All was silent but for Jonathan's hallooing at the trolls. When he paused in his cries for breath, he heard the drone of what sounded like a distant hive of very large bees. It was that noise, emanating from the very trees and growing in volume by the moment that had stupefied the trolls. Just as Jonathan became aware of the noise, it was drowned out by the furious barking of the courageous Ahab. The dog, apparently, had leaped overboard in the wake of his master and, finding the shallows of the sandbar too deep and cumbersome for his short legs, had swum along to the great alder woods and was barking and leaping in a threatening manner to the rear of the trolls. The Professor paused only long enough to tie the raft to outcropping roots before puffing along behind, weaponless but determined.

The Cheeser hadn't time to feel more than a bit of pride in his noble Ahab before throwing himself onto the shoulders of the nearest troll who was, oddly enough, thrusting the end of his bludgeon into the other troll's ear. It acknowledged Jonathan's presence only by leaving off his prodding, but the thrusts of the marlinspike merely glanced off the troll's greenish, scaly skin. Jonathan hung on though, perched atop the thing's huge shoulders. The second troll, who turned to reply to the poke in the ear, stood gaping at Jonathan lunging about wildly above his companion's head, waving his marlinspike and shouting. In the second troll's dim brain there registered the possibility that his companion had sprouted a second head, and it was all a bit much for him.

There was a good deal of shouting at this point, a tumult in fact. Between the howling of Ahab, the bellowed threats of Professor Wurzle, the cries of the stalwart Cheeser, and, finally, the amazed calling of Dooly, who had seen something strange away above the treetops, both trolls were, as the saying goes, out of their depth.

With a terrible cry that echoed away into the fringe of the wood, both trolls abandoned their supper plans and lurched about, sloshing through the shallows toward shore. At the sight of them, Professor Wurzle fled upriver along the bank, climbing among roots and around bushes, anxious, at that point, to slip away with as little ceremony as possible. The trailing whirl-gatherers of the oboe gun, however, brought him up short, and, faced with the idea of abandoning his weapon which hung tangled in the tree overhead, he chose instead to clamber up after it. He would be safer anyway, he decided, in a tree than on the ground.

He was hoisting himself into the lower branches, ripping a gaping hole in his shirt as he did, when he became aware of a great silence—a silence broken only by something like the whirring of a thousand sparrow wings and the hum of an army of bees. There, soaring along not twenty feet above the swirling waters of the river was an elfin airship which had dropped so swiftly from the heavens that rag-tail ends of clouds were dragged along and were rising skyward like misty bubbles here and there overhead.

The ship didn't exactly pursue the trolls, but clearly the beasts were uncommonly afraid of the airship and were making straightaway for the deep woods to avoid it. Ahab met them on the shore and generally raged about growling and woofing until both trolls lumbered off into the shadows of the alders and hemlocks and were gone. After that, Ahab sniffed about, raising a meaningful growl now and again and making an occasional dash in the direction of the forest simply to ensure that the trolls stay put.

The airship buzzed along upriver traveling only about as fast as a man might walk if he were in a moderate hurry. Jonathan, Dooly, Professor Wurzle—whose leg had become stuck in a crotch of the alder—and even Ahab watched wide-eyed the long, cylindrical ship.

A row of porthole windows as if built for sightseeing lined either side, and at each window was a grinning elf face, each gazing back at the four along the river as if *they* were the marvels. The sides of the craft glowed in the late afternoon sun as if lit from within, and the craft's color was that of a snowflake just as it turns to transparent silver and melts. It was some sort of precious elfin metal, no doubt, mixed high in the White Mountains and laced with enchantment and wind and sleet and glass and precious stones all melted down in a stew. Such, anyway, is how it appeared to Jonathan. The mere presence of the airship itself was enough to keep the company amazed for a week. The ship sported a pair of wings that thrust out from either side and were shaped very like the wings of a large but slender bat. The nose of the craft was translucent green, likely shaped from a monstrous emerald. Within sat another small party of elves, each wearing a pointed cap and gazing puffy-cheeked and pointy-eared through the green window.

The only markings on the vessel were a smattering of elf runes near the tail around a giant round face with wide goggling eyes. Although the image had ears, the face could have been little else but a comical drawing of the Man in the Moon in one of his most effervescent moods.

"My grandpa knows that man!" shouted Dooly as the craft began to round a distant bend in the river. And without thinking much about the consequences, he splashed along after the disappearing elves into deep water where he thrashed crazily until Jonathan dragged him to safety.

"My old grandpa!" cried Dooly.

"Was *he* in there?" asked Jonathan.

"No, he's been away for an age. But that man on the side with his cheeks all loaded up with cherry pits like a jelly man—him and Grandpa were friends."

"Ah," said Jonathan. "Then your grandpa was friends with the Moon, I suppose."

"I bet he was!" cried Dooly, doubly amazed. "He had such a picture on the back of a pocketwatch which he said was give him by a half-dwarf from the east. It was an amazing watch, Mr. Cheeser. You bet it was. You could stop it whenever you liked."

"I'll be a fried chicken," Jonathan said as the two waded chest-deep across the channel to shore. "You could stop it, could you?" But Jonathan wasn't feeling as flip as he sounded, for he too had seen such a face, and he wasn't at all sure whether he liked it or feared it or whether his mind might just be playing a trick on him.

"I should hope to shout," said Dooly. "And once it stopped, so did everything else."

"Bless my soul."

"And you could walk about and put people's hats on sideways and put their spectacles on upside down, and anything you want. Yes, sir. The Widow's pies weren't safe when Grandpa was about with his watch with the big face on the back."

"I should say not. I bet he ate his fill of pies, that grandfather of yours. He must have been the pie king."

"Oh yes. He was that. Everybody knew him as that up and down the river. Apple pie and a bit of yellow cheese. That was *his* idea of food. But I shouldn't mention the cheese."

"How come?" asked Jonathan, vaguely suspicious.

"Well he didn't take much."

"From whom?"

"From your old dad, I suppose. He was the Cheeseman back then. Do you remember?"

"Vaguely," said Jonathan, who actually remembered very well. He could close his eyes and see his father through a mist of rain coming out through the cheesehouse door with a great wheel of salted goat cheese as he himself had done a hundred times since. Old Amos Bing wore a wide-brimmed hat that rose to a stiff point on top and always had a leather pouch slung from his belt which housed a tiny ivory jar filled with snuff, a half dozen good luck charms, and four coins—possibly from the Oceanic Isles—that had wonderful pictures on them of strange deep water fish. Every time you looked at the coins there was a different fish on each side. You had only to turn the coin over for the pictures to change. And like the jeweled symmetry of a kaleidoscope, the strange fish wavered and reformed as the coins were turned and never, once they were gone, reappeared. Jonathan's father had told him that as each fish disappeared it found itself in the sea, and that that was why the ocean had so many marvelous creatures swimming in it. At least that was the story told originally by the bunjo man who had traded the coins to Amos Bing. Jonathan sat for hours after that revelation, turning the coins over and over and keeping tally of the hundreds of fish with which he stocked the oceans. Once, as he turned two of the four coins, a face appeared on all the coins instead of a fish, and it smiled and blinked at Jonathan and seemed to be looking around the room trying to ascertain where it was. Jonathan watched in startled silence as the face wavered and rippled as if seen through the haze of a hot August day. Its cheeks swelled and its smile grew until it was just this side of a leer, then it turned into the face that was on the side of the elfin airship—a great, round-faced moon which winked very slowly at Jonathan as if the two of them were in on the same secret. Then it, too, rippled again and was gone with the fish, and the coins became what they were before the face had appeared. Jonathan abandoned his task of calling up new fish and toyed with the coins only rarely in the years since. The face never reappeared.

Now those same four coins lay in that same pouch tied to Jonathan's belt. It still contained several good luck charms, most notably a red and black bean he'd been given by another wandering bunjo man from the east, which would sprout and grow in the shape of a house if you planted it, or so the bunjo man insisted. But Jonathan had never planted it and hadn't, in fact, even looked at the contents of the bag for a long long time. As long as his luck held, he thought, it was better not to go fooling with the charms.

Jonathan snapped out of his reverie and turned back to Dooly. "Was he a big cheese-eater, your grandfather?" he asked.

"Not so big as he was a pie eater. He ate all kinds of pies, but only ate cheese with apple pie. And he only had to borrow the cheese once when he was down and out. But he left pay, Mr. Cheeser. My grandpa always left pay. He told me himself that you could borrow just about anything if you left something in return. Then you could bring back what you took if it wasn't all ate up and get back what you left. He left something mighty fine for them cheeses though. It was what they call an octopus and it was pickled in a glass jar. It come all the way upriver from the sea with the traders. Grandpa had a batch of such things; he gave one to my old ma, who still has it though she don't let on in case someone might come to steal it."

Jonathan glanced sharply at Dooly and began to speak but thought better of it. Dooly had, no doubt, seen the encased octopus which had sat for years on the Cheeser's mantel and so had generated the story out of his fancy. But then it was true that Jonathan had never known where his father *had* actually gotten the thing. Dooly seemed to be intent upon having his grandfather embroiled in everything, like a colored thread that begins at one edge of a tapestry and seems to wind along through every scene on the cloth, popping up here and there and disappearing again into the weave only to become visible somewhere else.

"Wish I had that pocketwatch today when them monsters was after me," said Dooly. "But the conjurer dwarf from the Dark Forest got it. Grandpa was lucky there."

"How is that?" asked Jonathan as they drew up to the tree where Professor Wurzle sat looking uncomfortable and pink-faced.

"The thing was a curse. You had to always be winding it. If you let it run down, there was only one man who could start it. If you couldn't find him, you'd have to walk around with nobody for company and everyone standing like statues. You and me and anyone else would stand still as a tree until the man started it up again."

"And what man might that be?" asked Jonathan. For

some reason he knew the answer to his own question as soon as he asked it.

"It was the man on the elf airship," said Dooly. "The same one as was on the pocketwatch, like I told you."

Dooly, Jonathan, and Ahab looked up at the Professor lodged in the tree. "Up in the tree, are you, Professor?" Jonathan asked.

"Yes, I am. The opposite pressures exerted by these angling limbs seem to be holding my leg in sway."

"Does he mean he's stuck?" asked Dooly.

"I believe he does," replied Jonathan. "Why don't you climb up there and untangle the Professor and the elf gun, and we'll be on our way before the trolls come back."

Dooly did, and the company set out briskly for the raft. Dooly found a chain of several links on the shore and kept it, for it had, very apparently, belonged to one of the trolls who had lost it when fleeing. And although it was greasy and smelled abominably, Dooly intended to nail it to the mast as a trophy. They set out as evening fell and didn't anchor for the night until they had put several long miles between themselves and the forest of the trolls.

Chapter 5

Ahab Adrift

❦

T HE company spent most of the next two days rafting downriver to Hightower Village. They breakfasted the second morning on bread which had already begun to look a trifle greenish about the top and opened a jar of strawberry preserves with a layer of paraffin over it. Professor Wurzle graciously pointed out that the wax kept certain "things" from getting in. Organoids he called them. Dooly understood him to mean bugs and determined that the lid of the jar, if it wasn't twisted on by a fool, would keep out any bug he'd ever seen. The wax therefore, said Dooly, was placed in the jar to be chewed on. And a dabble of jam on it, as there was bound to be, made it tolerably good.

About five miles upriver from the village the alder and hemlock forests began to thin, and wide meadows full of columbine and skunk cabbage and lupin rolled away toward the White Mountains in the east. Rivulets tumbled along across the meadows and rolled on beds of smooth stones down into the Oriel where tall stilt-legged waterfowl plunged through the shallows. The meadows, fresh and green at first, became boggier and overgrown as they flattened out above Hightower. About a mile from town, the countryside became a wide impenetrable morass. Hightower itself, with its cold, stone crenelated walls like the fortress of some somber and ageless wizard, stood atop a prominence that poked above the motionless green of the swamp and looked down and across toward the village that lay along the river.

Although it didn't mean much either to Dooly or Ahab, Professor Wurzle was astounded to see white smoke whirling from a chimney lost amid the thrusting towers, many of which were crumbling away slowly. Hightower had the reputation of being curiously old and had been abandoned, or so the Professor insisted, for an age.

"Something afoot," the Professor stated.

"I'll say," said Jonathan. "Something I'll just keep my nose out of. There are too many such things afoot for my comfort: trolls not a league beyond Twombly Town, elfin airships having a bank holiday and buzzing up and down the river, Willowood Station lost. I'll just ask no questions about abandoned castles coming to life, if you please."

"Well, Jonathan," the Professor replied with a profound wrinkling of the forehead, "it's scientific blood that beats in my veins. The blood of the alchemists; and such as we are spurred along by mystery. It's bread and wine to us, meat and drink."

"I prefer my meat on a plate, fairly well done—and speaking of wine, a dribble of port tonight to celebrate our arrival at Hightower might do something to take the chill out of the evening air."

"It might at that," the Professor agreed.

Every so often they passed a lone cabin. Most of them stood up above the marsh on stilts, and the glow of lantern light could be seen through chinks in the weathered plank walls. Great drooping trees bent branches over the tops of the cabins, and drops of moisture plunked perpetually onto roofs carpeted with thick layers of mosses, green and purple in the evening twilight. From one cabin some hundred yards above the river came the *plink, plink, plink* of a tinny banjo, and the sound wafted out over the silent river in such a way as to make the three companions wish they were somewhere else with a good fire at their backs and a rice pudding and beef rib in front of them on a plate. They were, all of them realized, a very long way from home.

But the company, all in all, was a very stiff-lipped bunch. They were vaguely troubled though to observe that about half the cabins they passed seemed empty. In fact, not until they were beyond the fringe of the marsh and below Oldgate Bluffs did there begin to be signs of life.

The town itself was only modestly awake in an early evening sort of way. A group of school children tromping along the riverside waved and shouted and held up crayfish for the rafters to have a look at. Ahab wandered out of the cabin and barked once or twice cheerily, and one of the boys, no doubt well versed in the biological sciences, pointed at Ahab and shouted something about "a hi-yoona with a puff-head." The children immediately took up the chorus and went prancing about waving their crayfish. Shouts of "Puff-head! puff-head!" followed the rafters downriver for another quarter of a mile. Ahab took the chiding rather well and didn't seem at all put out.

Finally they could see the rocky outcropping that marked the edge of tiny Hightower harbor. Jonathan steered the raft into the quiet bay, and they tied up. Dooly and Ahab had to stay on board although both would have welcomed a stroll through town. It would hardly have done, however, for the entire company to traipse off and leave the raft unattended.

Jonathan and Professor Wurzle really had little business to transact, the raft being only three days out of Twombly Town. They intended to visit a baker and a butcher, and to purchase a few pounds of coffee, a commodity that had been forgotten. Also, they had to buy a jacket and bedroll for Dooly, who had come aboard woefully unprepared.

As they wound up the road into town, it began to look as if it were some holiday or another, for half of the shop windows were boarded up and signs hung on the doors reading "Gone Away" and "Closed for the Season." It all sounded suspiciously final, as if "the season" would apply to any one of the four as its turn came round.

The two unexpectedly came upon a large party of mice, of all the strange things, in company with a bug-eyed toad. The mice were busily engaged in chewing a hole through the side of a tack-and-feed store that looked particularly abandoned. The toad sat blinking placidly on a little tuft of moss nearby like a sultan trying to determine whether the labor of his minions was worthy of his attention or whether he ought not to drop off to sleep for an hour or so.

Professor Wurzle was taken aback at the sight and shouted incoherently at the mice more out of surprise than anything else. When the mice only paused and then returned to their labors, his surprise turned to curiosity, and he went stomping away toward them, an air of the researcher about him. At his approach, the toad shuffled off into the bushes and the mice followed—not in a rout, mind you, but very orderly.

Professor Wurzle said he'd be darned, and Jonathan said he would too. Then both agreed that something fishy was going on and that the mice were strange sorts altogether. As they reached the center of town, however, things began to take on more of an air of normality. Few people, however, seemed particularly glad to see them, and a few even ducked away furtively down alleys at their approach. But shops were open and doing business.

A wooden placard clacking on its stays advertised a public house and the Professor suggested they go in to see, as he put it, the lay of the land. Jonathan agreed and said that he'd like to see a mug of ale as well as the lay of the land. The Professor could find no fault with his logic.

The interior of the pub was not the cheerful sort that people of Twombly Town might boast of. It was littered with scraps of food and assorted bits of trash; a dozen layers of sawdust had been thrown on, one after another, as if the shreds would produce brooms and dust pans and mops and set about cleaning the floor. Instead, the sawdust simply messed about and mingled with the debris and produced a most disagreeable smell. The tavern was dimly lit, to boot—not in a warm and rosy way like Jonathan's living room, but simply in a bleak way as if candles and oil were running low and the place were too fallen to bits for anyone to bother going after a fresh supply. It was not at all the sort of tavern in which anyone would wish to spend his dinner hour.

Half the tables were empty, although glasses and dishes lay piled on most. The proprietor was sleeping on a stool behind the counter, his mouth having fallen open to reveal the fact that he had only two visible teeth, square in the center of the top of his gums; both, apparently, were made of solid gold and held in place by a complicated arrangement of tiny wires.

"Man needs a new set of teeth," said the Professor to Jonathan as they stood looking about the gloom.

"And a dozen candles," replied the Cheeser.

"He only wears them for show," came a halting voice from behind them. The two turned to see a plump, bearded man in a huge overcoat sitting alone at a littered table.

"I beg your pardon," said the Professor, addressing the gentleman.

"I say, he only wears them for show."

"Ah yes. For show. And very elegant they are, those teeth," the Professor replied diplomatically. "I met a dwarf in Beddlington once who had such teeth. He was an animal trainer. Marvelous man with gibbon apes and orangutans."

Jonathan tried to get the attention of the sleeping proprietor as the Professor sat down at the overcoated man's table and launched into his story of the Beddlington Ape. The sleeper lurched as Jonathan tapped him on the shoulder, then nodded pleasantly, smacked his lips, and toppled off his perch, crashing to the ground, stool and all. *"What! What! What!"* He shouted in a flurry of bewilderment. The Cheeser felt responsible and hoisted the man to his feet apologetically. None of the several people in the pub, aside from the Professor and his companion, took any notice of the misfortune. The collapsed chair was righted, with no damage, finally, seeming to have occurred. The be-tumbled man stared bleary-eyed at Jonathan, smiled idiotically, and clambered back onto his stool. He closed his eyes and nodded off again.

"Just draw one for yourself," said the overcoated man who, it turned out, was named Lonny Gosset. "Put five pennies in the can and draw it yourself."

Jonathan did and as soon as he tasted the ale he was sorry he'd ever undertaken the venture, for it was flat, tasteless liquid related more closely to the swampy pools upriver than to anything drinkable.

"This is Mr. Lonny Gosset," the Professor told Jonathan as the Cheeser sat down. "He's a milliner, a hat maker, and he was telling me that business isn't worth a peach hereabouts."

"Not a peach," assented Lonny Gosset, shaking his head in a befuddled way. "Not since that cursed Selznak arrived with his toads and such. Bloody awful beasts abroad on th-the highroad. People moving off downriver."

"Who is this Selznak?" asked Jonathan, gazing into his glass of ale and wondering what sort of a fiendish thing Gosset had encountered. He offered some of his ale to the Professor, who looked at it then shook his head. "He's not an altogether nice chap, I gather."

"Nice chap!" Gosset almost shouted. "A curse is what. A dwarf of some sort from the Forest. Came upriver six months back through Willowood. You heard about Willowood?"

"Yes," said the Professor.

"And Stooton-on-River?"

"No."

"All gone by the boards. Empty! Things are . . . abroad in the land," Gosset said darkly.

"I don't like things abroad in the land," said Jonathan in a practical tone of voice. "Not by half."

"I'm afraid," responded the Professor, "that things abroad in the land might not care for you or me much either. Now you know me as a man of science. And you know that I hold with fact. Observation and deduction are man's most useful tools, Master Cheeser, but I'd have to say, if pressed, that they're sometimes overshadowed by premonition."

"I don't go much for premonitions either. Let's get the supplies and see what mischief Dooly and old Ahab are up to, shall we?"

"Like a shot," said the Professor. The two shook Gosset's hand and left him muttering darkly beneath his breath about silk hats and things abroad and wretched little beasts.

They popped into Hobbs' General Merchandise where they were scrutinized by the owner, old Hobbs, who was whiskered and stuffy-looking and all bound up in buttons and collars and tight fitting, starchy clothes. Jonathan muttered to the Professor that Hobbs' tailor had the same sense of humor as had the sleeping pub man's dentist. Although the Professor had to agree, he replied that it was good to see such a staunch and solid member of the community.

"Someone, at least, is bearing up," the Professor observed.

Quick as you please, the two were loaded up and heading raftward, back past the abandoned tack-and-feed store where the party of mice overseen by the blinking toad were still gnawing away at the wall. Jonathan waved his arms and cut a caper or two as if preparing to lunge at them, but Professor Wurzle indicated that it might not be a good idea to go stirring up the local forest denizens. In light of their conversation with Lonny Gosset, the Cheeser had to agree. Both men made away down the road to the harbor where, in the late evening gloom, no raft was to be seen.

Jonathan's first thought was that they somehow reached the wrong harbor. Then it occurred to him for the briefest of moments that there never *had* been a raft at all, and he felt a strange relief momentarily as if he had awakened to find out that the dark fears of a nightmare had been just that—a dream.

Suddenly the Professor shouted "Foul play!" and began examining the frayed ends of the trailing ropes that had tied the raft to the dock.

"Dooly wouldn't have played us foul," Jonathan responded. "He's a peculiar enough lad, to be sure, but as trustworthy as either of us."

"Not Dooly," said the Professor, holding the rope and aloft. "These ropes have been chewed through. Our raft was set adrift."

"By the powers!" cried Jonathan, remembering that old Ahab was aboard. "The fiends. It was those mice and the toad. They've done this out of spite for us having scattered them on our way into town."

The Professor gave Jonathan a sidewise look. "Mice and toads don't do things out of spite. They don't think up reasons. I fear that our friend Gosset is correct. Something has come upon the land!"

"There you go again. Things 'walking abroad' and 'coming upon the land.' It's enough to make a body tired. Our raft, somehow, has come upon the river, and we've got to go get it." Jonathan began striding back and forth trying to think. But the more he tried, the harder it became. Following the river overland wouldn't do, for beyond Hightower travel was wretchedly slow and the two of them, even on horseback, if they had horses, would have to pick their way along the treacherous paths of the Goblin Wood: they might never catch up with the raft until Seaside. What they needed, clearly, was an airship full of elves, but such a thing wasn't to be had. Jonathan furrowed his brow and continued to stride about. The Professor didn't seem nearly as perturbed.

"We'd better start walking, my boy," he said, shrugging his shoulders with an air of finality.

"Where?" cried Jonathan.

"Why downriver, of course. Dooly must have been napping, but he'll put in to shore as soon as he finds he's adrift. There may be precious little sleep for the two of us tonight though if he puts in much below the village."

"Dooly!" shouted Jonathan. Of course. He felt a fool. Dooly was on board and would eventually put in to shore. The filthy mice didn't know they had Dooly on board. Good old stowaway Dooly!

Then from up the hill toward town in the darkness of the unlit road, the two heard a shout, as if someone was hailing them. A lone figure came jogging down toward the harbor in a wild side-legged run shouting, "Ho, Mr. Cheeser! Ho, Professor!" The two on the dock felt their hearts sink as Dooly, out of breath, lurched up and looked with amazement at the empty dockside. "The raft is gone!"

"And Ahab on it," said Jonathan. "We'll have to walk aways downriver before Ahab puts into shore."

Dooly was in a state. "Oh, Mr. Bing Cheese," he almost wept, "they said you wanted to speak to me. They said you and the Professor had need of me, so I come right along. I said to myself: if you please, Dooly, says I, don't hesitate. Bung right along. And I did, but I couldn't find neither one of you and no one would say a thing when I asked them."

"Who told you such a thing?" asked Jonathan, flabbergasted.

"It doesn't matter now," the Professor broke in. "We have to go after that raft."

"We need a canoe, that's what. A canoe for the three of us." Jonathan looked about, noting several that were tied up in the harbor.

"My old grandpa would find one and would have it too. Borrow it if he had to," Dooly chimed in. "Like that one there, down along the rocks."

"We can't just go stealing a man's canoe," said Jonathan, even as the three of them were heading for it.

"I think we'd best follow the example of Dooly's grandfather in this case," said the Professor. "I'll leave my card, though, here under a rock by this stake, and he can send for some money in pay."

In a trice, Dooly, Professor Wurzle, and Jonathan Bing were swirling downriver in the borrowed canoe, paddles dipping furiously, in pursuit of the disappeared raft.

A gibbous moon crept out from behind a swirl of cloud and seemed to smile down on them as they sped on their course. Its pale shape reflected on the water in front of the canoe, and they seemed to be racing along in pursuit of it, the only bright spot ahead in the dark night. The shores along either side became forested once again, and vague shadows crept along the fringes. Jonathan looked over his shoulder, but because of the bend of the shore and the thickness of the forest there was no sign of Hightower Village. In truth, it might not have been there at all except for the dim light in the windows of the tower on the ridge in the murky distance. Even from where he sat on the cold river, Jonathan could see what must have been the red glow of embers churning from the great chimney and the gray phantasmal shapes of the swirling smoke. The night seemed to grow colder as he watched, but the certainty that they were leaving such a strange place rapidly behind helped to offset his dread. He dipped his paddle earnestly into the water and turned his face toward the retreating silver moon.

Chapter 6

Fog Along the Goblin Wood

❊

LONG into the night it was dreadfully still as the three companions canoed wearily in the moonlight. After an hour's hectic dipping, they wisely decided to work in shifts, one of them resting for a quarter of an hour while the other two paddled on apace.

Overhead, the heavens hung thick with stars, each a bright jewel in the night sky. Their cold light, however, seemed to make the air even more chill. Frost had already begun to form its tiny crackling patterns on the shore grasses, and most of the wild things in the forests were giving serious thought to whether they ought not to bolt the burrow door, throw an extra quilt or two on the bed, and nod off for a good, four-month's sleep.

Jonathan, relatively warm in his heavy coat and fur cap, had similar thoughts. But Twombly Town and the cheese-houses and the chair with the stag's head carved on the seat might as well have been on the moon; they seemed as distant. Though merely a journey of several days upriver, it was as if they were in some comfortable foreign land away over the seas.

In his weariness, Jonathan's head kept slumping, his

chin almost bouncing against his chest. But each time just as sleep would overcome him, it would be his turn to take up a paddle. Once he managed to fall solidly asleep and began to dream of the round-faced man of the four coins holding out a wedge of green cheese on a glowing platter while a great wooden clock behind him chimed the hours and paintings of the sun and moon on the clock face spun dizzily, lopping off the days as if they were seconds. But when Jonathan reached for the cheese, a wrinkled face peeked out from behind the swinging pendulum in the clock and a hand leaped forth and snatched the cheese from the plate. The wedge of cheese turned just then to a tiny heap of dust and blew away across a long, pock-marked, empty plain, and Jonathan lurched awake with a shout to find himself once more on the wide river.

Dooly was, in truth, the only one of the three who didn't appear to be tired. Jonathan and Professor Wurzle had to force him to give up the paddle now and again for a rest, and it seemed that he grew more energetic as the air grew colder. To the horror of his two companions, he continually stood atop a thwart to get a better view of the river ahead. The canoe rocked crazily each time and caused the Professor to launch into a discussion of gravity and the other six major forces, especially those of toppling and upending.

"It's nearly midnight," the Professor observed, consulting his own pocketwatch.

"It seems like twice that to me," said Jonathan, immediately wondering exactly what he meant by it. "But the odd thing is we haven't yet come upon the raft."

"Dangerously odd," the Professor agreed. "Should have caught up to it an hour ago. Given the rate of river flow and a double paddle dip increase. Let me calculate for a moment here. Two, aught, aught, carry the five, round off for decimalia—" The Professor gazed shrewdly at Jonathan. "Even given an hour's head start, it shouldn't have been more than four hours ahead of us. We should have overtaken the raft two hours back."

Jonathan was struck with a grim thought. "What if it drifted ashore and we passed it?"

"If you please, sir," Dooly put in, "I been keeping a powerful lookout along shore, your honors, and I didn't see no raft yet. Maybe I'll just clamber up here atop the thwart and have another go at it."

Jonathan and Professor Wurzle grasped either side of the canoe and held on, expecting momentarily to be catapulted into the cold river.

"Sit down there, Dooly!" shouted the Professor.

"Yes, sir, Mr. Wurzle, sir. Right away, sir. Bless me, sir, I was all come over with a fit, sir, and forgot about what you said back there about the twirl of the land and the 'petual spins of this and that."

"Quite all right, Dooly. Try to remember next time."

"If we did pass it," Jonathan said, "say if it was in the shadows or something, then we'd have to paddle upriver to fetch up with it again."

"You're very right," said the Professor. "That's a fact which, right now, in itself, isn't as frightful as it might become."

"How so?"

"As it will be, let's say, two or three hours from now when we're twice as far downriver."

"Then let's either turn the canoe about or put into shore and discuss the matter," Jonathan said, feeling a bit lost.

"I could almost be sure, sir, that the good dog and his craft aren't in no shadows. My eyes go right through shadows like they weren't there at all. No, sir, I believe we'd best plunge on, as my grandpa said. He used to say a poem to me what ended so: 'Plunge on, plunge on, plunge on, da-dah, da-dah, da-dah,' it went, or something like that."

"Your grandfather was what they call a sage, Dooly," said the Professor. "But do we trust to Dooly's eyes and to his grandfather's da-dahs, or do we beat back upriver? I'm inclined, given the scientific facts of the matter, to turn her about like you say."

"*Yiii!*" howled Dooly, waving his paddle aloft.

"It's not as bad as all that," the Professor began, but Dooly continued to wave and point skyward. "The moon, the moon!" he cried.

Jonathan, startled by Dooly's shout, saw nothing but the round white ball, glowing as ever, floating in the darkness and encircled by stars. The tail end of a tiny dark cloud obscured a chunk on the lower edge for a moment but disappeared into the night, leaving the moon's surface unbroken. "Do you have to shout so, Dooly?" asked Jonathan, worked up, in truth, by his fears that the raft and Ahab were now behind them. And as if to make matters worse, wisps of fog came floating out over the river just then from the pond-dotted downs along shore.

"Fog," said Jonathan to no one in particular. "We'll lose our way in the fog." And it suddenly felt to him as if it was very late at night indeed.

"There it is again!" cried Dooly, pointing. "Them's no clouds. No, sir. Witches is what it is, and not just one but a fleet. There's witches across the moon!"

The Professor sputtered. He was more concerned, as was Jonathan, with the fog wisps that were beginning to blow out over the river and with the curtain of it that rose from the downs like a gray cloak. But he could see, as Dooly said, dark shapes in the sky. Silhouetted against the circle of the moon as if cut of black satin were the figures of three conical-capped witches. Dark robes trailed out behind like the tattered sails of ghost ships adrift in the sky. To Jonathan's amazement, each was astride a long broomstick, a thing he'd heard about but, of course, had never believed. Shrill cackling laughter wafted down on the night wind, and as the three witches passed across the face of the moon into darkness two more appeared, and three after them. When the fog finally enfolded the canoe and only gray mist could be seen, the grim laughter continued to clatter earthward like a fall of icicles.

Dooly groaned, his head in his hand. "Old grandpa knew those ladies," he said. "Yes, sir. And I don't imagine I want to. He come upon them once in the wood. In the Goblin Wood, in fact, if my memory serves—which wouldn't make if far off, would it, Professor?"

"Less than half a league, Dooly."

"Aye, grim luck. They was having a sort of thing in the woods. And there was goats there with two heads and a bubblin' pot and there wasn't one of 'em that didn't have a big sickle—"

"And I think we'd best keep the story for another time. For the daylight, let's say," said Jonathan.

Dooly was hunched up in the bow. The memory of his

grandfather's story was something he shouldn't have ferreted out, not just then.

"Well now," said Jonathan, "we're in a pickle. Do we come about?"

"If we can't see the shore, Jonathan," said the Professor, "then we can't know whether we're making headway, marking time, or losing ground. We certainly can't paddle upriver in a fog."

"Perhaps the fog will lift." But Jonathan knew it wouldn't, even though a good breeze was springing up at their backs. The fog was thick as a shroud and there were fewer clear patches all the time.

Laughter still rang strangely in the distance—laughter broken by an occasional shriek like the wail of a banshee. Although the eerie sound waxed and waned as if at the mercy of the winds, the three in the canoe seemed to be drawing nearer to it. All three paused in their paddling and listened, eyes peering widely into the murk ahead. Distant chanting, buried amid the clamor of laughs and shrieks and mingled with the occasional thudding gong of a great club whacked against an iron kettle almost drowned the sporadic barking of a terribly upset dog.

It was Ahab, ahead on the river and in the midst of some deviltry. The canoe cut through the standing mists as Jonathan, the Professor, and Dooly dipped their paddles as one, the grim sounds growing louder in their ears.

In the fog it was impossible for them to guess just how far they could see into the murk ahead. To the three in the canoe, the river water immediately around the boat was visible, but it was of the same pale gray color as the night air and two or three yards away the air and water blended so that no one could be sure what it was he was seeing. Jonathan feared they would run right up against the raft in their haste.

They saw the lights glowing in the midst when they were still some ten yards distant. The hooting and gonging and shrieking and laughing was not so much ahead of them on the raft as all around them—in the woods along the invisible shore.

The barking had ceased which Jonathan did not like by half. He felt like calling Ahab's name, but the unlikelihood that he could be heard over the din—and his dread of whatever made that din—kept him silent. He looked over at the Professor, who simply shrugged, leaned forward, then whispered, "Goblins."

Dooly seemed to shrink down even lower, if that were possible. Jonathan felt himself turning spongy. It was likely that they had already passed within the fringe of the vast, dark expanse of the Goblin Wood which separated the outposts of Willowood Station and Stooton-on-River from the upriver villages. It was a particularly bad place to be at night.

All of the running lights around the raft were lit, and, to Jonathan's amazement, the masts were rigged and the raft was sailing with the breeze at a good clip, accounting for the extra hours the companions had paddled in search of her.

The glow of the torchlight reflected off the fog and stained the air a ruddy pink roundabout the raft. Strange shadows undulated against the fog on all sides as if the torchlight were shining against a dim gray curtain. On deck were a dozen capering little men, tilting this way and that and howling and cackling and pounding away with their feet and fists against anything handy.

Dooly cringed before this fearful drumming; Jonathan gave him an encouraging nod in an attempt to look stalwart and quell his fears. Because the three in the canoe were in the darkness and looking into the light, they could see the goblins clearly before the goblins could see them. But the stalwart looks were all for naught when they drew near enough to glimpse the hideous faces of the goblins on board.

Although each was smaller even than a dwarf and thin and bony like a skeleton with a skin of leather stretched over it, Jonathan found it hard to convince himself of the facts. The figures seemed to grow and shrink on the mist like their leaping shadows. One moment they looked like smiling, prancing elves and the next like grim shadows of death with sunken eyes and protruding teeth and ghastly, misshapen hands like the claws of crabs.

There was no order to their leaping about nor rhythm to their gonging and pounding, and though no fires save the torches burning on deck, were in evidence, their cauldron sent steam bubbling up into the fog. One great goblin, taller than the rest by a grisly head, howled and cursed as he stirred the contents of the pot, his eyes glowing like embers in a ruin of a face. His companions, seemingly without purpose, toppled past and dropped random objects into the bubbling cauldron: the sextant, a cheese, the keg of nails, a length of rope, and all manner of lunatic things. It was all done in a rout—all mayhem done for the ghastly pleasure of the thing. Jonathan, whose teeth were chattering, didn't like the affair at all.

A cry like the wail of a marsh devil at sun-up went up from one of the leaping goblins. The three companions had been seen. The troupe of goblins lined the rail, pointing and beckoning and howling and laughing. Jonathan saw one rolling the dill pickle keg along the deck and off into the river, and it bobbed along near the canoe for a moment before the current took it and swept it on toward the sea.

Then one of the goblins yanked a torch from its fastenings and Jonathan was certain it was intent upon firing the ship. Instead, the creature set fire to its own hair and leaped blazing to and fro about the deck. Wild laughter issued from between its pointed teeth, and the fire seemed to melt the skin from its face and it ran down and left only a grinning skull with flaming hair.

Jonathan was caught between terror and disgust, but Dooly felt only terror as he sat curled up in the bow with his head buried in his arms. Then the goblins, each produced a long curvy-bladed knife and waved it about. Jonathan and the Professor backed water like sixty, both deciding without discussion to reconnoiter and consider strategies. But when a goblin lurched along carrying Professor Wurzle's oboe gun and dropped it too into the cauldron, the Professor decided he'd backed water long enough.

"By golly!" he shouted, brandishing his paddle. His outburst seemed to send the goblins into a wild fit, and they stamped about as several others set themselves afire.

The canoe was in a pretty pass because Jonathan wasn't quite as anxious to save the oboe gun as was the Professor, and he was still backing water as the Professor was dipping forward madly.

While the canoe hung there suspended, moving neither forward nor backward, Jonathan was amazed to see Ahab, huge in relation to the goblins, burst forth from the cabin door like a whirlwind. The goblins had clearly supposed he was secured within because he took them unawares and sent them into a mad caper.

It was a curious sort of rout altogether though. Howls of laughter rolled out over the water, and within the space of a moment, all the goblins were blazing like little upright bonfires. Ahab leaped up behind the great pot-stirring goblin and, unmindful of his grim, melting face and flaming head, picked him up by the seat of his trousers and, with a shake and a bit of prancing, flung him overside and into the river.

The thing shrieked as it fell, hissing and bubbling. When it finally sputtered to the surface, the goblin didn't appear half so terrifying as when it went in. Now it looked simply like a very wet, evil, sorry little man. Its companions on the raft, however, remained flaming and ranting and took to throwing things at the floating goblin.

Ahab was pleased with his work and wasted no time before latching onto another and sending him riverward. Jonathan, bucked up at the sight of the courageous Ahab, and Professor Wurzle, fearing that his oboe gun would be lost in the river, shot across the final few feet of water between them and the raft and looped the painter around the bolt in the stern.

Then it was but a simple thing to climb up over the rail because the goblins—the six or so that were left—were dashing in a fiery circle about the deck, round and round the hold. It was impossible to tell whether Ahab, smack in the center, was chasing the goblins or the goblins were chasing Ahab.

What stirred the Professor into action was the sight of one of the goblins brandishing the dripping oboe gun above his head. The weapon had clearly been cranked up, for the whirl-gatherers were twirling and it seemed as if at any moment the thing would wrench itself free and sail off on one of its lunatic journeys.

The Professor went for the goblin and grabbed at the gun, but the goblin held on, hooting and shrieking and tearing at Professor Wurzle with its talons. Old Wurzle, unmindful of the pain, flew into a very pretty rage when the oboe gun pulled free and sailed out over the river. Through a clear space in the fog the Professor saw the gun sail fifty feet or so, bury itself in the water, and emerge again a bit further on only to disappear into the swirling mists. His oboe gun was lost, and this time there were no handy trees to climb to fetch it back.

Professor Wurzle, in a fit of rage, dumped the clawing, flaming goblin, still laughing and hooting in a tiresome way, into the river.

Jonathan and Ahab pursued the last of the goblins around the deck. Finally, Dooly, plucked up enough courage to clamber up onto the raft and, emboldened by the sudden lack of goblins on board, collar the last one. Then, shutting his eyes so as not to have to look it in the face, Dooly pitched it into the river.

Goblin heads bobbed out of sight in the direction of the far shore. Their laughter, now somewhat dampened, faded in the night. Besides the gallant Ahab, the three companions sat puffing on the bow, Jonathan tut-tutting over the loss of the oboe gun. If truth were told, however, he wasn't as concerned as he seemed, for he had never been entirely convinced of the thing's usefulness.

It must have been close to three in the morning when finally they sailed out of the bank of fog into the clear night again. The Goblin Wood was a dark, misty blotch on the hillsides behind, and the bright moon shined once again along the riverside. Hillocky grasslands ran away for miles on either side toward the sea.

It took an hour of puttering about for the crew to straighten the mess and tally the losses. The strangest thing was that the cauldron had entirely disappeared. Where it had been, or had appeared to be, was a heap of scrap and trash: several broken barrel staves, some rusted bits of metal, fragments of crockery, Dooly's troll chain, and the skeletal remains of a half dozen oddly shaped fish no doubt caught from the river by the goblins.

They threw the whole mess overboard with the exception of Dooly's chain which they hung once more on the mast. Jonathan swore he'd seen a cauldron and the Professor agreed. Dooly was too baffled even to know he was baffled until the Professor told him it was all an illusion.

"Enchantment!" cried Dooly, familiar with goblin trickery due to the tales of his old grandpa.

The Professor explained that that was exactly the case. Coming out of the cabin door, Jonathan stated that the case was that the goblins had drank half the rum and ruined the rest. Sure enough, floating in the half-drained rum barrel were another dozen or so partially consumed fish. There was nothing to be done but dump the stuff overboard, keg and all.

This was a disappointment to say the least, because both Jonathan and the Professor had been keen on the idea of a mug or so of hot buttered rum. But they'd see precious little of it, at least for awhile.

So the pickles were gone and the rum ruined, and all the remaining loaves of bread had their centers eaten out and looked more like hats or helmets than bread. The Professor said that *he*, at least, didn't too much rue the loss of the rum which was pretty clearly responsible for the goblins having been in such a state. Sober goblins, it seemed certain, would have been a bit more dangerous. Everyone agreed that they had gotten off easily, all things considered. Just then Jonathan remembered the port that Mayor Bastable had laid in, and he went off to fetch a bottle and three glasses.

It seemed that the moon no sooner sank behind the Elfin Highlands than the sun came peering up over the White Mountains and it was morning. As the Professor had predicted, they had gotten little sleep that night; but they *had* gotten their raft back and could feel a hint of honest pride in having set to flight a party of marauding goblins.

Chapter 7

Magicians and Axolotls

❧

THE river carried them along toward the sea, and for three days they did little else but eat, sleep, and throw out an occasional fishing line.

Professor Wurzle found that his arms and chest had been scratched fairly thoroughly during his tussle with the goblins, and the long red scrapes insisted upon becoming infected, swelling to nasty-looking welts. The Professor hobbled along gritting his teeth each time he moved, but demanded to be allowed to take his turn at watch with the others.

They were miles from Willowood Station when it became clear that something had to be done for the Professor. He had, finally, taken to bed, and food and water were brought to him. He was so thoroughly sore that he even ached, he explained, when just blinking his eyes.

"I'm afraid, Jonathan," he said that afternoon when they were but a few short miles above Willowood, "that I'll need more than rest to make a recovery from these scratches. The goblin must have had some filthy substance on his hands."

"Ah, yes," agreed Jonathan, who was at a bit of a loss.

The only disinfectant on board was a sort of salve that smelled of eucalyptus and didn't prove to be of much benefit. "Between Stooton-on-River and the sea there's not even an outpost. What with Willowood gone and Stooton, according to old Gosset, gone too, I'm not sure where to find any medicines. I've been thinking, though, that whoever looted Willowood no doubt made off with valuables, but probably not with medicines. There might still be a few lying about the old apothecary. What thief would steal medicines?"

"What thief indeed?" asked the Professor. "But I don't believe that it will matter much anyway in this case. When do we pass Willowood Wharf?"

"In about an hour."

"Then put in, boy, put in. Have you any knowledge of herb lore?"

"Only in making tea."

"Then I'll have to explain a bit. Fetch up that pen and paper and write this down. I'll need arrowroot first off and the flowers of oxalis, about a handful, and a good deal of spearmint. Can you find such?"

"So far, so good, Professor."

"Then," the Professor continued, "I'll need a half dozen of those yellow tree fungi—the ones that look like clam shells and have the pink dots all up and down one side. I shouldn't wonder if you have a difficult time finding them. Look on the underside of old, fallen hemlocks."

"Old, fallen hemlocks," Jonathan wrote dutifully, "underside. How large are these fungi, Professor?"

"About the diameter of a man's head, when they're ripe. If you find them much larger they're useless. They go all to slime when you touch them. Slimy ones are no good at all."

"No slime," wrote Jonathan.

"And then I'll need a jar of cobweb—dusty cobweb if you can manage—and a half dozen little axolotls, preferably speckled ones."

Jonathan shook his head as if amazed. "Will this accomplish the cure, Professor, all this vegetation and such?"

"I hope so. I got the recipe from a wandering bunjo man who came through town years ago. Claimed he had beans that would grow into houses. A lot of foolery I told him."

"Of course," said Jonathan. "Of course."

"But I couldn't argue with his poultice. No one can deny the curative properties of fungi and axolotls."

"No one would dare," Jonathan assented.

No sooner had they settled on the recipe list than Willowood hove into view on a distant headland. The wharf, which had once been the center of most of the valley's river trade, was smashed to bits. Broken pilings jutted through the shallow river water but supported nothing but birds. Only a small section of dock remained whole, and it had been hacked up and was leaning in such a way as to make it of doubtful use. But it was the only place to dock so Jonathan angled in toward it. Dooly perched on the bow with the painter, ready to leap ashore and tie up.

For a moment Jonathan considered the possibility of tieing up to one of the pilings twenty or thirty feet off shore and paddling the coracle ashore. The raft would be a bit safer from deviltry that way. But then it was true that whatever sort of fiends were likely to be lurking about the station could just as easily steal the coracle and paddle out to the raft, so Jonathan figured it wasn't worth the trouble. They tied up at the dock.

The Professor lay on the bunk covered with several blankets against the chill. He had a mug of tea, some cheese, and a wrinkled apple for lunch. Beside the bunk was a good, stout oak truncheon should there be uninvited guests. Dooly and Jonathan stuck their heads in at the door and waved goodbye, then tromped off along the path toward the remains of the station.

The boathouse beyond the dock was a wreck. The roof had caved in and it looked as if someone had set in to build a cabin and then slipped up and put the roof of a lean-to on it. The windows were absolutely gone. There were only a few shards of glass laying about. Planks of ship-lap had been torn out of the walls and dashed to bits; they lay scattered outside. All in all, the boathouse wasn't much good any longer.

The several buildings that had been Willowood Station were in much the same condition as the boathouse. Roofs had collapsed, doors were broken and dangling from ruined hinges, walls were caved in, and the wind blew along through everything as if it were meant to. Nothing remained in the houses but broken furniture and ragged curtains. Food and clothing and everything of value had disappeared. Dark weeds sprouted through collapsed stoops and stairways, and forest vines crept in and out of broken windows and chimneys as if the forest were reclaiming the town for its own. And over all hung a dreadful silence that was broken only by the cries of an occasional bird. Dooly was certain ghosts were about but didn't let on to Jonathan for fear that he would agree.

"What do you suppose, Mr. Cheeser, sir, about this here wreckage? Was it a hurricane that came through?"

"I don't believe so, Dooly," Jonathan replied. "Although I rather wish it were. But what confounds me is that everyone is gone. I don't want to be morbid or anything of the sort, but one would suppose that there might be such a thing as a body or two left lying about, if you see what I mean?"

"Maybe the storm blew 'em all away down the river. Just sent 'em flying like bugs."

"That's one possibility, surely," Jonathan said. "But something, as they'd say at Seaside, is fishy here. What storm knocks the corner posts out of a house simply to allow the roof to cave in? And what sort of wind pulls entire planks out of walls and takes the time to smash them against things and break them into splinters? Craziness is what it is. And the worst of craziness, too?"

"Like them goblins all burning up and shouting," Dooly offered by way of illustration, "even after we put 'em in the drink."

"Exactly like that," Jonathan agreed.

"Pah!"

"Excuse me?" Jonathan sounded surprised.

"I didn't say it," said Dooly. "I thought you did."

"Pah, sir! I say," came a piping voice from within the wreck of a pub, and a gaunt sort of a man in a tall hat poked his head out a window. "Nothing, my friends, is done with no purpose. Goblins haven't the sense to do anything themselves. They're set into motion and caper away until someone sends them home."

Jonathan bowed, and Dooly stepped behind him and goggled at the man. "A wizard!" Dooly exclaimed, astounded.

"At your service, sirs," said the wizard. "How perceptive of you to notice. I suppose my hat rather gives me away. Something of a beacon, I don't doubt." His hat was pretty much that, tall and cone-shaped with stars and crescent moons all over it. All in all it couldn't have been more wizardish. It kept sliding over his brow and back down the rear of his head as if it belonged to Gilroy Bastable. The wizard yanked at it once or twice, then disappeared, reappearing momentarily with a bit of elastic which he attached to either side of the hat and tucked under his chin.

"Makes me go blue," he said.

"Quite," said Jonathan, not knowing how else to respond.

"But if one must go blue, he'd better pop right at it and see it through. No use expecting the cap to stay on its own. It'll have its way or know the reason why unless I lash it on with a strap and choke."

"Perhaps if it weren't quite so tall," offered Jonathan. "But then I know nothing of wizard hats. I suppose it must be as tall as that."

"Sometimes even taller. I have this extension." The wizard pulled a sort of tube with a carved ivory baby's face on top out of his cloak and attached it to the peak of the cap. The whole works balanced there like a flag pole atop a tower. The wizard looked ponderously uncomfortable and began to gasp, finally giving up the effort and holding the cap upright with his hands.

"Frightful nuisance, this, but a wizard needs such props if he's to be more than a carnival magician with a deck of playing cards tied together with string. And speaking of cards, allow me to give you my own."

Jonathan took the proffered card and read the name aloud for Dooly's benefit. "Miles the Magician," he read.

"Meelays, if you will. It sounds rather commonplace otherwise. If you stress the first syllable and accent the final *e* it gives it an exotic flavor. Rather an oceanic touch, I believe."

"Meelays then," said Jonathan pronouncing it in the odd way the wizard had requested. In truth, Meelays sounded about twice as foolish as plain Miles which is a simple and honest and pleasant sort of name. "Are you the only one about? No traders anymore?"

"Traders, is it? No, I don't suppose there are. Haven't been for nearly four months."

"Been deserted that long, eh? Four months?"

"That's about how I judge it. I've only been here three though."

"You've seen it pretty well go to bits then, I'd guess," said Jonathan. "Big storm or something?"

"Or something is just about the case. I believe you were hinting fairly strongly at it a moment ago. In fact, I couldn't help overhearing your mention of goblins. One wouldn't normally expect to find them outside the Wood, at least not in any quantity. But such times as these aren't what a wizard like myself would call normal. No, normal is hardly the word." The wizard dismantled his cap and hooked the pinnacle with the ivory head to a band inside his robe which at one time had been of a salmon pink color. Now it was simply brown and needed a cleaning.

"I've heard a great deal these past weeks about 'strange times' and such," said Jonathan, "and can only advise you to come up to Twombly Town for a bit. We don't much go for alterations of any nature; changes in the weather and the seasons are enough for us."

"And for me, dear sir!" the wizard cried, spreading his hands before him in a gesture that looked as if it was intended to assure Jonathan and Dooly of his innocence. "But none of us," he continued mysteriously, "are immune from adventure and change when such things come calling. Do you follow me?"

Jonathan nodded, more out of politeness than anything else. Then Dooly, in a state of marvel over the wizard's cap and sure that it provided some nature of wonderful talent, asked, "But did you send everyone away? Make 'em dry up and sail off like bugs, Mr. Wizard, sir, if I might ask, as it were?"

"Oh indeed no," replied the wizard. "Didn't you just understand me to say it was goblins? The traders wandered off, one by one, long ago. Six months maybe. And there weren't more than twenty or so at the station anyway. Most of them, I suppose, went downriver to the sea, being sailors by nature as well as trade. I passed a raftload, in fact, downriver, and they were awfully tight-mouthed about their reasons for closing up shop. It seems there was this dwarf," the wizard said in low tones. And Jonathan, fearing that he was going to touch on that very subject, rolled his eyes. "Do you know of him then?" asked the wizard. "I shouldn't wonder. We'll all know of him, I fear, before this game is played out."

"Who is this dwarf?" asked Jonathan. "And how can he go about chasing folks up and down the river? Why doesn't someone up and whack him once or twice with an oak branch—teach him to go parading around scaring folks so?"

"Don't think no one has tried. But he's not your common dwarf—not a field dwarf from the coast or a mason from the White Mountains. He's from the Enchanted Forest, and he seems to have a power over the beasts of the land. He can stop the wind from blowing," said the wizard darkly, "and cause the fog to rise at the worst possible time—and he has powers even more terrifying than those. They say that he can make the land go still—freeze men's souls. And they're right, I've seen him do it." The wizard gave his robes a bit of a swirl, and the tattered hem danced about for a moment even though the air was still. Dooly stepped behind Jonathan again and peered over his shoulder.

Jonathan felt as if he were just beginning to make out the pattern in a very complicated spider web, but that to see it any more clearly he would be compelled to get nearer than he'd like. It all gave him a creeping feeling roundabout the small of his back. He decided that he and Dooly needed to be furthering their business. The poor Professor was bedridden on the raft while the two of them passed the time of day with a wizard who had nothing but bad news. "See here," said Jonathan, "I'm afraid that Dooly and I must be off. We've a sick friend to attend to."

"And who might you *be*, sir?" the wizard asked in a tone of voice a bit too commanding for Jonathan's liking.

"Jonathan Bing of Twombly Town, at your service," he said, bowing stiffly and removing his cap. "I make cheeses."

"Cheeses," cried the wizard. "I know another man who makes cheeses. Huge cheeses. Cheeses that would drive men mad with wonder."

"Well," said Jonathan, "I don't suppose my cheeses amount to quite that much, but they aren't really too bad. They're rather in demand, in fact. Very popular out on the coast during the holidays."

"Then it's you who makes the raisin cheeses!" cried the wizard. "Why I'll be a laughingstock."

Jonathan, was favorably impressed at this outburst, and although he was fairly thoroughly swelled up with pride, he blushed a bit and felt sheepish.

The wizard insisted upon shaking his hand, then called to Dooly, who had found something amid the debris of the old pub, and shook his hand too. Jonathan thought that perhaps all this handshaking was laying it on a bit thick, but he only thought so out of modesty.

The wizard seemed to be incredibly interested in Dooly's hand. "That's quite a ring, my man, quite a ring."

Jonathan saw that indeed Dooly did have a rather marvelous ring. It was made of gold and had what appeared to be an odd, spiral-shelled, sea creature raised cameo style on the surface. The sea creature was peeking out of the shell with a cryptic eye. An elf from the Oceanic Isles could have told Jonathan that it was called a chambered nautilus, perhaps the most wonderful beast in the sea.

"Where did you get such a ring?" asked the wizard casually, as if he didn't care much one way or another.

"From my old grandpa," Dooly replied proudly. "He had four such rings, each one with a different beast—all fish of course. And he gave one to me and said it had magic in it, though he didn't say how."

"I believe he might have been right about that," said the wizard. "Who is your grandfather that he had such fine jewelry? A rich man, surely?"

"Not a word of it," said Dooly, warming to the task, as he always did, of talking about his grandfather. "He's been rich fifty times, maybe a hundred, but he gave it all away. Some here, some there. He was a Stover, of course, as I am, he being, as I've often said, my old grandpa which does, you see, connect us." Dooly paused and nodded as if he'd explained things pretty clearly and was waiting for a reply. He took another look at the ring on his hand, then a quick look at Miles' hand. "That's another such ring you've got there," he cried.

Miles shrugged. "It's a strange world, isn't it?"

Jonathan was about to admit that it was getting stranger by the moment, but Miles went right on, forgetting about rings altogether.

"Haven't seen any elves lately, have you?"

The question was rather abrupt, and Jonathan looked askance at the wizard, and, though suspicious without knowing why, answered, "Yes, an airship full about a week ago."

"A week was it? Well, you may see them again. They're particular friends of mine and altogether nice chaps, though a bit on the merry side. Wizards, as you know, are an uncommonly solemn lot, if I do say so myself. And elves must always be laughing and singing and larking even when they're out on serious missions. Good chaps though; you'll get on well with them."

This was all a bit mysterious for Jonathan and Dooly, but what was even more so was the little pile of fish skeletons Dooly was pulling out of a heap of smashed-up wood.

"Goblin food!" shouted Dooly, it being clear since the fog adventure along the Wood that goblins were voracious fish eaters.

"Goblin food indeed," said Miles. "All left over from the lot that ransacked the town a few months back, as I was saying. They just tore the place up: smashed windows, knocked over chimneys, dumped trash into mail slots, kicked the wharf and boathouse to bits—had a time of it, actually. It wasn't their doing though. Nothing ever is. He set them going just like he did at Stooton right afterward. Only three people left in town then, and they sailed downriver like geese when they got wind of the goblins. They knew he was behind it.

"The woods come creeping in now. Weeds and vines and such which, under normal circumstances, are fine things. But we needn't go into that now. Things were far worse at Stooton, I fear. But what about this sick friend you mentioned?"

"Yes," said Jonathan, pulling the list of ingredients from his pocket. "Perhaps you know where these things might be found?"

The wizard cast one eye up and down the list and looked pleasantly surprised. "It's the poultice," he said. "Yes, this will do the trick. Fancy the poultice being required down here. What is this gentleman's malady?"

"Goblin scratches and a bite or two."

"Oh my," said the wizard. "Why do we stand and talk? How long ago did he get them?"

"Three days ago."

"Oh my, my, my. You should have come to me sooner. But then you weren't coming to me at all were you? But you found me, and a good thing that is too. I have the poultice already mixed. Never go about without it. And that's fortunate for you. There isn't any spearmint in these parts. Far too wet, it is. You'd look high and low for spearmint and not get a sprig."

The wizard disappeared into the pub, and Dooly and Jonathan heard him rummaging around inside for a moment or two, although they dared not look in at the door. Miles was far too secretive and mysterious for them to go spying after him. He returned almost at once carrying a glass jar sealed with a great cork, the entire jar having been dipped after corking into hot wax.

"All we need are axolotls. A man can't keep live axolotls with him all the time, you know. What we have to do is find an axolotl den and borrow a few. They don't mind. Not a bit. Glad to do it, in fact, as long as they're returned to their den afterward and given a bit of salt."

The wizard began rummaging through the pockets inside his cloak. There were a good many of them, and he'd turned four or five inside out before he came up with what he was trying to find—a dusty leather pouch with a loose bit of rawhide tied about the mouth. Miles fiddled with the knot and worked the pouch open. He looked at Jonathan and Dooly who, in truth, were wondering what sort of marvel was likely to emerge. "Have you seen one of these?" asked the wizard as a lumpy-looking mottled thing crawled into his hand.

"It's a toad," said Jonathan.

"It's a great, fat bug." Dooly's eyes were wide with wonder.

"Actually," said the wizard, "it's what you'd call a Familiar. I'm not sure what he is, really. Sometimes I think he's a toad; sometimes, as the lad here pointed out, he seems a bug. Once I'd have sworn he was a turtle with the head of a pig, but that sounds so unlikely now that I won't even mention it. I inherited him from my old master, who used to tell the weather by him. He knows the secrets of the seven major amphibia and of the four true beasts, the platypus and dugong and such as that. If he can't find an axolotl, then no one can."

Miles the Magician bent over the Familiar and whispered at the blinking thing for a moment. Then, reaching into yet another pocket he fished out a slice of bread and tore off a piece for the Familiar. The thing poked a few good-sized crumbs away into a flap in its greenish skin, and blinked placidly. The wizard listened intently for a moment with his ear up close to the Familiar, then he carefully put the creature back into its pouch with another bit of bread and returned the pouch to his pocket.

"Well, boys, we're in luck. He says we're to look for a clump of pansies, as I already knew, down at a place where two forks of a stream merge and ferns grow high as a house top. That has to be where the Weaver and the Wincheap meet above town. You see, there are axolotls everywhere, a fact most people don't know, and they always like a bit of pansy for some reason or another. If you find pansies growing wild, you can count on axolotls being thereabouts, ready to lend a man a hand."

"Let's fetch up a score or so then," Jonathan urged, "and get back to the raft."

"Do let's," said the wizard.

The three of them clumped along for forty yards, crossed the highroad, and with the wizard leading, slid and leaped down the side of a bush-dotted hill and in among a thicket of willows. In the midst of the thicket a little brook no more than five or six feet across babbled cheerily along. They hopped from rock to rock down the center of the stream until it merged with another, larger brook and formed a stream that dumped into the river some quarter mile farther on. Among the willows, in vivid green thickets, sprouted clumps of curling ferns, towering, in places, over Jonathan's head. In midstream on a bit of an island was a little garden of pansies, purple, yellow, and violet with huge drooping petals. Within the pile of sand and soil and rock from which the pansies sprouted, were a maze of tiny crevices and caverns, and from each peeked the feathered head of an axolotl, speckled and foolish.

The wizard crouched down on the rocks and plucked forth a couple. "Slimy things, to be sure," he said, handing two over to Jonathan. "But indispensable. Half of the workings of the bestial sciences somehow depends on these things. One of the Six Links, actually, and not the least of the Six. Out in the Isles they grow to twelve feet long, they say, and go about on little wheeled devices which the elves make for them in return for services. That might be a lie, I'm not certain."

Jonathan let the two axolotls, who seemed well enough satisfied, lay limp in his hands. They were like long lumps of jelly—not something that anyone would look forward to handling.

"Four should do it," said the wizard. They all then clambered back up the hill, Jonathan remembering not to squish the axolotls, and made away through the ruined town toward the raft.

The Professor opened an eye when the three stepped into the hold but didn't do much else to acknowledge their entrance.

"Tch, tch, tch," the wizard clicked as Dooly fetched in a plate. Miles uncorked the jar and scooped out a spoonful or so of the poultice, which was a gooey and unlikely looking mixture altogether. Then, to the amazement of the two onlookers, he set the four axolotls on the plate, and they immediately began to dance about as if they were having a wonderful time of it. They dashed this way and darted that way and made little axolotl footprints throughout, pausing now and again to lick their feet clean before prancing off again through the goop. After a minute or so of such foolery, Miles plucked the four axolotls out and handed them to Dooly, who was rather at a loss over what to do with them.

"Apply this to the wounds five times a day," said the wizard, daubing a bit of the poultice onto the Professor's arm where a particularly evil-looking scratch puffed. The red seemed to go out of it immediately, and the Professor smiled and managed a nod. They smeared the stuff about on the several other scratches and helped the Professor to a sitting position on the bunk. He squeaked out a hoarse sentence at the wizard, who cautioned him against strain and then proffered a card.

"Explain the pronunciation of the name to him," he said to Jonathan. "And look me up on your way back toward Twombly Town if you have the opportunity. I'd like to hear about your adventures."

"We will," said Jonathan, "though I hope there'll be few adventures to relate."

"I wouldn't be surprised if you were wrong about that," the wizard replied shaking his head a bit and corking up the poultice jar.

Jonathan stepped across to one of the storage cabinets and fished about inside for a moment, coming up finally with a carefully wrapped cheese. He handed it to the wizard, who bowed. "Not one of the famous raisin variety?"

"The same. I hope it's worthy of its reputation."

Miles smiled and nodded. "Thank you. It's been a year since I've had a cheese of any sort and here I am with one of the true cheese wonders." He called after Dooly and retrieved the axolotls, and then with a last farewell, stepped ashore and disappeared around the ruined boathouse.

Jonathan was put out with himself because he hadn't asked the wizard to stay for supper. But they had several hours of sunlight left and might just as well press on. The Professor seemed much improved, and there was enough of the poultice on the plate to last a week. So Jonathan and Dooly cast off once more and sat together in the stern with old Ahab, watching the deserted ruins of Willowood disappear in the distance.

Chapter 8

Whacked to Bits

❈

THE day was windy and cold. Jonathan sat huddled at the tiller steering the raft around and through quick little channels between rocks in the river. It wasn't what you'd call a rapids, certainly, so there wasn't much excitement involved, just the barest chance that they'd come up against a rock if Jonathan didn't look sharp. And so he had to sit in the cold and push on the tiller now and then.

Dark clouds had sailed along through the skies for days but the wind managed to keep them in continual rout. During the past night, however, they began to bunch together and by late morning the sky was fairly black. It had, no doubt, been raining heavily behind them in the high valley. Jonathan thought that the clouds should be made to explain themselves when they acted that way—when they decided to quit fleeing before the wind and get down to business. Perhaps they had sailed entirely around the earth and met themselves again and gone bumping together and crowding up until all the blue spaces between were filled. That certainly seemed likely.

The wind tossed the branches of the hemlocks along the river and made them bend, then jerk straight, then bend again like spindly, many-armed giants waving frantically to ward off buzzing mosquitoes. It blew down the center of the river, as luck would have it, and it didn't seem to care a bit about coats and hats and mufflers—just whistled through them.

Jonathan anticipated the splash of rain—had been anticipating it for hours—but somehow it didn't come. Apparently the clouds were gathering force, which didn't at all seem like a good idea. Jonathan was reminded of gathering snowballs as a boy in preparation for a snowball war. He could recall once when he and two friends had piled snowballs until they had a dozen neat pyramids completed, each as high as their shoulders, in preparation for an impossibly huge battle. It had turned out that they hadn't time actually to have the battle; they'd spent so much time in preparation, that the afternoon sun started the piles melting. That night they froze solid once again, the melted snow turning to a sheet of ice. When Jonathan returned the following morning to carry on the campaign, he found a dozen ice pyramids clustered in a circle—the sort of thing that would set Professor Wurzle's brain bones twirling with wonder and generate theories of the pyramidal propensities of snow and of the five standard shapes. Professor Wurzle's great joy was his discovery of such phenomena. He was what Jonathan liked to call an explainer.

Five days had passed since the wizard had run the axolotls through the poultice, and Professor Wurzle was fit as a fiddle, as he liked to say while slapping himself on the chest. A dab of the poultice was left on the plate after the Professor's wounds had healed, and they saved it carefully in a little jar against future misadventures.

Stooton-on-River, or rather what remained of Stooton-on-River, they had passed morning before last. From all appearances, it hadn't a building left whole. If the waterside homes were any indication, the goblins had done a thorough job—most lay in a heap with even their chimneys knocked apart. All was abysmally quiet—so quiet that none of the three companions felt like breaking the silence because of some unnameable dread that seemed to hang in the air. Not until they had passed the ruined cottages of Little Stooton and were passing Stooton Slough did they hear again the sounds of birds and frogs and the occasional cry of an animal off somewhere in the swamps.

The Professor had begun to puff at his pipe with the fervor of a blacksmith puffing away at a forge when they came upon the great lily expanses of the slough. Old Wurzle, pretty thoroughly worked up, pointed out the spot where he'd first seen the masts of the magic galleon and then, some two miles downriver, the place among the reeds where he and Flutesnoot had come upon the broken section of mast, the oboe weapon, and the incredible gems. Dooly was for putting in to shore and wading about in the shallows in search of leftover treasure, but Professor Wurzle reminded him that five long years had passed and that any jewels which had escaped had long since found their way to the sea.

There followed a discussion of just how anyone, even elves, could have sailed such a wonderful craft so far upriver when there were leagues of overland portage to contend with where the Oriel dropped the final miles to the sea. They themselves would be weary as tramps before they even arrived at the coast since they'd be forced to leave their raft at the final upriver portage station and trek overland to the funnel of the delta. How then, asked Jonathan, could a boat of *any* nature make the trip in the other direction. It looked impossible to him.

And it looked much the same to the Professor, as the Professor admitted. "Just between the three of us," Wurzle had said, "I wouldn't say, if anything depended on my being right, that the elf galleon came upriver at all. The runes seemed to hint at islands and so I assumed, naturally, that the islands spoken of were the Oceanic Isles. Who wouldn't? But, in truth, I couldn't decipher the runes in any other way than to make them come out looking like 'sky' instead of 'sea.' But that, of course, is impossible. It's preposterous. There aren't any islands in the sky, are there?" The Professor had puffed away at his pipe, the thick smoke curling about his head, and he squinted first through one eye and then the other, looking convinced then unconvinced. "And they referred to *one* island in the sky particularly and to a sort of king. It was when deciphering those runes that I got all twisted up, to be frank. The thing seemed to hint at jewels with eyes in them and, pardon me, Jonathan when I say this, of cheeses of one phenomenal sort and another. All lunacy, you'll admit."

Somehow Jonathan was of two minds. The sensible one, the one that longed for the fireside and the beef bone and the shelf of books, had to admit to the lunacy. The other, which caused him to bolt his windows and heap oak logs on the fire whenever he read the wild and unlikely tales of goblins and trolls and dark night things written by G. Smithers of Brompton Village, didn't find the rune tales quite as lunatic. Vaguely unsettling glimpses of twisted patterns, patterns turned inside out, were demanding space in his mind somewhere even though Jonathan, in the sensible and altogether preferable light of day, tried to keep them out.

So there Jonathan sat, five days beyond the wreckage of Willowood Station and two beyond Stooton-on-River. Almost a week had passed without adventure, though that was all right with all three of the rafters, all four if you include Ahab, who had taken to sleeping most of the day atop the sailcloth in the hold. What with the wind and lowering skies, the lack of adventure was doubly welcome, since adventures in the cold and rain are about twice as likely to make you uncomfortable.

The Professor, having awakened from an afternoon nap, wandered out of the cabin with Dooly at his heels at about three o'clock—just when Jonathan was beginning to want a bit of company. They hadn't sat for more than a moment, Jonathan and the Professor making several vain attempts at getting their pipes lit and keeping them so, when the first drops of rain plunked down onto the deck. One, amazingly enough, landed with a hiss in the bowl of the Professor's pipe, putting out most of the fire that poor Wurzle had managed, finally, to stoke up. He looked at Jonathan and then at his pipe and said it was a stroke of bad luck, perhaps even an ill omen. Jonathan agreed that when water comes out of the sky to put a man's pipe out, it certainly can't be good.

But good or ill, the rain did nothing but increase, and the drops seemed to be something near the size of goose eggs. They pulled the canvas canopy across over them, optimistically figuring that the rain would take note of it and give up. It didn't though. Instead the drops grew bigger and the wind blew harder and the rain simply ignored the canopy and came charging in as if it were great fun.

Within a few minutes, Dooly and Ahab were high-stepping along toward the hold, and things were banging about the deck. The hatchdoor whacked shut about sixty times in quick succession until Dooly secured it from the inside. The Professor and Jonathan shouted across the few feet that separated them just to be heard.

Both were stupefied to see a tall hemlock growing along the larboard shore teeter in the wind, then continue to teeter, its roots tearing up from the ground in a muddy tangle and the whole thing collapsing crash splash into the Oriel.

"Seems to be a major blow shaping up," said Jonathan. "If this goes on we'll sail to the sea like the airship."

"Skip?" the Professor shouted. "Skip what?"

Jonathan waved at him to indicate that what he had said really didn't much matter. And actually it didn't, for just as they had ceased shouting, two of the empty kegs which stood against the side of the hold pitched forward and rolled smack up against the bulwark. Professor Wurzle went scooting along after them, but before he could right them three others mutinied and all five rolled this way and that as the raft bumped along in the choppy water.

The Oriel was running high, and there seemed, right then, to be little danger from rocks. But the high water rolled and bounced along in such a wild manner that Professor Wurzle hadn't a hope of keeping things righted. He was forced, finally, to summon Dooly from the cabin, and together they pounced on this keg and that, one after another, lashing them to the deck and the mast and the bulwark.

They went along so for the space of an hour, the rain falling in sheets and buckets and angry rills appearing here and there along the shore and cascading through forests and meadows into the swollen river. The wind skittering along the river whipped up little wavelets which, along with the natural roll of the current, bounced the raft along with a slap and a bang. The whole thing creaked woefully as if warning the rafters that it had had enough.

It was then that the Professor and Dooly changed their plan. Professor Wurzle had seen his own raft whacked to bits in a storm some five years back when he and Flutesnoot and the other two traders had crouched in a shallow cave above the riverbank. The storm that nearly brought round the fate of the trip hadn't sprung up with even half the rapidity and violence that this storm seemed to boast. Whole hemlocks and the limbs of alders along the unprotected bank were toppling and cracking with enough regularity that floating trunks and tangles of limbs shot along in the current beside the raft, bumping and scraping and hurrying toward the sea.

Now the Professor wasn't what you'd call a pessimist, quite the opposite in fact, but here were signs of disaster. And when disaster looms ugly before you, there's nothing for it but to light in and, as the poet said, set accounts in order.

So Dooly, directed by the Professor, began dragging the kegs along and stacking them beside one another. He was as wet by then as if he were working beneath the river rather than atop it, but so were the others. Dooly, to everyone's good fortune, hadn't yet figured out the seriousness of their straits. He liked a good storm as well as the next person and it was still all rather grand. He'd set up a keg and then lurch away after another, speaking to them as if they were chickens in a barnyard or dogs in a kennel. "You there, Mr. Keg," he'd say, grabbing for one just as it began to roll away across the deck. "Enough, sir!" And he even added a bit of sea-wise talk he learned from the Professor, shouting, "Avast, ye keg!" and threatening the rampaging things with keelhauling and plank-walking and all manners of fearsome ends if they didn't leave off and cooperate.

As each was righted and stacked next to another, the Professor looped a rope through the metal eyes on the tops of the kegs and bound them together. They hadn't gotten more than a dozen or so lashed tightly, most of them full of cheeses but with an occasional empty keg for the sake of buoyancy, when the Professor noticed that Jonathan was having a bit of a time with the tiller. They were charging along between the Highland banks like a mad buffalo, and the Cheeser couldn't hold on to the tiller. Each change in the direction of the current wrenched the slippery thing from his hand, and it flapped back and forth with a will of its own. Jonathan wrestled with it, leaning away to steady it while the rain whipped into his eyes and the wind ripped the little canvas awning above him into tatters that blew straight out in the gale like ragged banners flying above a besieged fort.

He no sooner regained control when the tiller tore loose again from his sore hands and went off on its own. Clearly he was gaining little and was losing the skin on both hands and getting thumped resoundingly by the arm of the tiller each time the raft decided to surge off on a new course.

After being whacked two or three times running, Jonathan was in a state. He couldn't wipe his eyes dry quickly enough to be able to see clearly, and a rivulet of rainwater charged continually down the back of his shirt, despite the brim of his hat which had worked well to keep out the rain until it filled up with water. So while he was being sloshed and wrenched and smacked, he went so far as to lose his temper and, between lunges at the tiller arm, to shake his fist at the whirling skies. He even shouted something at the heavy clouds, but the wind took the words away.

It struck him that shouting and raging, under the circumstances, was pretty theatrical; behavior that smacked of the dramatic was almost sure to appear foolish. Shouting at the heavens was as futile as wrestling with the tiller, so he gave up both at the same time—at about the time, in fact, that Dooly and the Professor finished getting everything lashable lashed.

The three of them stumbled dripping into the cabin where Ahab, unable to sleep, waited. The raft churned along on its own jolly course, pitching and rolling in the current and flying toward the sea like the wind.

With the storm howling outside and the drumming roar of rain on the roof, the Cheeser and Professor Wurzle once again discussed strategies. However, when all was said and done, there were no strategies worth a flea, for the four of them were trapped aboard the runaway raft, powerless to alter her course. They had to wait, they knew, for the storm to slacken and the river to go down. Though none of them had been much below Stooton before, they were fairly sure that there were no rocks or rapids about that might trouble them. Sandbars and islands were no doubt well covered by the rising waters, and it was quite possible they could plunge along for hours without much danger. Theirs was a sturdy craft, and though it creaked and cracked in the rolling current it showed no signs yet of breaking up.

None that is until with a snap and a crash the mainmast broke away, splintering a section of railing as it smashed against it and tumbled over into the river dragging along a mass of rope and furled sail. But there would be plenty of fallen trees along the riverside out of which to hew a new mast, and the extra rope and canvas that Jonathan had insisted upon taking were still piled there in the hold. So, all in all, their position remained much the same, or so Jonathan thought as he and the Professor peered out through the cabin door which they held against the wind.

Dooly was the first to notice that the speed of the raft had increased and that the bow seemed to be dipping as if the whole raft were careening forward. Jonathan and the Professor, watching the fall of the snapped mast, pointed out at almost the same instant the tangled branches of a clump of cottonwoods seemingly sprouting from midriver.

"Odd sort of cottonwoods," Jonathan said, "to be growing in the river." But then he noticed that the shore off to starboard seemed to be about a mile away and that the raft was rushing along amid occasional clumps of tree trunks. The Oriel was no longer a river, or at least it wasn't paying any attention to its banks. It had broken out over them, increased by the torrential rains, and gone lapping away over the meadows of the Elfin Highlands shouting and booming and uprooting bushes and trees.

Jonathan had hardly had time to wonder at their having abandoned the river and to consider the amusing but grim possibility of their finally being left high and dry in the middle of some meadow or other on the Highlands, when a roaring, bursting sound reached his ears—the sound perhaps of a mountain taking a rumbling stroll through the woods.

The raft tilted dizzily, slamming all four in the cabin against the forward wall, cascading the accumulated contents of the hold against them in a tangled heap. Dooly was shouting and the Professor was calling for order. Jonathan seemed to have the end of a coil of rope against the tip of his nose, but he couldn't yank his hand free to push it away.

The roar increased. Then, through the door that had crashed open, Jonathan saw a strange sight. The water all along the larboard side was eight or ten feet higher than it should have been—higher, in fact, than the top of the cabin. It was this wall of water, gray and muddy beneath the sky and littered with debris, which was doing the roaring.

Jonathan hadn't time to do much more than shout and pull himself free from the tangle when the bow of the raft dipped even farther, and they were running across the face of the wave. They no longer bumped and rolled but simply tore along over what had been a vast expanse of meadow. Pressing against the wall, Jonathan pulled himself to his feet as Dooly and the Professor endeavored to do the same.

The open door drew Jonathan forward, partly because of the tilt of the deck and partly because of the wonderful sight outside which was terrifying and thrilling at the same time. The raft quartered across the unbroken surface of the wave as it folded and boomed behind them. It was as if they were on a giant skate gliding down the surface of a frozen hill of ice. The sensation was short-lived, however, for a clump of lonely cottonwoods loomed up before them, and, with a crash and a slam, the raft caught and spun and broke into two pieces.

Jonathan and Ahab somersaulted forward through the open door, onto the ruined deck. Jonathan slammed back-foremost against the stump of the mast and Ahab slid yipping into him. Scrabbling to hold on to Ahab and to the mast at the same time, Jonathan slipped and tumbled. When the raft smashed again into the trunk of a great lone alder and went to bits for good, Jonathan and Ahab tumbled away together into the water, both of them shouting and flailing legs and arms.

When the Cheeser popped to the surface he was pleased, as anyone would be, to see the wave a hundred yards before him, dissipating in size and strength as it rolled away. The roar of the wave was gone and even the howl of the wind had decreased, replaced now by the barking of the befuddled Ahab, who paddled in tight circles around his swimming master. Jonathan, for some odd reason, was very happy, as if he'd just accomplished some grand feat.

A hard object, just then, cracked against the back of Jonathan's head. It was the little coracle which had been tossed from the deck in the crash; it had floated along upside down to crack Jonathan in the head and remind him, no doubt, that this was no time to go about feeling satisfied. On the other hand, a boat isn't at all a bad thing to come upon when you're overboard in a flood. After rubbing the bump on his head, Jonathan set about trying to right the craft. He could get one side up out of the water, but with nothing to brace his feet against, it was impossible to fling the thing over. Finally Ahab showed uncommonly good sense by trying to climb up on to it as onto the back of a great turtle. Tired from fighting to overturn it and from treading water, Jonathan followed Ahab's example and dragged himself up onto the flat bottom. Then he helped Ahab up. The craft turned out to be steadier upside down than it had been right side up.

The sky, which had been dark all day, was growing steadily darker. But a lone star on the eastern horizon showed that the onset of night, not clouds, was causing the darkness and that, in fact, the clouds were breaking up and going on their way. In a few minutes the wind fell off almost altogether, the rain decreased to a drizzle, and the coracle bumped up onto a hill and sat there.

They were perched, for the moment, on what seemed to Jonathan to be the top of a fairly round hillock covered to the depth of a foot or so by the floodwaters. The Cheeser sloshed around for a bit, toppling Ahab into the water, until he managed to right the coracle—a simple enough task with firm ground beneath his feet. Then he helped Ahab over the gunnel and stepped in himself. He was pleased to find the two paddles, wet but undamaged, still lashed securely beneath the thwarts. He untied them out of instinct, but with no real thought of where in the flooded, night landscape he might paddle.

He decided finally to stay atop his hill in hopes that the half of the raft the Professor and Dooly were on had fared better than his own and that the two might come to find him. Bits of wreckage floated roundabout from time to time although nothing salvageable presented itself. The night began to grow chilly. It had been chilly all along, of course, but the excitement had made him oblivious to the cold. Sitting now on the skinny thwart without a dry rag on him, he began to shiver. He decided that something, by golly, was going to be done. Having nothing else better in mind, he shouted once or twice, "Hallo! Hallo!" with his hands cupped over his mouth. It seemed reasonably certain to him that the Professor and Dooly were far downriver by this time, no doubt having been borne along on the crest of the wave after his own piece of raft collided with the alder. But it was a good idea to shout anyhow. If no one was about, then he'd simply waste a bit of breath. But if there was someone, anyone for that matter, then Jonathan wanted to find him. They were far too deep into the Elfin Highlands for there to be any danger of trolls or goblins, and bears and wolves would have moved to higher ground long ago.

"Hoo-ha!" Jonathan shouted, not much caring whether he made sense or not, and he went on shouting so while slapping his hands against opposite shoulders to warm himself. When he paused to say a few words to Ahab, who slumped in the puddle on the deck, looking thoroughly miserable, he heard a distant echo—a "hoo-ha" just like his own, but drawn out and mournful.

He was surprised at the echo, but imagined that the broad expanse of water surrounding him must have something to do with the phenomenon. "Hello, old Ahab," he said to the dog. "Wet are you? Wet as a sponge from the look of it. And cold, I shouldn't wonder." Just then, in the midst of his sympathizing with Ahab, the echo repeated itself a bit more clearly. "Aaaay!" it seemed to echo. Then, unmistakably, "Mister Cheeser!" with the drop of a note or so between the two *ees*.

"Hallo!" Jonathan shouted, standing in the boat which sat firmly on the little hill. "Dooly! Professor Wurzle! Whoo-hoo!" This went on so for a score of minutes, Jonathan half the time listening and half shouting, while the answering shouts drew slowly closer.

Overhead the clouds were in a whirl of activity, dashing this way and that at tremendous speeds. It looked as if they'd heard that something was brewing up toward the White Mountains and were determined to be there by morning or know the reason why. The moon, not much more than a crescent, seemed to soar out into clear spaces in the sky every few moments to get a look at the earth. It glowed silver white, tilting crazily and outlined so clearly that it appeared to be an immense hook for some heavenly giant to drape his overcoat across.

But even though the moon was just a slice, its pale rays lit the surface of the water when it loomed free of the clouds. Jonathan could now make out tousled clumps of trees roundabout him hoisting up out of the water like little clusters of vegetables clamped into an asparagus cooker. From between two such clumps, about a hundred yards off his port bow, there appeared a weird but welcome sight. It was Dooly and the Professor, sitting waist deep in the water and paddling along slowly with pieces of plank, no doubt once a part of the cabin. There was no sign of any boat beneath them, and Jonathan marveled at the sight of the two rowing boatless through the flood—probably one of the Professor's ideas. What cheered him most though was the string of kegs that trailed behind them, looped together with rope.

They looked like a little keg armada off in formation to do battle. In a minute or two they drew up with a lurch onto the hill. Then Jonathan saw the little fiddlehead which he recognized as part of their borrowed canoe.

"You might have drained it," Jonathan said smiling. "It rides higher that way. Keeps you dry, too."

"I'm afraid, Jonathan," the Professor replied, "that this is one canoe that would be easy to drain but difficult to keep so. It met with a tree stump once or twice some half mile below here and took on water, as they say. But a submerged canoe is better than no canoe at all, eh, Dooly?"

"Oh yes, sir," began Dooly. "Especially, sir, if you flap about in the waters as I do, sir. Flap about drowning whenever I'm in it, I do. If it weren't for the Professor, Mr. Bing, I'd be laughing out of my other mouth, as my grandpa liked to put it. It was what he called a shave, on account of it being so close."

"Yes, well, eh?" Jonathan said. "You've got the kegs and I the coracle, and I suppose we can eat cheese as well as anything else for a few days."

"Better yet, Jonathan," the Professor said, "we've got a bit of raft salvaged on high ground beyond that stand of trees you see off to the left, and a few yards of sailcloth and a bedroll and Dooly's coat. With a bit of luck, we won't entirely freeze, and this infernal water will drop away by morning."

"I believe it will," said Jonathan. "The storm is past, along with our chances of getting home by Christmas."

The Professor nodded "First things first. Why don't we drag these boats free of the hill and tie this keg line to the coracle with the painter, and perhaps we can tow our kegs to where the piece of raft is. Of course we can! Where the mind mutinies, the spirit stands fast! Those were the words of Captain Standish, the great dwarf general."

"Righto," said Jonathan.

"Aye, aye," Dooly agreed. Together they tugged and tied and paddled, finally, through the still waters to where the remains of the raft—a seven-foot-wide chunk with part of one wall of the cabin still attached—floated before the clump of cottonwoods to which it was tied. The weight of the four rafters as they scrambled aboard caused the raft to settle onto solid ground, there being only a few inches of water below. Within a half hour they were clear of the water altogether and sitting on a grassy hill. The flood was dropping quickly away.

There they sat, long river miles from home, the four of them on a ruined raft marooned somewhere on the Elfin Highlands. It was well on into November and no time to be wet and cold and surrounded by floodwaters. Without their raft they might just as well be destined for the moon as for Seaside.

Chapter 9

Dooly Eats Cheese with the Squire

No one got much sleep that night because it never seemed to stop growing cooler. Being wrapped up in wet sailcloth wasn't Jonathan's idea of a jolly, warm bed, but he found that wet blankets were better than no blankets at all. He and the Professor had a long discussion about the stars, and in the early morning darkness they pointed out constellations—a dipper here, an elk there and even what appeared to be a grinning, spectacled face—all revolving very, very slowly in the night sky.

To the east was a long river of stars leading along into the deep void. They were so close together that they shone like a white splash across the sky. Although the Professor pointed out the broad patch almost at once as the Milky Way, Jonathan was already aware of the name and was wondering what it might be like to be rafting away down a river of stars. What distant seas might lay deep and shifting at the mouth of that river, and what weird sea creatures might be swimming and splashing in the shallows and deep canyons of an ocean such as that? The more he thought about it, the less he really liked the idea of making such a journey. The old Oriel was enough of a river for him—too much, apparently.

Jonathan was the only one of the four of them awake when the sun came peeping up above the eastern horizon. The first bright tinge of red immediately reminded him of the morning he'd sat on the log below the mill plunking stones and watching the frogs sail past. It seemed like a year ago, even though it was only a couple of weeks. He hoped the sun would be warm enough to dry things out. If a person were dry, warm, and fed he had little to complain of. A good book and an easy chair would add a good deal, of course, but good books and easy chairs were as far off as was Twombly Town and the log below the mill where the frogs sailed along. Jonathan dozed off just at sunrise and immediately began to dream he was sailing seaward in pursuit of Mayor Bastable's hat which tumbled along in the wind before him, always just out of reach.

When he awoke, the sun was high in the sky. It must have been nine o'clock or so. Roundabout on the meadows lay pools of bright water, but most of the river had returned to its usual course. Flood debris—broken limbs and bushes and such—was lodged in among the branches of the cottonwoods and alders and occasional willows which dotted the meadowland. Below them ran the Oriel, acting as if nothing were out of the ordinary, as if she had been doing nothing for the last twenty-four hours but minding her own business. Above them and off to the south toward Seaside, the trees thickened until they added up to a full-fledged forest. They quickly turned into the Elfin Highlands as the thick, forested slopes rose away into the misty distances.

The Professor sat hunched and sleeping at the base of a tree, and Dooly could be seen hiking halfway between the river and the remains of the raft. He seemed to be intent upon clambering up into the branches of a tree and was being fairly secretive about it. He would take a hop at one of the lower branches, flail about with his legs, then drop groundward and crouch for a moment peering around the trunk toward the river. Finally, he flailed up against a limb, caught, and yanked himself into a sitting position. Soon he was in among the uppermost branches, crouched and watching.

Jonathan, noting Dooly's odd behavior, took a listen or two himself, and from somewhere downriver he heard just the breath of a tune and perhaps a song. He waited, straining to hear. Evidently the singer was approaching, for the tune grew by the moment. Jonathan could make out the words of the jolly song almost at the same instant that two figures strode into view along the muddy river road.

They were linkmen, of that he was sure—jelly men as the children of Twombly Town called them, and here they came carrying baskets of blackberries and great, green pippin apples. Both of the tiny linkmen were weighted down like hod carriers.

They were almost copies of the several linkmen who had come into Twombly Town selling jams and jellies some years back. But to Jonathan, most linkmen looked pretty much alike anyway. They all wore pointy hats like elves and had long slender legs and noses and perpetually grinning mouths. They almost always wore short pants and high woolly socks in season and out, and if it weren't for their size it would be tough to tell them from elves. Elves, of course, are a head or so taller and are altogether too secretive to be strolling along the river road singing ridiculous songs. One of the linkmen hummed loudly, rather more of a shout than a hum, while the other sang in a clear falsetto:

> *I've a basket and a berry, tra-la-la*
> *And I'm singing oh so merry, tra-la-la*
> *For the sun is shining yellow*
> *And the clouds go sailing by,*
> *And I'm such a jolly fellow, tra-la-la.*

Jonathan remarked to himself that linkmen, although superb jam makers and fruit pickers and, no doubt, altogether fine chaps, weren't poets. But almost as soon as the first fellow's verse ran itself out, the second took off and added a stanza or so.

> *Well I'm on my way to eat 'em, tra-la-la*
> *With a pleasant bit of sweetum, tra-la-la*
> *And a touch of golden cream*

With a pink and rosy gleam
That will please the dusty palate, tra-la-la.

He wrapped the verse up with such a wild and yodeling tra-la-la that Jonathan cringed even more than he had at the "eat 'em/sweetum" part.

Jonathan decided that the only thing to do would be to leap about and catch their attention, both to explain being marooned and to have a glance at the contents of their baskets which, illuminated by the sunshine, looked awfully good. Apples and berries aren't normally breakfast foods, but when it's a clear choice between fruit and cheese, cheese, although clearly one of the food marvels, is best left alone until lunch.

So just as Jonathan began a hearty wave and opened his mouth to shout, the two linkmen spied him there on the hill and began jabbering excitedly and waving their arms. They were about six feet from the base of Dooly's tree when, with the sound of snapping branches and a lunatic shout, Dooly himself plummeted from his perch and crashed wildly to the ground. He was immediately up and sprinting toward Jonathan on the hill where the Cheeser and Professor Wurzle watched the stupefied linkmen, hoping the while that the linkmen wouldn't think Dooly mad and run off with their baskets.

In truth, the linkmen looked momentarily puzzled. But when it became clear that Dooly was fleeing them and was not, apparently, a menace, the two simply shrugged and climbed along in his wake.

"Hallo, hallo, hallo!" called one of the linkmen—the one who had gotten so carried away with his singing. "Here we are now. A cheeseman and two cheese companions. No, three, clearly. There's a beast among the ruins. A wonderful thing from the high valley."

Jonathan began to introduce himself until he realized, abruptly, that an introduction appeared to be unnecessary. They had, oddly enough, called him a cheeseman. First Miles the Magician and then linkmen. It seemed that everyone knew what he and his companions were about. "Yes, indeed," Jonathan said, not so much in reply as for lack of anything else to say.

The Professor, however, was bowing and waving his cap and ay-aying it like a medicine man selling elixirs to a batch of church ladies. Dooly crouched behind the Professor, grinning. He poked old Wurzle in the back and pointed along toward the river where yet another pair of linkmen were striding, one enormously fat and the other seemingly taken with fits of dancing and leaping. They too carried baskets of goodies. The big linkman's basket was loaded with loaves of bread, some long and white, some round and very dark. There was enough bread to feed a dozen people, probably twice that many, although Jonathan noted that the linkman was stuffing bread into his mouth with his free hand as if he were shoveling coal into an oven. He looked, Jonathan thought—a bit unfairly—like a creeping pyramid. His head angled immediately up from his shoulders without leaving room for a neck, and his cheeks were so round that the top of his head appeared to taper up into his pointed hat. Somewhere below his waist, Jonathan knew, were legs. But at such a distance they sort of blended together within the floppy pants to give him a conical, shuffling look, like a little hill having come to life for the purpose of robbing a bakery.

The first two linkmen produced great flowery oil cloths from their baskets and began flapping them out in the breeze and laying them about.

"Excuse me," said the Professor. "I am Professor Artemis Wurzle; this is my good companion Dooly; and here, as you are apparently aware, is Jonathan Bing, the Cheeser of Twombly Town."

The linkmen paused during the Professor's introductions and listened respectfully. "We're poets," the linkman in the green hat explained. "You might have heard us coming along the river road." He gave the Professor and Jonathan each a squint in turn as if to say, "Pretty rare stuff, eh?" But linkmen, of course, are a very humble lot and wouldn't think of complimenting themselves.

"Oh, indeed," said Jonathan. "It sounded like quite an epic. Is there more of it?"

"Not at the moment," said Yellow Hat. "But there will be. It strikes us now and then like—like—"

"Like a stone on the forehead," his companion chimed in.

"Just so. Like a bonk on the head. That's the beauty of poetry. It just sails in on the wind."

"Sounds a bit like what you'd call inspiration," said the Professor helpfully.

"Oh it is that," Yellow Hat agreed. "It's that in a nutshell. And you never know when it might strike. Watch this." The linkman stepped off to the side a bit and a gleam appeared in his eye. "Hark! Ye late rising tornadoes that doth from the sea foam spring! Do ye shout now of this and that? Do ye rage of things foul in the heart of the Goblin Wood? Do ye blow, ye foul hermitage, full-throated like some great beast afoot—" He was striding back and forth at this point, one hand pressed to his head and the other flailing wildly. Dooly stood amazed. The Professor nodded seriously, and Jonathan was afraid the linkman was overdoing it a bit. "Like some great beast afoot in—. Where the devil is he afoot?" Yellow Hat asked his companion.

"In the halls of stone?"

"Of course not."

"In the land of the mig-weed?"

"I won't stand for your jokes!" shouted Yellow Hat, and he gave his companion a look. "Like some great tramping beast—" he went on, striding about lost in his poetry.

Jonathan was wondering aloud whether the line he searched for might not suggest itself during breakfast, having heard food recommended highly by G. Smithers of Brompton Village. The linkman in the green cap agreed and set about spreading silverware around the cloths. He seemed to think that "in the land of the mig-weed" was a pretty significant contribution to the poem which was progressing up a small hill nearby, and muttered as much under his breath once or twice.

The words, "Some great slippery beast," could be heard from atop the little hill where Yellow Hat had settled down to compose. But further lines were interrupted by the arrival of the two who had been advancing along the road. The pyramidal linkman was devouring what looked to be a loaf of rye bread.

"Squire!" shouted Green Hat. "Let me take your basket, Squire!" The Squire was apparently hard of hearing. He continued to grip the basket and to tuck into the loaf of rye. "There we are, Stick-a-bush!" cried Green Hat. "You've let the Squire carry the bread, haven't you, and it's half gone. You know the Squire was to carry only plates and cups."

"He said he wouldn't have no plates," replied poor Stick-a-bush. "He said he only wanted to peek at the bread to check it for mold. Then he snatched it up and said it was his. Said he was fairly sure the bread was poisoned and would eat of it to see. Then he wouldn't give it back but must sample every loaf to be sure, and he ate and ate and ate all the way along the river road. That's the truth, Mr. Bufo, the honest truth."

Mr. Bufo, the green-hatted poet, tried to pry the Squire's fingers from the handle of the basket. "Squire Myrkle!" he shouted. "We must save the bread. There are hungry people here. Squire, let me introduce you to these fine raftsmen. That's right, you can lay the basket there on the cloth." Bufo tugged on the basket, but the Squire, with a faraway look about him, seemed glued to it. "Right there on the cloth, Squire. This is Mr. Bing, Squire, the cheesemaker, and this is Professor Wurzle, the famed explorer. And this is Mr. Dooly, whose grandfather you're familiar with."

Jonathan was taken aback by the comment. The Professor had a shrewd look in his eye, as if he suspected this was evidence of more things abroad in the land. Dooly began to say something about his grandfather, but didn't get much of it out before Bufo began shouting at Squire Myrkle again as the Squire began to search through the bread basket.

"Do you see that beast?" cried Bufo into the Squire's ear. "He's made entirely of cheese!"

The Squire dropped the basket of bread and lumbered along toward Ahab who, until then, had been lying very still. At the approach of Squire Myrkle, however, Ahab arose and stretched, alerting the Squire to the sad fact that he wasn't, as rumor had it, made of cheese.

The Squire sat down in the middle of the tablecloth and

looked as if he were going to cry. Jonathan marveled at the fact that, aside from being considerably shorter, the Squire looked the same sitting as standing. "Cheese!" shouted the Squire shaking his head sadly, whereupon Ahab wandered over and sniffed at him.

"That's it!" came a cry from the hill, and Yellow Hat, Bufo's poet companion, came lurching down toward them in a sort of theatrical tragic stride shouting and gesturing. "Do ye blow, ye creeping beast, full-throated through the land of cheese?"

"I rather like that," said Bufo. "Yes. It has a ring."

"I should say it has. Thank you, Squire, for the suggestion," said the Yellow Hat. "You're a good man."

But compliments weren't worth much to the Squire, who was patting Ahab absently on the head. "Cheese!" he shouted. "A bit of cheese for the poor Squire. The poor languishing Squire cries out for cheese!"

Jonathan was overwhelmed. Being the only Cheeser present, it seemed as if the Squire's cries were directed toward him, and there was nothing to do but break into a cask and hoist out a cheese. "Here you are," said Jonathan, handing a chunk to the Squire, who nodded very civilly. "Thank you, my man." Turning to Ahab, he continued, "Good fellow, that. Always a cheese at hand for the Squire. The Squire will make him rich. The Squire will eat this cheese now." And the Squire did, sharing a bite now and again with Ahab. The two of them quickly became good friends. Dooly finally tramped over and had a bite himself, and the three of them made such a hearty show of it that for years after, Jonathan and the Professor looked back on that as the time Dooly and Ahab ate cheese with the Squire.

The rest of the company joined in and set to with a will, saying little for a quarter of an hour as they tucked into breakfast. The wild berries were sweet and big as the Squire's thumb and stained beards and faces purple. Loaves of bread, puffy and white, thick and dark, vanished as if by magic, and two of the remaining cheeses in the rafter's keg followed suit. Jonathan was tempted to pry the lid from one of the kegs of raisin cheese, but he wisely decided otherwise. Those, after all, were for trade and weren't, strictly speaking, his at all; not since Mayor Bastable had purchased them from him in the name of the people of Twombly Town that night before their departure.

Linkmen, Jonathan noted, enjoyed eating even more than did the people of the high valley, amazing as that might seem; their conversation, what little there was of it, ran to comparisons of ales and porters and pies and pastries. The famous dwarf, Ackroyd the baker, was held to be the last word in baked goods—mainly because of his honeycakes—and even the linkmen had to admit that their own bakers, although extraordinary in their way, didn't hold a candle to Ackroyd. Only Dooly, who most likely wasn't aware of the extent of Ackroyd's fame, contested the assumption that the dwarf baker was the major name in cakes. Dooly said that as far as he knew, there was a land among the Wonderful Isles where loaves of cinnamon bread sprouted from trees, and where a man might toss out all the crusts in the world without worrying about wasting food. So, at least, is what old Grandpa had told him.

Jonathan was a bit embarrassed for Dooly since tales of old Grandpa were perhaps too farfetched to be passed off on strangers as truths. Much to his surprise, however, the linkmen nodded in agreement, and Bufo pointed out in his poetic way that no loaf of bread made by a mortal could hope to compare with one from Mother Nature's oven. Jonathan wasn't sure if Bufo were being philosophic or diplomatic or if he actually believed in Dooly's grandpa's cinnamon-loaf trees, but it turned out in the end that it didn't much matter. The conversation, in fact, changed direction abruptly when Bufo arose and wandered over to have a look at the remains of the raft.

"Something's gone wrong with your craft," Bufo said, poking at it with a bit of stick. "I wouldn't sail this across the Squire's mill pond, much less down the Oriel."

"Who's sailing on my pond?" asked the Squire, who was squeezing little round sections of blackberry, trying to shoot the seeds through a circle formed by the thumb and forefinger of his free hand. "They must ask me from now on before they sail on my pond. It's all right this once, but next time they'll have to give me some marbles. And they shan't chase my ducks again either."

Yellow Hat rolled his eyes and, winking at Jonathan, rotated a finger through the air around his ear. Bufo scowled at him then said to the Squire, "No one's on the mill pond, Squire, nor has been since those filthy goblins cut up rough on your island last Saturday." The Squire shot a seed at him and jiggled with laughter.

"Goblins," said the Squire, "haven't any sense. Their heads are filled with webs and dust."

"Goblins is it?" asked the Professor. "I don't suppose you get many of them down your way. Too close to elf country, I'd think."

"None at all until a few weeks ago," replied Yellow Hat. "Since then they've been breaking up the orchards and sneaking into people's houses at night to pour things into their shoes. A bunch of them went out punting on Myrkle Pond and set the Squire's boat on fire. But that didn't make 'em half as warm as they were when the Squire got hold of 'em."

"Good for the Squire!" cried Jonathan.

"Good for the Squire!" shouted the Squire, shooting another seed at Bufo. "The Squire put them in the dungeon. Set them to cleaning fish."

"Just where they deserve to be," said the Professor. "But what about this raft, Mr. Bufo? As you say, it's in pitiful condition. All due to an unfortunate collision with a tree." And the Professor's mind, of course, was whirling with ideas for patching up the old raft and sailing away.

Chapter 10

Pickle Trickery

✖

THE lot of them sat there for a time, the Squire occasionally squashing another berry. It was difficult for Jonathan to tell whether Bufo was concentrating on the problem of the ruined raft or was once again being smitten by poetic inspiration. The day had warmed up nicely by that time. It was warmer, in fact, than it had been for weeks, as if the storm had dragged any hint of poor weather away with it toward the sea. There would be pruning fires and autumn dances at Seaside for the next few nights, Jonathan was fairly sure. And if things hadn't run quite so amok the previous afternoon, he and Dooly and the Professor would have sailed right into the midst of them.

"It isn't bad as all that, actually," said Bufo. "We'll just pop down to Seaside—we're heading that way anyway— and send the dwarfs upriver to rescue you and the kegs. A few days should do it. They won't mind. Not much anyway. They're cheerful sorts, really, dwarfs. For the most part. They may require a bit of a fee, however . . ."

"Which we haven't got," said Jonathan, "and besides, we don't want to wait for a few days or get rescued by anyone.

113

This is *our* problem. We promised to get these kegs to Seaside and we will."

"Hooray!" shouted Dooly, very patriotically. "We'll ride inside the kegs, Mr. Cheeser, just like I did when I stowed away. Mr. Bufo can put on the lids and push us into the river."

"Maybe so, Dooly, but then again maybe not. We'd likely sail through Seaside at night and wind up in the ocean, halfway to the Wonderful Isles. If we're going to do that, we might as well just shove the kegs of cheese into the Oriel and walk down."

Addressing Bufo, the Professor asked, "How long would it take us to sail to Seaside from here, Mr. Bufo? Two days?"

"Just about," said Bufo. "The white water is pretty much behind you now. It would be a pleasant sail, in fact. And the first outpost is about a day away—an easy sail. Perhaps we could repair this raft."

The Professor nodded. "Just what I was thinking."

"And I," Jonathan chimed in. "We'll use these kegs, just as Dooly said. If we can find a log clean enough to lash onto the bottom of the starboard side there where she broke in two, we can get her fairly level and raise the deck high enough to stay dry. Then we can tie the casks around the outside so as to have less weight on deck."

"And for the purposes of flotation," the Professor added. "We've plenty of line, and a bit of sail, so we can rig a lean-to to keep the wind off. If it rains though, we're done for."

"Let's get going then," said Jonathan, who was always happier doing almost anything than doing nothing. "Let's patch her up while the weather holds."

Squire Myrkle seemed pleased with the whole idea. He rose slowly to his feet and lumbered toward the raft, Ahab following along behind. It occurred to Jonathan that the two looked like kindred souls. "We'd best drag the thing down to the water's edge to work on it," Jonathan suggested. "And we'll need to search for a good, straight log in the debris along the shore."

Dooly dashed off toward the Oriel along with Ahab, insisting that he knew where there was just such a log.

Jonathan was pleased to find that the kegs which the Professor had towed to safety were roped together by the entirety of the extra two-hundred-foot length of line he'd insisted Mayor Bastable add to the provisions. The hundred-seventy-five odd feet dangling from the final keg had been neatly coiled and tied off and was, aside from being a bit on the muddy side, in perfect condition. They'd have enough and to spare. Among the ruins still attached or hanging from the halved raft was one wall of the cabin, knocked askew and splintered up, but with a dozen lengths of board fairly whole. The walls were redwood plank, about a foot wide. Jonathan set about pulling the planks apart, carefully levering them out with a piece of driftwood so as not to split them and to pry the nails free along with the planks. Some of the nail heads, although broad and square, tore through the soft redwood, but most came out with the boards. After being whacked on the tip a couple of times with a flat stone, the nails loosened up. Jonathan wiggled the things loose with his fingers and lay them inside his cap. Only two or three weren't bent all wiggly, but it would be little trouble to smack them fairly flat again against a rock.

Stick-a-bush, tired of squabbling with the Squire over which of them was going to lug the dishes down to the Oriel and clean them up, abandoned the whole idea and stood about watching Jonathan salvage bits of the raft. The Cheeser took advantage of his curiosity, sending him along with the cap full of nails to a shelf of granite protruding from the hillside nearby with instructions to straighten out the nails.

The Professor and Bufo were involved in a heated discussion about principles of flotation. Everything, the Professor insisted, was irresistibly drawn toward the center of the earth due to the whirl of various pendulous masses. Mr. Bufo pointed out very simply that such wasn't always the case. The Squire, he insisted, could float like a bubble all day long on the surface of his mill pond with a glass of lemonade balanced on his stomach. That, insisted the Professor, was what science referred to as shortsightedness. In time, he said, the Squire would sink, along, doubtless, with his glass of lemonade.

Just what all this had to do with repairing rafts, Jonathan couldn't quite see. But then theory, more often than not, was his weak side. Jonathan's father had always held that it was elbow grease and not theories that got the job done, and Jonathan had come to pretty much the same conclusion. The only way he knew to float the raft was to roll up his sleeves and whack away on it until it would work like a raft again and not a bundle of sticks.

Off beyond the river road along the water's edge he could see Dooly and Yellow Hat—whose name he still didn't know—at work on a buried log. Yellow Hat was trying to induce the Squire to help dig it loose, since ten feet of it or so was buried beneath tangled brush and mud. The Squire, however, had hauled his bread basket with him down to the river along with a basket of plates and cups, and he was selectively gouging hunks out of the center of two round loaves.

Dooly abandoned his submerged log when Yellow Hat began arguing with the Squire. Jonathan watched in wonder as Dooly sloshed out into the Oriel a foot or two, stared a bit into the swirling waters, then carefully inched out a bit farther, nearly overbalancing and plunging headlong into deep water. Jonathan jumped up with a shout that drew the attention of both the Professor and Bufo, but Dooly righted himself and, pointing at a clump of bushes protruding from the water, began to holler and wave his arms and point. Everyone, including Stick-a-bush, gave off their theorizing and pounding and raced across the meadow. Even Squire Myrkle hulked along behind Yellow Hat shouting gleefully, a round loaf of bread with the center plucked out was pushed over either wrist like bracelets of dough.

All of them reached the side of the Oriel and stood in a little knot on the green clover and oxalis of the bank and searched for the cause of Dooly's concern in the surprisingly clear water. The river was running swift and high and clumps of prickly bush and snag were growing out into the rush of water. Entangled in the branches was debris, mostly limbs and pieces of wood and flotsam which would, if no more storms added to the river's depth, be left high and dry on the riverbank within a day or two. Dooly, addled and waving one hand while pointing with the other, seemed to see something amazing down among the leaves and branches.

Everyone crowded even closer roundabout, but it was Jonathan who first made out the cause of Dooly's excitement. Half submerged and almost invisible amid a tangle of brush was the crank device of nothing less than the Professor's oboe weapon, the phenomenal, goblin-routing bird gun hidden in the weeds. By following the crank down into the shadows, Jonathan could make out the trailing whirl-gatherers and funnel nose of the singular machine lodged firmly just out of reach.

Dooly, without waiting to be asked climbed out of the Oriel, sprinted up the slope toward the remains of the raft and untied the line that threaded the cheese casks together. He puffed back into the group of onlookers, all baffled except Jonathan and the Professor. "Tie me up!" Dooly shouted bravely. "I'll go in after it!"

Jonathan thought it a bad idea, given the fact that Dooly couldn't swim a stroke. He himself had no desire to plunge into the cold water, having been thoroughly dry for about an hour and a half out of the last two days, but he could hardly expect any of the linkmen standing about to wade into the Oriel. And the Professor, although game for anything, had complained mildly that morning of his rheumatism which the wet weather and continual dunkings had set going afresh.

"No, Dooly," Jonathan said, wrapping the end of the rope around his own waist. "I'll go. It's a fine day for a swim, what with the sun and all." He tied a bowline in the rope and gave it a yank or two. Squire Myrkle latched on to it to prevent Jonathan's being swept away in the current. Shouting directions and encouragement, the Professor leaned out over the river, as Jonathan waded forth. Somehow the warm sun overhead served to make the water seem even colder than it was, making Jonathan gasp and breathe in little gulps. He wriggled in among the branches, the water about waist deep, and plunged his hand down beneath the surface to grasp the stock of the weapon. He feared at first that he'd be forced to use both hands to free it, a process that would require ducking his head. But the oboe gun seemed to free itself, and he pulled it forth and handed it up to the anxious Professor.

The Squire, at the other end of the rope, relaxed his grip to goggle at the wild-looking thing which was, the Professor was relieved to discover, entirely whole and unharmed. The slack rope allowed the current to give Jonathan a quick shove, nearly upsetting him and pushing him deeper into the bushes. He caught himself, as Bufo and the Professor took up the slack and hollered apologies before reminding the Squire to pay attention.

Beneath the water, Jonathan could see before him the shadow of something too symmetrical to be a rock. He focused and squinted and determined it, finally, to be a keg of a size a bit smaller than those on the raft. Pushing a prickly bush aside and scratching his arms and hands a dozen times, he burrowed even deeper into the bush. An overhanging branch snatched his cap from atop his head. Turning to retrieve it, he was astounded to see *two* caps hanging in the branches above him. One was his own, suspended from a broken twig. Another, waterstained and battered but obviously of good make, hung a foot or so higher up.

He yanked his own free, and then by pulling on a fairly stout limb, he managed to retrieve the second. "I've found something here, Professor," Jonathan shouted.

"He's found something! He's found something!" came a chorus of voices from shore. "A treasure!" cried Dooly.

"A hat," said Jonathan, sorry to disappoint anyone. "And a keg of some sort. I'm going to untie the rope and fasten it to the keg, Professor, then climb out. We can haul in the line from shore." Jonathan began to do so as the Professor shouted assent. He found a ring atop the keg simply by feeling about and poked the free end of the line through it, tieing it securely. "Keep the rope taut," he called, then pulled himself hand over hand through the bushes, wearing both hats at once. In a moment he stood shivering beside his comrades.

Stick-a-bush and Bufo stood some distance away, near the oboe gun. The Professor looked happy as a lark and not a little proud after having revealed himself to be the original discoverer of the thing. The rope was being slowly reeled in, the keg apparently not tangled too thoroughly in the brush.

"I found a hat," said Jonathan.

"And a good one too," the Professor observed. "Or it was once. The Oriel seems to have been wearing it for a few weeks. Rivers have little concern for hats."

Jonathan inspected the hatband. "Look here," he said, pointing. And there, stitched into the band very elaborately, was the name G. Bastable, Mayor. "It's the mayor's hat, lost in the storm!"

"Not surprised are you?" asked the Professor.

"Why I suppose I am."

"It's scientific law, my boy. Nothing extraordinary. The third law of stasis and termination, and nothing less."

"Of course it is." Jonathan nodded. "I should have seen it at once."

"The law of accumulation," said the Professor. "All things seek like things. The lost seek the lost, the found the found."

"Ah!" nodded Jonathan in full agreement. "But here's the keg. And it's a familiar-looking keg too."

The Professor cast Jonathan a knowing look. "Looks rather like a pickle keg, what?"

Jonathan admitted that it did, whereupon an argument ensued over whether the pickles inside were ruined with the river water or not.

"They'd bloat," said Yellow Hat, who seemed to know what he was talking about.

"They'd rot," Bufo added.

"Pickles exist in a state of passivity," chimed in the Professor. "They are impervious to the processes of leeching and bloating. I'll stake my reputation on their being unharmed."

"Pickles!" shouted the Squire, who still wore his bracelets of bread, now and then taking a bite out of one, being careful not to break the ring.

There was no choice but to pry off the top and have a go at the pickles. Since he was perhaps the most learned of them all in the way of tasting food, the Squire bit into the first pickle, fished forth another, and declared that to be positive, to be absolutely sure, he'd have to taste a third. He squinted thoughtfully and demanded a fourth which he devoured with a mouthful of bread.

"It's a trick," shouted Stick-a-bush. "He'll eat them all!"

"The Squire will have another pickle," said the Squire, giving Stick-a-bush a fish-eye. "Squire Myrkle will test each pickle."

"See!" Stick-a-bush cried. "He'll do what he did with the bread basket. Devour 'em all. Every one."

It seemed fairly clear that Stick-a-bush was right, for the Squire submerged both hands into the keg and drew forth clusters of pickles, chomping away at them noisily. He offered one to Ahab, who was sniffing roundabout. Ahab accepted the morsel gratefully, sitting down to eat it as if it were a beef bone. The Squire smiled cunningly at his companions and dipped again into the barrel as Bufo shouted, "Pickle trickery!" Then, following the Squire's example, Bufo began handing pickles, and very good pickles at that, to everyone. It was a trifle odd that pickles seemed such a delightful food in midmorning. Like cheese, they seemed more of a lunchtime food. But the fact that they had been recovered from the river must have added a certain something—a mystique perhaps—and they tasted very good indeed.

Bufo cleared his throat once or twice in the manner of someone trying to gain attention. He held a pickle aloft and, eyeing Yellow Hat all the while as if to say, "Listen to this!" began a peculiar sort of poem.

> *A pickle in a hat and with a cat upon his lap*
> *Came riding in a cart along the road.*
> *He met upon the way, in a rather sad toupee,*
> *A wrinkled and quite beastly seeming toad.*

> *I have come, he told the toad, from mig-weed*
> *   land which o'er*
> *Looks the forest near the lands of rocky shore,*
> *And I have with me a cat and a timid sort of bat*
> *From the caves of inky-blinky-dinky-nor!*

"Hurrah!" shouted Stick-a-bush, breaking into applause.
"A mighty line that last," said the Professor.

"Very substantial," Jonathan agreed.

"Mig-weed my foot," said Yellow Hat, who was apparently dead set against poems involving mig-weed.

Stick-a-bush and Dooly clambered to hear about the traveling pickle again, and Bufo thundered out the verses a second time, then said that he intended to add a few more verses later. He gave Yellow Hat a look which could only be described as hoity-toity.

After the bunch of them mooched around by the side of the Oriel for a half hour, it occurred to Jonathan that, as the saying goes, talk won't cook rice. Given the nice weather it seemed a bad idea indeed to dawdle there. If they were to finish the voyage at all, they must do it in good weather. Another storm would doom them.

He said as much to the Professor, who had, by then, decided that his bird weapon was in tip-top shape. Old Wurzle quite agreed with Jonathan and said that, in fact, he'd like to be away by morning. Spending nights on shore in such goblin-infested times seemed unwise. Jonathan hadn't considered the whole affair from that particular angle, but when he did he had to admit the wisdom in it. So they set to with a will.

Stick-a-bush and Dooly whacked away at nails and untangled tattered canvas while the rest of them, Squire Myrkle hunching along before, dragged the remains of the raft to the waterside. Dooly's log was fairly easily wiggled free of the debris once they found a hold to pry against. Although a tad short, all agreed that it would do nicely, being for the most part free of interfering branches. Those few which would have gotten in the way when it was lashed beneath the supporting cross joists of the raft's deck, Jonathan broke off. Then, with a sizable rock, he smashed away at the short stumps of removed branches until the log was comparatively smooth and altogether serviceable.

The Professor and Jonathan undertook the actual lashing after Bufo and Yellow Hat fell to arguing about suitable knots and then tied a couple which were so mushy and loose thay hadn't a hope of remaining knots. The Squire, who proved to be amazingly strong as well as easily distracted, obliged everyone by obediently lifting corners of the raft into the air so that Jonathan and the Professor could poke one rope end through here and tug another out there.

It was easy work late in the afternoon to pound together a rough lean-to which Jonathan anchored to the deck with a pair of redwood slats. In the front they managed to rig a canopy tacked securely in place and made from the remains of the sail, the whole thing appearing a trifle ramshackle and worn finally, and shearing from port to starboard if anyone pushed on it. Jonathan nailed the remains of a battered plank diagonally across the back of the angled wooden wall of the lean-to, fearful as he did so that he was about to knock the whole structure to bits. He didn't though, and in the end the structure proved solid and large enough to hold the three rafters and Ahab with room to spare, although not much room.

They rolled the kegs down and with the remaining line secured them round the perimeter. Jonathan could only hope they were tied fast enough so that, bobbing in the current, they wouldn't continually whack against the sides of the raft and fall to pieces. The coracle, still being serviceable, was to be tied to the rear of the raft. The canoe, however, was a lost cause, the hole in the bottom rather diminishing its value. But they saved a paddle from it and that was better than saving nothing. It began to look to Jonathan as if he might, with luck, see Seaside yet. The whole lot of them looked the raft over from this angle and that and found, with the fall of night, everything shipshape.

The rafters and linkmen had been so busy with their repairs that none of them had noticed evening coming along. When the Professor finally called everyone's attention to the fact, the sky against the horizon was a deep purple that faded gradually to an aqua blue. It wouldn't be long—a half hour perhaps—before the first stars would twinkle into life. The line of trees along the edge of the Elfin Highlands was just a dark smear in the gray distance, hardly distinguishable from shadow. The moon obligingly sailed out early like a phantom galleon on the purple sky. Jonathan hoped that beneath such a bright moon the night wouldn't be altogether dark and foreboding.

Not building a good-sized fire was unthinkable to any

one of them, but a problem arose when they ventured to gather firewood. Although wood a-plenty was scattered about the meadow, most of it was water-soaked and good for nothing but smoking out bees. Finally, several hundred yards downriver, one capsized hemlock was discovered that sported a few dead, beetle-eaten limbs which had risen high above the mushy meadow and had managed to dry out some. Jonathan and Dooly clambered atop the log and set to stomping as many free as they could. Everyone else hauled bundles along toward the raft where they heaped up a great whacking pile of the stuff. Four smaller piles were stacked, and the little camp was finally bordered on one side by the Oriel and on the other by a half circle of little crackling fires.

Jonathan was afraid, was certain in fact, that the dry wood wouldn't last out the night, but he counted on the possibility that they were too close to the Elfin Highlands to be in danger of encountering any really fearful creatures. And such, in fact, seemed to be the case for a time. The night was unusually warm for late autumn, and although no one would have complained at the idea of another blanket, everyone got on well enough, for there was no lack of room around the various fires.

A cloud or two sailed skyward over the northeastern horizon as evening drew on, remnants, perhaps, of yesterday's storm. The moon tilted its way across the heavens. A bright star, another world likely, trailed along for a bit to keep it company. About the meadow, each tree branch and stand of willow, each outcropping of rock threw a weird moon-shadow which pointed away downriver toward Seaside. As each cloud wandered across the face of the moon, the shadows on the meadow would fade and the evening landscape would dim away into night. The cloud, for the few moments it passed in front of the moon, seemed to catch fire and glow, and it appeared as if grand things were occurring inside—great rolling oceanic tides and plunging surge. Then the glow faded in a second and was gone, and it was impossible to tell whether the cloud was full of rain or was empty or whether anything at all was going on within.

The entire company lay about munching pickles and

cheese and the few remaining loaves of bread, and poking at the embers of the fire. Squire Myrkle was asleep and had been for an hour, but the others chatted softly and idly about this and that. Dooly contributed oddball tales concerning the doings of his old grandfather, most of which the linkmen seemed to take pretty much at face value. Bufo, in fact, pridefully admitted to having met the old man some years back on his way to market at Seaside. Old Escargot, as Bufo referred to him, had traded him a whale's eyeball for his horse. Escargot, with frequent glances back over his shoulder, had leaped upon the beast and pounded away down the river road toward the sea, a gloomy fog rising up in his wake.

"Odd chap, your grandpa," said Bufo. "I never saw him again, even though he had some dealings with the Squire not long back. Something to do with a handful of marble-sized emeralds. The Squire is rather fond of marbles. Has dungeons full, actually, that he clambers through."

The conversation popped right along for a space, then fell off. Then it picked up again for a bit, then lazied away to nothing again. The silent spaces between grew longer as the night grew late, and everyone talked in low tones as if it weren't quite proper, or perhaps safe, to speak aloud.

When the moon was overhead and Jonathan assumed it to be about midnight, a deep, distant rumble sounded way off upriver. It was a low, mournful sound and made Jonathan feel uncommonly lonely, even though he was in the company of good friends. He reached out and patted old Ahab, who lay curled beside him, warm as a baked apple. It was a moment before Jonathan considered the source of the rumble, not, in fact, until after it occurred a second time, Ahab's ears pricking up at the sound; the stalwart beast jumped to his feet and growled off into the darkness.

"Just a bit of thunder, boy," Jonathan said, hoping, of course, that it wasn't. More storms wouldn't do any of them any good. It wasn't however, until another noise joined the first that Ahab's odd reaction was explained. The muted echo of copper gongs and the cackle of goblin laughter wafted past on the winds from the direction of the Goblin Wood, and Jonathan could see the goblin fires burning in the distant hills, miles and miles away upriver in the direction of Twombly Town.

The eerie shadows of the trees around the rafters and linkmen flickered and danced in light of their own campfires, now and then seeming to be the upraised arms of a great goblin or hunched troll set to rage in upon them. Jonathan was happy to see that Dooly, asleep next to the Squire, had not awakened when Ahab barked. Stick-a-bush, however, was wide awake, his eyes goggling and one arm pointed off toward a thick stand of oak atop a small rise beyond the camp. Amid the crooked limbs blinked a bobbing jack-o'-lantern, its eyes flickering weirdly and its grinning mouth agape. No one moved or spoke while the thing bobbed there. When it winked out and disappeared there was a simultaneous *whoosh* of air as everyone began to breathe again. Professor Wurzle, happily possessing a mind curious enough to consider the grim vision from a scientific slant, said simply, "Can you beat that?" Then, when no one apparently could, he added, "Someone's playing a bit of a gag on us. I've half a mind to hike up that hill and play one of my own on the top of his head."

"Perhaps we should leave whoever it is alone," Jonathan suggested. "Let them have a bit of fun. Jack-o'-lanterns don't amount to a bit. We'd best stay together here and wait for the sun."

"That's right," said Bufo. "It's a good idea to be in the open at night. No one with any sense goes prowling about in the woods."

The Professor wasn't convinced. "This all strikes me as damnably familiar. It reminds me, in fact, of a poem that an ape up in Little Beddlington used to chant. His master was a dwarf, a crafty-looking sort with a great cap and eyepatch. The ape would shout "The Madman's Lament" as clearly as you or I, unless, of course, it was a trick of ventriloquism. There was another poem he'd chant—you know which ape I mean, Jonathan—but I can't remember just how it went. Something about pumpkins in trees and a great deal of cheese."

"I think I know it," said Bufo. "Although it's strange that it would mean anything to an ape. If it's the one I believe it to be, it was written by Lum Blimp in 'The Song of Ildor's Domain.' Tell me if this is it:

> Bottle cork, bottle cork
> There's naught within but lees.
> The glowing eyes of Jack O'Lantern
> Dance on evening's breeze;
> Goblin fires light the wood
> And flicker through the trees.
>
> The clouds, they say, are whipping cream,
> The oceans seas of teas,
> The rain a fall of diamonds,
> The moon a ball of cheese."

"That was it," cried the Professor. "That was it exactly." And he scratched his head in wonder.

The goblin drumming and gonging rumbled along until one by one the various rafters and linkmen forgot it was even there and began to nod off and fall asleep. Jonathan, fearful the fires would burn themselves out, piled on most of the remaining brush before finally turning in, grateful for the loan of one of Bufo's blankets and for the company of the steady Ahab, who nestled in beside him.

It seemed that for hours he was haunted with the same fitful dream. He was captive, in the dream, within a great house, many stories tall and with long, dim, and very wide stairways throughout that he seemed to be perpetually climbing in search of a way out. He happened, finally, upon the trapdoor of an attic that promised the chance of escape. But the attic, once he pulled himself up through the trap, was cluttered with ancient furniture and dusty, rolled carpets and such a pile of antique clutter that he was forced to worm his way along through it, always squinting to peer through the twilit distance for a door into the open night.

Finally, in the midst of the attic, Ahab seemed to be barking up a storm, not a bad thing, really, since the dream was giving Jonathan the creeps. He called to Ahab to come and show him the way out, but Ahab simply continued to bark. Then Jonathan was shaken awake by the Professor only to discover that he lay wrapped in a blanket by the glowing embers of a burned-down fire and that Ahab was actually barking.

The Professor pointed toward the heavens where a cloud or two still scudded along and where the moon had traveled across the sky and fell away toward the treetops along the Elfin Highlands. At first Jonathan thought his eyes were still full of sleep and that what his mind told him he saw was a figment. But then the Professor obviously saw it too, and so, apparently, did Mr. Bufo and the Squire, both of whom seemed strangely unperturbed.

There, sailing through the channels between the islands of clouds was a ship. It was awfully far away—no more really than a shadow on the winds. It was not an airship like that of the elves, but a rigged ship of the sort you'd expect to see plying the trade lanes beyond the Pirate Isles. The galleon tossed upon currents of air rather than water. Painted sails billowed out along the masts and glowed for a moment in the light of the moon. Jonathan thought he could see sailors, such as they were, scurrying about the decks. The four of them watched as the ship sailed earthward, disappearing from sight beyond the distant hills.

The night suddenly seemed strangely quiet, and Jonathan became aware that the goblin drums had ceased to pound. There was no hint of any far-off fires, only the dark woods in the distance and the broad Oriel running through the night toward the sea.

"The drumming stopped when the ship appeared in the sky. Stopped dead, Jonathan, and the fires flickered out almost as quick. There's some sort of elf magic afoot, if you ask me, and that's something I'll not complain of. Better elf magic than goblin magic."

Jonathan agreed. The Squire, smiling broadly, said, "It's Mr. Blump with a gift for the Squire. Blump, Blump, Blump, Blump."

His chatter made no sense to Jonathan, but Bufo agreed. Yellow Hat woke up and asked what all the commotion was about, but Bufo told him to shut up and go back to sleep, which he did. Ahab looked for a moment as if he were going to do the same, but then leaped up and, with a yip, bounded across to the far side of the raft and began scrabbling furiously at it, sniffing along the kegs on the repaired starboard side. He seemed so earnest and worked up over the whole thing that Jonathan and the Professor stepped across to see what the dog had managed to corner. They caught a brief glimpse of a strange animal, about the size of a squirrel but unlike any squirrel either of them could remember seeing, scurrying away into the river and disappearing beneath the dark surface. It seemed, Jonathan remarked, to have had the head of a beaver balanced on the little body of a squirrel and was, as the Professor would have said, damnably odd. Ahab wasn't half interested enough to follow it into the Oriel, so he clumped back to the fireside and fell asleep.

"What was it?" Jonathan asked.

"I've no idea," the Professor replied, "but it's been having a go at the ropes. See here."

And sure enough, there were the lashings, chewed to the point where a particularly sizable wavelet might well spring the whole thing loose. "Well I'm awake anyway," said the Professor, and he rummaged around and came up with the remainder of the coil of rope. In gray light of dawn the Professor and Jonathan made the corner of the raft secure once more, both of them troubled by the appearance of the little beast that had seemed intent only on sabotaging their craft.

They shook Dooly awake just as the sun peeped up over the hills to the east and called Ahab aboard. Then with Squire Myrkle, Bufo, Yellow Hat, and Stick-a-bush pushing and pulling the raft, they prompted the thing into the river and let the current carry them slowly out toward midstream. On the rise above the meadow lay the ruined canoe, and dotted about the green below little pondlets caught the light of the morning sun and sparkled. The linkmen waved a cheerful goodbye, shouting that they'd see who'd get to Seaside first, although it was certain that, barring mishap, the raft would sail in long before the linkmen could get there on foot, toting their nearly empty and frightfully impractical baskets.

Jonathan considered the wisdom of introducing them to

the idea of knapsacks sometime, but then perhaps linkmen wouldn't look like linkmen any more if they hadn't any baskets to tote around—and by this time Jonathan rather liked the whole lot of them, baskets and all.

Chapter 11

At the Cap'n Mooneye

❊

THE Oriel two days above Seaside was an uneventful river, which was certainly all right with Jonathan. There were one or two spots where the raft found its way into water that was comparatively shallow and so raced along and bounced over submerged rocks. But the river was high, and although such rapids might have posed problems in summer months, they caused nothing more than a bit of excitement in autumn. Once or twice the roped kegs bobbed and bounced so energetically that Jonathan feared they would smash down onto a rock beneath the surface and break to bits. Such wasn't the case though.

When they were first underway, the Professor knuckled his brow and smacked himself in the forehead a bit. He had an aren't-we-all-morons look in his eye—and rightfully so. The raft lacked, it turned out, one important piece of equipment—a tiller—and neither Jonathan nor the Professor had thought to rig one. It turned out, however, that the raft tended to swirl around the edges of shallows and find its own way into deeper water. Once the stern swung about and scraped across a bar, but the three rafters were alerted to the danger and immediately poled their craft away.

They attempted to control their course by paddling frantically on one side or the other with the small planks but that only worked when they were on a wide, calm stretch and no eddies or quick currents got hold of them. They were hopeful that on the broad delta at Seaside they'd be close enough to shore to guide her in along the bank. Otherwise, especially if they slid past at night, they may well, as Jonathan had warned earlier, find themselves adrift on the open sea. But all that was speculation, and too much speculation only leads to worry; at least that's how Jonathan often felt.

The Oriel seemed to Jonathan to be broadening out. At times the far shore appeared to be a mile away. The foliage along shore became greener with each passing mile. Jonathan could see, during one swing in toward shore, that the berry vines were still hung with black and purple fruit which was odd, given the time of year. But the Professor speculated that the coastal berry season was later than the inland season due to the climate, especially the perpetual fog which kept things wet and cool most of the year around.

Sea birds began making an appearance late in the day— first gulls, squawking like lunatics and flapping along as if toward a distant but monstrously important destination. An occasional white pelican sailed by, sometimes several at a time, looking foolish behind their preposterous beaks, or noses as Dooly liked to say.

The whole voyage was starting to seem altogether pleasant in fact. They breakfasted on a last loaf of bread, some berries and cheese. They could have had a pickle or two if they'd had a mind to, but the previous day's feast had allayed their pickle hunger nicely. Dooly mentioned that his mother was quite a hand at making pickle pies, but the very idea of it seemed so ghastly to both Jonathan and the Professor that they asked Dooly not to talk about it anymore.

Around midmorning, after navigating the craft became more or less routine, the Professor and Jonathan each pulled out a pipe and smashed the bowl full of tobacco which had, by that time, dried out enough to burn. It tasted vaguely of river water, however, and Jonathan admitted that the effect of the river on tobacco was comparable to its effect on hats—that is to say, it gave the tobacco a romantic, weedy flavor, and a rather comfortable flavor at that. The Professor suggested Beezle might be interested in a formula for it, so as to offer it for sale in his smokeshop. Old Water Weed Blend he could call it.

Once his pipe was smoking well, the Professor put away the nail he used as a tamper and settled back. "This has been a strange voyage so far. It shouldn't have been half so strange."

Jonathan nodded. He had, of course, thought about the same thing more than once. "What's peculiar," said Jonathan, "is that somehow we seem to be a party to all this odd business. Why do weird little animals keep trying to scuttle our craft? What do they care whether or not we get to Seaside with a load of cheese?"

"This thing goes deeper than cheese." The Professor was squinting along with one eye at Jonathan's nose. "There're elves flying about in impossible ships in the middle of the night and traveling parties of linkmen who, for some inexplicable reason, know who we are. Seemed not at all surprised to see us marooned there atop the hill. It was as if they'd packed that lunch with us in mind."

Jonathan thought for a moment. "This whole rat's nest can't have stirred up over the doings of that conjurer dwarf. The elves would simply fly about over Hightower for a while and drop bricks on his head."

The Professor nodded. "You'd suppose so. Unless this dwarf is more powerful than we suppose. He has some terrible control over certain beasts; that much is clear. And he seems to have the same control over the weather. Who knows where that storm came from? I'd give my eyeteeth to know whether it swept through the entire valley or just sprang up below Hightower somewhere. I wouldn't be surprised at the latter."

Both of them sat there for a moment, pondering the whole affair. Finally Dooly, who sat on the bow with a pole watching for rocks and shallows, piped up, "You can bet, Mr. Cheeser, that old Grandpa is somewhere about. There's not much goes on that he don't have a hand in. He foreshortened all this business anyway."

"Pardon me, Dooly," the Professor put in, "do you mean he forecast it?"

"That's just it, Professor. That's just what he did. A powerful bright man is Grandpa, and nothing goes on that he don't know about. He told me about this here king friend of his, you know. A cheeseman like yourself, Mr. Bing. Has a ship that sails in the sky and fishes in the clouds with great huge nets for elf crystal. Takes it all back up to the moon."

"Is that right?" The Professor favored Jonathan with a wink. "Airships like the one we saw upriver, are they?"

"No," said Dooly. "Not flying machines, ships. Sails and rigging and all that sort of thing."

"I see," said the Professor. "There's more inside a cloud than meets the eye, apparently."

"That's what Grandpa would say. Pretty much exactly." Dooly went back to looking for shallows. He shouted and pointed at an odd creature near the shore, and the Professor and Jonathan at first feared that it was the little rope-chewing beast. But it turned out to be nothing more than a normal, unremarkable platypus that blinked at them in a friendly way as they drifted past. Ahab barked a greeting and seemed for a moment inclined to swim across and play with it, but they were so soon past and clipping along downstream that there was no opportunity.

Jonathan resumed the conversation. "I believe we're what they call fated, Professor. These cheeses are going to Seaside and we along with them. So far we've had no choice but to be part of hatching plots."

"You're no doubt correct, Cheeser. It seems more likely the case all the time. I joined this party, as you know, in order to record a bit of natural history. But my pens and paper are gone, and, I'll admit, I've become quite unnaturally lazy. When we get to Seaside, however, I'm going to do a paper on these airships. The bat-winged craft strikes me as implausible, while perhaps possible. But the schooner last night was a clear-cut impossibility."

"It didn't appear to be an impossibility to me, Professor. I believe I even saw the crew moving about on deck."

"Hallucination, likely."

"All of us hallucinated?"

"Mass hallucination. Entirely possible, Jonathan. It's happened before, you know. I've often thought that the Beddlington Ape never shouted poetry at all. The audience just thought he did."

"A talking ape isn't half as weird, as I see it, as that ship last night. I'm glad that it belongs to the elves and not this dwarf."

"According to Dooly," the Professor whispered, "it belongs to this cloud-fishing, cheesemaking chap from who knows where. I'm not sure I like the sound of that entirely either."

"Well, if he's a cheesemaker . . ." said Jonathan, trying to add a bit of humor to the conversation.

But the Professor, apparently, didn't catch on, for he was swept up in theories of hallucinations and clear-cut impossibilities. It was about then that a sizable group of pelicans came winging past, each one flapping its wings in long, easy strokes. The Professor pointed the stem of his pipe at them.

"There you are," he said in a tone of voice that made it seem as if the three words were, somehow, an explanation of a mystery. Jonathan listened intently without inquiring as to the Professor's intended meaning, since he knew from experience that a scientific revelation was in the offing.

"Wing flappage," the Professor stated, "is the key to heavier-than-air flight. Only two forces are known to science which overcome the inherent nature of objects to seek solid ground—to plummet, that is, groundward: wing flappage and heated air. Pelicans make use of the former; the bloated fire toads of the Wonderful Isles utilize the latter to fly from island to island. Yet this ship, with a quantity of weighty passengers aboard, whirls aloft as it will."

"You're absolutely correct, Professor," said Jonathan as he watched the pelicans sail away upriver. "Although I remember that G. Smithers wrote a story about flying carpets that could carry whole trunkloads of diamonds back and forth between two kings of Oceania. They were such fine friends and were so generous that they gave increasingly finer gifts to each other daily. Finally they reached the point where they gave away the entirety of their kingdom to each other every afternoon for a week, until one, having waited some years for just such a thing to happen, accepted the other's gift one afternoon and neglected to give his in return. It made a beggar out of the other king, but things turned out well."

"How was that?" asked the Professor.

"The point was that it's better to be a wise beggar than a foolish king, I think."

The Professor thought about it, then decided that G. Smithers was a nincompoop. "That's all lies, all that kings of Oceania business. G. Smithers made it up. But science, my good Bing, can't be made up. It has its roots in deeper seas, in the forces that make order a certainty and hold the flux at bay."

"Flax?" Jonathan repeated, wondering why in the world grain had to be held at bay.

"Order over chaos," the Professor continued wisely. "The immutable governing of disorganization by scientific law! That's the secret of the flappage of wings and of the flying fire toad phenomena of the Wonderful Isles. Everything has its explanation. Every marvel is as common in the eyes of science as a strip of cured ham."

"That ship last night was a trifle more astonishing than any cured ham I've ever seen," Jonathan said. "Not that I'm questioning scientific principle."

The Professor sat thinking for a moment, nodding vacantly at Jonathan's comment. When he spoke finally, it had nothing at all to do with science or cured ham. "That was the same sort of ship," he said softly. "The same bloody sort of ship. It had to be."

"The same as which?"

"As the one on Stooton Slough. As the elf galleon from the Oceanic Isles." The Professor was fairly whispering.

"I thought you said it wasn't from the Oceanic Isles," said Jonathan.

"I'm not at all sure. It's a quandary. The rune could have read either sea or sky, that much I know. And now we'll assume it's the sky. But an island in the sky?"

"Of course," said Jonathan.

"You don't mean?"

"What else?" asked the Cheeser.

Just as Professor Wurzle was about to utter the truth,

Dooly, grinning like a hippo, blurted out, "The moon!" in such a wild voice that Jonathan and the Professor jumped in surprise. Ahab, supposing that some fearful segment of his dreams had become a reality, awoke with a lurch and nearly bowled off howling across the raft. He came to in a moment, however, only to doze off again.

"Dooly," said the Professor, in a kind but very authoritative and condescending voice, "recently I've seen two inexplicable marvels. Indeed both might have been the same marvel. I'm not at all sure. They involve weighty objects sailing in the heavens with a blatant disregard for scientific principle. I don't pretend, of course, to be learned in that field, but given a sufficiency of paper, a universal calculation chart, and a volume of Lord Piedmont's observations on physical laws, I could, in time, explain such phenomena away.

"But nothing, sir, not Lord Piedmont nor the Seven Sages of Limpus, could prescribe a method by which a terrestrial object could overcome the atmospheric tides and the pressures of the suspended globes of the heavens in order to sail to and from the moon!"

And he emphasized the word "moon" in such a final sort of way that Jonathan was half afraid Dooly would never gather enough courage to speak again. But he merely grinned and nodded and said that he didn't know this Piedmont, nor any of the rest of that stuff neither. Then he shrugged at the two of them and said simply, "Magic."

The Professor looked saddened, no doubt regretting having gotten into an argument with, of all people, Dooly.

Jonathan patted his shoulder. "Remember what you said, Professor, about science holding the key to the side door?"

"That was stuff. I was under the influence of the rays of the moon. No, Jonathan, I much prefer a scientific explanation."

But the Professor's preferred explanation never suggested itself. It's the wondering and speculating that's worthwhile in the end anyway—all the solved puzzles in the world aren't worth the one that's unsolved. Or at least that's the way Jonathan looked at the whole thing. He often thought, in fact, that *he'd* like to be a scientist instead of a cheeser. It would be a grand thing indeed to have great

rooms filled with bubbling this and thats and coiled appa-
ratuses and devices. Scientists always seemed to have something stewing, some weighty problem to ponder and could
jump and race off in the middle of a conversation without
seeming rude in order to put to the test some vital new
theory that had sprung upon them unawares. It wouldn't be
a bad thing at all if, when a friend called, his housekeeper
could say simply, "The master is in the laboratory," and
usher in a wide-eyed visitor goggling at the terrible equipment heaped roundabout. He'd have to buy a long, white
coat and spectacles that made his eyes look like plums and
talk like the Professor—all that stuff about whirlabouts
and universal calculation charts.

But then, of course, he couldn't take Dooly's side anymore in learned conversations. And he'd be busy all evening constructing graphs and charts and reading about the
mutability of duck feathers or the properties of frozen water. There'd be precious little time for G. Smithers and all
his magical kings of Oceania. That would all start to look
like "stuff" to quote the Professor. Also he'd have to be
perpetually doing something—a condition which, that afternoon in the thin sunlight of early November and from
the perspective of one lying on his back and drifting pleasantly with a pipe in his mouth down the old Oriel, seemed
like far too much work. Besides, there probably wasn't
enough science to go around, and if he horned in on the
profession it would be that much more quickly used up.
Then the Professor would have to turn out and maybe become a cheeser and it would all add up to the same thing
anyway. Jonathan sailed along thinking about all this but
keeping it all pretty much to himself. Somehow it was a bit
too cool for a nap; it was just a good day for doing nothing.
Jonathan remembered G. Smithers having said that doing
nothing was the most tiring job in the world—simply because you can't quit and rest. Maybe G. Smithers *was* a
nincompoop.

That afternoon they lunched on more cheese. The bread
was gone, but there were berries and pickles aplenty. With
each mile that fell away behind them the sun seemed to
lose some of its sharpness, some of its radiant heat. A cool
breeze sprang up after lunch, a coastal onshore wind that

blew straightaway upriver and likely did so almost every afternoon. It brought with it the smell of the ocean every now and then, a smell of salt spray and kelp and fog and fish—maybe the finest smell there could be. Jonathan, anyway, thought that such was pretty much the case. But it was a sort of cold and lonely smell at the same time, a smell that carried with it the vastness and depth of the sea and everything those depths conjured up somewhere at the base of his mind.

Around two o'clock they passed a dwarf outpost. They halloed at the closed door, but it wasn't until Ahab barked once or twice that anyone appeared—a dwarf with a beard nearly to his toes who carried a fearful-looking axe. The rafters waved at him, and he raised his axe in the air by way of returning the greeting.

"Rather short with us, wasn't he?" the Professor commented.

"Well," said Jonathan, "he can't answer for his size." Then he looked at the Professor out of the corner of his eye.

"I was referring to the look on his face, although it's hard to tell with that beard and all whether he was smiling or frowning. Looked rather like a frown though, to me. And that was a pretty halfhearted wave, too."

"He's probably had visitors over the past weeks who didn't agree with him."

The Professor nodded. "Either that or he thought a pile of kindling wood was shouting to him from the river. I hope he's more amenable to the idea of travelers by the time the Squire and Bufo and the others come along. They'll be ready for a bit of a rest by the time they make it this far."

Beyond the outpost, the river widened even more, and its pace slowed to such a leisurely crawl that Jonathan began to wonder whether they *would* beat the linkmen to Seaside. Presently an island sprang up ahead of them, a thickly wooded, hilly sort of island which was likely covered with all nature of grand caves and turtle ponds. A single loghouse perched atop one of the hills, and a jolly plume of white smoke rose from a stone chimney. Beyond the first island were two more, splitting the Oriel into thirds. The river seemed to have lost most of its vigor by that time, and would submit without complaint to being partially dammed up by a family of beavers or a tangle of pond lilies and driftwood.

When night fell finally they were drifting lazily, almost in midriver. The Professor tasted the water and declared it to be brackish—a sure sign that they were nearing Seaside. They decided to draw straws and keep watch in two-hour shifts. Jonathan pulled the first watch and puffed away on his pipe until the Professor and Dooly were sleeping away, then he too dozed off. The gray dawn broke without incident, and the rafters awoke to find themselves wet with foggy morning dew and passing the scattered grove of an outlying farm.

Piles of prunings from apple, cherry, and peach trees were heaped here and there amid the wide orchard rows that crackled with smoky fires. A stalwart dwarf stomped about close by watching the stuff burn. Some of the groves were spindly and unpruned, and all were leafless above a carpet of lush grass.

Jonathan imagined the pancakes and syrup being tossed down inside the farmhouse, the fresh eggs being fried, and the strips of bacon sizzling on open griddles. If he'd been tempted, he likely would have traded away every bit of cheese on board for a cup of coffee. The farms, as the day wore on, became more numerous and generally smaller. Clusters of cottages began to pop up here and there—little villages surrounded by acres of orchards and cozy beneath the pleasant smoke puffs of pruning fires. Long, narrow canals wandered off into the lowlands around the Oriel, canals lined with reeds and cattail and marsh lily. Jonathan could see someone, now and then, with a fishing line cast into one of the waterways.

The raft seemed to Jonathan to be moving at a frightfully slow pace, and there was no real hint—aside from a sort of feeling in the air—that they were nearing the sea. About noon, however, their speed appeared to increase, a phenomenon which the Professor said indicated a receding tide. Within an hour, that certainly looked as if it were true, for the closest bank of the river showed great patches of mud, and parties of dwarfs slogged upon them harvesting oysters from broad beds and moon snails from sand flats.

All in all it was a pleasant day for the rafters. They considered, at first, asking a passing craft to tow them along to port, but finally decided against the notion, choosing instead to laze along toward the sea and enjoy themselves. Around four or five in the afternoon a fog began to blow in, first in little wisps and snatches, then in banks of cottony white which sailed away upriver to leave a clear space for a bit before another wandered through. A foghorn moaned somewhere in the distance, and it was apparent to the rafters that the boats out on the river were becoming few, and those still out were hurrying away toward port. It occurred to Jonathan and the Professor that they'd be wise to do the same.

The fog got thicker though. The three of them paddled away on the portside hoping to run up on the left bank somewhere since it seemed to be the most populated. But it was impossible to tell whether they were making toward the bank or just splashing aimlessly in the water. During one last gap in the mists Jonathan saw the bank—he supposed it was the left bank—directly ahead and about two or three hundred yards distant. Dooly shouted that they were "on course," but it seemed more likely to Jonathan that the raft was merely swinging about in slow circles, still adrift in midriver. When the fog closed in they had no more idea of their direction than a blind man. The Professor and Jonathan stopped paddling simultaneously, as further paddling didn't make much sense. Dooly, however, paddled away, taking short deep strokes.

The foghorn sounded again, but they couldn't agree on where. It seemed to come first from forward and a bit to starboard, then to port, then, strangely from aft. Jonathan took this as evidence that the raft was slowly spinning, but the Professor said that the phenomenon was due to the muffling effects of the fog.

"What do we do?" Jonathan asked. "We can't be too far from the river mouth."

"Aye," said the Professor, shaking his head. "This is no good at all."

"I for one would rather swim to shore from here than from a half mile out to sea. Why don't I just swim in, find some help, and try to head the raft off at the river mouth?"

"You'd never find us," the Professor replied wisely. "You'd no more be able to see the raft in this fog than we can see the shore now. Besides, how do you know, absolutely, where the shore is? How do you know we're not already at sea?" The Professor pushed a thatch of wet hair out of his eyes, paused, and held up a finger for silence. A creaking and groaning sounded behind them. Jonathan leaned out beneath the canopy, peered into the mists astern, and saw the hull and bowsprit light of what appeared, in the few seconds he had to consider, to be the ghost of a small schooner cutting in upon them out of the fog at such a rate that he hadn't time to do more than shout.

There was a tearing of wood as the deck plunged beneath him and he tumbled backward into the water. He rose to the surface sputtering and gasping and was immediately conked on the back of the head by a floating section of the raft with the forepaws of a wet and amazed Ahab hanging onto the edge. Ahab pretty much looked like Jonathan felt—cold—and was beginning to think that having one's raft smashed to bits and being flung into rivers and bays were simply a rafter's unfortunate lot in life. "Hello!" Jonathan shouted, grabbing Ahab's ruined piece of raft and squinting off into the fog. "Hello! Professor! Dooly!"

From somewhere behind him Professor Wurzle replied, "What-ho, Jonathan. Out for a swim, are you?"

Jonathan thrashed around and encountered the Professor and Dooly both clinging to the redwood wall of the lean-to, the only piece of the raft that bore any real resemblance to anything but a stick of wood. Laying atop it were the oboe weapon and, of all things, Mayor Bastable's hat. Kicking his feet, Dooly propelled the thing along gleefully and shouted, "Look at old Ahab! Ain't he wet!" Jonathan had to admit that he was.

A voice in the mists, however, silenced them. The slap of oars on the surface of the water preceeded the arrival of a long rowboat in which sat two grizzled dwarfs, one rowing and one craning his neck to see into the fog. "Who's there?" one shouted.

Jonathan feared at first that they were all to be run over a second time, so he yelled, "It's us!" in reply to the dwarf's question.

"I see it is," the dwarf said as his partner shipped the oars. "Is this all of you?"

"Quite," replied Jonathan.

Without further discussion, the two in the rowboat set about hoisting the three rafters and the dog Ahab aboard without submerging everybody involved. The task was finally accomplished with much joggling and shouting and leaping to this side and that. Jonathan kept a sharp eye out for floating kegs. It would be a rotten thing indeed to suppose his cheeses were at the bottom of the Oriel or that the kegs, roped together, would drift oceanward on the tide and never be seen again. The Professor insisted he'd seen the kegs drifting off together and that they seemed fairly well intact. Sure enough, as they rowed slowly through the muffling fog—the dwarves whistling, then listening for a returning whistle from the schooner—Dooly spied a phantom keg bobbing along on the waters of the bay. Tied to it were all its fellow kegs, some empty, most filled with raisin cheeses, and all, apparently, sound as tubs. They tied the keg line to a ring in the sternpost and towed it along behind.

Jonathan found he was shaking with cold in the few minutes it took them to whistle themselves into sight of the schooner. Untying wet knots with cold fingers was proved an impossibility—one which, no doubt, the Professor could have easily explained. Explanations would have done the Cheeser precious little good though, for not only could he not untie the keg line in order for the dwarfs to haul the thing aboard, he could barely grasp the ladder and haul *himself* aboard. It was a numbing shaky cold which was a product not only of the waters of the bay, but even more so of the onshore wind which blew straight in off the open sea.

The dwarfs, mindful of the shivering rafters, brought out a heap of blankets and slickers and dry socks, most of which were too small by far to fit any of the rafters. But just getting in out of the wind seemed to do the trick—that and a blanket or two. Even so, everyone was thankful when the ship finally rounded an island with a lighthouse perched atop it in the mouth of the bay, and they could see harbor lights and the tip of a long pier fifty yards off the port bow.

The wharves were nearly empty, almost no one being foolish enough to want to have anything to do with the ocean in such a fog. Two frazzled-looking dwarfs fished from the pier, never even moving their lines when the schooner was hauled in and tied up. They shared a steaming cup of coffee between them and continually looked over the edge of the pier at their dangling bait which hung a foot or so above the gray water.

"They're looking for fogfish," the Professor explained, nodding at the two. "It's a good night for fogfish, if you like them. I tasted them once, years ago, fried up with mushrooms. Too many bones for my taste. There's always one going down your throat. Taste like trout, though, actually."

Dooly was so cold he couldn't speak. He could barely revolve his eyes in order to glance at the three fish that lay in a heap on the pier. The fish were fat-headed foolish things with fins like wings and spiny crenelations which shone phosphorescently in the fog. Jonathan wasn't any more interested in the Professor's observations than was Dooly, until a bloated, glowing fogfish, swimming through the mists as if underwater, came flapping out of the fog making a sort of *whooshing* sound and goggling roundabout. One of the fishermen cast his pole to the deck and grasped a net, pursuing the fogfish across the wooden boards on tiptoe. The thing apparently grew suspicious, however, for it flew—or swam, as the case may be— zigzagging away into the murk. The dwarf returned with an empty net only to hear some rough words from his companion. Moments later a muffled splash sounded off the end of the pier as the fogfish returned to the sea.

It occurred to Jonathan that fishermen often seem oblivious to the weather, a condition he could never entirely figure out. He could remember Mayor Bastable on more than one occasion, crunching out through a snowy December morning, fishing pole in hand, toward the icy banks of the Oriel. It bespoke inexplicable enthusiasm and heartiness; but in his numbed condition, heartiness of any sort struck him as worse than tiresome—perhaps even criminal.

At the end of the wharf they were met by an elf, puffing along up the road for the sole purpose, it seemed, of taking charge of them. He introduced himself as Twickenham, shook their hand a time or two, and led them off to an inn half a block from the ocean and within the confines of a tremendous rock wall. A wooden sign, darkened with age, swung on hooks outside the door of the inn—a sign which read "Cap'n Mooneye" and depicted a carved piratical dwarf, his beard knotted and his eyes wide and wild. It was altogether the most romantic inn Jonathan had seen, like something out of G. Smithers.

The inn was warm as a goblin pot, due to a great fire burning in a fireplace big enough to set up housekeeping. A wide clock sat atop a deep wooden mantel over the mouth of the fireplace, its hands pointing to nine o'clock. On its face a grinning gibbous moon was rising, a moon with two long, thin arms, one of which was placing a star in the dark blue night sky. The clock chimed the hour almost as soon as the troupe walked in and hurried across to the fireside.

"This is the ticket!" Jonathan told the Professor. "This makes the whole lot of it worthwhile."

"I quite agree." The Professor smiled.

Dooly, still too cold to show much enthusiasm merely nodded. Ahab stood smack in front of them on the hearth and shook so much water out of his coat that the embers in the fireplace hissed. Then he lay down in front of it and almost immediately fell asleep and started to snore. Dooly livened up fairly quickly and even noted that Ahab was "dog tired," laughing at his own joke. Jonathan and the Professor smiled, although probably not so much in approval of Dooly's humor as at the mugs of mulled ale and the beef joint that Twickenham and Monroe, the jolly, fat innkeeper were lugging forth from the kitchen.

The three rafters set upon the fare as if they'd been fasting for a week, and even Ahab woke up and got his share. He, of course, drank warm buttermilk rather than ale, but then he didn't care a great deal for ale and probably didn't see much purpose in it.

Twickenham spoke little that night aside from assuring Jonathan that the cheeses had been taken to Ackroyd's bakery where the casks would be checked for leaks. Having been dipped in wax before packing, the cheeses, would no doubt have survived, leaks or no. If the rafters would condescend, he said, to stay at the old Mooneye for a day or two to rest up, then no one would worry about business of any sort until the day after tomorrow.

Jonathan assured his host that he would probably sleep until the day after tomorrow and didn't want to hear about business until after he had.

"We're waiting," said the elf, "for a party of linkmen coming along the river road. They should be here late tomorrow afternoon if nothing goes amiss."

"We've seen them," Jonathan explained. "Ate half their food, in fact. Fine chaps, linkmen, all the way around."

"They are that," Twickenham agreed. "Was there a large one among them? A round sort of linkman tremendously fond of food and larks?"

The Professor nodded. "The Squire. He was there. He and Dooly got on famously. When we left them they were a day's walk from the first outpost, and they seemed fairly anxious to get there. We had a bit of trouble with goblins now and then. Seem to be a lot of them afoot—almost to the Highland edge."

"That's part of the business we'll attend to shortly, as soon as the Squire's party arrives."

There was not much more in the way of conversation. When Jonathan was full and warm he found himself dozing, his head slumping forward onto his chest. But it was no more possible to remain awake than it had been to make his frozen fingers cooperate on the knotted keg line, and finally there was nothing to be done but slouch off down the hall to their respective rooms where they fell asleep atop wide beds with feather comforters.

Chapter 12

The Moon Man

❈

A long time later, although it seemed but an instant or two to Jonathan, he felt himself being shaken awake by a dwarf lad wearing an idiotic suit of clothes, serving livery perhaps. "Wake up, Master Bing. The others are already about."

Jonathan slurped away at his coffee while he pulled on his breeches and shirt and suspenders, all of which had been cleaned and dried while he slept. His leather pouch full of coins and charms hung over the edge of a chair. He was pleased that the dwarf lad had brought along a bowl of buttermilk for Ahab, but he was probably not half so happy about it as Ahab.

He found the Professor downstairs tieing into toast and jelly and waiting for a plate of eggs and ham. Jonathan joined him, noting the presence of an empty plate at the table with traces of egg yolk and crusts. Dooly, then, had already eaten and disappeared. There was no sign of Twickenham, but when Jonathan offered to pay the rotund Monroe for breakfast he replied simply, "The elf has seen to it, sir." Jonathan took this to mean Twickenham and decided that it seemed reasonable that this Twickenham

147

was deeply involved in all the mysterious doings which Jonathan wanted to ignore until after a bit of a vacation. He assumed rightly that the elf wouldn't stay away too long.

After breakfast they wandered off into Seaside. The fog had lifted, so the city didn't seem quite as murky as it had the previous evening. There still wasn't much sun, and the air was cool and damp. Off to their left not twenty yards distant was the stone wall which, in the light of day, they could see encircled the entire city. It was about fifteen feet high, and judging from the depth of the arch that led through the wall into the open docks along the wharfside, it was about six feet thick. The Professor speculated that the wall was a defense against pirates. Jonathan liked the idea fairly well, and as they proceeded uphill toward the center of Seaside, the whole suggestion became more certain. The city was built upon low, coastal hills, and on two such hills, visible over the tops of the buildings and houses, were what appeared to be forts. Jonathan could see the barrels and muzzles of cannonade protruding through the porthole windows and pointing variously toward the bay and playing out over the open ocean.

On the whole, Seaside was a clean and neat sort of city in its way, even though it was overshadowed most of the year by gray weather. As is true of any port city, much of the waterfront flotsam—dried kelp and tar-smeared wrecks of packing crates and rusty bits of scrap—and the smell of fish and salt air were a continual presence. Even a half mile inland, pelicans padded up and down the avenues, and the foghorns in the bay could be heard off and on, warning trawlers and barges and sloops away from the rocky shores.

Along the streets, the homes were tall and thin—most of them three stories high plus an attic above. Wooden arms with pulleys attached angled down from the peaks of the houses. In front of one house, a block up the street from the Mooneye, a piano dangled from the end of one of these pulleys. Workmen in dungarees scrambled about below, shouting orders, pointing and looking as if they were ready to cut and run at the slightest indication of a problem.

An effort had been made to cheer things up; most of the houses were painted in bright colors, although the effect was subdued and dimmed, more often than not, by the fog. Almost all the windows up and down the streets were lined with boxes containing potted plants. These plants grew abundantly in the wet coastal weather and drooped out over the fronts of the houses. If a person liked the fog and the rain, he'd like Seaside. It seemed to Jonathan to be the sort of a place where a chap could write great poetry while peering down at the fog-shrouded streets from a fourth-floor attic study. It would be perfect for Bufo and Yellow Hat, although the poetry they were likely to write under such conditions would be, doubtless, foggier poetry, not nearly so full of cherries and sweetum.

On a hill in the center of the city was the palace, and a very functional palace it was—not one of those gaudy, spired affairs lived in by the kings of Oceania. A heavy, gloomy-looking palace of gray stone, almost the color of the fog that so often surrounded it, it was a fortress in the midst of a fortress city.

The Professor suggested they mosey on up that way, and Jonathan, who had no better plan, agreed. Ahab tagged along happily. They passed through two streets—named, appropriately, Second Street and Third Street—that immediately parallelled the bay. Dim pubs and shops with flats above lined the street, and serious dwarfs hunched along through the cool morning toward the bay. Every now and then the foghorn lowed, and sometimes a cloud of fog trailed through as if to justify the sound. The cobbled streets slanted this way and that, and the occasional carts that clattered past listed frightfully. They passed two interesting-looking bookstores, filled to overflowing with a likely hodgepodge. It looked like G. Smithers country to Jonathan, and he noted the cross streets, intent upon stopping in for some browsing on their return.

Up and down each street were arched streetlights, most eerily aglow, even though it was getting on toward late morning. When a particularly dense bit of fog rolled in, the lamps glowed through it, seeming to make the atmosphere even more ghostly. The Professor pointed out that Seaside was a strangely silent city, that individual noises, even though muted in the mists, stood out against the silence of the morning. The clatter of hooves on the pavement, the cry of a wheeling gull, the shuffle of leather boots along the cobbles—all forced themselves into a person's consciousness instead of simply being background noise as they would have been in Twombly Town.

They wandered up a street full of greengrocers and fishmongers. But November really isn't much of a month for fruits and vegetables, so the produce was a bit thin. The seafood, however, was a different story. They saw great heaped piles of periwinkles and mussels, of moon snails and oysters, and deep vats of squid and clams and shrimp. Fogfish were in particular abundance and were cheap; wide slabs of pink salmon were visible everywhere and weren't cheap. Jonathan always liked the idea of strange seafood, but somehow it never tasted quite so interesting as it looked or sounded. One vendor had a bubbling tank of water in which he was boiling whole crabs. The Professor suggested they return at lunchtime with a bottle of white wine and a loaf of bread, and the idea sounded brilliant to Jonathan.

They found Dooly about two-thirds of the way up toward the palace. He stood atop a cask and talked to a dwarf who didn't seem to be paying him much attention. Dooly was telling about the siege along the Goblin Wood and tossing in trolls and treasures and all such things to glorify his story. The dwarf, red-faced and sweating, held a long tube with a ball of glowing glass attached to the end in his hand. He was very carefully daubing colors of molten glass onto the outside of the ball and swirling them about with a metal pick. It occurred to Jonathan at first that the dwarf was constructing a tremendous glass eye, perhaps for a cyclops who had lost his own—bad luck for a cyclops— but it turned out that he was making paperweights. They were little globes of crystal that were not quite like anything Jonathan had seen. They were larger than marbles and some even had tiny gardens of little glass flowers inside. Some of the glass flowers were so small that Jonathan had to study the paperweight to see them. Others were larger and strangely shaped, more like animals or sea creatures than flowers. Even the Professor *oohed* and *aahed* over the things for the space of ten minutes. There was one which was a deep blue, scattered through with chips of glowing gemlike stars. When he put it to his eye and stared inside, the noises roundabout seemed to dim and he felt as if he were falling forward into the jeweled darkness of space. It was a very fearful feeling and yet one which was literally quite wonderful. He stood staring until he heard his name being called and realized that Dooly was tapping him on the shoulder.

"Mr. Bing Cheese," Dooly shouted. "Come along, sir. We're off, sir, to see the palace."

Jonathan put the paperweight down and saw that the Professor was a good way up the road. Feeling a bit foolish for having stared at a globe of colored glass in such a way, he turned to the dwarf still hunched over his work. "Good piece this; one rarely sees better," he observed in a voice intended to sound knowledgeable.

The dwarf smiled up at Jonathan pleasantly, winked, then added mysteriously, "One rarely sees at all." Then he went back to his work.

"Funny little man," Jonathan thought, wondering about the odd statement and, at the same time, convinced somehow that there was truth in it.

The palace wasn't half as interesting as the paperweights. There didn't seem to be anyone around aside from two dwarfs who leaned on impossible axes at the monstrous oak door. A chap with a penknife, Jonathan thought, could slide in and do away with both dwarfs before either could heft his axe, let alone swing it. But he supposed that the guards were primarily there for effect anyway. The king, it turned out, had gone fishing on his trawler and wouldn't be back until the following afternoon.

They decided at last to see about the bread-and-wine business as the Professor had suggested. After enjoying a most satisfying meal, they cut along back toward the Mooneye, where all three of them slept the afternoon away.

The following day was spent pretty much the same way, Jonathan engaging at noon in the rigors of eating periwinkles which he discovered didn't want to come out of their shells for any purpose. He found it such trying work just digging the things out that his appetite grew more quickly than he could satisfy it.

It was a pleasant two days. The Professor complained mildly about the gray weather, but Jonathan rather liked it. It had a sort of "mood" to it, as Dooly pointed out more than once. Twickenham popped in on the third morning and announced the arrival of the linkmen the previous evening. There was a meeting brewing at the palace which the three rafters, Twickenham insisted, wouldn't want to miss. Apple pie and cream and hot coffee were to be served, and so it was important they hurry, for the Squire couldn't be held off much longer. Ackroyd the baker himself had made the pies, and if it wasn't that Ackroyd and the Squire were such fast friends, the Squire would have set out in search of the pies an hour ago.

So they popped right along toward the palace where the same two dwarfs with their awesome axes stood guard by the entrance. Behind the palace on a sort of hedge-fenced green, the type where you'd play croquet, lay an elfin airship. The same ship, Jonathan was sure of it, that had routed the trolls below Willowood. The puffy-cheeked countenance of the Man in the Moon, the mysterious winder of clocks, smiled from the side of it. Once again Jonathan thought of his magical coins and felt for the leather pouch tied to his belt.

Above the hedgerows, the masts and furled sails of a good-sized ship could be seen, a fact that struck Jonathan as peculiar since the ocean was a half mile behind them. The Professor explained that there was likely a backwater or canal that led up behind the palace. They hadn't any time to investigate though, for a party of elves, all chattering and laughing and pointing toward the three rafters, filed through a gap in the hedgerows. Like Twickenham, they were slightly larger than linkmen and not nearly as stout as dwarfs. The odd thing was that in the dim sunlight some of the elves seemed almost translucent. Jonathan fancied he could see one elf through the first and again through the second as if they were all made of shadowy glass. When a patch of fog obscured the sun, however, the illusion vanished, if it were illusion, and the elves looked very real indeed, much more handsome and less comical than the linkmen. It appeared to the Cheeser, however, for a brief moment, that they were putting on airs, for one or two had a superior look about him. But Jonathan soon discovered that the elves went in for songs and joking even more than linkmen did.

Twickenham seemed a little put out at the crowd of elves, as if he thought them rather tiresome. One very fat elf who looked remarkably like Mayor Bastable strode along in front. He was very businesslike, although a businesslike elf is still a very cheerful sort of fellow. Jonathan supposed that a speech was in the offing.

"Hullo, ullo, ullo, ullo!" said the round elf. "Gentlemen, gentlemen, gentlemen! Uh? Well, well!"

Jonathan whispered to the Professor that the jolly elf had what might be described as a way with words, and the Professor agreed. They were soon compelled to shake hands all around, although so many hands shot forth from the cluster of elves that Jonathan was never sure whose hand he shook. Hands kept bursting out in the heartiest manner until Jonathan realized that he had shaken at least three or four times as many hands as there were elves and began to catch on to the fact that he was involved in a sort of elf joke.

The round elf laughed uproariously when Jonathan caught on and made a point of shaking his hand one last time, wiggling his own hand back and forth in a jellylike way while doing so. Jonathan thought the whole ritual pretty peculiar, but he liked jolliness as well as anyone and so acted very pleased when the round elf explained that he'd been given the fish shake. The balance of the elves exploded once again into laughter, amused no end over the old fish-shake joke. Bursts of laughter erupted fairly often after that amid shouts of "Twenty hands apiece!" and "Took him right in!" and "Shook his hand nearly off!"

Twickenham himself laughed a bit, although he looked as if he had seen rather more fish-shake larks than he cared for.

"Twicky, Twicky, Twicky," said the round elf who turned out to be named Mr. Blump. "There is food inside, sir. Food and drink for the light elves in the winged craft. The bird that flappeth not, eh?" And this last comment was also, apparently, a vastly amusing joke, for the elves hooted themselves blue over it.

"Hello, good Blump," said Mr. Twickenham. "This, as you know, is Jonathan Bing of Twombly Town, Professor Wurzle the historian, and Dooly the grandson."

"Clever, clever, clever chaps!" shouted Blump, reaching for Jonathan's hand again. But as Jonathan very courteously extended his own, Mr. Blump yanked his back and jerked it twice over his shoulder with his thumb extended, laughing like a lunatic. Jonathan grinned to show that he was one of the lads, but the Professor gave Twickenham a look, as if he was tiring of Blump's unyielding humor.

"Where's his Highness?" asked Twickenham mysteriously. "We have tidings."

"Ah, tidings," said Mr. Blump. "Tidings is it? His Highness has been hunting along the canal with his platypuses."

"Platypi," corrected the Professor very respectfully.

"Of course," said Blump. "But he'll no doubt be along shortly."

Suddenly, through the great door of the palace, strode Bufo, the Squire, Stick-a-bush and Yellow Hat. Stick-a-bush was railing at the Squire for some unknown reason, and the Squire was stuffing a piece of cake or bread into his mouth, no doubt having convinced someone to find him a bit of a snack to tide him over until Ackroyd's pies were served. Shouts of "Ho! It's the Squire!" and "Squire Myrkle is here!" went up from a half dozen of the elves as the Squire lumbered into view, grinning hugely. After quite a bit of pushing and shoving and hand-shaking one elf in a conical cap presented the Squire with a leather bag encircled on top by a drawstring.

"Marbles!" Bufo whispered to Yellow Hat, and Dooly pushed to the front of the throng to see if it were true. Sure enough, the Squire sat upon the green and loosed the bagful of marbles onto the grass. The tinkle of little glass spheres seemed to fill the quiet air roundabout as everyone watched the marbles flow from the bag into a little marbles stream. It soon grew to a marbles river, then into a bit of a pond, then a lake—hundreds of marbles poured out, their rainbow spirals throwing glints of sunlight into the morning air.

Clearly this was no ordinary bag of marbles. Even Squire Myrkle had enough sense to pull the drawstring tight before having loosed more than the linkmen could carry back in their baskets. It seemed a bottomless bag of marbles, and Jonathan wished *he* had such a thing. He'd always been fascinated by the idea of something without end—of coming across unlimited shelves of books all written by G. Smithers of Brompton Village, or of finding rooms and rooms of cut gems and gold coin, enough to burrow about in like a mole. Here was just a thing—an elfin marvel. Jonathan decided that once this journey was done and springtime made travel a bit of a wiser idea, he'd come south again to the land of the linkmen to visit Squire Myrkle and see his marbles treasure.

The Squire sat on the green staring into a deep red orb the size of a plum, with swirls of color within encircled by clear glass, as if he were looking through an enchanted cavern into the center of the earth.

Away across the meadow just then, Jonathan spied the top of someone's head. He expected it to be the head of the dwarf king, what with all this talk of highnesses. But when the entire head appeared, finally, with a body attached to it, it proved not to be a dwarf of any nature, but someone who looked oddly like the face on the airship—like Dooly's pocketwatch man.

Walking along toward them over a little path bordered by hedgerows of dogwood, he seemed to be very leisurely about the whole thing. As he approached, however, he appeared to Jonathan to be stooping just a bit, as if he carried some fairly heavy weight on his shoulders. He was clearly warm—exerted from his exercise—an odd thing indeed on so cool a day.

He was dressed in a tweedy sort of coat, and wore a vest beneath it that was covered with moons and stars and whirling planets. As he strode near, he hailed the elves and rafters and squinted at the lot of them through a pair of spectacles that made his eyes look as if they were being seen through a telescope. His trousers appeared to be spun of gold thread, which might, of course, have been the case. His head was bald but for a peculiar thatch of hair over either ear—it was almost a Mayor Bastable haircut, but not nearly so wild.

The Moon Man—for that's how Jonathan thought of him—was a peculiar-looking person, there was little doubt about that, but it was easy to see that he might well be a king of some nature. Behind his spectacles his eyes were very jolly, but Jonathan could see that there was some nature of seriousness on his mind. As with the Squire, however, Jonathan would find that the Moon Man liked the right sorts of things: eating apple pie and cream for breakfast, capering with platypi on the riverbanks, strolling along between hedgerows, admiring marbles with the Squire and, it turned out in time, investigating the mysteries of kaleidoscopes and paperweights.

He shook Jonathan's hand, addressing him as a "cheeser" and saying hello, then mentioning that he dabbled in the cheesemaking arts himself. "Nothing so wonderful as raisin cheese," he said, "just some fairly tolerable green cheese."

Jonathan regretted he hadn't any raisin cheese with him and was tempted to inquire more deeply into the nature of local cheesemaking facilities—to "talk shop" as they say. But he decided to wait for a more leisurely moment. He had always disliked bringing about discussions that concerned himself in which others of the company could take no part. Such a thing smacked of a type of selfishness he didn't at all like.

The Squire had gathered all his marbles and returned them to the leather sack, miraculously grown to a sufficient size to house them all. He rose, hoisted the sack over a round shoulder, and nodded toward the Moon Man. "Where is Mr. Ackroyd? We must see Mr. Ackroyd. The Squire has business with him. Pie business."

"Mr. Ackroyd is inside," said Bufo. "He's fetching out the pies at this moment, Squire."

"I will speak to Ackroyd," replied the Squire.

The Moon Man, a jolly enough sort it turned out, and a great friend of the Squire, took his arm and set out toward the palace door. "We'll find Mr. Ackroyd together, sir." The Squire looked very pleased.

The palace, although rocky and somber, was very satisfactory inside. Long halls led off in every direction from a great antechamber, and thick rugs, woven in pleasant springtime colors, lined the stone floors. Clusters of glowing crystals, rose quartz from the look of them, hung from the ceiling and served admirably as lamps. Jonathan was at a loss to understand how they glowed by themselves until the Professor, anticipating his wonderment, leaned over and explained: "Fire quartz. Very rare stuff. The dwarfs mine it beneath the Emerald Cliffs. They say the stuff glows for five hundred years."

The party trouped along into a great hall bisected by a heavy, battered and age-darkened table set with mugs and forks and plates and such. Two young dwarfs poured thick coffee into the mugs, the steam floating about the hall carrying the odor of coffee and cinnamon.

Twickenham introduced Jonathan to another dwarf who unloaded pies from a wooden cart on wheels. He was a stout, bearded sort, and he shook Jonathan's hand until Jonathan began to wonder if he ever intended to stop. "So you're the famous Bing?" said the dwarf, nodding shrewdly at him.

"I am indeed," Jonathan replied.

"I," said the dwarf, "am Ackroyd the baker. You may have heard of me."

Jonathan of course had—not only because his cheeses were housed at Ackroyd's bakery, but because Ackroyd the baker's name was known for miles beyond Twombly Town in the high valley, mostly because of his honeycakes. Ackroyd was tall for a dwarf, coming up almost to Jonathan's chest; his beard hung below his belt. It was a patchy, ragged sort of beard due to being singed in one way or another almost daily while Ackroyd loaded ovens in his bakery. The dwarf opened a flap in his coat and removed an object wrapped in waxed paper, inviting Jonathan to take a peek at it as if it were contraband. It turned out to be a honeycake. "First of the season," said Ackroyd with a note of mysticism in his voice.

"Indeed," said Jonathan, looking at the little cake which was so phenomenally good. "Sorry not to have come round to talk business, by now, Mr. Ackroyd."

"Just Ackroyd, if you will. And it's quite all right. Your cheeses are in tiptop shape, and we've plenty of time for business. Too much time. Damn all business."

Jonathan rather liked the baker's attitude. He was far more concerned with his honeycakes than with transactions. That was a healthy sign.

The Squire lumbered toward them with a wild but identifiable look in his eye. Bufo, seeing that only half the pies were on the table, made an attempt to waylay him. Ackroyd said to Jonathan, "Do you know who gets this cake?"

"I haven't any idea."

"The Squire. No one appreciates a good cake as much as the Squire. You wouldn't know it to look at him, but the Squire is an important sort."

"Is he?" asked Jonathan.

"Oh my, yes. When old King Soot passes on, it'll be the Squire who replaces him. King of the linkmen he'll be, from Seaside to the Highland Top to the White Mountains."

Jonathan glanced over at Squire Myrkle supposing that somehow his eyes had betrayed him into supposing the Squire slothful. But no, there he stood, listening politely to one of Bufo's poems while eyeballing the pies. He broke in, finally, not being able to hold out any longer. "The Squire will have some pie and cream. The Squire will taste a pie."

"Odd sort of king," said Jonathan.

"Not at all. He's a perfect linkman king. He has two passions, eating and collecting marbles. They say he has deep cellars filled with chests of marbles and that he has one huge crystal globe—a marble fit for a giant—that has little stairways cut through it so that the Squire can climb about inside through rooms of glass. Just the sort to be king of the linkmen." And with that, Ackroyd presented the Squire with the cake.

"A cake, a cake!" the Squire cried, smiling triumphantly. "Here we have a cake!" Squire Myrkle looked solemn for a moment, and everyone around fell silent. "Jolly good Ackroyd," he said, "has brought along a cake for the Squire!"

"Good old Ackroyd!" Dooly shouted.

"Hurrah, hurrah!" everyone yelled, and the Squire

smashed the honeycake down his throat, nodding heartily and reaching immediately for a mug of coffee to wash it down.

They all finally sat along the table. Jonathan, Dooly, the Professor, the linkmen and Ackroyd the baker sat on one side and Twickenham and Blump and the rest of the elves sat along the other. At the head of the table sat the Moon Man, and opposite him, twenty feet away, sat a grizzled, serious dwarf in a brown robe who turned out to be the fisherman king, Grump. It occurred to Jonathan that King Grump had been given an unfortunate name, although it was a name that seemed to fit. His face was lined and weathered like the pilings of the pier to which he no doubt moored his trawler. He looked entirely out of place here, as if he wished he were casting cod nets off the Channel Islands. Although he proved genial enough as kings go, he took little obvious interest in the proceedings. When Ahab wandered past, however, and sniffed at him once or twice, King Grump fed him a piece of crust and patted his head. Jonathan decided that he was all right.

They tied into the apple pie and cream. It was very thick and, like all good apple pie, had a good deal of cinnamon in it. After the first slice another was heaped on Jonathan's plate, and his cup was filled again with the rich and powerful coffee. Jonathan noted that no one in the room refused a second slice and that the Moon Man seemed to be eating his piece with at least as much pleasure as anyone else. He declined a third slice, however, as did Jonathan and everyone else except Dooly and the Squire.

Finally they all sat sipping at coffee and chatting pleasantly, and Jonathan thought to himself that if all "conclaves of war" were conducted in this manner he'd volunteer as a general or admiral or something. But he feared that they'd all been summoned to the castle for other reasons than simply gobbling up Ackroyd's pies.

It was Twickenham, who rose and waved everyone silent. All of a sudden he looked very important and dignified. He cleared his throat several times and strode back and forth purposefully in front of a diamond-paned window. In the rays of sunlight shining in through the window he too looked as if he were vaguely transparent. Twickenham as well as Blump's company were what were known as light elves. Though it had always seemed outlandish to Jonathan, he had heard it said that the light elves rather dissolved away as they aged and that after hundreds of years they seemed to be made of bands of translucent rippling color, then, as time passed, of clearest crystal, finally disappearing altogether from the sight of mortals. No one knew for sure, of course, aside from the elves themselves, since disappeared things can never be entirely counted on. The Professor, no doubt, knew of a scientific theory to account for the phenomenon, and Jonathan intended to inquire about it at a more convenient moment.

Anyway, Twickenham paused and raised a finger in a gesture of seriousness. "We're not here . . ." the elf began, only to be interrupted by young Stick-a-bush, who burst into laughter over the fact that the Squire hadn't eaten any of his pie crusts. He had left them in a little heap on his plate.

Twickenham scowled at Stick-a-bush, and he was immediately silent. "We're not here," he continued, "to lark about!" He squinted a bit severely again at Stick-a-bush, who slumped. "This is a serious day, a momentous day. A day on which the gate of the fates hinges."

The crowd was silent. There were few days that could be considered momentous in the course of the year, and when one arose it wasn't to be taken lightly. Bufo cleared his throat loudly. "I have a poem here, Mr. Twickenham, that, I believe, is appropriate. If I might have everyone's attention . . ."

"Save the poem, Bufo," said Twickenham. "Keep the poem in your hat. We haven't time to dawdle over poetry or larks."

"Or mig-weed," said Yellow Hat.

"Or, as you say, mig-weed," Twickenham continued. "We have visitors here—and important ones at that. Each in his own way important. And the most important of all, begging everyone's pardon, is this lad here." He waved his hand in Dooly's direction.

Dooly looked about to see who this important person might be. Surely he must mean the Cheeser. But no, there sat Jonathan Bing and the Professor. No one was pointing at them. There was no one else. It was Dooly they were after. He wasn't sure what to say, and his first response was to feel guilty, only because there was nothing he could think of to feel proud about.

At the other end of the table Squire Myrkle had been fishing marbles out of his bag, examining them, and handing each in turn to one of the elves who sat on either side of him. They seemed monstrously pleased. Jonathan would have thought that the elves would have long since tired of such wonders, having an abundance of them on call, but then we never tire of those things we honestly enjoy any more than we tire of eating good apple pie. Anyway, Twickenham shot the two elves a stern look, and they put the marbles away. Twickenham seemed to be giving looks to a lot of the company that morning, but it's true that they had very serious business to attend to. "Show friend Dooly your ring, Squire, like a good fellow," Twickenham said.

The Squire put his bag of marbles away and winked at Dooly. Then he very slowly said, "Twicky Twicky Twicky Twickenham—ham sandwich," and waved the ring on the middle finger of his left hand in Dooly's direction.

"Have you seen such a ring?" Twickenham asked Dooly.

"No, sir," Dooly replied, taken aback by this sudden concern with rings. "I mean, yes, sir. I mean to say, your honor, that such a ring has passed by my eye globes at one time, sir. But only for a bit. It wasn't me that borrowed it, I'm sure." Dooly said all of this with one of his hands buried in his coat pocket.

"Might I see your own?" asked Twickenham of Dooly.

"My own, sir?"

"Ring, my boy. Your sea ring. The ring of Oceania Profundis. The one with, if I guess rightly, the squid upon it. The chambered nautilus."

Dooly reluctantly drew his hand from under the table and showed Twickenham the ring. The elves and linkmen rose and bent toward Dooly to have a look at it as did Jonathan and the Professor.

Dooly's ring and the Squire's ring had both, undoubtedly, been cast by the same smith. The Squire's was larger and pictured the raised form of one of those feathery plant-like fish with flaps of skin waving about as if they forgot to tuck in their clothes—and commonly called frogfish. In its eye was a blue diamond.

"Where, Squire Myrkle, did you obtain your ring?" asked Twickenham.

"It was a gift, Mr. Twickenham." The Squire paused for a moment then said in a deep voice again, "Twicky Twicky Twickenham," and laughed heartily. Everyone but Mr. Twickenham laughed.

"A gift from whom?"

"Why from Theophile Escargot, who I gave a little cart to once. Carrying things, he was, which he had found, he said. Traded him straight across for this ring."

"Just so," said Mr. Twickenham, who seemed pleased to have gotten a sensible answer. "And you, Dooly, do you know this Escargot?"

"Yes, sir. No, sir. Yes, sir," replied Dooly.

"Contrary sort, aren't you?" said the elf.

"Yes, sir, sir. Begging your pardon, but that isn't his real name, although he likes it well enough."

"And how would you know?"

"Because, sir, he's what you might call my grandfather, sir, and my mother's father to boot. And her name, if I might carry on some, was Stover, sir, which would make his the same and not, begging everyone's pardon, Escar-what-is-it. He was a great one for fun, was Grandpa."

Twickenham strode back and forth behind the Moon Man, who seemed about to fall asleep. "Did your grandfather, by any chance, Dooly, my lad, ever come across a pocketwatch that was at all out of the ordinary?"

"Not really," said Dooly casting his eyes groundward.

Jonathan cleared his throat meaningfully.

"Well, once," Dooly added.

"Ah," said Twickenham. "And did it have a face upon it?"

"Yes, but I didn't never have nothing of the sort," Dooly said, lapsing into bad grammar because of his excitement.

"Of course not, of course not," Twickenham assured him.

Dooly looked as if he were about to cry, sure as he could be that he was guilty of some dread thing, although he had no idea what dread thing that was. Surely they couldn't hold him responsible for the fact that his grandfather loved to borrow things, names included. He was relieved when the conversation passed on to something else.

Twickenham gestured at the wonderful oboe weapon which the Professor had brought along to the gathering. "And you, Professor, do you know what that is, that thing you carry?"

"Indeed, sir," said the Professor, exhibiting the odd device to those around the table. "It is an apparatus I found several years ago along the river near Stooton. It was entangled about the ruined mast of a certain vessel."

"That would be the Galleon of the Lakes of Luna, mired in Stooton Slough?"

"Uh, yes," said the Professor after a moment's hesitation. "This is, I have determined, a weapon which works according to the three major urges: velocity, pendulosity, and whirl."

"A weapon?" said Twickenham, smiling a tad for the first time. The Professor looked just a bit put out. His assumption that it was a weapon had been reached after some fairly painstaking study.

"May I have a look at it?" asked Twickenham.

"Of course."

Twickenham looked it up and down thoroughly as did the other two elves. All of them chattered with excitement. "It's perfect," Twickenham concluded.

The Professor smiled triumphantly.

"But it's not a weapon."

The Professor sputtered, feeling foolish. He'd gotten all his understanding from elf runes, so it was likely that elves would know the truth about it.

"It's of far greater worth, sir," said Twickenham. "And I think it may be useful to us all. What do you think?"

"Just as you say," said Professor Wurzle. "I ask only to be useful."

Twickenham bowed in response, handed the Professor his device, and cast a look at the Moon Man, who was polishing his glasses.

He tucked the glasses into a case, then put on a spectacularly large pair which made his eyes look as if they were in fishbowls. He paused for a moment and wearily lit his pipe, at which point several of the elves in the hall did the same. Jonathan, knowing that it was correct to follow his host's example, lit his own. He didn't at all like the tone of the conversation so far, and he liked it even less when the Moon Man put away his tamper and said in a grave voice, "Christmas is coming on and every day we slide farther into a season which may well be grim beyond our fears. We must prepare for it!"

Jonathan puffed thoughtfully. Dooly seemed to be melting away into his chair, fearing, of course, that the grim fears were somehow his fault. Jonathan wasn't at all sure why the approaching season was to be so fearfully rotten. He knew, it's true, that all wasn't well along the Oriel, but how the goblins and the strange doings at Willowood and Hightower and Stooton could concern the Moon Man or even the dwarfs in their fortified city of Seaside was beyond him. It was true, thought Jonathan with a bit of a shudder, that the Moon Man's face had turned up rather often in the past, but that didn't make all this business any more evident. Perhaps it *was* all a bit like a spider web. From a distance the pattern is clear, but for a bug caught up in it, it's just a tangle of threads running out in every direction toward the horizon. He had hoped that the Moon Man would sort things out for him—that he and the Professor and Dooly would be able to do a bit of fishing off the pier and have a leisurely supper or two with the linkmen and then have a cheerful trip home carrying a paperweight and a carton of books.

But that prospect didn't look likely. It started to look even less likely when Jonathan noticed what was sitting atop the table in front of the Moon Man—an oddly shaped jar with a glass and cork stopper in which floated a tiny pickled octopus. Dooly saw it at the same time.

"Old Grandpa's been here!" he shouted, gesturing at the octopus.

The Moon Man smiled at him. "He has indeed, Dooly," he boomed. "And quite a grandpa he was."

"Oh, yes, Mister Man-in-the-moon," said Dooly, hugely pleased at the compliment. "There was times, sir, if your grace will pardon me while I carry on, that Grandpa had what might be called adventures. He was a powerful smart man, was Grandpa. And rich! Let me say! He had more

than one of those octopods!" Dooly winked meaningfully at
Jonathan, partly because Jonathan was in on the octopus
secret and partly because of Dooly's pride in old Grandpa's
reputation.

"It's been many years since your grandfather and I last
struck a bargain," said the Moon Man.

"Back in the octopus days," said Dooly. "Later on it was
whale eyes, then horned frogs in little cages, then finally
little marbles with a sea horse frozen inside which he said
he got from the linkmen. Only I didn't know he meant jelly
men until just a few days ago when we came on Mr. Bufo
and the Squire and Yellow Hat and Mr. Stick-a-bush along
down the river."

The Moon Man seemed anxious to say something, and
he took advantage of Dooly's catching his breath to say,
"Yes, it was during the octopus period. He traded, if you
like, this octopus and a quantity of magic beans for four
coins, some golden rings, and a pocketwatch.

"Of the rings, three have been found. Miles the Magician has one, Squire Myrkle another, and you, Dooly, the
third. Where the fourth is is unimportant. It's likely that
your grandfather traded it finally also. Rumors came along
several years ago that he was spending a good deal of time
of late beneath the sea in a submarine contraption and that
he had as a companion a pig of exceptional intelligence
dressed as a clown. It was kept previously in a teakwood
cabinet above Seaside by a bunjo man, or so the story goes.
I'm beginning to suspect, however, that something is amiss
in the tale.

"Your grandfather, Dooly, traded the ring and the coins
for the undersea device and possibly for the bunjo man's
pig. The bunjo man wandered away upriver. We know this
because the four coins came into Amos Bing's possession
several months later."

Jonathan thought for a moment and then began to untie
the bag on his belt. He had an odd affection for the coins
even though they'd come to terrify him in some undefinable way, but if they belonged to the Moon Man and had
been stolen, or traded, from him by Dooly's grandfather,
then there was no choice but to return them.

The Moon Man smiled and held his hand up. "Keep

them, Mr. Cheeser, if you wish. But only if you wish. They
are what you'd call magical. You know that by now.
Through them I can see a great distance, as you, years ago,
found out. What good are they to me where I dwell? Real
evil hasn't come there yet. But in the river valley, on the
ridge above Hightower Village, lies something I can neither
see nor, I admit, fully comprehend." The Moon Man
paused, adjusting the heavy glasses which slid continually
down his nose. He narrowed his eyes, as if to see more
clearly. "So I'd like for you to keep the coins, Mr. Bing,
and I'll show you their secret—that which you stumbled on
years ago. And they'll be my eyes, so to speak, through the
coming winter."

"Yes, sir," said Jonathan, not as entirely overwhelmed
by the gift as he might have been.

"One last bit of business here," said the Moon Man, "before we turn to more pleasurable topics. Dooly lad, to
whom did your grandfather give the pocketwatch?"

Dooly looked up and down the table noting fearfully that
the elves had turned a bit pale, just as if they were coming
onto the part in a ghost story where the ragged skeleton
peers in at the window. "To . . ." Dooly began. "To . . ."
he continued, "To a conjurer dwarf from the Dark Forest."
Dooly then slumped in his seat and closed his eyes.

The Moon Man removed his spectacles and wiped his
forehead. He had suspected, of course, that such was the
case. It had to have been. What other device could have so
completely overwhelmed the galleon while it lay in Stooton
Slough, the elves on board searching for that very pocketwatch? What else could account for the desolation along
the river, for the weird twistings of nature roundabout
Hightower and Willowood and Stooton? The Moon Man
had suspected and at first blamed Dooly's grandfather for
stealing the watch. Then he blamed himself for having
allowed it to be stolen. Finally he blamed no one, for blame
rarely accomplishes anything and it's best to let it wear itself out. The time to act was, it seemed, upon them. Doom
was closer to them all than Jonathan feared. As the Professor had aptly put it, things were abroad in the land.

"And how do you know, lad, that the watch fell into the
hands of this dwarf?"

"I was there, sir."

"Indeed," said the Moon Man. "And did the dwarf have only one eye, the other covered by a black patch?"

"Yes, sir."

"Did he have a long walking stick, oddly carved?"

"Yes, sir."

"And had he a pipe in his mouth that billowed smoke like a grass fire?"

"He did, sir. All of that, sir."

"It's as I thought. When was this last trade accomplished?"

"Oh, years back, sir. Just before Professor Wurzle found the boat."

"Have you seen your grandfather since?"

Dooly hesitated, but because of the spectacled stare of the round-faced Moon Man finally said, "Yes, sir. A few times."

"What did he say to you, Dooly?"

"He said, sir," Dooly replied in a voice so small that everyone leaned toward him to hear, "that he'd been a fool, your honor, sir, and that there was winter coming on. But it was April then and it was all gibberish to the likes of me. He told me to take care of myself, sir, and watch for squalls, as he put it, and to come along to the coast if things got bad. That he had a device that would take us to the Wonderful Isles."

"And where, Dooly, were you to find him? The coast is a long, long place."

"I can't say, sir," said Dooly, his voice breaking and tears starting from his eyes. "I told him I wouldn't tell no one. Not even Mr. Bing Cheese, sir. Not even old Ahab." Dooly began sobbing and looked as if he were getting set to crawl under the tablecloth.

"I say!" said Jonathan, not at all happy. "It wasn't Dooly here who took the bloody watch. It was his grandfather, and the boy can't be blamed for it."

"Be quiet!" the Professor whispered into Jonathan's ear in such a way that Jonathan obeyed.

"Dooly," said the Moon Man, "it's for your grandfather that I ask you, as well as for your friends. It's for all of us."

Dooly sniffed twice and smeared the back of his hand across his eyes. "Are you sure?"

"Very sure," said the Moon Man.

"He said he'd be at the caves of Thrush Haven during fall and winter each year and that I was to wait for him there if ever a time came that I needed to."

"Perhaps that time is come, Dooly. Perhaps it's come." A silence followed.

"Well!" said King Grump rising. "Let's have a round of ale, shall we? It's early, but this is thirsty talk, thirsty talk. And we'd best fetch a lager and lime for the lad here who needs bucking up."

The Moon Man rose, nodded to them all, put a hand on Dooly's shoulder, then said he was tired and supposed he'd take a bit of a nap. They all watched him walk out of the hall while glasses of ale were brought in and passed down on a tray. He walked slowly as if he were either very tired or very thoughtful. Most likely he was both.

Chapter 13

News of a Fourth Companion

❧

AND that, apparently, was the end of the "conclave of war." It hadn't been much of a conclave. Most of those present hadn't spoken a word. There hadn't been any talk of battles or strategies or anything else—only questions about Theophile Escargot and his habit of borrowing jewelry and such. He seemed to be uncommonly ubiquitous, always racing about stealing rings, trading rings for pigs, pigs for beans, beans for octopuses, octopuses for undersea devices. He seemed to be a rather notorious and effective thief.

On the walk back to the inn, Jonathan and the Professor pondered all this, but came to no conclusions. Jonathan was relieved that he hadn't been drummed into any army, but suspected that they hadn't seen the end of all this business yet.

After a lunch of plaice and chips and a pint of ale, Jonathan and the Professor left Dooly to his own devices and walked the half mile along the coast road to Ackroyd's bakery. The fog had pretty much cleared by midafternoon, and it was a fine autumn day, all things considered. The road wound in and out of the walls of the city, in among the shops and homes for a bit, then through a massive arch and along the seashore. The rocky coast was peopled by little islets, many of them simply clumps of weedy rock beaten by the tides and wind, and many with lighthouses atop them. One or two appeared to be forts, for again the muzzles of cannon were visible through dim ports. It would be a difficult coast to attack, all in all.

Children played along the sandy beaches, none of which were more than fifty yards across; and a fair number of dwarfs, some in hip boots, some with their pant legs rolled, clammed in the shallows, shoving long-tined forks beneath the sand.

The two rafters paused once or twice to peer into a particularly promising tide pool. Bright orange fish—garibaldi, likely—sported among sea-green anemones and purple urchins. Preposterous crabs and willowy nudibranchs wandered about, scavenging food and accomplishing necessary fish business. Obviously they could spend a day, a week even, fooling about in tide pools and never wear out, so they decided to press on toward the bakery and have done with their business. It took them all of two hours, in the end, to walk the half mile to Ackroyd's bakery.

The bakery itself was a tremendous stone affair, and as soon as they got around to the leeward side of it they were overwhelmed by the smell of warm bread. It wasn't a bad smell at all, but Jonathan puzzled over the fact that two loaves of bread in an oven smell far more wonderful than two hundred. It seemed to prove what his father had always said about moderation being a finer thing than whatever its opposite was—satiation or gluttony or something.

Ackroyd himself oversaw all the operations at the bakery, and throughout most of the year spent the better part of his day peeking into ovens, poking loaves of bread, directing lads with mops and buckets about the bakery and that sort of thing. Today, however, he was covered in baking flour and was mixing up a complicated batch of spices—most of them White Mountains spices from the elfin groves and ground barks from the Wonderful Isles. Until Christmas Eve, he told Jonathan and the Professor, he'd be at work on honeycakes. It was nothing but honeycakes after the first of November for him, for he was the only one who knew their secret.

He shook a bottle full of amber powder in the copper vat of spices, threw a linen cloth over the top of the thing, and led Jonathan and the Professor into a sort of office in the back of the factory. But it wasn't the usual, dreary, and uncomfortable office; it had a window that opened up onto the sea, and it was lined with bookshelves. Across one wall was a tremendous fireplace with a hearth and face of carved tile and a mantel of some nature of translucent marble, almost the sea-green color of the tide pool anemones. On the walls were, appropriately enough, intricate pen-and-ink sketches and watercolors of astonishing pies and cakes, and one, amazingly, of Squire Myrkle nodding as if in approval over a monumental loaf of glazed cinnamon bread. The Squire had been younger when the painting was finished, but it was clearly he, with the same shoveled-into-his-clothing look about him.

Jonathan never cared much for business transactions, although that wasn't because he didn't, as they say, have a head for it. He knew, for example, the exact weight and value of his cheeses and, to the penny, the amount of Twombly Town coin in his sack. They would return with more kegs of cakes, finally, than the number of kegs of cheese they'd arrived with. And the elfin gifts which he would purchase from Twickenham would fill several more. Elfin gifts don't take up much room, however, for they are usually small—the smaller the more wonderful, in fact. Sometimes they grow a bit later on or change shape, but four kegs of elfin gifts would satisfy all the children in Twombly Town.

It was only right that Jonathan made a bit of a profit on the whole affair; the cheeses, after all, were from his cheesery, and he had spent the past weeks out on town business. Although his profits were moderate, moderate profits being the only acceptable sort, they would be rather nice. It looked, however, as if he'd immediately have to give up most of the profit, for he'd lost his raft or what was left of it, in the bay. Not only did he feel responsible for the raft, but they'd have no way to get home unless they bought or rented a new one.

So he decided to broach the subject with Ackroyd who, after all, had done enough trading in his time to understand the niceties of river-rafting. "We have a problem with our raft," said Jonathan.

"What raft?" asked Ackroyd. "I heard it had gone entirely to smash. Sounds to me like you don't have any raft at all."

"Quite," said Jonathan. "You've touched it exactly. We haven't any transport upriver. Even our coracle is gone. Drifted away in the fog."

"Then you'll need a new raft."

"Precisely," the Professor put in. "And a not inconsiderable raft at that. Something substantial. Rafts seem to run into rough times on the Oriel."

"Well," said Ackroyd, "you needn't worry about rafts. There'll be one for you to use."

"And the cost?" Jonathan asked uncomfortably.

"I can't say," replied Ackroyd. "But I'd guess that a raft would be one of the advantages of the position you're about to volunteer for. Don't quote me on that; I've heard rumors."

"Ah," said Jonathan.

"Position is it?" The Professor sounded interested. "Volunteer?"

"So to speak," said Ackroyd, figuring like sixty on a sheet of paper and piling little stacks of coin. "I shouldn't have mentioned it at all. You'll hear about it soon enough. Nothing dangerous, of course, just a journey upriver. An uncomplicated journey." Ackroyd looked addled, as if he had spoken out of turn. The door sailed open just then, and a wild-eyed dwarf lad with a face full of gooey dough charged in shouting about "the bread oven" and "Binky the yeaster." Ackroyd leaped up and ran off, shouting that he'd come round to the inn for a pint later in the evening.

After that puzzling exchange, there was nothing for Jonathan and the Professor to do but gather up their receipts and coin and head back to the inn. They were both thinking all sorts of things. Jonathan felt downcast on the one hand, for he was coming to believe that he'd likely not see Twombly Town again, but he was happy about the possibility of obtaining a raft without having to spend every cent.

He'd come to look a bit sourly on adventures by that time, having had his fill, and yet he couldn't help but feel a bit puffed up over the notion of being a central figure in the river doings.

"Professor," he said, "there's one thing now that would make me a happy man."

"What's that, Jonathan?" asked Professor Wurzle, who seemed to be lost in thought.

"I'd feel vastly improved, Professor, if you'd be willing to take half of this coin. I quite literally wouldn't have made it this far without your help. You were the one, after all, who saved the kegs after the storm, and you're an altogether fine traveling companion. What do you say?"

"I say, Jonathan," said the Professor, "that I fully intend to profit from this venture. There will be books written and scientific grants obtained, and, quite possibly, not a little fame. I won't take away your profits now just as I know you won't take mine away six months from now. I was an uninvited guest anyway. It's out of the question. Out of the question."

Jonathan shook his hand, and they ambled up to the old Mooneye. "Then let me buy you a pint," said Jonathan.

"Buy me two," said the Professor.

"Done," said Jonathan.

Later in the day the Professor decided to take a bit of a nap while Jonathan just sat and squinted out into the afternoon sunlight. Dooly and Ahab put in a brief appearance, Dooly having somehow obtained a magic toad—although in what way the toad was magic he couldn't say—and a bagful of paper seeds that would sprout into curious flowers when dropped into water. The Cheeser left the two experimenting with the wonderful seeds. He decided that Dooly had the right idea, that it would be regrettable to come home from Seaside without souvenirs—and he knew exactly what souvenirs he wanted.

At the glassblower's shop Jonathan found the celestial orb he'd been so carried away by two days before. The price was dear, but seemed fair given the amazing nature of the things. The dwarf slid it into a little velvet bag and put the bag in a wooden box with a hinged lid.

Jonathan still had a good bit of coin left after the purchase, and he considered that it would likely be folly of some sort to return upriver with *too* much money. They'd probably just get waylaid and robbed by highwaymen or goblins. Therefore, all things considered, it would be wise to spend most of the rest of his money on books. Few thieves, when you think about it, bother stealing books. They either don't go in much for reading or would have an impossible time carting away the books.

So he cut along back to one of the bookstores he'd been intending to investigate and found it open. A dwarf sat atop a stool within, playing chess with himself and seemingly in a rage about the way the game was progressing. But he was polite enough when Jonathan wandered in. Books were piled everywhere, on shelves leaning this way and that and angling up to the ceiling—everything covered by a thick layer of dust. Books which were out of reach overhead were gray with it, and Jonathan reflected that somehow the dust added to their appeal, as if books which had aged a bit like wine improved in some measure.

"Everything's half price," said the dwarf, one hand poised above a rook, "except the almanacs."

"Almanacs too popular for that sort of sale?" asked Jonathan.

"Not at all," said the dwarf. "The almanacs are free. Nobody wants them except the mice." He pointed to a heap of paperbound almanacs on the floor beside the counter. Three mice, one white and two white with brown spots, were methodically chewing strips of paper from the pages and hauling the scraps through a hole in the wall. Other mice could be seen capering along across the doorway that led into a second room of books. "The best mouse library on the coast rests within that wall," said the dwarf. "The little buggers must read like whizbangs. I can't figure it out."

"They have a lot of free time," said Jonathan, who liked to think that mice would enjoy books as much as the next man. He started poking along up an aisle, leaving the dwarf to his chess game, and found no end of good stuff almost immediately. The first shelves were loaded with pirate adventure novels—something he'd never been able to pass up. If he were in Twombly Town he'd buy the entire lot of them, but he'd have to be selective in Seaside. The more books he bought, the more he'd lose if they were dumped into the river. On the other hand, what did it matter if he lost fifty books into the Oriel or if he lost a hundred? He'd end up with no books either way. The outcome was identical. He might as well buy what he wanted, after all, and worry about it later. It was far more fun that way. He held up a dark copy of a book called *The Pirate Isles* by someone with the ridiculous name of Oodlenose, and he asked the dwarf the price.

"The price is on the inside cover," said the dwarf, moving his queen several squares ahead and then over two. Jonathan didn't know much about chess, but he'd played enough to know that such a move was unsound. The dwarf slammed his hand against the oak countertop, the chessmen hopping and dancing in a little cloud of rising dust.

"Did you see that?" asked the dwarf.

"I believe so," said Jonathan. "Odd move, that."

"Cheating, that's what I call it! How can I win if he cheats?"

"You can't," said Jonathan. "Who is he anyway?"

"My opponent," said the dwarf, motioning to a book lying open before him on the counter. The book, entitled *Peculiar Chess Moves*, was about three inches thick and had seen some use.

"I'd use another book," said Jonathan. "Find another opponent."

"It's the only one I have," said the dwarf. "It's awfully rare. Paid a fortune for it actually."

"Ah," said Jonathan, seeing the logic of it. "It sounds like you'll have to cheat too then. It's only fair."

"I don't do that," said the dwarf seriously.

"Of course not," Jonathan said. "By the way, there's no price at all in here, actually."

"Well how much is it worth, do you suppose, six pence?"

"Easily," said Jonathan.

"Then half that. Everything here is half price. Didn't I tell you that already? Seems like I did. The almanacs are free, but you'll have to wrestle the mice for them."

"Fine," Jonathan said, picking up an empty wooden crate and putting the pirate book in the bottom with a few others by the same author. Then he ran across a shelf of books by Glub Boomp, the elf author from the White Mountains who wrote about lands way off in space and about the Wonderful Isles and a country beneath the sea called Balumnia that was peopled by mermen. Needless to say, Jonathan stacked those away in his crate too.

But he really struck paydirt when he stumbled upon the collected works of G. Smithers of Brompton Village. At home Jonathan had a dozen or so volumes, most of them dog-eared and falling to bits after having been read and re-read and loaned out and so on. But there was a complete set of G. Smithers, one hundred-twenty-nine volumes in all and every one as good as the other. After a couple of hours of browsing, he hunched out into the evening mist. He had to hire a wagon to carry his books back to the Mooneye. It had been an amazing afternoon all in all and was even more satisfactory because he had found, in a room of illustrated science and philosophy classics, the phenomenal *Tomes of Limpus*, great aged, vellum-covered volumes full of scientific arcana—a collection for which, Jonathan knew, the Professor would gladly sell his oboe weapon. They'd make a fine gift, something the Professor couldn't refuse.

Ackroyd the baker came round that evening, as did the four linkmen, and all sat about before the fireplace gobbling down roast goose and oyster pie and cranberry jelly and pints of ale. Jonathan settled into bed late with Ahab curled up on a rug beside it and lost himself in a G. Smithers he hadn't read before—a book about buried treasure and goblin wars and all manners of things. He dozed off, however, before he was through twenty pages, and he slept through the night, his candles burning themselves into little waxy puddles.

He seemed to be involved in the same dream for hours, a dream in which he and the Professor were walking with the Moon Man across broad meadows of clover and lavender. It was a sunny day, a spring day, and the path they ambled along led to a heavy oak door set into the steep side of a small grassy hillock along the path. A huge bar and lock bolted this door, and the Moon Man toyed with a chain of keys in search of one which would fit the great lock. When the door swung open it revealed nothing but a dark hallway running down and away beneath the meadows. The Moon Man produced a lamp from a shelf just inside the door, lit the wick, and stepped in, followed by Jonathan and the Professor. Their footsteps echoed along the dim, stony passage. Jonathan became aware, in his dream, of an odd, musty, sharp odor in the air roundabout—not at all unlike the smell of the inside of a cheesehouse.

"Smells like a cheesehouse down here," he said aloud.

"Just so!" said the Professor. "That's just what it smells like. Rather nice, actually."

"Watch your step here," the Moon Man warned as the three of them clumped down a long batch of stone stairs into an immense underground gallery.

The Moon Man turned the flame up on the lamp, and the yellow glow lit the entire cavern. The walls, pockmarked and cut into odd geometric forms, seemed light green like very pale jade. There was an overpowering smell of cheese in the air.

The Moon Man was grinning widely. With his penknife he cut a chunk out of one wall and broke it into three pieces. All of them popped a bit into their mouths, and Jonathan was vaguely surprised to find that it tasted good, very sharp and with a smooth soft texture. The whole thing struck Jonathan as funny all of a sudden, for the Professor stood goggling, chewing slowly. He was smack up against another impossibility and was trying to study it out. Jonathan couldn't contain himself; he began to laugh like a lunatic. The Moon Man joined in, and finally the Professor did the same. All of them laughed their way out along the passage and into the open air. Amazingly—though it seemed natural to Jonathan in his dream—it was dark out—dark as midnight—and the meadows roundabout stretched off in every direction, lit not by the pale rays of the moon but by the blue-green light of the earth which swung overhead in the night sky like one of the Squire's marbles.

It was altogether a pleasant if mysterious dream, but it ended abruptly when Jonathan became conscious that someone was whacking on the door. He awoke, sat up, and shouted, "Green cheese," very loudly before realizing that he wasn't in the land of dreams anymore but was sitting in his bed at the Cap'n Mooneye and that, according to his pocketwatch, it was nine o'clock in the morning.

There was a whacking at the door again, and Ahab bounced about the room, rushing to the door, then to the side of Jonathan's bed. "Jonathan!" the Professor shouted from behind the door. "Wake up, man. We've an appointment with your Moon Man." Jonathan stepped over to the door and opened it.

"I rather thought something like this was coming up," he said.

"It had to be," agreed the Professor. "There's more to our trip upriver than just gifts and cakes. You can count on it."

A short hour later they found the Moon Man waiting at the Seaside dairy, a mile inland from the coast. He wore his tweed coat and leaned heavily on a carved stick. But the countryside roundabout and the bustle of the dairy seemed to buoy him up a bit, as if he felt at home. In truth he had nothing to do with the operation of the dairy, but he liked to point out that he and Hodgson, the master of the Seaside dairy, were thick as thieves, especially when it came to the making of cheeses. Jonathan was pleased when Hodgson, a cherubic-looking dwarf with a pointed beard, insisted that the Professor was witnessing a meeting of the three finest cheesemakers in the Western lands. The elves, he said, couldn't make cheese worth a bob. They were always dumping magic crystals or impossible spices into them and ruining the whole lot. They insisted it was all very gourmet, but, if the secret were known, they wouldn't even eat their own cheeses. They sold them to the coastal villages to be used as fish bait.

The dwarf cheesehouses looked pretty much as you'd expect—much like Jonathan's, in fact, only vastly bigger. Enormous wheels of cheese hung from the high rafters, some wrapped in gauzy cheesecloth, some covered in coatings of wax and wound round with rope, some encased in great crystals of rock salt.

Along one wall of the cheeseroom were stoves and cutting boards and presses and a dozen or so dwarfs all up to the elbows in tubs of curds and whey. The cheese presses were huge affairs, one almost as large as Jonathan's house, and they were an absolute wonder of cranks and gears and sieves. Great dollops of whey dripped into long troughs cut into the floor beneath, and a rush of canal water was allowed in through a trap in the wall every ten minutes or so to wash the troughs clean.

Jonathan was treated like a prince by the cheese-hands who assured him that his name had been well known for years around the Seaside dairy. Jonathan doubted that such a thing could be and blushed a great deal, assuring them that his cheeses were paltry things at best when compared to dwarf cheeses. The dwarfs, however, slapped him on the back and said that they enjoyed a humble nature as much as the next dwarf.

Hodgson led them along to the milking parlors—long rooms with a maze of stalls and a line of cattle coming along on a sort of treadmill device. The cattle were clearly Seaside hybrids. They seemed easily twice as large as any cow Jonathan could remember having seen around Twombly Town, but such a phenomenon might have been an illusion caused by the fact that they towered over the dwarfs who scuttled about milking them. They were ponderous, low slung beasts with round, lumpy hooves and legs like the stumps of trees. Their eyes were small, far too small to seem anything but foolish, and the folds of flesh on their faces made them look as if they were squinting and always deep in thought.

Ahab didn't know what to make of the beasts, but he seemed to sense that in many ways he bore the things a family resemblance and, as a consequence, felt at home with them. He went sniffing about and, as if he hadn't any manners, pretended to peer into a bucket of milk for some apparently philosophic and innocent purpose, when what he intended, Jonathan knew, was to have a go at it. Jonathan warned him away, after which a dwarf poured the pooch a dish of the stuff and patted him on the head.

Hodgson stormed about overseeing the milkers and so left the rafters and Ahab and the Moon Man to go about their business. Jonathan and the Professor followed the Moon Man out onto a pasture, then sat down on a long bench, gray and pitted from years of coastal fog and rain.

The Moon Man didn't waste words. "Gentlemen," he said after clearing his throat and pushing his spectacles higher up onto the bridge of his nose, "I've had correspondences last night from upriver, and the news, I fear, is disheartening."

Jonathan thought immediately that whatever curse seemed to be plaguing the high valley had spread to Twombly Town. But that, it turned out, wasn't the case.

"The town of Hightower, gentlemen, has been deserted by the townspeople. Not more than a handful remain—half a dozen at most. The houses are inhabited now by things from the swamp. Goblins and hobgoblins and animals behaving in odd ways go about freely in the town and even carry on trade with two or three of the merchants who have elected not to give up their shops."

"Staunch sorts, those," said Jonathan, who remembered his meeting with Old Hobbs who, as the Professor had stated at the time, was the sort to "bear up" through a crisis.

"All gone daft, actually," said the Moon Man with a sad shake of his head. "Every one of them, I'm afraid, and the rest off upriver and down with nothing but baskets of clothes and food. It's a sad pass."

Jonathan shook his head. Three villages between Twombly Town and Seaside lost. Nothing lay between Hightower and Twombly Town to slow the creeping spread of horror but a few short miles of forests—forests already frequented by trolls and wolves and, no doubt, goblins. "It seems to be time, sir, that the Professor and Dooly and Ahab and I got about our business. We're needed in Twombly Town while we're here on a holiday of sorts in Seaside. That's not a good thing, I believe."

"Not a bit," the Professor agreed.

"No, I suppose not," said the Moon Man with a sigh. "One likes to think that trouble will dry up and blow away on the wind, but that's rarely the case."

Jonathan agreed, apprehensive over all this trouble business and fearing that his return to Twombly Town wouldn't be a simple matter. "We've only a little more than a month before Christmas," Jonathan said, "and trouble or no, we've got to get these cakes and gifts home before Christmas. We can't very well forego tradition."

"I should say," said the Moon Man. "Traditions such as those mustn't be foregone. We can't change such things with our whimsy; they're rooted too deeply in us all. No, Mr. Bing, you're very right. You'll all be on your way in due time on a raft that should be quite suitable. I have high hopes that you'll be home in time for the holidays. In time to put up a jolly good Christmas tree and light the fire in the fireplace and appreciate your pipe and your dog and your merry companions and everything else that the holidays are. Because, Mr. Bing, it's those traditions that see us through each winter and will, I hope, see us through this one."

"Yes, sir," said Jonathan, seeing some truth in the Moon Man's words. He suddenly felt a funny sort of sad regret for the passing of the few days he'd spent in Seaside and for knowing that the future, whatever it held, would as surely pass away in time. But perhaps that's what made such days seem so wonderful, finally, in his memory. So Jonathan told himself to buck up and cheered himself at the thought of the coming holidays and of seeing good old Mayor Bastable again and talking about philosophy with him in front of the fireplace.

"Well, sir," said the Professor, always the one to get down to brass tacks, "this is all just a bit too mysterious for my liking. I'm ready to lend a hand, and I think I can say the same for Jonathan here and for Dooly too. And Ahab's no slouch either when it comes to the dirty work." The Professor patted Ahab atop the head. "You should have seen him routing goblins there below Hightower. He was inspired.

"We've been led to believe, sir, that we can obtain a suitable raft, and as far as we're concerned, Jonathan and I, there's no reason not to bung straightaway upriver tomorrow morning. We've had quite a stay here these past days, but time is growing short."

"Shorter than you suppose, perhaps," the Moon Man said cryptically.

"That's just the sort of thing I mean," said the Professor, getting his dander up. "Anyone with any sense can see that things have run fairly well amok along the Oriel. There's no end of marauding goblins and trolls and menacing toads and such, but what has it to do with us? It's time, in other words, for Jonathan and Dooly and me to have a look at the script, if you follow me."

The Moon Man nodded in agreement, as did Jonathan. Ahab trotted away to sniff at two cows who wandered past munching clover. He didn't care much for scripts of any sort.

"I won't tell you that the whole thing is very simple," said the Moon Man, "because it most decidedly is not. The danger grows daily, and the future is a muddle of possibilities. But your part is not complicated. I'll merely ask you to transport a certain party upriver—to give passage to a gentleman whom you've heard something of, I dare say. In exchange, you'll have your raft, as well as the knowledge that you've played a part—and a very significant part at that—in what will most assuredly be a momentous event. I'd like to say a momentous victory, but I've seen far too many odd turns of event in my time to be so optimistic." The Moon Man removed his fish-globe spectacles and wiped away at them with a checked rag he kept in the pocket of his tweed jacket. He began to replace them on his nose, then seemed to see another speck and polished the things again. Then he blew his nose ponderously into the cloth, plucked a clean cloth from a trouser pocket, put the clean cloth away in his coat and shoved the used cloth into his trousers. It was an altogether odd exchange of checked cloths, but it seemed unportentous to the Moon Man so Jonathan didn't comment on it.

"Who is this chap," asked Jonathan, "that we're hauling along? Some elf warrior or dwarf axe brandisher?"

"Not at all," the Moon Man replied. "I sincerely hope it will be Mr. Theophile Escargot, a gentleman with whom you're to some degree acquainted."

Jonathan wasn't entirely dumbfounded. Escargot obviously figured heavily in the doings of the high valley—perhaps he was responsible for them in a way. Certainly he and this oddball pocketwatch were the Moon Man's major concern.

"You hope," said Jonathan in a questioning tone, "that

Dooly's grandfather will travel upriver with us. But you don't know?"

"Not until we ask," the Moon Man replied. "But I rather believe he can be convinced to come along. Young Dooly himself will help with that angle. He'll come, sirs, like it or no."

"But he can't be forced," said Jonathan. "Not if we're to be responsible for him. And what can he do by himself, anyway?"

"Well," said the Moon Man, "there's a certain pocketwatch. Rather an odd pocketwatch, actually . . ."

"Which," interrupted Jonathan, "can be used by nefarious types like Escargot to steal apple pies and lumps of cheese."

"Without question it can," replied the Moon Man. "And it can overwhelm elf galleons in Stooton Slough and bring about the ruin of a fine and trusted crew. And it can send Willowood Station all to smash and do the same, my dear fellows, to Stooton and Seaside and Twombly Town and Brompton Village and who knows what all else. Theophile Escargot, gentlemen, is going to steal that watch. He stole it once, excuse me if I don't mince words, and he's going to steal it again with, hopefully, the help of the Professor's odd device."

The Professor scratched his head. His oboe weapon was at the inn, but he wished he had brought it along, since the Moon Man very obviously knew what it was and could have enlightened him to one or two features about it—its unfortunate desire, for example, to sail around in big circles—which the Professor was still uncertain about.

"The device," said the Moon Man, "was built by Langley Snood; you may have heard of him."

"Who hasn't?" asked the Professor. Jonathan was fairly sure *he* hadn't, but nodded his head in agreement with old Wurzle.

"It was Snood and his company," the Moon Man explained, "who were very unfortunately surprised and overwhelmed by the strange storm on Stooton Slough, but it wasn't the storm alone that accounted for their defeat. Snood's device, gentlemen, was designed to find that selfsame watch—possessed now by the insidious Dwarf on

Hightower Ridge. It serves no other function. If the watch is within shouting distance of Snood's device, the device will lead you to it. Infallibly. The watch must be found and it must be stolen, and all must be done with great secrecy, unless the thief is to meet the same fate met by Langley Snood on Stooton Slough."

The Professor was awed, but was hugely pleased. His finding and repairing of the wonderful device was of far more consequence than he had hoped. "We'll do what we can," he said.

"Of course," agreed Jonathan. "And the sooner we launch out, the better. It sounds as if our journey upriver will be at least as adventuresome as was our journey down."

"Do as you like," said the Moon Man. "If you'll agree simply to cart Escargot upriver, I'll be obliged to you. You need promise nothing more. And as to launching out, we'll do so this very afternoon. After you gather Dooly up and eat a bite of lunch you can meet Twickenham and his crew at the palace around one. Mr. Twickenham, gentlemen, is my lieutenant and will henceforth be, as they say, in charge. I'm afraid that I must sail along home. It doesn't do me any good to be gone long. Brings on something frightfully similar to rheumatism, if you follow me."

Jonathan didn't, entirely, but he admired Twickenham, and, although he didn't much care to either take orders or give them, he'd as soon take them from Twickenham as from anyone.

"About the coins," said the Moon Man, almost as an afterthought. "Do you have them with you?"

Jonathan untied his bag. "Of course. You were going to show me how to order them, weren't you?" Actually, he wasn't keen on knowing much about their order. He was happy with the idea that things *had* order, but he found that they often remained more mysterious and wonderful if the order wasn't revealed. Also, with each revelation lately he seemed to become that much more tightly ensnared in the whole dark pocketwatch business. He held the coins in his open palm.

"Their secret is simple," said the Moon Man. "Point the

noses of the fish toward each of the four points of the compass."

Jonathan did, and there, shimmering into focus on the coins, was the winking face of the Moon Man. Jonathan flipped one of the coins and the face disappeared. "Simple as that?" he asked. "No abracadabra?"

The Moon Man shook his head. "No magic words. Nothing mysterious." He stood up and dusted off the seat of his trousers. "That's all I have to say, gentlemen, beyond thanking you for being so cooperative."

"Our pleasure," said the Professor, extending his hand. The three of them parted company, Jonathan and Professor Wurzle departing for the inn.

Having nothing else in particular to say, Jonathan quoted a line from Ashbless, a favorite poet of his: "When at last the die of battle cast by fates has tumbled still, in feathered expectation, wait I will."

"Sounds apt," said the Professor. "Is that G. Smithers?"

"Ashbless," said Jonathan.

"I should have known," said the Professor. " 'Feathered expectation'? It sounds as if it were narrated by a bird."

"A man disguised as an ostrich, actually," said Jonathan.

The Professor nodded, then pointed off toward a point midway down the block and at the other side of the street. There stood Dooly next to a fountain—a cut stone circle with a bronze fish spouting water in the center of it—and Dooly seemed to be floating scores of miniature paper flowers on the surface of the water. Pretty as it was, the flowers would inevitably foul the works of the fountain, and the Professor said so, in a kindly way. They cleared the fountain and floated the flowers away down the running gutter before proceeding to the inn, Dooly in tow. At one o'clock they were there at the palace with Twickenham, his crew, and the elfin airship, amazed to find themselves actually climbing aboard the craft.

Chapter 14

The Hum of the Devices

❧

THE idea of flying—of being more than a few feet above the ground in fact—all of a sudden seemed a bad idea to Jonathan. Dooly, apparently, thought it an even worse idea. He slumped into a padded seat and sort of scrunched his head down between his shoulders as if trying to disappear. The Professor, however, was in his element. Jonathan could almost see the gears whirring and spinning inside his head. An elf in the seat in front of them took the whole affair matter-of-factly. His name, it turned out, was Thrimp. The Professor immediately began to question him about the nature of airships, but didn't seem at all satisfied with Thrimp's explanations.

Meanwhile, the four linkmen were engaged in squabbles of some sort—Bufo and Yellow Hat insulted each other, and Squire Myrkle tickled the inside of Stick-a-bush's ear with a duck feather, hiding the feather each time Stick-a-bush lurched around. When the commotion finally ceased, the Squire poked Stick-a-bush with the feather again, which somehow caused them all to start thrashing and shouting and arguing. Of the four of them, only the Squire seemed to be enjoying himself.

Jonathan, worrying mildly about the likelihood of flying machines, was amazed to see the meadow dropping away below them. There was no roaring or lurching—they simply floated upward as the green meadow seemed to grow beneath them. Soon the long hedgerows could be seen ambling away in no particular pattern. They could see that the top of the palace was in need of repair, many of the tiles on the roof being broken and all of them covered with a thick layer of moss.

To the north, up the coast, a dense forest grew almost to the edge of the sea. Dim hills could be seen miles and miles away to the northwest, hunching up and up until they disappeared in the misty distance. Inside the airship all was quiet. Squire Myrkle no longer larked about, but stared through the window in wonder. The hum of the mechanisms, which were so clearly audible to Jonathan on the day of his adventure with the trolls, could barely be heard. Everyone, including Thrimp the elf, had his face plastered against the window.

As Jonathan stared groundward, the view was suddenly lost in a swirl of mist. "Fog!" Jonathan thought, as he peered out and saw, not fog, but a little puffy cloud directly below. It was floating like a crazily shaped balloon and looked rather like Squire Myrkle.

But for the cloud the day was really very clear. Away upriver Jonathan could see farmhouses and barns nestled among orchards, and dark willow-lined canals winding through. Tiny rowboats or canoes dotted the canals— dwarfs out fishing for catfish and squibalump, no doubt. Looking at the pleasant landscape below, it was difficult to imagine that a few miles upriver tendrils of evil were spreading out through the countryside as weird vines covered the ruined houses of Willowood. With smoke floating up out of chimneys and pies being baked in ovens, the farmhouses and cottages below made Jonathan homesick. He wished, just for a moment, that he was in one of those cottages with a couple of Ackroyd's cakes and a mug of hot punch. But then he considered the fact that he was already in a fairly wonderful place. Mayor Bastable, Jonathan thought, would trade away every hat he owned and take a job as a stableboy if such things would gain him a ride in an airship.

Soon they passed above the great wall, and Jonathan could see the roof of the Cap'n Mooneye below and the winding streets that led along the water and up toward the palace on the hill. Shielding their eyes from the afternoon sun, people on the street gazed skyward as the airship passed overhead.

Seaside disappeared behind them, and they sailed peacefully above the rocky coastline for a bit, Jonathan catching a glimpse now and then of what seemed to be a tremendous bank of clouds moving toward them in an awful hurry. They sailed in and out of patches of mist until, finally, instead of sailing out again, the ship whirred deeper into the clouds.

Jonathan was disappointed since the air journey would be much more interesting with the ground visible below. But then here was an opportunity to see what the inside of a cloud was really like. He was pretty sure there would be no lakes full of colored fishes as he'd once imagined, yet there might be something wonderful, who could say, in among the clouds.

But between the layers of clouds were spaces of air, and the only surprises were occasional forks of lightning that would crack along frightfully close to the ship and make them all jump and shout and hold their hands over their ears. Dooly was white and shaking and peering out through his fingers which he smashed against his face. Ahab, sound asleep on Dooly's lap, emitted a snort now and again— usually a moment before thunder cracked—that would set Dooly trembling in anticipation. The Professor had told Jonathan once that dogs, being one of the four major branches of domesticated nature, were, as he put it, "Alert to the profundities of weather."

They were out of the other end of the cloud bank fairly quickly, however. They had passed through what might be called a squall that apparently was dashing along down the coast toward Seaside, as if trying to arrive before dumping all its rain.

Below them, when they were out of the weather, were high cliffs and rolling ocean. Dark forests covered the hillsides above the cliffs, and for as far as Jonathan could see—miles and miles and miles—there were no houses or farms or villages, just deep woods cut here and there by a winding river.

Dooly seemed to cheer up somewhat after the thunder and lightning fell behind, and he and Stick-a-bush chatted about the storms they'd been involved in. The Professor and Thrimp exchanged theories about lightning, none of which sounded at all likely to Jonathan. Somehow the lightning conversation went the way of all good scientific discussions; that is to say, it moved along from lightning to weather in general, then to other sorts of natural marvels. Finally they came round to flying, whereupon the Professor, rather oddly, insisted that what they were at that moment doing was, if not impossible, at least highly unlikely.

"Ach!" said Thrimp. "Flying is nothing. Any elf child over the age of three can explain it away in a moment. Just look at the pelican, Professor. He is, you'll admit, the most foolish bird of all, and yet he has no trouble flying. Flying is nothing."

Jonathan thought that Thrimp's argument about the simplicity of flying was what one of his teachers had called a logical fallacy. But it didn't much matter who called it what, the Professor wasn't about to be convinced without seeing some proof—some evidence.

Old Wurzle was thoughtful for a moment and then said, "I once saw, Mr. Thrimp, a sight that even you and your people would goggle at. There was a dwarf up in Little Beddlington with an ape—I believe it was an orangutan— that would shout 'The Madman's Lament' as if it had been treading the boards for a decade!"

Thrimp screwed up his face and chanted:

> *"Woe unto drunkards bloated with ale*
> *Chased beyond darkness where creeping things pale*
> *At the sight of a gibbering, floundering torment—*
> *The thing on all fours, the Madman's Lament!"*

"You've seen it!" cried the Professor.

"The thing on all fours?" Jonathan, who hadn't heard the stanza of the poem before, gasped.

"No, the Beddington Ape," said the Professor.

"At the fair at the City of the Five Monoliths," Thrimp replied. "The 'Thing on all fours' I have no wish to see."

"But science, my good Thrimp," the Professor, brought the discussion back around to his original point, "has a place for the Beddlington Ape. It's a matter of rays emanated from the lower reaches of the eyeball. Somnambulism it's called, as you are no doubt already aware. But science, with its charts and forces, has no room in it at present for the flight of an airship. No, Mr. Thrimp, I prefer a scientific explanation, and would like to have one in regard to the operation of this ship."

Thrimp nodded. "I suppose I can arrange it, Professor. You are, of course, absolutely correct. I'll ask Twickenham for permission to tour the propulsion apparatus room."

"This is more like it," the Professor said to Jonathan as Thrimp disappeared through the door which led to the forward compartment, the room with the emerald walls. "I can barely imagine the gyros and combines and anti-force apparatus that operate this machine."

"They must be compact," said Jonathan, unable to determine where such things could be hidden on the tiny cylindrical ship.

"Oh, elves are immensely clever," said the Professor. "Especially with miniatures."

Thrimp returned and beckoned to Jonathan and the Professor to follow him. They passed through the door into a room of glowing green light where Twickenham and another elf engaged in conversation. Twickenham doffed his hat and bowed.

"Professor," he said. "I have infinite respect for a man of science. It's not to anyone that I'd reveal the workings of our craft which is, you'll find, very deceptive and improbable. But to you and Mr. Bing I'm honored to grant such a boon." Twickenham bowed again as did Jonathan and the Professor and Dooly, who, fearing to be left behind, had followed his two companions forward. Ahab, who didn't care a penny for either science or airships, remained sleeping in Dooly's seat.

Jonathan noticed a rather small door in the side of the ship which, anyone would assume, led into empty space. In fact, swirls of clouds were visible through the deep green of the emerald from which it was cut. Thrimp led them toward that door which seemed to swing open by itself, or rather to simply fade from green to blue to black—the same sort of black the night is made of. The three companions peered into the darkness. Then the Professor began to step through, but Thrimp put a hand on his arm and restrained him.

"I can't see a thing," the Professor reported.

"It's cold," said Dooly.

"It's dark as pitch," the Professor said, "but I think I hear the hum of the devices."

Jonathan held his breath and could hear, very faintly, a roaring sound—more the shouting of wind in a deep canyon than the hum of a machine. He began to wish he were elsewhere.

The darkness, however, either began to brighten or their eyes began to grow accustomed to the dark. They could make out the vague outlines of a vast, dimensionless room without any observable walls or floor or ceiling. The echoes of shouts and creaking ropes and the clacking operation of vaguely outlined machinery became clearer and clearer—great millwheel devices and a slowly spinning cube suspended in air; a forest of hanging ropes and chains attached to pulleys and cranks were almost invisible in the air above. A host of little men dressed in leather coats and white aprons, many with pencils stuck behind ears, scribbled on paper note pads and shouted incoherent orders to one another. Jonathan could hear words and phrases which he supposed the Professor understood. Things like, "Treppan the lumen!" and "Haul on the crank-about!" and "Overcome the sky tides!" were tossed back and forth by the little men in a haphazard but essential way as they worked furiously, yanking on pulleys and twirling little merry-go-round apparatus that glowed in the deep reaches of the room miles and miles away, it seemed, like wild pinwheels.

Thrimp, somehow, shut the door, and the three found themselves looking at clouds through an emerald wall.

"That's the most amazing thing I've seen." Professor

Wurzle had a look of awe on his face. "What were those spinning devices?"

"What do you suppose?" asked Thrimp.

"Why I've no doubt they're gyros of a sort," Wurzle replied.

"That's exactly it. Gyros is what they are. As many as you please."

"Ah." The Professor shook his head, obviously puzzled. "As many gyros as I please," he muttered as they trooped out and resumed their seats.

Jonathan wasn't sure what he'd just seen, but he was fairly sure that whatever it was, it had very little to do with the running of the ship. Or perhaps, it had everything to do with it. Perhaps he had seen the secret of the operations of everything—of all of the Professor's forces and laws and such. Who could say?

Soon they found themselves flying above Thrush Haven—nothing more than a section of rocky shoreline, smashed in the winter by long north swells that wrapped around the tip of Manatee Head and made it idiotic to bring a ship of any size within a half mile of shore. Jonathan thought it peculiar that the place was called a "Haven" since it was so clearly the opposite, and neither the Professor nor Thrimp nor any of the linkmen could explain the thing. Although it was a pleasant enough day now that the clouds were far behind, the surf appeared to be running high; waves broke against the mountainous rocks along the shoreline, sending cascades of spray fifty feet into the air. Beyond the surfline, spotted seals sat about in clumps, one now and again sliding off into the water and disappearing, no doubt, in search of a passing fish.

"Tough way to make a living," Jonathan pointed out. "You'd think those seals would have seen through this 'haven' business and moved on long ago."

"Seals haven't any sense of irony," the Professor said. "And they trust anyone—rather like old Ahab here."

Ahab's ears wiggled at the sound of his name. He seemed fairly pleased to be compared favorably with seals.

The airship zoomed along above the sea but below the tops of the cliffs that rose several hundred feet above the shore. Sea birds by the thousands, nested along the cliff face, were dashing off in all directions, skimming over the tops of the waves and soaring on the breeze.

"Thrushes?" Jonathan asked.

"Not a one," answered old Wurzle, who, as a naturalist, knew about that sort of thing. "There aren't any thrushes this far down the valley. Never have been."

"I see," said Jonathan.

The airship circled once, and Thrimp pointed out a dark slash at the base of the cliffs. As the surge washed out, it was revealed as the mouth of a long, low cave. Jonathan could see enough to realize that the thing must be sixty or eighty yards long. When the surge *whooshed* back in, the opening disappeared and only the arched top of the mouth was visible.

Dooly watched the activity below as if he wished he were back in Twombly Town. Jonathan felt bad about the whole thing. Although he knew that Dooly had not, in effect, betrayed his grandfather, Dooly's guilty face and general slump made all the logic in the world beside the point. Jonathan half hoped that Old Escargot would be long gone—off stealing emeralds from the jewel elves or trapping nautili and frog fish in the kelp-choked seas south of the Wonderful Isles.

The ocean disappeared behind them as the airship topped the cliff and settled onto the grasses of the heath beyond. Jonathan half expected the ship to go sliding in, bouncing on rocks and lurching over hillocks, but it simply ceased to hum all of a sudden and sank groundward at a leisurely rate, barely bumping at all when it settled.

"Smooth landing," Jonathan said to the Professor, who was crammed against the window so as to get a clear view of their descent.

"That would be the gyros." The Professor looked to Thrimp for support.

"Of course it is." Thrimp hopped up, then headed off down the aisle toward the hatch. Squire Myrkle bulked out behind Thrimp, squeezing between the seats. He made a sound like bubbling laughter. "Thrimp, blimp, gimp, wimp, dimp." Thrimp responded in kind, calling over his shoulder, "Squire, wire, cauliflyer." Then he popped on through to open the hatch and down the stairway onto the meadow. Dooly perked up at the cheerful mood of Thrimp and the Squire. Watching Dooly laugh at all the name calling, it occurred to Jonathan that the Squire and Dooly had the same sense of humor—a very peculiar sense of humor to be sure, but one which seemed to make any situation a bit lighter. That, as far as Jonathan was concerned, was always a good idea.

It seemed as if Dooly had forgotten for the moment that his grandfather, although no doubt looking forward to seeing his favorite grandson, would frown at the idea of being visited by a party of elves and linkmen intent on persuading him to undertake a difficult and dangerous task. Worse, even, Old Escargot obviously wasn't hiding from enemies of any sort, but from himself. And Twickenham was determined to change all that.

What they would accomplish by strolling on the meadow, however, Jonathan couldn't say. He followed along as Twickenham, urging Dooly along ahead of him, made off toward a stand of blown and bent cypress trees that formed a forest of sorts in a little valley between two grassy hills. Twickenham pointed and gestured while Dooly shrugged repeatedly as if he had an itch between his shoulder blades that he couldn't reach. Finally Dooly nodded and seemed to slump a bit, whereupon Squire Myrkle patted him on the back and cheered him. Jonathan could never be sure about the Squire, who seemed to be the dimmest sort of good-natured half-wit one moment, then oddly shrewd another. He was a marvelous sight though, hurrying along at the head of the procession, his arms swinging about his body as he lumbered puffing forward on bulky legs.

They paused in the midst of the stand of cypress, and Twickenham began stomping about with one hand cupped at his ear and prodding and poking with his walking stick as if searching for a buried clam. He thumped, finally, against something hollow and wooden. Then with the help of Bufo and Dooly, he scraped away dirt and brush from atop what turned out to be a trapdoor made of heavy wooden planks, worm-eaten and dark from having been buried. The whole thing was nestled into a hole in the earth. Mr. Bufo, a theorist in the manner of the Professor, found two rocks nearly the same size—and shape, in fact—as the Squire's head; he hauled them over. They set one at each of two corners, and using two oak walking sticks pried away at the heavy door until it popped loose. A dozen hands hauled back the door to reveal a dark passage dug out beneath the twisted roots of the cedars and shored up with heavy timbers. A ladder of sorts led down into the depths.

"Is this it?" Twickenham asked Dooly.

"Yes, sir," Dooly answered. "Begging your honor's pardon, sir, but old Grandpa described just such a hole, and it ain't a goblin hole neither, but leads to the caves."

"Shall we?" Twickenham asked the company in general. Everyone nodded and chattered and gathered round the mouth of the hole as Twickenham scrambled down. Each one followed in turn until only the Squire and Ahab remained above, peering down at them grinning. Clearly, when Squire Myrkle stepped onto the first rung, the ladder would be tried fearfully by his weight. It bowed downward, creaking and snapping; those below pushed back deeper into the dark corridor.

"Hold on Squire!" Bufo shouted. "Don't come any farther!"

"Here comes the Squire!" the Squire shouted and lowered himself a bit farther, one leg swinging ponderously back and forth as he groped for the second rung.

"Wait, Squire!" Bufo shouted again. "You'll break it all to smash, and none of us will get out!"

The Squire stopped and peered back down into the darkness. "The Squire will stand guard outside, with the beast," he said, as he crawled out of the hole.

"Me too!" shouted Stick-a-bush, who scrambled out after him. "I'll keep the Squire company."

"Me too!" cried Dooly, charging after Stick-a-bush, but Twickenham latched onto his belt and brought him to an abrupt stop. "Maybe I won't," said Dooly, scratching his head. "Maybe two guards is enough."

"Perhaps so," said Twickenham. With Dooly in tow, he led away downward. A blast of sea air, moist and salty, blew up the tunnel at them. The walls were wet with it and mossy to the touch. Each member of the party hung on to the belt or shirt of the one in front of him so as not to fall behind or take a wrong turning. When Twickenham stopped abruptly, everyone pummeled together like toppling dominoes; Jonathan fell in a heap on top of Bufo and the Professor. There was a general shouting and scuffling, but when things were sorted out, Jonathan marveled at the sight that lay spread out before them.

Chapter 15

Theophile Escargot

❧

It was a tremendous vaulted cavern, wide and deep enough to house a fleet of ships. Sunlight streamed in from shafts in the rocky ceiling, and great stone pillars angled away toward the cathedral ceiling a hundred feet overhead.

Below them and away to the right a path stretched over the stone, chiseled clear here and there and leading past what appeared to be other tunnels cutting away into the cliffs. Directly below was a wide and peaceful lagoon, green and murky within the twilight of the cavern. The mouth of the cavern, which they had seen during their flight along the cliffs, was visible in the distance, a sliver of light which opened to a half circle as the surge ebbed, then closed again to a sliver a minute later. At each surge a glassy swell humped across the face of the lagoon, swishing quietly up onto the rocks some few feet beyond and below where Jonathan stood with the rest of the company.

Aside from the swish of the rolling surge, the only sound within the cavern was the occasional echoing cry of a sea bird that sailed in and winged around for a few moments within the cavern before either sailing out again or disap-

pearing into one of hundreds of weedy-looking nests clinging to crags and depressions in the walls above.

The whole quiet vista was something close to awesome;
it silenced all of them. But perhaps most awesome of all
was the weird ship that floated at anchor off a sandy spit
halfway around the lagoon and at the end of the path
across the rocks. It was an astonishing craft, obviously built
either by elves or by one of the tribes of marvel men in the
Wonderful Isles—built by someone, anyway, who knew
what such devices ought to look like. It was a spiraly affair, with odd, seemingly senseless crenelations and spires
and a series of what might be taken for arced shark fins
down the center of its back. On a foggy night the thing
would certainly resemble a sea monster more closely than a
ship, for it had several round portholes at the front, two of
which, on either side of its pointed nose, glowed from some
inner light and looked for all the world like eyes. On the
sides were protruding fins, shaped like the fins of an enormous tide pool sculpin. Seawater to the rear of the vessel
seemed to be churning and bubbling, and a *whoosh* of water shot out of the end every minute or so.

"That's old Grandpa!" Dooly said. "Sure enough and no
doubt. That'll be his undersea device there." Dooly pointed
proudly toward the submarine. Twickenham, followed close
on by the rest of the company, hopped across a couple of
rocks and climbed along up the path until he reached a
little rocky peak from where they could see the entirety of
the beach off which the device was moored. The beach
sloped away into the mouth of another cavern, and hustling
through the cavern's mouth came Theophile Escargot, perhaps the most noted thief and adventurer in the land,
carrying an armload of goods which he piled into a canoe.
He pushed the canoe into the lagoon, produced a paddle
from beneath the thwarts, and dipped away stiffly toward
the submarine.

"He's onto us!" said Twickenham. "And he's going to
run."

"Not Grandpa," said Dooly. "He said he'd wait until December for me."

But it was clear that Escargot was in a huge hurry, for
he made the little canoe skate over the surface of the la-

goon. Dooly leaped ahead of the rest of them and charged down the path toward the beach shouting.

"Grandpa!" he shouted when first setting out. Then just, "Whoooo!" and, "Hey!" as he pounded along, moving too quickly to bother with any actual words.

Old Escargot, shoving odds and ends through an open hatch, turned to see who was making such a fuss, paused, caught sight of the rest of the party clambering down the path. Without more than a moment's hesitation he climbed down into the submarine. The hatch slammed shut, two or three blasts of water shot out behind, and the whole craft sank bubbling away beneath the waters of the lagoon.

Dooly stood on the sand, waving slowly at nothing, puzzled, probably, that old Grandpa had disappeared so completely. "He must not have recognized me, Mr. Bing. He thought I was a ghost or goblin or something. Maybe I shouldn't have made such noises."

"Perhaps that's the case, Dooly," Jonathan agreed.

"He seemed in a powerful hurry to get away."

"That he did." Jonathan looked back up the beach. In the mouth of the little cavern lay a heap of supplies. A fire crackled within a pit encircled by stones; an odd fish, half-cooked, hung spitted over the fire.

"Left in the middle of lunch," Jonathan said, "and without half his supplies."

"The old scoundrel," said Bufo, shaking a fist at the empty lagoon. Near the mouth the surge ebbed and two spiraling towers were briefly visible cutting along through the swell. "Hah!" Bufo shouted as they disappeared, the submarine passing away into the open sea. "I'll compose a poem about this treachery! An epic." Bufo stomped around, possessed by the muse.

Jonathan could see that Dooly was making a grand effort not to cry. "Why don't we talk about treachery some other time," he said to Bufo. "It won't do us any good now anyway."

Bufo looked at Jonathan, then at Dooly. "I believe you're correct." He followed Twickenham and Thrimp and the Professor over to where the fish was still roasting to pieces. Its underside was charred and going to bits, but the top side was barely done. The Professor, idling about while

Twickenham picked through Escargot's abandoned supplies, turned the spit.

Jonathan sat on a rock and picked up a hermit crab as it scuttled past, big as a fist. The crab poked its head out of its seashell, looked at Jonathan, then pinched him on the finger. Jonathan shouted and pitched the thing into the lagoon, although he was immediately sorry he had, afraid that the crab might have suffered in some way. It occurred to him that it was foolish to go about picking up crabs if you didn't want to get pinched.

Dooly, who still stood near the water's edge, began to shout and dance. "Hooray! Hooray!" He pointed out toward the water. Jonathan jumped up, and the others stormed across the sand toward him, for, surfacing amid a flurry of bubbles and steam, was the undersea device, Old Escargot was clearly visible within, working a complexity of controls. The thing motored into shallow water, and an anchor splashed out from the stern. As the hatch shot open, a grizzled head popped through.

"Grandpa!" Dooly yelled. Old Escargot, smiling as if he were just pulling into port after a fairly successful fishing trip, shouted, "Dooly, lad!" He waved heartily.

The man wasn't at all what Jonathan expected or remembered. For the last ten years he'd been nothing more than a rumor, a shadow around Twombly Town, known to everyone but well known by no one. Somehow Jonathan expected a dapper sort of gentleman thief—someone who looked a bit like the Professor perhaps, or like a retired schoolteacher. But Escargot more closely resembled a madman or a pirate or someone who had been off digging for buried treasure in the White Mountains for a year. His beard was simply grizzly and gave him the look of a fanatic. His hair should have been cut months before; it was swept back away from his face to some extent as if he were standing in a stiff wind. His eyebrows were on the bushy side. He wasn't a particularly large man, was small in fact, but the spectacular appearance of his face made him look larger. Jonathan was fairly sure that any self-respecting person would take one look at him and think, "There's a man who's up to no good," and set about locking doors and patting his back pockets to see if his wallet were secure.

Escargot stood looking at them from the open hatch. "Would one of you gentlemen be so kind," he said, "as to fetch my canoe there and paddle her out? I'd swim, to be sure, but the water this time of year doesn't agree with me. A bit cold, you see."

Fifty feet down the strand lay the abandoned canoe, which had washed ashore on the swells. Since no one else made a move toward it, Jonathan stepped along, pushed off, and paddled out to the submarine, He grabbed hold of a protruding bit of metal alongside a brass ladder, holding on until Escargot climbed aboard; the little canoe tilted dangerously, then righted itself.

"What ho," called Escargot, winking at Jonathan as he paddled ashore. "Didn't I know your father, lad?"

"That's so," said Jonathan. He knew, as Bufo had pointed out, that Escargot was treacherous, although that certainly sounded like a harsh word. It wasn't, on account of that, easy to make small talk. Escargot, however, didn't seem overmuch concerned with the problem.

"He was a good man," Escargot continued. "We did a bit of trading, him and me. He made a good cheese." Escargot smacked his lips appreciatively.

The canoe bumped ashore, and an embarrassed silence ensued. No one knew quite what to say. Twickenham, after all, was the one among them who was running the show. Bufo looked as if he were stewing, and the Professor looked pretty much the same. Dooly, however, capered up as if to hug Old Escargot, stopped, then thrust out a hand. Escargot shook it. "You're looking fit, lad. You've brought along some friends, I see. Mr. Twickenham," he said, and shook hands with the elf. "And Artemis Wurzle, if my eyebones don't deceive me. It's been a while, sir."

The Professor, disgruntled, shook hands anyway and admitted that it had been a while.

"You'll excuse my appearance," Escargot said, "but I've been living at the Haven here for the last two months. Haven't felt much need for the social graces. Didn't expect any visitors, you see."

Twickenham nodded. "Dooly here has been telling us that perhaps you did, that you had reason to believe that trouble was brewing up along the river. That you and he might take a bit of a cruise to the Isles."

"Yes, that's so. It is at that," said Escargot, who seemed a trifle uncomfortable. "Trouble you say? Upriver?"

"That's right," said Twickenham. "A certain dwarf—Selznak his name is—has gotten hold of something he shouldn't have."

"It's come to that, has it?" asked Escargot.

Twickenham seemed to be considering his words carefully before speaking. He might succeed by being stern, or then again he might not. He might be patriotic or he might appeal to Escargot's sense of duty. But he wasn't sure Escargot had any sense of duty or that he cared a penny for patriotism of any sort. There was the possibility that he could use Dooly, so to speak, to persuade Old Escargot to cooperate, but the idea likely seemed distasteful. It turned out, however, that Escargot needed no persuasion at all.

"You might have seen me motoring my submarine around the lagoon," said Escargot.

"Out of the lagoon," corrected Bufo.

"Quite right," Escargot continued. "I was checking her ports and mungle bars. She has to be shipshape if I'm to lay her over here for the winter. Wouldn't want to come along in April and find her at the bottom of the lagoon."

"That's understandable," said Jonathan, who was happy to go along with the old man's lie. "And will she hold up?"

"Like a queen. I myself haven't been upriver for a year. I thought I'd mosey up that way. Funny that you chaps should show up. Tomorrow would have been too late."

"I dare say." Bufo gave the Professor a knowing look.

Twickenham saw that he had an advantage. "Perhaps, Mr. Escargot, you'd combine pleasure with business and do us all a grand favor. His majesty would be grateful."

"I know that he would, and I'd be delighted to help out. There's sure to be profit in such a venture."

"Profit indeed," Bufo almost shouted, still in an ill-humor about the whole thing. But Twickenham shot him a look and shut him up. There was no need to strew rocks in the path, after all.

They clumped across to where the fish still smoked above the fire. "There's lunch," said Escargot, pointing at the sad object. All the meat had fallen off into the fire, and only the thing's skeleton hung there skewered.

"Looks like a goblin meal," Dooly pointed out. "Like them fishbones in Willowood among all them smashed up buildings. You should see it, Grandpa. All up and down, there's goblins about and ghost towns and everyone carryin' on like crazy people. Makes a fellow wonder."

"Is that so?" asked Escargot. "Willowood you say? How about Hightower? Everything well at Hightower, is it?"

"Worse yet," the Professor replied.

"I see," said Escargot. "I'd like to visit Hightower again. See what's up."

"That would be capital," Twickenham put in. "Just the ticket." And with that they began rummaging around, breaking camp. Jonathan and Dooly doused the fire, although there was nothing about for it to burn aside from the fish skeleton and skewer stick. Escargot gathered a packful of odds and ends together, paddled out once more to the submarine, then hid his canoe among the rocks out toward the mouth of the cave.

They found the Squire and Stick-a-bush above eating cold fried chicken and a loaf of bread from one of the two baskets of lunch Twickenham had packed. Ahab trotted from one to the other, helping with the meal. The Squire had gone a long way toward reducing the lunch to nothing, but there was enough left for each of them to have a bite or two during the return flight to Seaside. Escargot ate almost as much as the Squire, seeming happy to have something other than fish for lunch. He was as bluff and merry as any of them—more so, in fact.

Although Dooly's spirits rose in proportion to his grandfather's heartiness, Jonathan was just a little suspicious of the whole thing. Bufo was still acting like a sourpuss and was scribbling away in a note pad; pausing now and then to knuckle his brow or to ask Yellow Hat for a word. By the time they were halfway to Seaside, however, Escargot's cheerfulness had spread fairly thoroughly through everyone aboard, and he and the Squire led the whole party in a chorus of "Old Dan's Demise." Bufo was persuaded finally to recite his poem about the traveling pickle, and Old Escargot made such a show of appreciation over it that

Bufo admitted to Jonathan and the Professor that perhaps he'd underestimated Escargot. Late in the evening they landed finally at Seaside, all of them in fairly good spirits. Twickenham and Escargot disappeared into the palace. Jonathan, Dooly, Ahab, and the Professor set out for the Mooneye, anxious to be gone early next morning.

Chapter 16

Fishbones at the Mooneye

❄

LAMPS were lit up and down the streets, but fog had rolled in to enshroud them and dim their glow. It was a cool and murky night—one of the sort that frazzles your hair and makes you wish you'd put on a sweater under your coat. When the rafters clumped into the Cap'n Mooneye, the dining room and lobby were empty. Although that in itself wasn't so peculiar, it was odd that no kitchen smells wafted out to greet them as Jonathan had hoped. All of them were powerfully hungry and wanted only to eat and go to bed.

"Monroe!" Jonathan shouted, hoping to rouse the innkeeper. But the only answer was a furious banging and kicking above them on the second floor. "Monroe is pounding on something upstairs."

The Professor nodded, "I hope he's tenderizing a chunk of meat."

The pounding paused momentarily then began again. Someone, Monroe probably, stomping away like crazy. In between knocks a muffled sound could be heard, like someone shouting through a wad of cloth. *"Mmmph! Mmmph!"* it went, then more pounding. The Professor slumped into a chair by the burned down fire as Jonathan tossed three or four wedges of split cedar onto the coals, squeezing away at them afterward with a bellows until they began to pop.

"Careless of Monroe to let the fire burn down," said Jonathan. "He usually has it so warm in here that you can't breathe."

"Just my style." the Professor pulled his chair a bit closer.

Dooly and Ahab disappeared up the stairs, off to see what foolishness Monroe was up to. Immediately the stomping and banging ceased, and the muffled sounds were replaced by Dooly's shouts. Jonathan sprinted up the stairs four at a time, the Professor close behind, and found in the upper hallway poor plump Monroe, trussed up and gagged and making the "*Mmmph!*" noises through the end of his wadded up shirt that was jammed into his mouth. His eyes bugged out and he had a knot on his forehead where someone had, apparently, clouted him with one of his own frying pans. As soon as his shirt was pulled from his mouth, Monroe began shouting madly about goblins and throwing arms about in an effort to illustrate the tremendous size of the one who had smacked him with the pan.

The hallway roundabout was a clutter of strewn clothes and trash. Jonathan noted disapprovingly that his own tweed coat lay among the debris. Professor Wurzle plucked his oboe device from a pile of nightshirts belonging to another lodger. In the funnel mouth of the thing was a weedy looking fish head, jammed in as if looking down inside for some lost object. Other fish skeletons lay about the hallway, one across the threshold into Jonathan's room. The Professor was in a rage, almost as much of a rage as Monroe. Wurzle pulled the fish head from the nose of the device and threw it with disgust into a hat that lay upended on the floor. "Damnation!" he cried, furious. Then he swabbed out the funnel with one of the nightshirts. It appeared to Jonathan that the nametag in the hat and in the nightshirt were one and the same, and he hoped that their owner had a sense of humor. He sent Dooly off toward the palace to find Twickenham and to alert King Grump of the goblin affair, for it seemed to him to be a particularly bad portent. Jonathan had heard of no goblin activity of any nature in Seaside. But Dooly wasn't gone five minutes before dashing back in with both Twickenham and Escargot.

Their rooms were almost as wildly strewn with odds and ends as the hallway had been. Not only were their few clothes tossed about, but a tree limb had been dragged into Jonathan's room along with a length of clothesline strung with strange undergarments that were a perfect wonder of whalebone stays.

"Why they've been at my wife's stuff!" shouted Monroe, waxing furious again. "It's unheard of! What were they after, do you think? If it's money, they're a sorry lot by now."

"Well it isn't books," said Jonathan, happy to see that his cartons of books in the closet were unharmed.

"It isn't anything," said Escargot. "What could anyone have that goblins want? Tearing things up is enough for them. I would have said it was impossible for them to be this far below the Wood, though. But these are strange times. Very strange indeed."

"There's the chance," said Twickenham, "that their master put them up to it."

"More than a chance," agreed Escargot.

"Let me at him!" cried Monroe. "We'll see who he's master of and who he ain't!"

Jonathan and the Professor, however, weren't quite as anxious as Monroe to encounter this master. They were pretty sure they'd run into him in due time. Escargot was a bit on the pale side and looked unhappy—even more unhappy than he had looked when he had first spied them all that afternoon before making his escape in the submarine. "Aye," said Escargot in low tones. "It's his work."

They cleaned the place up and tossed trash and fishbones out the window. Jonathan was sure that he heard the cackle of weird laughter through the fog more than once, but after alerting the Professor to it the first time it occurred, he decided to ignore it. There was nothing to do about it anyway.

Around midnight, after a meal of cold meat pie and cheese washed down with a pint or two, they went to bed. Jonathan kept his window locked even though he liked a bit of a breeze at night. He had agreed with the Professor and Escargot that they'd be wise to awaken at six. There was a sort of unspoken assumption since that afternoon that Escargot was to travel along upriver. He himself acted as if he'd been planning to do so for weeks.

Daylight came quickly, and Jonathan was disappointed that he hadn't insisted on rising an hour or two later. He seemed to have just gotten to sleep. Ahab was fresh as a cucumber, however, and ready to go. It was as if he knew that in a couple of hours they'd be heading for home. Jonathan busied himself with packing—a chore that only took a few minutes since he had almost no clothes with him—and then hauled his books and bag down to the lobby where he found Dooly and the Professor.

Monroe had recovered vastly from the day before; even the lump on his forehead had gone away and been replaced by a purple spot. He brought round mugs of coffee for them all and sat down at the table. "That old boy upstairs," he said, jerking one thumb over his shoulder back toward the stairs, "is a strange one. Carried on fierce last night about three, pacing up and down. Did he have a bottle with him? Crazy-looking old boy with that beard and all."

"In fact," said Jonathan, "the gentleman upstairs is Dooly's grandfather. As for the bottle, I haven't any idea."

"Oh, yes. Of course, of course. Young Dooly's grandfather is it? Interesting sort, as I was saying. Must have been struggling with the window. It sticks in the wet weather. Needs a spot of paraffin."

"Where is your grandfather, Dooly?" asked the Professor. "Late sleeper is he?"

"Not old Grandpa," Dooly replied. "Up with birds is Grandpa. 'Time flies like an arrow,' Grandpa used to say, 'but fruit flies like bananas.' "

Monroe nodded assent then thought about it for a moment before getting up and disappearing into the kitchen, shaking his head.

"Brilliant man, your grandfather," said the Professor. "He should have been a philosopher."

"I'm pretty sure he was," Dooly replied. "But he didn't make no money at it."

"They never do," Jonathan observed, "and neither will

we if we sit here tossing off coffee all morning. See if you can rouse your grandfather, Dooly. Bring him a cup of coffee."

Dooly stomped off noisily up the stairs, balancing a cup of black coffee. He always seemed to have a sort of early morning cheerfulness, something Jonathan found vaguely irritating in anyone but Dooly. When Dooly didn't return for five minutes, the Professor volunteered to see what was up. His shout brought both Jonathan to his feet and Monroe out of the kitchen, and they dashed upstairs in time to find Escargot's room empty as a balloon. The window was open entirely, and lace curtains blew through on the warm air that was sailing out of the house into the cool morning mists. The bed hadn't been slept in during the night; it had just been rumpled up by someone sitting atop it.

"So he took off!" Monroe almost shouted, not angry really, just astonished at the fact that Escargot had thought it necessary to go through the window and down a drainpipe rather than out the front door like anyone else would have.

"The goblins got him," said Dooly tearfully. "Took him right away, they did. They was lookin' for him last night."

That didn't seem at all unlikely to Jonathan, and in a way, for Dooly's sake, he wished it were true. The Professor, however, didn't think much of the idea.

"You may be right about the goblins last night, Dooly," he said, "but they didn't come back and haul off your grandfather. Now I'm no detective," he continued, squinting over his glasses at them, "but there's nothing here to show that he fought with any goblins. And that pacing about last night that Mr. Monroe spoke of, I don't like the sound of that. I'm inclined to agree that Escargot made off in the night, blast him, and he could have gone anywhere. I'm damned if we wait around while Twickenham searches for him. If he doesn't want to go, he won't go. We can't hold the man prisoner."

"Well we'd best let Twickenham know anyway," said Jonathan. "He's running the show, after all."

"Twickenham knows," came a voice from behind them; all turned to see Twickenham standing in the doorway scowling. Elves have a difficult time scowling convincingly, being such cheerful-looking little fellows for the most part, but Twickenham managed nicely.

"He stole a horse at the south gate about four," Twickenham explained. "Gave the keeper some sort of sleeping draught and bunged away up the coast."

"Back to Thrush Haven," said Jonathan.

"Maybe," said Twickenham. "But maybe not. Who can say? There's nothing between here and there but hundreds of miles of forest. We'd be weeks catching him. You're right, Professor. We've delayed you long enough. Your raft and supplies are waiting about two miles up the harbor. We'll leave now. There's horses out front."

"Horses!" cried Dooly, who had never ridden a step. "Perhaps, sir, begging your pardon, but maybe I'll just walk and meet you there. I'm powerful quick once I get my knee bones limbered up."

"You'll enjoy the ride," said Twickenham in a manner more of command than of simple observation.

They trooped out into the street, arranged their goods in a little dog cart, and, happy to see that the four linkmen were along, clopped away up what were the first miles of the river road. Dooly actually had been fairly accurate in supposing he could move as quickly on foot, for the little dwarf horses weren't as quick as they might have been—especially the Squire's horse, which seemed distinctly put out. Dooly's horse stopped continually along the way to munch at shrubs and grass. Dooly yanked on the reins and yelled the familiar horse shouts, but all to no avail. Finally Twickenham took the reins in one hand and led Dooly's horse along. Dooly appeared to be slightly embarrassed, but had been happy enough to let the horse eat since it seemed to be enjoying it so.

The raft was moored at a little pier above town. It was much the same as Jonathan's old raft, aside from the fact that it had added a sail and a larger paddlewheel. They'd be able to make good time, winds or no. They needed only a moment to throw their goods on board, check the supplies and cast off. The saddest part was saying goodbye to the four linkmen, who were themselves ready to set out up the river road toward the Elfin Highlands and linkman territory.

Squire Myrkle seemed so merry, however, that it eased things a bit. "We're off to war!" he shouted, waving one lumpy arm about his head. "We'll whack them with sticks!"

"That we will, Squire," said Jonathan. "We'll see you lads along the way somewhere, I trust."

"More often than you'd care to, probably," said Bufo. "We're off to the territory to raise an army, then up to Stooton on a goblin hunt."

The Squire pulled a short sword from a scabbard attached to his pommel and thrust it this way and that shouting, "Avaunt, spooks!"

"Hey!" cried Stick-a-bush, nearly speared.

The Squire calmed a bit and replaced the sword. Jonathan could see that all of them were pretty fairly worked up. A good breeze was blowing onshore, and the tide was rising. The company shook hands all around and, there being no time like the present, as Twickenham pointed out, pushed off and slid out and away from the dock. They waved as the four linkmen pounded away up the road. Twickenham sat on his horse atop the dock while Jonathan unfurled the sail. With the tiller hard over to drive in toward the dead water near shore, the rafters began their journey home. The sails billowed in the breeze, filled, and the raft sailed along. Twickenham watched them disappear upriver. The morning was a good one, and Jonathan found himself vastly relieved that he was moving once again.

Chapter 17

Mysterious Traveler

❧

T HE fog never lifted that first day out from Seaside. It was thick and wet, and Dooly spent most of the day in the cabin. Out in the open was like being in a drizzle. Jonathan's coat was limp with moisture, almost soggy, and his hair curled and sort of frizzed as if it had suffered an electric shock. One thatch of it insisted on dangling itself in front of his eyes, and all the pushing and combing in the world had no effect on it.

Both he and the Professor sat on the deck on two of the three wooden chairs that Twickenham had provided. It made Jonathan feel touristy. If any fishing boats or trade barges had come by with the usual assortment of seafaring types on board, he would have felt positively foolish, sitting there on deck as if waiting to be handed a cup of tea. But it was so foggy that few boats were out at all, and those that were stuck fairly close to midriver, not wanting to run aground. Every now and again Jonathan could see the ghostly shape of a boat somewhere off the port bow, just a shadowy pile of spars and rigging and running lights, crawling its way downriver toward the harbor. The muffled voices of crewmen crept out over the river. He heard

one gruff, low voice, even before he could see the shape of
the trawler it came from, say in a tired way that it seemed
like twenty years since he'd been in at the old Mooneye for
a pint. Another voice replied simply, "Aye." Then there
was silence.

It seemed to Jonathan like an awfully sad thing to say,
and he felt like shouting to them that he felt the same way
even though he had gone through a pint or two just last
night. It was probably just the fog that made it such a gray
day.

By running along close to shore they could just make out
the occasional farmhouses that appeared and then disappeared in the mists. They passed the mouth of a little river,
overgrown on both sides by a tangle of giant alders hung
with wild grape. Both Jonathan and Professor Wurzle remembered the place from the downriver voyage although it
had seemed far more cheerful and less forbidding then
than it did now with the great trees dripping through the
fog. As they passed along thirty feet offshore they heard
the growl of a beast—a bear, hopefully, or a moose—and
then listened as the creature splashed away up the shallows
of the river deeper into the forest.

It was fortunate that Twickenham had given them a
map of the river. Although there was no way to become
lost, neither of them were familiar enough with the Oriel to
determine how much progress they were making. They recognized an occasional landmark, like the river mouth or an
island that passed by slowly off to port, but they had no
idea of the distance from one to another. They might be
plodding along like snails, or then again they might be sailing like birds.

Twickenham's map was a long, rolled-up affair, something like a scroll. Unrolled it was ten or twelve feet long,
and it had markings for almost every little riverside farmhouse
and way station, of every little rapids and sandbar, and
even of certain fallen trees and of the skeletal hull of a
ruined trawler some twenty miles upriver. They spent most
of the morning looking over the map and pointing out land-
marks and watching for boats that might have wandered
out of the midriver channel in the murk.

Neither Jonathan nor the Professor liked the idea of being smashed up by a schooner again. They hung lanterns in the bow and stern—something they would have done on their trip downriver had they had any lanterns to hang.

Jonathan finally rummaged about in the cupboards of the cabin, being careful not to awaken Dooly and Ahab, who were asleep on a bunk, and found the coffee pot, coffee, and a nice little dwarf camp stove—a big tin can filled with heavy, rolled paper and candle wax. Several wicks protruded from the wax, and the whole can sat on a metal frame with a grill atop. There were several other cans of fuel in the cupboard. It was all just the right equipment for brewing up a pot of trail coffee on deck, something that seemed to Jonathan a fairly romantic notion, given the fact that there was a good wood stove which they could have used in the cabin.

The smell of the ground coffee was perhaps the finest thing either Jonathan or the Professor had experienced to that time. Jonathan wished that Bufo or Yellow Hat were around to compose a poem about it. Considering the number of ghastly love poems that had been written and which seemed fairly clearly to be a waste of everyone's time, Jonathan couldn't help but be surprised that coffee hadn't been thus immortalized. There were certainly plenty of poems about other sorts of drink, although the only verse he could remember went, it seemed to him then, something like, "Beer, beer, beer—never fear," When he thought about it, it was nothing worth writing down.

Anyway, the coffee as it brewed smelled so rich and deep that it woke Dooly up. He and Ahab came out onto the deck, Dooly carrying several slices of bread and a toasting fork. The day brightened up a bit and took on more of a merry tone with all of them sipping the strong coffee and toasting the slices of bread from Ackroyd's bakery.

The farms along the riverbank were fewer and fewer, and the woods in between were darker and more vast. For the last two hours no boats at all had slid past aside from a single canoe which had appeared to be empty. Jonathan decided too late that he should try to retrieve the canoe, but it had swirled away downriver before they had a chance at it. There was no clearing at all that afternoon. Jonathan thought that the two on the fishing trawler were probably drinking their pint at the old Mooneye right at that moment and that old Monroe was likely shoving a joint of beef up onto a spit while his wife cleaned potatoes and rolled out crusts for pies. He sipped his coffee and thought for a bit about those pies until he very nearly dozed off.

But he was awakened abruptly by a voice. "I could go for a cup of that coffee."

Jonathan looked up at the Professor, who was working the tiller. "Have some then. I'll make a fresh pot."

Dooly was looking roundabout him as if he was sure it had been a ghost who had spoken.

"I didn't say anything," said Wurzle. "If I drink anymore of your coffee I'll have the jitters all evening."

Jonathan recalled that day out of Twombly Town when Dooly had first made his presence known. His theory concerning talking dogs had seemed a reasonable enough explanation at the time, but it wouldn't do here because Ahab, although asleep, didn't care a bit for coffee, and it was unlikely that he'd dream about it one way or another.

"Are you deaf, mates?" The voice came again.

"It must be another boat," said the Professor. "Look sharp."

Jonathan stood up to turn up the wicks on the running lights, and he looked off into the fog and listened for the creak of rigging or the slap of water on a hull. But the fog wasn't as thick as it had been, and there were, quite clearly, no boats within a couple hundred yards of them. It was a puzzle. Jonathan sat down again and stabbed another piece of toast with the fork. He was just smearing preserves on it when, seemingly from atop the cabin, came the following odd song:

> *"Oh there was a jolly miller*
> *Who lived upon the sea;*
> *He looked upon his piller*
> *And thar he sawr a flea.*
> *Ho ho, har har, hee hee,*
> *And thar he sawr a flea."*

Then, in a trice, the toast was snatched from the end of the toasting fork, and it floated along through the air for a moment before being gobbled up by an invisible mouth.

The Professor was astonished and started to reach for the oboe gun with which he'd been tinkering before remembering that it wasn't a gun at all. "Watch out here," he warned, squinting this way and that. "There's deviltry afoot, and plenty of it." Then the Professor's cap, a battered-looking tweed affair, floated up into the air and settled again on his head, backward.

Dooly laughed like a hyena and held one hand over his mouth to smother it. "Well, Dooly lad," the disembodied voice said. "You've got a sense of humor for sure. How do you like my cloak?"

"What cloak?" Dooly asked, looking about himself a bit more furtively now that it was he being spoken to. "I don't see no cloak, sir, begging your honor's pardon. Are you my old Grandpa?"

"Of course I am," said old Grandpa from somewhere above—on the cabin top again, probably. "Who did you think I was, Selznak the flaming Dwarf?"

Jonathan exhaled a lungful of air in one resounding *whoosh,* and Professor Wurzle put his cap on straight.

"I've been here all along, lads, quiet as a mackerel. Didn't want to make a sound until we were upriver past civilization. No telling who might be lurking about. Still best not to shout, I suppose." There was a brief clatter and stomping as Escargot climbed down from the roof of the cabin. "Can I use your cup, Professor?" he asked, and the cup sailed up into the air, dipped itself into the river, and shook itself out. The coffee pot upended and the last of the coffee, black by now as coal dust, poured in a steaming stream into the deep cup. One of the deck chairs creaked and settled and the coffee cup waved in the air.

"I knew you didn't climb out no window, Grandpa," said Dooly. "They said you took off and went down the coast."

"They was fools, Dooly, lad. The innkeeper was dense as that forest yonder. He kept peeking in at the keyhole all night. Thought I was stuffing the towels into my bag I suppose. So I peeked back out at him, I did, and winked. Threw him into the hallway, that wink, and as soon as he crawled back into his room I went out the front door. What kind of fool climbs out a window when there's a front door at hand?"

"Hah!" shouted Jonathan. "I knew it. Twickenham set the whole thing up."

"Almost, lad," said Escargot. " 'Twas me set the thing up. Now this Selznak, you see, don't like me a bit. We had transactions a while back. And I admit; he got what he shouldn't have got. But I got myself a few of his creatures, mostly small ones that didn't amount to a thing but came in handy for trade. But one was a good one, mates. A pig, it was, and lived in a special box. Leastways it looked a pig, excusin' its nose and its hands. It could sniff out elf silver from a half mile away like one of them mushroom pigs the linkmen keep. I let on that I got him from a bunjo man and kept him pretty secret. We had some luck, I can tell you, up in the White Mountains."

"What happened to this pig?" asked Jonathan.

"Died, poor devil. Had to sooner or later. He didn't have but half of him that was his own; the rest was bits and pieces. Crazy damn thing. Evil, I called it and still do. But it was better off with me than with that damned dwarf. He was setting in to attach wings."

"Vivisection!" cried the Professor.

"Then that beast by the river that chewed through the ropes—" began Jonathan.

"An abomination," said the Professor.

"Didn't you have one of them once," said Dooly. "One of them abomi-what-is-its?"

"More than one," said Escargot. "But that's why I'm here, see. No one but me has been in that bloody tower. And I swore I'd never go back, not for all the goblin treasure in the Wood. Not for a bucket of troll gold."

"So why *are* you going back?" asked Jonathan. "You could have been half way to the Isles by now."

"Well," said Escargot ponderously, "that I could. But I could go to the Isles come spring, too. Me and Dooly could go in the submarine. What's a few months more or less? And I wouldn't give it to them to say that Theophile Escargot, Gentleman Adventurer, ran when the fight started. No, sir. If this dwarf cuts up rough—and he will, mark me—then I'll be there to speak to him, I will, and not in no Wonderful Isles."

"Hooray!" shouted Dooly. "We'll smack 'em, won't we, Grandpa?"

"Aye, Dooly. Rough and ready, that's us in a nut."

"You haven't heard anything, I suppose, of the Lumbog globe?" asked the Professor.

"The which?" asked Escargot.

"The globe that was stolen from the elves a hundred years back, maybe more," the Professor explained. "It was pure crystal—elf crystal, not just soda glass—and big around as a melon. I haven't seen it, but I was told that clouds swirl through it and it was deep blue like the night sky. And there was a silver moon inside and stars all around. There was magic of a sort in it when you set it up in front of a lighted window. Those stars and moon started to swing round inside and the clouds blew about, or seemed to, and whoever gazed into it would find himself within the globe and could sail through space along with those stars to wherever it was he wanted to go. And your man Boomp, Jonathan, wrote most of his books after talking to old Lumbog up in the city of Couch. They say the old glassblower was three hundred years old by then and had been to places no one else had ever been nor ever will be either. I didn't believe a bit of it," said the Professor, trying to qualify things, "but I thought I'd ask whether or not you'd gotten wind of the story."

"Interestin'," said Escargot. "Seems like I have heard of it, now that you mention it. Seems I heard that some dwarf has it now."

"I thought maybe you had," said the Professor. "This Selznak has quite a collection of elf marvels. More than his share, no doubt." The Professor seemed as if he were going to give Escargot a look, but then he wasn't at all sure where Escargot was, so he didn't.

"Why didn't this Lumbog make more?" asked Jonathan.

"He tried," answered the Professor. "He and every other glassblower. That paperweight you bought in Seaside—that was a copy; I'm sure of it. But the original was a mistake. Even old Lumbog didn't know what happened. Got the fire too hot maybe, or spilled elf dust into the glass by mistake, or sloshed ale into it and didn't know, or any of a thousand things."

"Well," said Escargot after a long pause, "if old Selznak gets this cloak he'll have the three major elf marvels then. Those elves are pretty loose with their marvels, aren't they? You can steal 'em blind one moment and they're handing you a magic cloak the next. Sounds like there's a moral in there somewhere. Either that or a lot of stupidity."

"I suppose we'll find out before long," said the Professor, "one way or another."

Jonathan realized at that point that they'd been talking to a phantom. He decided he wanted to know more about that cloak. "What sort of cloak is this then, anyway?" he asked.

"It's what Twickenham called 'the cloak of invisibility.' *The* cloak, mind you, not *a* cloak. Fits a bit tight on me, but it must be like a tent on an elf. Watch this." The three of them stared as the coffee cup hovered in the air for a moment then disappeared. Then, as abruptly as the cup had gone, it appeared again. The cup finally settled on the cabin roof, and a second later a cigar appeared in the air. Then it disappeared and a pair of spectacles hovered about, opened up, and sat atop the bridge of an invisible nose. "I need these things to read," said Escargot about the spectacles. "This getting old is bad business. You don't get any more wise; you just fall apart."

"But where did all that stuff go, Grandpa?" asked Dooly, slow to catch on when the glasses finally disappeared.

"Into the blasted cloak. It's really more of a coat than a cloak as far as I can tell. It has sleeves at least. And it isn't warm worth a damn—like having nothing at all on. I'd appreciate it if you could see clear to giving me the spare bunk inside boys, if you would. I most froze up here this morning. Twickenham said I wasn't to come down too soon, and who am I to argue with Twickenham? Never argue with an elf who gives you a cloak of invisibility, that's my motto, and so far it hasn't steered me wrong."

"I dare say." The Professor, who, Jonathan suspected, actually thought Escargot a trifle glib, smiled. Jonathan didn't mind a bit though. He rather liked Escargot's attitude.

Confidence, in fact, was just what he himself could have used a bit more of. He wondered, however, whether or not Escargot was as untroubled about returning to Hightower Ridge as he seemed. If he was, then he was an altogether astonishing grandfather indeed.

They ran along after dark, not wanting to miss any of the breeze that was still being very cooperative. They were well above any section of the river that was likely to be frequented by boats of any sort, and the Oriel was still broad enough and lazy enough so that they hadn't any fear of rocks or bad water. Late in the evening they hit stretches of river free of fog, and in the glow of the lantern-light felt safe enough to press on, the Professor at the tiller and Jonathan sitting forward.

But by midnight both of them were done in. As it grew later it seemed less profitable to push along. By twelve-thirty if someone had offered Jonathan a choice between eight hours sleep and a treasure map, sleep would have won hands down.

"I've had it, Professor," he said, stretching and pulling his coat tighter. "Let's throw out the anchors right here and call it a night."

But there was no response from the Professor, only a fairly revealing snore. Jonathan turned and saw that his friend had fallen asleep, his head slumped forward onto the tiller arm. The raft was still maintaining a rather straight course, although the wind had fallen off somewhat. It was a simple thing to reef the sails and heave out both anchors, one on either side of the raft. The raft was on its way back to Seaside when the starboard anchor dug in and the bow swung round, almost pointing the raft downriver. The port anchor caught a moment later and the raft lay still as a pond lily in slack water. Jonathan wished he had a snag to tie up to. He could imagine himself waking up several hours later only to find that the raft had broken loose and drifted halfway back to Seaside. But, being seafaring dwarfs, they likely knew a bit about anchors, though the only way to find out whether the anchors were trustworthy was to try them. At last he blew out the running lights and then almost immediately wished he hadn't. The sliver of moon above gave off almost no light, and the night was so utterly dark that he stumbled over the deck chairs on his way to the stern.

He rousted the Professor out of a sound sleep and the two bent in through the cabin door and collapsed into their bunks.

Chapter 18

Corned Beef and Cabbage

❈

THE second day out was as uneventful as the first. More so, in fact, for the coastal fog finally cleared up and the sun favored them with a visit during the afternoon. Escargot felt it best that he keep his cloak on all the time, day and night, just in case they were visited by some creeping thing from the river or in case one of the crows that occasionally flew over was somehow a minion of the terrible Dwarf.

Jonathan quite preferred it that way. Enough mysterious occurrences had taken place already on the downriver voyage to satisfy any desire for adventure that he might have had. Besides, he and Dooly and the Professor amounted to nothing more than bystanders. If it were known that Escargot was aboard, who could say what sorts of terrible times might lay ahead?

So Escargot only took the cloak off to wash up. Oddly enough, it wasn't until he pulled his arms out of the sleeves that he suddenly appeared, as did the cloak, looking altogether normal. Even one arm in a sleeve was enough to remove him and the rest of his clothes entirely from sight. Escargot was as grizzly as he had been on the day they found him at Thrush Haven. He explained he was "cultivating an image" and hoped to pass as a pirate come the following April. The wilder a pirate looked, it seemed, the more highly he was regarded in certain circles.

Jonathan had always thought of Escargot as an old man—probably because Dooly constantly referred to him as "old Grandpa"—but he thought that the man couldn't be as old as all that, though it was hard to tell. His hair was black as a tunnel, and although there was a fleck or two of gray in his beard, there wasn't enough to bother about. When Jonathan had first seen Escargot, years before, he had seemed something of a dandy. His beard—probably more of a goatee than a beard—had been trimmed neatly. He had worn a top hat, carried a cane with a silver knob atop and was never seen around town in the daytime without a tie with a stickpin stuck through it. He affected a cultured speech then, not the seaworthy tone he was using lately. It was a bow here and a "Good day to you, sir," there and a prithee this and that whenever possible. Considerably younger at the time, Jonathan had been greatly affected and had even tried to act the same way. Eventually, however, he determined that he himself was destined to be no more than Jonathan Bing, and that anything else was foolishness.

Several years later Escargot reappeared—actually he wandered through several times but rarely stayed—wearing a pair of round spectacles and a tweed suit; he was selling cookbooks door to door. Then he vanished again, and wild and unlikely tales filtered upriver from the sea and down from the White Mountains.

Whenever he took the cloak off it too became visible, and although he wasn't sure what he had expected, Jonathan was a little bit disappointed in it. In fact there was nothing about it at first glance that would lead anyone to suppose it an elf marvel of any sort. It was white, mainly, although within the wrinkles and folds of material it appeared to be pink. And it wasn't until they had been three days on the river that Escargot held the coat up in the sunlight streaming through an uncovered window, and Jonathan saw its true colors. The thing shone like a rainbow in the sunlight.

In the sunlight, the cloak became a rippling mass of

color, almost alive with it, though it was abruptly still and pale when in shadow. As Escargot's arm slid down the sleeve, the coat very simply vanished, as did Escargot. Jonathan once again had to be careful not to step on invisible toes and to question seemingly empty bunks and deck chairs before sitting down on them. Cupboards opened and shut, the water jug upended itself into cups that floated about, hovering knives spread peanut butter onto floating slices of bread. All that took a bit of getting used to, as did the disembodied voice that was likely to speak to you when you expected nothing of the sort. But apparently it doesn't take an overwhelmingly long time to get used to living with invisible people, and, all things considered, everyone got along smoothly. On the third day the voyage became somewhat more arduous because the wind fell off almost entirely. It seemed to Jonathan that it would be pleasant merely to lay about and read a book and wait for things to pick up again. The wind was sure to blow up sometime. But the Professor, insisting that the entire valley was falling to ruin about them, thought it best to crank up the paddlewheel.

Jonathan suspected that what the Professor meant was that he wanted to investigate the workings of the thing which, it turned out, was operated to fairly good effect when two of them pedaled simultaneously. One man, likely, could have made headway alone if he were on a lake and the water were very calm. On a river, however, even a lazy river like the Oriel, the going was more difficult. Together he and Dooly pumped away until the raft was sort of skimming along. Actually, though, it only seemed so in relation to the river water that was streaming past. In relation to the shore, they weren't doing quite so well. The Professor said they were making about three knots; Jonathan determined that if a man were walking along the river road, he and the raft would keep about even. He started to calculate exactly what that meant in terms of the miles that lay between them and Twombly Town. Then, for fun, he counted the number of times he pedaled in twenty minutes, figuring that they had covered about a mile in that time. It turned out that he and Dooly—or whoever else did any pedaling—would pedal about sixty zillion times before they were halfway home. Just thinking about it was lunacy. When he checked his figures with the Professor, old Wurzle pondered for a time and said that, give or take a billion or so, Jonathan was tolerably close. The best thing he could do, all things considered, was not think about it at all.

But the more Jonathan tried not to think of pedaling along, the more he thought about it, or else thought about not thinking about it, or thought, every fifteen seconds or so, that it had been some time since he had thought about it last and then felt like a fool. The whole thing was maddening. After about twenty minutes he forgot all about not thinking of it and so didn't. The pedaling itself, once the paddles were slapping easily through the water, wasn't much of an effort—no more, certainly, than riding a bicycle. When the Professor offered to take over for a spell after an hour or so, Jonathan replied that he was just getting into his stride. Dooly said the same, proud, no doubt, that he was an important member of the crew.

Escargot, invisible atop the cabin, cheerfully volunteered to have a go at it himself, but the Professor pointed out that such a thing might, as he put it, tip their hand. Escargot agreed, but not as quickly as Jonathan had expected. Instead he told them the story of when he had taken a job logging and had to run rafts of logs downriver from the City of the Five Monoliths to Willowood Station. It would have been an exciting job under any circumstances, but to hear Escargot tell it, there was no end of trolls and goblins and wildmen and outlaws who wanted those logs or who simply wanted to run mad for a bit at Escargot's expense.

Dooly prompted his grandfather to relate the tale of finding the stick candy treasure, and after a few moments hesitation he did. Jonathan was fairly sure that Escargot was laying it on pretty thick for Dooly's benefit.

The afternoon passed along into evening, and as the sun went down the wind came up. They gave up their pedaling and sailed for about three hours. The night was so dark, however, that they ran up onto two sandbars, one right after another, and had to pole themselves free. Night travel seemed to be a bad idea, and—as Escargot pointed out—

they weren't in such an incredible rush as all that anyway.

So they threw out their anchors about ten o'clock when they were in the midst of a wide spot in the river—one of those lily-covered, swampy areas that threatened now and again to choke the Oriel entirely. The countryside roundabout was particularly low and the floodwaters of the preceding week's storm still covered the meadows. Thick stands of willow poked through the still waters, and just to be safe, they tied up to a thicket.

Escargot dug around in his bag and came up with a bottle of cream sherry and a bag of walnuts. In the light of one of the lanterns the four of them sat about on deck chairs cracking walnuts and sipping the sherry which was very good—made across the sea in the sunny Oceanic Isles. Jonathan was surprised to discover that Ahab liked walnuts as well as any of them—even more than Dooly, who simply cracked them for the sport involved and fed every other one to the dog. It was a little cool to be picnicking on deck that late in the evening, but the night was so wonderfully clear and the stars so bright that it would have been a shame not to. When the moon finally peeked up over the hills it was just a little scrap of a moon, only two days away from being nothing at all. Still, it was a friendly sight.

Dooly, still awed by his grandfather's tales that afternoon, insisted that Escargot "spin the yarn" about when *he* went to the moon and fell in among sky pirates. The word yarn struck Jonathan as being particularly appropriate, but Escargot's reaction to Dooly's request made him wonder a bit. In fact, the old man changed the subject rather abruptly after saying only that it had been "quite a time" and nothing more. Either the sky pirate story was a trifle far over into the realm of the tall tale or else, quite possibly, it involved the theft of the pocketwatch—something that Escargot regretted. Jonathan couldn't be sure which, but one way or another, no one heard any more that evening about the moon and sky pirates.

Changing the subject wasn't difficult. Escargot called their attention to several flickering lights moving among the trees upriver on the far side. Jonathan jumped up and blew out the lanterns. They waited in the darkness. The moon didn't even cast enough light for them to see one another's faces. Only the rustle of creatures alongshore and the noise of crickets or an occasional frog could be heard. Jonathan found that he was staring at the approaching lights, his eyes wide as saucers in an attempt to make some sense out of the night around him. Dooly started to whisper but Escargot shushed him. For five minutes they sat in silence and watched what had to be sixty or eighty goblins trotting down the river road. They were surprisingly sensible goblins compared to the lot that had attacked the raft. Half a dozen flaming torches lighted their way. Among them were several goblins of tremendous size—easily twice the size, say, of the average elf. Oddly enough, however, it was impossible to say which of them were the big goblins. When they were directly across the river—perhaps fifty or sixty yards away, Jonathan spotted a tremendous thing, a ghastly, pale, disfigured goblin more horrible that any of his fellows. But just as Jonathan picked him out of the lot, he seemed to shrink and change and reduce himself to half his size, and the goblin beside him, up until then a sort of nondescript pixie of a goblin, puffed up incredibly, dwarfing his fellows.

"They're up to no good," whispered the Professor when the party was once again only flickering torchlight through the distant trees. "Where do you suppose they're going?"

"The first outpost maybe," said Escargot.

"Then they'll get a warm reception from the keeper," said the Professor. "He didn't half like the look of Jonathan, Dooly, and me on our ruined scrap of a raft; imagine what he'll think of a party of torch-carrying goblins."

"They could just as easily be heading for Snopes' ferry," said Escargot.

Jonathan chuckled. "In which case, they may well run into the Squire's party. Bad luck if they do."

"Let's hope that they don't run into anyone at night," said Escargot. "There're too many goblins there to mess with, mates, and they ain't just out to pour honey into people's hats."

"This is unprecedented," said the Professor, lighting his pipe. "I don't like the look of it much."

"What is it?" asked Dooly.

"Bad business." Escargot said to Dooly. "In more ways than one."

Jonathan could imagine the squint-eyed look on Escargot's face: and hoped he was as sure of himself as he sounded. It was more than acting and rough talk that they'd need before the voyage was through.

They decided to keep a watch that night. Escargot volunteered to take the first and was to wake Jonathan at one. The Cheeser would rather have taken the first himself, but the day's pedaling had done him in, and he felt a bit limp, almost as if he were floating. By one, after only two hours of sleep, he'd be in no shape to stand watch.

But when he was shaken awake, sunlight was pouring in through the cabin window and Escargot was slapping water onto his own face out of the bowl, his cloak of invisibility heaped on his bunk. The smell of bacon and coffee filled the small cabin, and the Professor clanged away with their two frying pans on the cabin stove, waving a fork over the crackling bacon.

"What time is it?" asked Jonathan. "I missed my watch." He swung stiff legs to the floor. His calves and thighs felt as they should after a day of pedaling.

"I missed mine for a week after I sold the thing," said Escargot. "Made a sundial out of a squid and it kept better time than my watch. Then I traded it away for that pocketwatch you heard about. Worst move I ever made. Nothing but pain ever come from that blasted pocketwatch. Gettin' rid of that watch was the second biggest mistake. But I'm going after both of them mistakes now. If I would have kept my squid clock none of this would have come up. Think about it. Could you see all them elves and dwarfs and linkmen and goblins and who knows who else up in arms over a squid clock? It ain't likely. They're the craziest-looking things there is."

Jonathan, by then, was up and testing his muscles. He walked like what one of those squatty-legged cavemen in the Twombly Town Museum must have walked like before he turned into a fossil. It occurred to Jonathan that it was likely that exercise caused fossilization—that it made you stiffer every day until you woke up frozen one morning and had to roll yourself out of bed. But he found that he limbered up fairly quickly. The smell of the coffee and bacon had a good effect.

"Someone should have woke me up last night," said Jonathan. "I never could have done it myself."

Escargot slipped the cloak on and vanished. "I didn't do nothing all day yesterday but talk. You talk too much and you go crazy. It's proven. Ain't that so, Professor?" The Professor nodded, but Jonathan suspected that he was just being polite. "So anyway," Escargot continued, "I figured that if I set up all night and thought about this and that but didn't say nothing it'd even itself out. The elves have a saying about that, about what a fine thing silence is. Leads to wisdom, they say. But you don't have to live among 'em for more than an hour or so to know how much philosophy is worth. Which reminds me; do you know what it was that Blump said to me, just as their ship was a-settin' sail the other night?"

"No," said Jonathan. "I thought Blump set sail before we ever left for Thrush Haven."

"Nope," said Escargot, "they waited around for me. Blump's a prize. Doesn't have quite the brains that Twickenham has, but he's a wit, I can tell you. Here he was, already aboard, sails spreadin' all up and down the mainmast, and he shouts at me as me and Twickenham are off to the Mooneye. He shouts this, mind you, waving at the Squire all the time so as to call his attention to it. 'Why,' he shouts, 'did the linkman put a chair in his coffin?' Twickenham was for going on, but I had to hear, so I shrugs up at him. And laughing like a crazy man, he shouts, 'So rigor mortis could set in!' Then laughs so hard he collapsed on the bloody deck and two elves had to help him to his cabin, him hootin' and shoutin' the damn fool punchline all the way. That's an elf captain for you."

"An undeveloped sense of humor, certainly," said the Professor. "But I find that any jolliness at all is better than none."

"I thought the joke was pretty good," said Jonathan, who was repeating it to himself so as to remember it to tell Gilroy Bastable. Dooly, who wandered in in search of breakfast, asked, "Who was it who set in?"

"Rigor mortis," Escargot explained.

"Was he some kind of elf or something?"

The Professor tried to explain, but it made the joke incredibly foolish. He finally gave up and told Dooly that it didn't make any difference anyway, that it had to do with being stiff.

"Then he must have set in last night," said Dooly, "because I can't hardly walk."

The Professor said that, on the contrary, Dooly could hardly walk, but his explanation of the grammatical arcana involved was no more successful than his scientific explanation of rigor mortis. They all forgot about it while they ate breakfast.

"Where can I get one of these squid watches?" Jonathan asked Escargot.

"I'll make you one. If we were at Seaside I'd have one this afternoon. We'll have to fish for river squid here, though. And you don't catch many of 'em. Tricky bunch of swabs. And they have too many legs too. You have to compensate."

"I had a snail clock once," said Jonathan. "It worked pretty well except when it snowed."

"Never heard of a snail clock," said Escargot.

"I made it up," said Jonathan. "I can only use it at home. At about five in the morning there's about six hundred snails out on the lawn, all of them going somewhere. Eating grass and such. You have to be careful not to step on them. Then at six-thirty there's only about twenty left, and they're all heading for the bushes before the sun comes up over the top of the house. By seven-fifteen there's usually only one left. I think he's sort of a village idiot snail, though, because he's likely to be out any time of day. He mucks the clock up a bit, actually. Then at night they do it all over again in reverse."

"Not too accurate, Jonathan," said the Professor.

"It's good for a break now and then," said Jonathan, supporting the snail clock. "Being accurate gets tiresome."

"Getting up early enough to use the bloody clock is what would be tiresome," Escargot put in. "I'll make you a squid clock, Bing; they work day and night."

Out through the window they could see trees swaying in

the morning breeze. It wasn't as good a breeze as it might have been, but they popped along and raised the sails anyway, tacking away slowly upriver in the cool morning sun.

For two days they traveled along just so, pedaling now and then when the wind gave off, poling their way through shallows, and all in all making fairly steady headway. That same afternoon they sighted smoke downriver on the Highland shore. It was a great billow of dark smoke that dimmed the sky to the east for hours—a forest fire possibly or perhaps a barn fire. In the evening a second billow of smoke appeared some miles distant from the first, but by nightfall it had vanished. There was little doubt among the rafters that the fires and the goblin party were somehow related. Jonathan had to agree with the Professor that there wasn't time to dawdle, that the high valley likely *was* falling to ruin.

But there was nothing they could do about any fires downriver. One night passed and then another, and by the morning of the sixth day out of Seaside they neared the remains of Little Stooton—which looked, oddly enough, as if it had decayed even farther in the past couple of weeks. Great tendrils of creeping vine covered the houses along the shore, snaking in and out of windows and prying shingles from roofs. Lamps or candles seemed to be glowing dimly within the shadowy recesses of a few of the houses, but that, perhaps, was a trick of the sunlight that still shone off and on through a darkening sky. A thin wisp of smoke rose from one chimney, striking the rafters as being altogether odd. They had no idea whether the smoke—or the lamps, if they were lamps—were a good or bad sign—if that meant that Little Stooton hadn't been entirely abandoned or if, on the other hand, the village were being resettled by goblins. The Professor said he'd like to find out; he was horrified by the idea of goblins living in abandoned homes. Escargot told him that he had heard of stranger things, that it wasn't uncommon, in fact, to come across just such a thing in the deep woods. Both Jonathan and Escargot, however, saw no value in stopping simply to satisfy their curiosity, and the Professor finally agreed.

There was almost no breeze at all until about nine o'clock in the morning when what wind there was turned round and blew downriver toward the sea. Even Dooly realized that a storm was brewing, for the wind smelled as if it were full of water, and off toward the White Mountains lightning arced out of the clouds every few minutes, though they were too far away for them to hear the thunder.

Rain began to fall at about ten—big round drops that came sailing out of the gray sky to plop on the deck and on the roof of the cabin and form puddles and little streams running this way and that across the deck. There was not much running around and lashing things down since most of the cargo was stowed inside the cabin. Only the deck chairs were hauled inside.

Jonathan and Dooly, both of whom rather liked rain, decided to continue pedaling in the hope that the rain would let up. The Professor ambled inside along with Escargot, apologizing for his rheumatism. It seemed great fun, at first, sailing along through the rain and watching the lightning flash in the misty distance. But when the first ball of hail hit Jonathan on the head, his mood changed a bit, especially since the hail balls were the size of big marbles. Though there was a canopy of sorts over the paddlewheel and its mechanisms, the hail came sailing and it bounced under the canopy and whacked Jonathan and Dooly on the head and back. They had to bury their faces in their arms during the first onslaught. Then, of course, they couldn't see where they were going, so it made little sense to keep pedaling.

As quickly as they could, they ran the raft up into the mouth of a little creek that emptied into Stooton Slough. The banks on either side were high and broke the wind, and there was such a tangle of underbrush and limbs that much of the rain was waylaid before it ever reached the raft. As Jonathan and Dooly pedaled in, Escargot popped out and tied the raft up fore and aft to twisted roots that jutted out of the bank. Dooly heaved an anchor overboard, but the water was so shallow that the anchor merely sat there as if wondering what to do, its length of line and chain still mostly heaped on the deck.

They sat about in the cabin all day playing cards and drinking coffee and reading books. Jonathan made an effort to teach Dooly pinochle, but it was too much for him.

They ended up playing Go Fish instead, which is not a bad game at first but gets old after a half hour or so.

The rain fell and the wind blew on and off through the afternoon, but it never turned bad enough so that they had to fear flooding or toppling trees. When the Professor began slicing up cabbages and boiling the corned beef for dinner, the four of them took a vote and decided to spend the night there in the slough, even though the rain had nearly fallen off and there were breaks in the clouds. They could have pushed on, but the few miles they'd travel before dark didn't seem half worth the effort involved. The inside of the cabin was so cheery and warm by that time that the idea of venturing into the breezy drizzle outside was unthinkable.

Escargot suggested that they eat dinner and then have a council of war to plan the siege of Hightower ridge. Both Jonathan and the Professor agreed, although Jonathan rather thought that any such siege was more Escargot's business than it was his or the Professor's. But the battle was obviously drawing nigh, and this was as good a time as any to make plans. All such plans are likely to go awry when the action heats up, but there is still a certain sense of security or purpose that goes with order and with planning.

So they ate a very good early dinner, and they opened a few bottles of ale they'd laid away against just such an evening. The rain and the wind fell away, and it grew very still outside. Dooly observed that they were in the "eye of the hurricane," but the Professor pointed out that there was no hurricane involved. Dooly concluded that they must be in some other kind of eye.

If there was any moon at all it was hidden away behind the clouds that still covered most of the sky. Jonathan suspected that the night was going to be very dark indeed when it arrived.

Chapter 19

Stooton Slough

❧

WHEN dusk was just turning to night Jonathan and Dooly took a look outside and found that the creek, although muddy, hadn't risen much at all. Dooly spotted a tangle of blackberry vines drooping over the bank, and he and Jonathan and Ahab took advantage of the last twenty minutes of daylight to pick a few quarts. A little trail ran along the bank and back up a wooded rise beyond, and Jonathan thought he could just see the corner of a cabin in the woods there a hundred yards or so beyond them. Dooly looked in that direction but said that he didn't see anything and didn't want to either.

They decided to make a cobbler out of the blackberries later in the evening, so Jonathan set about washing the bugs out of them and picking through to find the green ones. There's no use souring up a cobbler because you're afraid to waste a few green berries.

Finally the berries were cleaned, the dishes were washed, the cabin was neat as it had to be, and there was nothing left to do but read or engage in serious discussions—in councils of war, as it were. They thought about it for a moment and came to the conclusion that a council of war would go much better in an hour or two over a hot cobbler. The Professor offered the observation that reading was suspected by medical science to be a digestive aid, so each of them lit a pipe and lost himself in a book—each of them except Dooly. Dooly didn't smoke a pipe, and instead of reading he plunked himself down at the table and began working on writing a book. He wasn't sure what the book was going to be about, or at least that's what he said, but he had the feeling that it was going to be good. He was suffering from inspiration, he said, just like Mr. Bufo and Yellow Hat.

Jonathan opened a G. Smithers and loaned a Glub Boomp to Escargot. It was an amazing thing to glance over toward Escargot's bunk and see the business end of a pipe and an open book hovering about in the air. The Professor looked into one of the ponderous *Tomes of Limpus* and began almost at once to meditate deeply, looks of astonishment, puzzlement, horror and understanding popping up variously on his face. The inside of the cabin was silent as a clam within moments, the only sound being the scratching of Dooly's pen on the page.

For a half hour it remained so, everyone being pleasantly abandoned to his book. Professor Wurzle, first broke the silence, standing up abruptly and asking, "What was that?"

Jonathan started to say that he hadn't heard anything, but only about half of it was out of his mouth when the Professor held his hand up and stopped him. They listened in silence for the space of ten seconds; then, very low, as if it were coming from somewhere distant, they heard the sound of weeping—an anguished, eerie sound that made Jonathan apprehensive. It stopped for a moment and then started again, a bit louder. It sounded nothing like the moaning of goblins, but more like a woman weeping over a lost child or a dead lover.

Jonathan, Escargot, and the Professor stepped out onto the deck. Dooly volunteered to stand guard with Ahab inside. In the silent night air the weeping grew louder, more insistent. The forest roundabout was deadly still, and the faint glow in the sky did nothing to dispel the gloom.

Jonathan remembered having seen what he supposed to be the wall of a cabin in the woods, and he jumped across to the path by the berry vines, motioning to the Professor and Escargot to follow. They tiptoed down the path, Jonathan half expecting some ghost or troll or bear to leap out of the dense undergrowth. They didn't go far, however, when there in the distant clearing they could see what was clearly the candlelit window of a small cabin. The sloped roof of the cabin was a dark shadow among the trees, and it appeared as if smoke from a fire within was rising through the trees above. The weeping, louder there at the edge of the wood, sounded, if anything, more anguished.

Escargot tugged on the sleeve of Jonathan's jacket, and the three of them retraced their steps to the raft, finding that Dooly had locked them out. It took a bit of convincing to get him to open the door.

"Do you think it's goblins?" the Professor asked.

"Might be," said Escargot. "It's impossible to say what sorts of pranks they'll get up to."

"Doesn't sound like goblins," Jonathan put in. "It may be that people are still living in Stooton. That sounded like a woman crying."

"It could be," said Escargot. "But if it is, we should let her cry. She doesn't want us dropping in for a chat. Let's leave it alone and get out of here."

"But if Jonathan is right," said the Professor, "then there's been trouble up there. Might still be. We can't just sail away."

Dooly, round-eyed by this time, had Ahab on his lap. He looked as if he could sail away quite happily.

"I believe I'll take Ahab," said Jonathan, "and have a look in that window." He began to regret his decision almost immediately, for the weeping started up again and reminded him of the darkness outside. But he had his code, after all.

"You won't go alone, Jonathan," said the Professor. "Dooly and Mr. Escargot can stay on board and you and I will have a look at that clearing. If someone is up to shenanigans, we shouldn't leave the raft unguarded."

"Aye," said Escargot. "But make it quick. Whistle three

times so we know it's you. If this is some kind of set up, then make a racket. We'll beat a bunch of pans together if anything gets fishy."

"Okay," said Jonathan. "It won't take a minute to hike up to that clearing." He and Professor Wurzle stepped back out into the night, each carrying an oak truncheon. They jumped across to the bank and squashed along up the path which was spongy with rainwater. It struck Jonathan as odd and a bit eerie that there wasn't a frog or a cricket to be heard, only the deathlike silence broken now and again by weeping.

Jonathan immediately wished they'd brought a lantern along and had a wild urge to dash back to the raft and get one. But the path wasn't hard to pick out, and the lighted window of the cabin was clear ahead of them, so he resisted the urge and pushed on, the Professor close on his heels.

The path wound around through the trees which were thick overhead, blotting out the sky almost entirely. Jonathan looked above him before plunging deeper into the woods and saw dark clouds boiling across the sky and what appeared to be a great bat winging along toward the river.

The path, which Jonathan suspected should have led straightaway toward the cabin, angled sharply on the right. He and the Professor stopped, suspecting trickery, but saw a glow of light—the window which they'd lost sight of, evidently—off in the same general direction. The sound of weeping was louder than it had been. The glow through the trees, however, seemed to recede as they made their way along the path. Finally it blinked out altogether.

"There's something wrong here," said the Professor. "Let's go back. Look sharp."

Jonathan had to agree. The light was all of a sudden gone, the weeping stopped, and they were quite simply alone in the deep woods. He hefted his club and was reassured a bit by it, but he would have been reassured even more had they a score or so of dwarf axe warriors along.

They hadn't gone more than twenty feet along the way they'd come when, very strangely, the path forked. There was no way of knowing which of the forks to take, and neither Jonathan nor the Professor had noticed the fork five minutes earlier. In fact, neither of the paths seemed to be the one they remembered. They seemed merely gloomy tunnels leading deeper into the forest. After a moment's pause they took that path which led most clearly in the direction of the creek.

But that path came to an abrupt end a hundred feet along. There was nothing to do but retrace their steps once again. And that's just what they started to do when, away to the right, they saw the cabin window flickering with candlelight. The weeping began almost at once, louder than ever—weeping punctuated by a very tired and mournful moaning, again as if someone were grieving.

They paused to listen for a moment, but in the silent spaces between the fits of weeping not even a leaf stirred. For a mad moment Jonathan considered rushing off helter-skelter through the woods, making the racket that Escargot had advised. But considering it stopped him. Professor Wurzle had a very determined look on his face, a sort of lesson-teaching look. So Jonathan hefted his club and, crouching a bit, crept through the trees toward the cabin.

They were very near, about ten feet from the window, when the weeping began again. They heard a screech like the howl of a banshee, and the rush and whir of bat wings overhead. Jonathan felt something brush across the top of his cap, and he swung his club at it but hit nothing. The night grew immediately silent once again. He and the Professor smashed themselves against the wall and inched once again toward the window as the weeping and moaning began anew. With one hand on their clubs and one on the windowsill, both of them rose until they could peer inside.

It was a single large firelit room, almost empty of furniture and so dusty and hung with cobwebs that no one could have lived there for a long long time. Before the fire, sitting in a wooden rocker, head bent forward, was what appeared to be a hooded, black-robed woman who shook her head and wept into her hands. The embers of a fire glowed in front of her and cast a shadow onto the wall behind.

The figure paused its rocking, and in the flickering red light of the fire turned toward the window. The hood fell away and the robe fell open and there in the midst of the cabin a grinning skeleton stared out at them through empty eye sockets and wept through clacking teeth. It rose shakily in the chair, as if incredibly old, and beckoning with a bony finger, took two halting steps toward the window before bursting into wild cackling laughter.

Jonathan, at the sound of the thing's laughter, swung his club, more out of instinct than motive, and smashed the glass of the window. The light went out inside and the fire died. There was a scuffling of feet on the floor and a fearful moaning. Jonathan and the Professor took off like the wind for the raft.

The path, somehow, was where it should have been in the first place. Jonathan could almost feel dry fingers latching onto his shoulder, and could hear horrible laughter behind them, punctuated by dread weeping and gasping. From ahead, clanging through the night time, came the sound of pots and pans being beaten together and mixed with shouts and the barking of Ahab. The raft had been untied and had swung out into the river, but it had caught fast in the creek mouth because of the anchor. When Jonathan and Professor Wurzle pounded down the path to the creek and past the berry vines, they saw it, ablaze with light, swinging around into the shore some twenty feet or so beyond where they had tied up. On board was a confusion of howling goblins, of Ahab bounding back and forth, and of Dooly, who dashed about, clanging together a frying pan and a big sauce pan and pausing here and there to whack a goblin on the head with one or the other. Amid the entire swarm, an occasional goblin was suddenly spirited into the air, shaken, and thrown far out into the river. A little line of goblin heads bobbed away downstream.

Jonathan scrambled along the steep edge of the bank, managing more than once to squash one or the other foot down into the muddy creek. What with the tangled roots of the shoreside trees, though, it was a simple if wet task to reach the raft. The light glowing so brightly on board turned out, to Jonathan's dismay, to be a fire on the deck. The lantern had been knocked from its hook, and a circle of oil flamed away around the broken remains of the glass shade.

Goblins cackled and hooted past him—a couple of dozen—more than he would have supposed could fit aboard.

He took a moment right off to push a couple into the river. One paddled away after his bobbing companions, but the other, a great ugly thing who shrieked and babbled and rolled his eyes in a frenzy of strange goblin emotion, attempted to clamber back aboard. Jonathan, unknowing, whipped away at the fire on deck with his jacket and was joined in a trice by Professor Wurzle, who did the same. The second of the two goblins that Jonathan had sent into the river managed, finally, to boost himself up onto the deck far enough to grasp Jonathan's ankle in a taloned hand. The claws bit into the flesh of his leg, and he was jerked off balance, dropping his jacket into the fire and smashing backward into the cabin wall.

Professor Wurzle latched onto the sleeve of the jacket as Jonathan and the hooting goblin tumbled about, but when he pulled it out of the fire he saw that the whole thing was aflame. The Professor shouted in surprise and spun round to fling the flaming jacket into the river, only to see the wet and shrieking goblin flailing toward him. So the Professor, faced with such a scourge, flung the burning jacket onto the goblin's head, an action that didn't slow the thing down in the slightest. It continued to rage about waving both arms in a windmill of fury until Dooly pranced up behind it and slammed it in the back of the head with the cast iron frying pan, sending the thing headlong into the river along with the flaming remains of Jonathan's coat.

Jonathan dragged himself to his feet, rubbing the knot on the back of his head and marveling at the fact that his back and legs had been pretzeled so thoroughly in the tumble and yet still worked reasonably well. Around him things had quieted down somewhat. Ahab seemed to be playing tag with two or three goblins, one of whom had grabbed hold of the mast and was swinging around it, arm extended, like a twirlabout, laughing and shouting. One of the other goblins who seemed to have two heads in the weird flickering of the fire, dashed along up the deck and continued on to dash off the edge, legs running in air, sinking away in the end beneath the river. Another met head foremost with a mysterious floating truncheon and, staggered, was propelled from behind by an invisible boot into the Oriel. The Professor and Jonathan managed to smother the fire which, in fact, had consumed most of the puddle of oil and had pretty much burned itself out.

Both of them looked about, half hoping that another goblin would show himself so that they could dip him into the river. They were surprised to see no goblins at all aside from the one who, idiotically, was still twirling round and round the mast, yelling and cackling. Jonathan looked at the Professor and shook his head. "Stupid little chaps, aren't they?" he asked. The Professor quite agreed. The two of them along with Dooly, Ahab, and the invisible Escargot stood about for a moment watching the goblin twirl. He slowed down in time, let go of the mast, and staggered about in a little erratic circle, dizzy as a water bug until he slumped to the deck and lay there.

They let him rest for a moment or two until he began to look around him and blink, surprised to find that all his friends had flown. He was such a hopeless and disheveled little pile of goblin that any urge in Jonathan to pull his nose or whack him on the head was dispelled. The thing attempted a traditional goblin cackle, but it sort of petered out foolishly.

"What do you have to say for yourself?" Jonathan asked.

But the goblin looked at him stupidly, then made a noise that sounded more like the noise a duck makes than anything else. Dooly made duck noises back at him, but it didn't seem to have any effect.

"They can't speak like men," said Escargot. "All the bloody fools can do is gobble. Can't even understand one another as far as I can tell. Too stupid by half."

"What'll we do with him?" Jonathan asked. "Do we want to keep him?"

"Not a chance," said Escargot. "Have you ever seen one of these lads eat? Makes you sick. And they don't eat nothing but fish and river trash. Throw the bones all over the place and try to comb their hair with them. There's not a sane one among them."

"We'll make him walk the plank," shouted Dooly. "Poke him in the rear with a cutlass!"

"Aye!" shouted Escargot, who stood behind the goblin so as not to be found out. "I can use some practice in that art. That's not something you can find volunteers for, and in the pirate trade you're expected to do it right. There's regular methods, you know."

"I dare say," said the Professor. "But why don't we practice some other time? I'd like to take a look at Jonathan's ankle there, the one he's limping around on. And I think we should cast off and pedal out to midriver. This tieing up to the bank is dangerous business."

"True," said Escargot. "We don't have any plank anyway, and the deck's only a foot above the water. There wouldn't be any sport in it." Escargot picked the goblin up by the seat of his pants and the collar of his shirt and swung him back and forth a couple of times. He was just about to let the creature sail out over the river when Jonathan shouted for him to hold up. Escargot put the gobbling thing down, and Jonathan rolled it over. There, tied to the rope that the goblin used as a belt, was a leather bag. Jonathan untied the bag, opened it up, and spilled its contents onto the deck. A stream of marbles rolled out, sparkling in the lantern-light. There were ten, then twenty, then fifty and a hundred marbles, and still the bag showed no sign of emptying. Jonathan closed it up as Dooly scrambled after the marbles. Without speaking, Jonathan picked up the goblin and threw him into the river. He wished he had a brick to throw after him, but it wouldn't have done any good.

"I didn't see that bag," Escargot said, taking a close look at it. "Looks like some sort of elf design."

"It belonged to the Squire," said Jonathan, and he sat down tiredly on the deck.

Chapter 20

An Ultimatum

❈

THE Professor hoisted the anchor aboard, and he and Escargot poled the raft away from the bank and let it drift out into deeper water before tossing out fore and aft anchors. They spent the night in relative peace, not even bothering to keep watch. As soon as the sky turned from black to gray, about an hour before the sun rose over the mountains to the east, they were underway, full sail on a good morning breeze. They sailed and pedaled all that day and the next and then did the same the day after that. At night they could hear the distant pounding of goblin drums and could barely make out the gonging and cackling that seemed always to begin not long after the sun went down. Goblin fires lit the woods now and then, more often as they drew closer to the Goblin Wood. Parties of goblins came and went along the river road, paying the rafters little heed, although one small party paused long enough to throw stones out over the river—all of which fell far short of the raft. In fact, the goblins took such frightful aim that the stones flew in every which direction, but in no particular direction at all.

They passed Willowood in the afternoon; it stood as before, ruined and empty, pier pilings thrusting up through the green waters of the Oriel and the wrecked boathouse visible beyond.

"What do you say," asked Jonathan, "to pulling in and looking up Miles the Magician? He might give us a hand with this venture."

"I think we'd be bloody fools to pull in anywhere." Escargot replied at once. "And besides, Miles the Magician doesn't stay in one place. He's likely long gone since you saw him last."

"He's right," the Professor agreed with Escargot. "Besides this isn't his affair anyway. The man likely has enough to concern himself with. This project has spread itself about too liberally already."

"True," said Jonathan. "He was just such a jolly sort that I thought it would be nice to see him again. But we'd best not loaf now." So they didn't loaf or stop at Willowood, but sailed right on by.

Twice during those three days they were passed by rafts floating downriver toward Seaside. The first, as far as they could tell, was empty—the decks were clear, and no one sat at the tiller. The raft slid away sideways on the current. Dooly shouted wildly as it drew toward them, hoping that someone was in the cabin having a snooze. But if the cabin were occupied, whoever was in there wasn't in a listening mood; nothing but silence answered Dooly's calls. The second raft had a bit more activity aboard, but not much. A listless fellow with a tremendous overgrown beard sat at the tiller, and another lay on deck, sleeping. Smoke rose from the chimney shoving through the roof of the little shingled lean-to that sat in the middle of the deck; so someone, likely, was inside either cooking or keeping warm.

Again Dooly shouted, but got only a sour look from the helmsman who didn't seem at all inclined to be cheerful. He wore very somber, dark clothes and a black hat with a brim on it the size of a cartwheel. For a moment Jonathan considered trying out the rigor mortis joke on the man, but the raft had such a look of emptiness and ruin about it, and the fellow at the tiller such a look of narrowness and fanaticism about him, that the joke probably wouldn't have aroused much of a response anyway. The man appeared to be waiting for an opportunity to go mad—just the sort of person who is best left alone.

Late in the afternoon on the second of December, they found themselves fast approaching the Goblin Wood and hence the town of Hightower. They moored one evening in midriver, choosing a particularly wide spot at a point in the river some miles downstream from the Wood. It was as close as they dared come at night, and still close enough so that with luck, a bit of a breeze, and some active pedaling they might pass it entirely in the light of day if they set off early enough in the morning.

The weather had grown colder, as if having made up its mind to become serious about leaving autumn behind and to see about winter. With every mile they traveled the temperature seemed to drop a degree or so. In the morning, ice appeared on top of the cabin and frost on the deck. When not pedaling or steering the raft the group stayed pretty much inside the cabin and kept a jolly fire lit in the stove. Ahab was generally ready to pop outside if anyone made a move toward the door, but he was even more ready to pop back in after having been outside for a bit. Only Escargot seemed oblivious to the cold and spent as much time outside as in—"Getting some air," as he liked to say.

They discussed their goal a time or two, though the discussion accomplished little. Jonathan, in fact, was a bit put out at the very idea that there was any goal. His only goal, after all, was Twombly Town, and he had only three and a half weeks to get there if he were to make it before Christmas. That night below the Goblin Wood he decided to press the issue, for Escargot rather seemed to assume they were all about to advance some sort of lunatic siege on the castle at Hightower Ridge.

When they sat poking at the remains of the trout and potatoes they'd eaten for dinner, he brought the discussion around. "Well," said Jonathan, examining a fishbone, "day after tomorrow should see us at Hightower. What do you propose, Mr. Escargot?"

"Simple as a trout," Escargot said, picking up the pop-eyed remains of one of the fish and dangling it by a fin. "There's a creek a mile below the town. Something like that creek at Stooton we were tomfool enough to tie up in.

It's here on the map." Escargot pointed with the fish head toward Twickenham's map. "Hinkle Creek, it says here, though it don't much matter. I had reason to hide out there a few years back. Spent three days in a bloody thicket eating crusts, and was lucky to have them too. I say we run her up the creek thirty or forty yards. She should be high enough now to do it. Then we lock the goods in the cabin, nail the shutters down over the window, cut brush enough to hide her as well as we can, and blow into town through the back roads to see which way the wind blows, if you follow me."

Jonathan hated this sort of thing. He always found it much more pleasant to be agreeable. But there are times when it works best just to slam right along and say what you mean. "Quite honestly," said Jonathan, "it strikes me that somehow the Professor and Dooly and I have gotten roped into something none of us bargained for. We were led to believe that we would simply transport you to Hightower and be on our way. If our luck holds, we can be in Twombly Town a week before Christmas. If we, as you say, leave the raft unattended in Hinkle Creek, we'll likely return to find goblins sailing it up and down the river and feeding the honeycakes to the fish. What I mean to say here is that this watch-stealing business is none of our concern."

Escargot paused for a few moments before responding. He closed the shutters and removed the cloak, realizing no doubt that it's tough to have a conversation of any serious nature with an invisible man. Then he lit his pipe, puffing at the tobacco until it blazed like a lumberyard fire.

"Your luck won't hold," he said, looking at Jonathan. "As for concerns, like it or not this pocketwatch business *is* your concern—and you'll likely not see Christmas unless you make it so." Escargot's voice wasn't in any way threatening; he stated it all very matter-of-factly, and so it had more of an effect on Jonathan that it might have had. He was prepared to be angry. The Professor, however, didn't appear altogether convinced. He sat there deep in thought as Escargot continued. "And we might need the seeker. Who can say where he keeps the blasted watch. It may be in his pocket and it may be upstairs. It may be under a brick in the wall around the tower. Even if I walked in and beat the Dwarf senseless, I wouldn't come up with the watch. It isn't worth trying for the thing without the seeker."

"You can have it," said the Professor. "Take the seeker. I haven't any use for it. It's just a curio. None of us need be involved. And let me say right now that, speaking for all of us, we're not afraid of this Dwarf. I'm getting too old for that sort of fear. But, by golly, to speak the plain truth, this whole mess has your name written all over it, and you should be the man to clean it up! The risk is yours, not ours."

Escargot nodded slowly, as if satisfied with the Professor's logic. He puffed away thoughtfully. "Fear has little to do with your decision; I know that, Professor. But it has something to do with mine. I won't talk falsely now. I know this Dwarf. I know who he is, what he has. And, mates, I'm not going into that tower alone. Not for you, or Twombly Town, or for the whole damn valley. Not for a moment."

"For Dooly," the Professor suggested. Dooly stared at the plate of broken fishbones.

"I'll take care of the lad," said Escargot. "He doesn't figure in this. But I won't go up to Hightower Ridge alone. You don't know this Dwarf, even though you've seen him. He isn't any sideshow conjurer now. He has powers even the elves fear."

"I believe you're mistaken about my having seen the gentleman," the Professor said. "I haven't had the pleasure and hope that I won't, either."

"The ape," said Escargot. "He was the master of the bloody Beddlington Ape. And that wasn't no ape, neither, or at least it wasn't when you saw it. I can't say for certain what it was, but it was a man's voice that came out of it. It might have been part ape, but then it might have been part anything. Probably was.

"Even back then he was up to foul tricks up on the ridge, but no one could see it. Everyone thought the ape gag was some sort of prank—ventriloquism or something. It was a prank all right, but it wasn't any ventriloquism. And it ain't only animals he controls. He can do things to the weather. He can send rains up and down the valley and make a fog rise up off the river with a wave of his stick." Escargot paused for a moment, then went on.

"When I heard about that elf ship in the slough, I knew there was trouble ahead. There wasn't any doubt. There was only one reason for the ship to be upriver—they were looking for the watch. And they found it too, the hard way. This watch freezes everything. Just stops things dead. Lets a chap do what he will, if he has that watch. I had it once and it was worth a few larks, I can tell you. But I didn't know what in the devil it was. It ain't easy to work—not if you do it right. You have to study it out and get the feel of it. All I did with it was borrow a few pies and such. And I didn't need no pocketwatch to hook pies.

"Then one day I ran into Miles the Magician. I didn't let on I had it, but I got him to tell me what it was, really. He said that the watch tells time. I said that every watch does that, if it ain't broken. He said that with any other watch, it's *you* who tells time by it. With this, it's the watch that *tells the time*. Do you follow me?"

Jonathan supposed so, and nodded, although the whole story was sounding a trifle grand and unlikely. The Professor had a look of astonishment on his face. "I'm not at all sure I *do*. What does all that signify?"

"Just about everything there is," Escargot said mysteriously. "You don't think they had time before they had a watch to tell it, do you? Well, that was the watch. There's one man who should run it, and a Dwarf who shouldn't but does. It's lucky for us he ain't had it long enough to have worked the whole thing through. Because Miles told me that time ain't what you'd think. It's everything there is, and it's nothing. If you understand the watch, you can run it ahead and you can run it back and you can stop it from running at all. When I first used it, it didn't seem to have no effect farther than about ten feet. When I sold it, I could slow the whole show down and stop it for twenty-five feet around.

"But Selznak—there's no telling what tricks he's been up to with the thing. Stooton had a look of decay, like it's been a ghost town for twenty years. I don't like the look of it. And you tell me Willowood's the same way. People gone, houses smashed up. Some of it's goblins, but most of it's Selznak. Him and that damn watch. I'll go after it, like I said, but I won't go alone."

"For what incredible reason," asked the Professor, "did you sell the watch to that demon? I hope you got more for it than that ridiculous pig we keep hearing about."

"Oh I got more," said Escargot cryptically, "but I still didn't get half enough. Now I'm a little dry, and if you mates have no complaints, I believe I'll just uncork another bottle of that ale we stowed."

"Make it two," said Jonathan.

"Three," said the Professor.

Suddenly the plate of fishbones began to look horrible to Jonathan, so he picked it up, stepped out through the cabin door, and dumped the whole thing into the river. There was almost no wind at all, and the night was silent as a tomb. Even the Goblin Wood, a dark line of distant trees, seemed still. No fires burned and no drums pounded. It was likely too cold even for goblins to be out. The river ran deep and dark beneath the raft, and it struck him that the water which flowed beneath him at that moment had flowed past Twombly Town only a couple of days ago. Some of it likely curled about Mayor Bastable's fishing line and pushed the millwheel around a few times. Some days hence it would flow past Seaside and run smack up against old ocean. Then who could say what strange things that water would see. What Jonathan would see, likely, was the inside of the castle on Hightower Ridge.

Back in the cabin, the Professor and Escargot were taking a pull of ale. Neither was speaking; both were deep in thought. Dooly had abandoned the conversation and was sitting on his bunk writing away at his book which had evolved to the point where it had a central character—the Toad King.

When Jonathan sat down, Escargot wiped his mouth with his shirtsleeve. "So that's that, mates. You know me now. I been a lot of things, but I never been what I ain't, and you can lay to that. I got a cloak here that amounts to a heap more to the likes o' me than any infernal pocket-watch. And I got me a submarine back at the Haven that can get me and the lad out to the Isles in a week. There's lands beyond that, too, and someday, mark me, I'm a-going there. It might as well be now."

"How long will it take us to get the watch?" Jonathan asked.

"The way I see it," said Escargot, "either we get it or we don't. If we mess up, then getting up to Twombly Town by Christmas is the least of our worries. We won't get no second chance—not this time. If we get it, we'll be on our way upriver three days from now."

"Three days from now we're on the river, watch or no watch," said Jonathan.

"Done!" said Escargot, and he thrust out his hand. Dooly hurried over from his bunk and shook hands with the rest of them. He said it was a good idea to spit on your hand first and then shake before going into adventures such as this, but the Professor suggested they forego the routine this time—a handshake alone, under the circumstances, was enough. More, in fact, than he would have expected.

Chapter 21

'Possums and Toads

❧

THEY were away before dawn. It seemed frightfully cold, but there was no ice on the deck and only a very little bit of frost, so it clearly wasn't as cold as it had been. Jonathan never got on well in the cold and would much prefer stealing watches comfortably in pleasant weather, so he was happy to think that things were warming up some. He hoped it was a trend. The breeze was good, blowing almost straightaway upriver, and they found themselves clipping along past the banks along the Goblin Wood at a quick pace.

The limbs of the great alders that lined the riverbank drooped low out over the water, shadowing the mossy bank and giving the forest a sort of impenetrable look, as if all were darkness within and the forest floor never saw the sun. Long green vines twined along through the trees, and from the tips of the limbs bunches of gray-green moss drooped, dripping moisture from the morning dew. They rounded a bend in the river and surprised a troll attempting unsuccessfully to club a fish. The thing saw the raft while peering between its legs. It was bent at the waist and its nose was an inch or two from the swirling waters of the

Oriel. Somehow the upside down view threw the troll into something of a panic, for it stumbled forward waving its arms in circles as if trying to keep its balance, and it tumbled head first into the river. It leaped up immediately in a towering rage. Dooly shouted at it and put his thumbs in either ear and waggled his fingers just to show it that he was one of the boys and had dealt with a few trolls in his day. But the troll immediately broke a limb off a nearby alder and flung it out over the river, managing to smash the thing into the side of the cabin. Dooly threw it back, but it only flew about twenty yards before landing in the river. By then the troll had forgotten all about them and was slamming away at fish again.

Beyond that the banks of the Oriel were empty. No herons waded in the shallows, no beavers or muskrats were busy building nests. Everything was still. "Creepy place," Jonathan remarked to the Professor.

"The less movement here, the better," replied Wurzle. "If it's activity you want, come at night."

"No thanks," said Jonathan. "This is fine. Just so no one suggests we tie up to the bank and go exploring. Those woods look old enough to be petrified."

"It's a mushroom collector's paradise," said the Professor. "I'm going in there some day."

"I'll go too," said Jonathan. "Let's plan on it some afternoon about thirty years from now."

Escargot stayed inside all afternoon. He popped out once in his cloak of invisibility, but was careful not to carry anything around. He explained to the others that he was the "trump card," the "ace in the hole," and that they were too close to Hightower to take any chances. There were likely more than just a few odd silly goblins lurking about, and there was no use stirring things up.

They threw out their anchors below Hightower shortly after dark. Jonathan lit lanterns fore and aft, and the Professor, in order for them to appear very matter-of-fact, sang a couple of old songs in a cheerful sort of falsetto voice. They went to some length to make it appear as if they were simply spending an evening on the river and that nothing at all was going on. Each of them kept a sharp eye out for goblins.

In the distance, rising up out of the dark woods and the swampy lowlands above town, was the craggy peak of Hightower Ridge. Atop the ridge, dim and obscure in the dark of evening sat the castle, known up and down the river simply as Hightower. Pale smoke rose above the stone spires of the tower, and several lights burned here and there within—one in the uppermost reaches of the largest tower that angled up above the rest in gray immensity, almost indistinguishable from the rocky cliffside behind it. The yellow circles of light reminded Jonathan overmuch of eyes, and as he watched the walls of the castle fade into the obscurity of night, the topmost light blinked off, then, a moment later, blinked on again. It looked for all the world as if the thing had winked at him. Although he knew that such a thing was nonsense, he didn't like the idea anyway and so decided not to take such an interest in the castle. There were other things to occupy his thoughts.

About eleven o'clock he turned the lanterns down and, along with his companions, went into the cabin and set about turning in. They even went so far as to climb into their bunks and lay there in the darkness, none of them able to sleep even if they would have liked to. The hours passed: midnight, one o'clock, two. Finally at about two-thirty Jonathan and Dooly slipped out of the cabin and slid into the seats in front of the paddlewheel. Dooly kept signaling to Jonathan by putting his index finger over his mouth, alerting him, Jonathan supposed, that they were being very quiet indeed. Escargot padded invisibly across the deck and silently hoisted both anchors, then took a seat forward. The Professor took hold of the tiller arm and the raft began making slow progress up the river. Only Ahab stayed inside the cabin asleep, having no stomach for fooling about in the middle of the night.

They crept along for two hundred yards, silent but for the muffled splash of the wheel as it turned. Then they came about in a long arc, and the Professor headed the raft up the mouth of Hinkle Creek. Once shrouded by the trees and brush along the creek bank, Escargot grabbed a pole and pushed the raft away from the shallow water along either bank of the narrow channel. They were well up into the creek—thirty or forty yards—before it became too rocky and overgrown to proceed. Escargot and the Professor tied up, and as Dooly had luckily done that night in Stooton, they dropped both anchors overboard into the shallow water. Then there was nothing left to do but wait until morning.

"Have we fooled anyone?" Jonathan whispered when the four of them were back inside the cabin.

"We haven't fooled *him*, if that's what you mean," said Escargot. "Or at least if we have, we won't have for long. There's nothing that goes on along this stretch o' the river that he don't know. Nothing but about me, that is. We've got to hope he don't know about me. He likely won't care much about you, if you follow me."

The Professor grunted an ambiguous reply, but Jonathan was pretty sure that what Escargot said was true. Tomorrow would tell. He decided not to think about it, and did instead what he always did when he wanted to sleep but was too restless or excited—he began counting the holes in a huge, imaginary Swiss cheese. He made it to the eighty-second hole before growing drowsy. Then he counted the eighty-third hole four times, then couldn't seem to remember what came after eighty-three, then forgot all about holes and about Swiss cheese and was lost in sleep. When he woke, the sun was high.

Dooly was still asleep, but Escargot and the Professor were up and about. The cabin door was open, and Jonathan could hear low voices out on deck. He splashed some water on his face, brushed his teeth, and hurried outside without bothering to shave. He figured that either he'd catch up on his shaving in a day or two or would end up locked away in some dungeon where shaving wasn't required.

The day was overcast and dim, but it wasn't particularly cold. The forest on either side of the river was overgrown with ferns and vines and little, sprouting trees. The Professor was ashore, hacking at brush with a hand axe, and tossing particularly leafy clumps and branches back up onto the deck. Escargot's voice, coming, it seemed, from up on the mast, said in a sort of stage whisper, "Hand me up one of them branches, mate."

Jonathan shoved a branch up toward the top of the mast, and it was pulled out of his hand. He watched as the brush appeared to twine itself through the line wrapped around the crossbar. He shoved another in the same general direction, then another and another, until the mast appeared to be more a tree than a mast. Then they went to work on the foredeck, heaping brush about the deck and piling it atop the cabin. It didn't take too long, finally, to finish the job.

They looked it over from this angle and that, rearranging brush here, adding a bit there, and decided that from the starboard side—that is from the Hightower side—the raft was tolerably well camouflaged while from the downstream side it looked like a pile of ruined shrubbery heaped about the deck of an ill-hidden raft. But it was the best they could do. Escargot pointed out that there likely weren't enough townspeople left around to worry about, and that goblins, dim-witted as they are, could be taken in by anything. The Dwarf, of course, likely had better things to do than be off hiking through the underbrush along Hinkle Creek. So the raft was probably as safe and as hidden away as it was ever going to be.

They debated for a bit about whether to hang about the raft all day and wait until sunset to investigate the village, or to set out right off and do a bit of snooping. It seemed safer to wait, but on the other hand it would be far trickier poking around unfamiliar countryside at night. What it boiled down to in the end was that none of them wanted to sit and wait. There was too much anticipation, and that often led to worry and fear, neither of which would be helpful.

So they set out, about eleven or so in the morning, carrying a bit of lunch in a knapsack. Jonathan and the Professor elected to carry truncheons, and Dooly carried what he called his "whack-um"—a paddlelike slab of oak, more of a broken off boat oar than a club. Escargot carried nothing, neither a weapon nor a knapsack, since floating objects would no doubt draw undue attention. He insisted though that Dooly take along a coil of line—apparently an important item in a thief's line of work.

They set out sloshing along the bank, finding muddy footholds in the shore grasses and clinging to roots and brush. On occasion they hopped along atop rocks for a bit, but the rocks were so slippery that soon there was more than one wet boot among then. Ahab, somehow, pranced along as if he were on the boardwalk at Twombly Town. No clumps of weeds or slippery stone seemed too small for him to balance on. About halfway back down the creek toward the river, Ahab began sniffing along, then thrust his nose into the bushes and disappeared. Jonathan, not wanting to lose sight of the dog, jammed through behind, calling him softly.

He found Ahab trotting down a little grass trail toward the river following a fat raccoon. Jonathan whistled, and Ahab stopped and watched as the raccoon disappeared around a bend. Then he turned and wandered back.

"What ho, Jonathan," came the Professor's voice from the creek bank on the other side of the brush.

"There's a trail here," Jonathan replied in hushed tones. "Goes toward the river. No one but a raccoon on it."

A snapping of twigs and parting of bushes indicated that Escargot had pushed his way through to the trail. After him came the Professor and Dooly, hunching along through and pushing branches out of the way. They set off down the trail single file, sort of tiptoeing along stealthily until they sighted the river road ahead of them, winding along beside the banks of the Oriel. Dooly pulled himself up into the lower branches of an oak and managed to clamber high enough up to command a good view of the road and the surrounding woods. The other three hunkered down behind a tangle of brush and waited for Dooly to make a report. The brush seemed to be uncommonly full of spiders to Jonathan, and was still wet with morning dew. They waited five minutes as Dooly edged out onto a limb.

"What do you see?" Jonathan called, finally, becoming annoyed with the bugs.

"A house," replied Dooly in a loud whisper. "A big old house, Mr. Cheeser, and a cart in front. Windows on the ground floor are all boarded up, but it looks like someone's living there anyway."

"How do you know, lad?" asked Escargot.

"Because there's a guy hanging out wash," said Dooly. "Only it looks as if he's worn hats all week. That's all he's got hanging."

"Hats?" said Jonathan, thinking that somehow the idea of someone having to do with hats around Hightower wasn't altogether new to him.

"Gosset!" said the Professor. "Remember that man at the pub, Jonathan, on the way down."

"Lonny Gosset," said Jonathan. "He was at that. Strange he'd be making hats with no one about to wear them. And why in the world would he be hanging them out on the clothesline?"

"Likely just dyed the lot," Escargot suggested. "So you know this chap?"

"I believe we do," said Jonathan. "And we may be able to count on him. I'll just climb up into the tree and take a quick peek."

There, sure enough, hanging hats on a clothesline in a weedy yard hidden from the river by scrub oak and lemon-leaf, was Lonny Gosset the milliner. His hair was considerably wilder than Jonathan remembered, and as he pinned caps and hats to the drooping line he looked furtively over his shoulder every few moments. Dooly and Jonathan watched as an opossum with an amazingly long nose chased into the yard out of the woods. Gosset jumped, flinging an oddly shaped cap—a nightcap, probably—into the air, and dashing across the yard toward the house. The opossum, scouring along on ridiculous little legs, headed him off, dashing between Gosset and the stick that lay against the front stoop and which Gosset seemed intent upon. Gosset stopped and eyeballed the opossum warily as it too stopped and scratched at its nose with one, fingered paw. It was a momentary standoff until, something came hopping from the edge of the woods, something that appeared to be an immense toad. The thing appeared to be too much for Gosset, who edged away toward the door, watching both creatures warily. Suddenly a cackle of laughter, goblin laughter, sounded from the trees beyond the clothesline, and Gosset broke and ran toward the house, slamming the door behind him. The opossum and the toad wandered off and disappeared. As they did, three goblins capered out of the forest, howling and laughing and plucking caps from the clothesline and stuffing them in a sack. Jonathan could see Gosset in the upstairs window, watching as the goblins stole his hats, then pulled down the clothesline and deliberately knotted up the thing, thereafter dropping it down the well. They never stopped hooting and cackling as they went about their mischief, and they fought over who was going to throw the rope into the well, pushing one another down and jabbing one another in the eye. Finally they leaped away into the woods, each wearing one of Gosset's hats and jabbering like fools.

Jonathan and Dooly climbed down out of the trees, and Jonathan told the story to Escargot and the Professor. Upon mentioning the opossum, Dooly put in that it was one of them animals which carried its babies around in a spoon. Jonathan remembered seeing in an encyclopedia a picture of three baby opossums on a spoon, but the Professor clearly didn't for he gave Dooly a fairly puzzled look.

"Poor bloke's daft," said Escargot. "Goes crazy when he sees a 'possum and a toad. Maybe *you* can count on him, but he don't seem like any sort of prize to me."

"We have a chance," said Jonathan. "It's clear he's not in league with the Dwarf."

"Absolutely," said the Professor. "And Gosset was a good lad. We can't abandon him."

"I want one of them orange hats," said Dooly.

"Then you shall have one, lad," agreed Escargot. "Although it strikes me that this is uncommon crazy, hat or no hats." And with that, the four of them set out through the woods toward Gosset's house.

Chapter 22

A Visit with Lonny Gosset

❧

WHEN they got there a few minutes later, Gosset was bent over the well trying to fish out the lost line. He had one foot planted in the thick, green lawn and the other waving about in the air; his head and shoulders and right arm were thrust down the well.

Very wisely, none of the rafters spoke until Gosset had fished out the rope and there was no danger of frightening him into the abyss which, given his surprise at hearing the Professor's voice, would surely have occurred. "*Aaah!*" shouted Gosset, wheeling about and staggering back a step. He held the end of the line in his hand as if it were a weapon and menaced them with it, his teeth chattering like crazy. What he intended to do with the rope was unclear—likely it was the only thing at hand.

"Mr. Gosset, I believe," said the Professor, extending a hand. "Perhaps you don't recall having met us."

Gosset edged around the perimeter of the well and peered at them from the other side. He seemed to be thinking hard, as if wondering whether they were a pack of fresh devils from the woods or were, as they appeared to be, human beings. "You know me?" he croaked.

"We met at the pub," said the Professor. "Only a couple of weeks back."

"Long weeks," said Gosset.

"They have been that," said Jonathan. "You said you were a milliner, I believe. And from the look of those caps on the line, you still are."

Gosset tossed his rope to the ground, seemingly convinced that there was nothing threatening about the rafters. Escargot didn't make a sound.

"Bloody hats," he said, then paused. "Won't let a man alone."

"Hats?" asked Dooly, astonished at this new fear.

"Goblins!" shouted Gosset. "They're a filthy curse. Broke out my windows. Shoved toads into the living room. Howled down the chimney all night. A man can't sleep with that. They run off my rabbits and poured slime in the well. Now I have to haul water up from the river." The three rafters shook their heads and clacked their tongues over it.

"Foul creatures," said the Professor.

"They are that!" Gosset shouted a bit loudly. "Huh!" he said, capping it off. "But not half so foul as—" he began, then broke off, looking about him as if suspecting the very trees in the forest of listening in. Then he looked shrewdly at Jonathan and the Professor and Dooly, assuring himself, probably, that none of the three were disguised dwarfs. He shrugged and began to coil his rope.

"As who?" the Professor asked, and they watched as Gosset's face grew red as a beet. It looked as if the top of his head were going to turn into a little volcano and he were going to start spouting steam.

"As Selznak the Dwarf?" asked Jonathan.

Gosset seemed to be stricken by the very mention of the name. He began dancing about and flailing away with the coiled rope at the sides of the well. He lurched across and stomped on a soiled cap that lay on the lawn, dropped by the goblins. The rafters watched in amazement until Gosset's furious capering played itself out. Finally spent, he wandered in a small circle in the middle of the yard, seeming to have lost his bearings. Jonathan and the Professor latched onto him and led him along toward the house, neither of them wanting to say much lest they set him going afresh. The door shut behind them as Escargot followed them in.

The downstairs was a ruin of broken glass. One great chair was slashed to bits, and huge wads of stuffing were stuck to what had been a very noble marble bust atop a stand in one corner. The thing wore an impossible beard of cotton wad and had another pile of the stuff atop his head. Under any other circumstances it would have been funny. A small deal table was jammed into the fireplace and had been set afire several times but had smoldered out. Leaves and brush and a piece of tree stump lay heaped about amid the upset furniture.

Gosset, recovering, waved a hand at the mess. "Three nights ago they came," he said tiredly. "Twenty or thirty there were. Set the place to ruin. I bolted myself in upstairs. What could I do against so many?"

"Nothing at all," said Escargot unwisely.

Gosset paused for a moment in wide-eyed horror before asking in a hoarse whisper, "Who said that?"

The Professor decided to be truthful. "Our friend here," he said, gesturing toward the seemingly empty space beside him.

Not waiting for any further explanation, Gosset shoved past Jonathan and ran howling up the stairs in a single mad rush. Jonathan looked at the Professor and shrugged. "That was an ill-chosen moment to speak," he said to Escargot.

"True," said Escargot. "It was stupid of me. I forgot about this bloody cloak. We better go after him."

"I'll go," said Jonathan. "If we all go he'll likely run amok."

At the top of the stairs a hallway wandered away toward either end of the house. Goblins had quite apparently had as high a time upstairs as they had below, for scattered about the landing and down the hallway were odd pieces of clothing and the tattered remains of lace curtains. Two of the legs had been kicked out from under a carved sideboard, and it lay on its face in the disarray. Fish skeletons were tossed helter-skelter.

Some six doors opened onto the hallway. Two were ajar, but the other four were shut. There was nothing to be done other than to try the doors and seek out Gosset.

"Mr. Gosset?" said Jonathan tentatively. "Oh, Mr. Gosset?" There was no reply.

Jonathan tried the first of the closed doors and found it unlocked. He swung it open and peered into the room. It was empty. The second door was locked, but appeared to be nothing more than the door to a linen cupboard or coat closet. He wiggled the knob on the third door. Like the first, it turned and the door swung in on its hinges. "Mr. Gosset?" said Jonathan, peeping into the dim interior through a foot-wide opening. "We're friends, sir. We're here to drive this Dwarf away. Rid the woods of goblins."

There was no response from within the room. Jonathan poked his head in just a bit—just to the point where he could make out a four-poster bed and a massive frame and panel sideboard. Next to the bed was an endtable with a lamp atop. Below was a scatter of books and a coffee cup. He decided to check the final room, not wanting to go prying through Gosset's home unnecessarily. As he backed out into the hallway, however, he heard the *whoosh* of a breath being let out followed by a wild and ill-controlled shout. On the wall to Jonathan's right was Gosset's moving shadow, the arms upraised and hands gripping a wooden kitchen chair. The chair came smashing down, cracking into the edge and back of the door. The door slammed shut, shoving Jonathan over backward into the hallway. He rolled smack up against the rail that ran along the edge of the hallway and separated it from the open mouth of the stairwell, giving the thing a solid push. For one wild moment he thought he felt the railing give way, and he grabbed wildly about him for a handhold. The railing wobbled and tilted and snapped and cracked, but in the end it held.

The Professor and Dooly and Ahab and, likely, Escargot clattered up the stairs toward the upper landing, but Jonathan motioned them back down. He rolled forward onto his knees, then leaped to his feet. Clearly had he shoved any farther into the room Gosset would have smashed him on the top of the head with the chair instead of just wildly pummeling the door. He waited in case Gosset should come lunging out. When nothing happened, Jonathan crept forward and knocked lightly. He could hear sobbing of a sort within.

"Mr. Gosset?" said Jonathan. "The invisible man down-stairs is an elf warrior in a magic cloak. He's on his way to Hightower to have a word with Selznak the Dwarf."

The door inched open, and Gosset's nose appeared, the rest of him remaining in the shadow of the room. "What?" asked Gosset. "Elves?"

"That's right, Mr. Gosset," said Jonathan in a friendly way. "We have major elf magic here. Selznak's end is near. By Friday there won't be a goblin outside the Wood."

The door opened a bit more, and Gosset squinted out. He seemed to ponder for a moment; then he swung the door open and waved Jonathan in. The remains of the crumpled chair lay on the floor behind the door, but other than that the room was in fairly good order. It was a large room that opened onto another room through a pair of French doors. The second room was apparently a library or study that contained a couple of easy chairs, a comfortable-looking couch, and an old, dark library table. A door, the fourth of the six upstairs doors, led from the library back out onto the hallway above the stairs. From the look of it Gosset was a man who loved books. The titles seemed to Jonathan to indicate that he was an intelligent sort, driven toward desperation and lunacy by the goblin doings.

Gosset picked up the two rear legs which had been bro-ken from the chair. He pushed open a window and tossed them out onto the lawn, throwing the rest of the smashed chair after them. He stood unsteadily by the window and ran his hands through his hair as if to cool himself down. The effort seemed to have a calming effect, but it made his hair stand on end and he looked as if he'd just staggered in out of a tornado.

A decanter of spirits and several glasses lay on the li-brary table in the adjoining room. Although it would have been poor manners under normal circumstances, Jonathan pointed in their general direction. "Perhaps a drink would be in order." Gosset nodded.

Jonathan pushed open the french doors and walked into the library. He pulled the glass stopper out of the bottle and gave it a sniff, then tippled some of the brandy into one of the glasses. He handed it across to Gosset, who poured the liquid straight away down his throat, coughing and hacking over it for a moment thereafter.

It occurred to Jonathan that it was perhaps not a good thing that Gosset knew of Escargot's existence. They had taken great pains on their upriver voyage to keep his presence an absolute secret. Then, after sailing smack into the enemy's camp, so to speak, they had blundered into the first lunatic they could find and alerted him to the wild fact that not only was there an invisible man among them, but that he wore a magical elf cloak. In fact, there could have been no profit at all in approaching Gosset in the first place. They weren't, after all, going to lead a wild assault on Hightower or come raging through the town with an army. They were simply going to slide in secretly and wait about while Escargot stole the pocketwatch, or something like that. If it came to it, Jonathan supposed, they could tie Gosset to a chair until it was too late for him to reveal any secrets. But then if something went wrong and they didn't come back, Gosset would spend the rest of his life tied to a chair, and that wouldn't do.

The Professor looked in through the door about then, and Gosset sat down on the bed in a rumpled heap. Dooly and Ahab crept in last, or so it appeared. Gosset poured himself another glass of brandy and sipped thoughtfully at it. After a moment he sighed, messed his hair some more, and spoke in a comparatively calm voice.

"The boggers want caps," he said, musing over his glass. "All I can make. If I stop sewing caps I'd best find another home. That's what he said. His goblins must have caps. It's been terrible. They try to wear three at a time, and they tear each other's to bits. I could make a million a week and it wouldn't keep them in caps. Not for more than a moment. They do it for sport. What does a goblin care about a cap?

"And the blasted creatures of his. The toads and 'possums and such. Gone mad they have. He's seen to it. Has a spell on 'em. I come upon 'em chewing through the back door. They had a vine strung up over the garden wall and was climbin' up and down the blasted thing like apes. Exactly like apes!" Gosset took a sip of brandy, shook his head resignedly, and continued.

"I was putting out lettuce and onions for the winter garden. Had six lines of snow peas and cucumbers. All gone now. Not ate up, mind you, just dug to bits one night. Beat the stuffing out of the scarecrow and lit him afire. Danced around it, they did, six wolves and about two hundred toads. Rode about on the wolves' backs, croaking like devils!

"And two nights ago. In this very room. I opened up that wardrobe and there was a ghastly sight. There was moths. A dozen of 'em, and they had my sweater on the floor. Knives and forks, they had. The whole lot of 'em, and they were sawing the bloody sleeve off. Moths the size of golf balls with litle arms and hands. It was ghastly. A positive horror." Gosset drained the glass and tipped another drop or two into the bottom.

The Professor looked at Jonathan and rolled his eyes. He tapped a forefinger against his temple. Jonathan nodded just a hair to show that he understood, but Dooly was wide-eyed with terror. Gosset offered Jonathan a spot of brandy, and Jonathan began to refuse, then decided that if he didn't take a turn at the big decanter, Gosset would likely be seeing more fork-wielding moths before the day was out. So he accepted a glass of the stuff and winked at the Professor, who himself took a glass. Neither thought to offer Escargot any. Jonathan wasn't sure he was even in the room and hesitated to bring the subject up. As the bottle was being replaced on the table, however, a throat was cleared somewhere in the vicinity of the open french doors, and it had an instantaneous effect on Gosset, who began to tremble violently.

Jonathan feared that Gosset would cut and run again. "Allow me to introduce you to Mr. Theophile Escargot." He waved a hand in Escargot's general direction.

"Delighted," said Escargot.

Gosset looked about him wildly. The Professor, thinking quickly, plucked a cap from a hook on a hatrack alongside the wardrobe and waved it toward Escargot, who took it from him and put it on. Gosset seemed relieved, finding a floating cap less threatening than a floating voice. "Glass of the best?" Gosset asked Escargot.

"Aye, mate," said Escargot, plucking the glass from Gosset's outstretched hand. "Just the thing on a day like this."

"Warms me up," Gossett agreed. "I can't stand a chill. Never could." He slumped back as if exhausted and lay there for a moment. The silence was awkward, but it didn't last long. Gosset leaped up with a hand to his ear as if straining to hear something faint and far away. He tiptoed to the window and in a hushed voice said, almost to himself, "Fog!" then fell to his knees, staring trancelike out toward the river road. The four rafters stepped up behind him, and, sure enough, swirling along on a late morning breeze were billows of fog, very slow and languid fog—fog that seemed to know what it was about. Faintly, from the direction of town, there sounded a muffled tapping, as if someone were knocking against a hollow log with a stick. Gosset fell forward and pressed his face and hands against the window.

From out of the whirling mists below a Dwarf in a slouch hat appeared, tap tap tapping along the cobbles of Gosset's drive. He wore a dark cloak, almost black, but not quite—rather a deep shade of purple like the sky at night. A patch covered one of his eyes, and his nose was crooked and long, giving him the appearance of being very very old. His staff was a good six feet high, nearly twice as high as the Dwarf. Below his flowing cloak could be seen pointy-toed shoes which were silent on the stones below. All that could be heard was the insistent tap tap tap of the walking staff. In his mouth was a long pipe, the bowl of which glowed red and orange through the mists. From the burning pipe billowed white smoke, and it seemed as if the Dwarf alone were responsible for the fog that floated roundabout.

When he stood directly below the window, the Dwarf stopped and looked up toward the gaping Gosset and the rafters clustered behind him. It was useless to attempt to hide, although Escargot was quick-witted enough to jerk off his cap and toss it onto the bed. There wasn't the slightest doubt that Selznak was paying Gosset a visit in their honor. He stood for a moment as if fondly contemplating Gosset's wild face. He nodded very slowly, and idly touched two fingers to the brim of his hat as if wishing them all a good day. Then he removed the pipe from his mouth and puffed forth three bluish smoke rings that

floated up toward the window, slowly widening and undulating on the breeze. When they drew even with Gosset's face they seemed to burst like bubbles and disappear
into the fog.

Gosset groaned and slumped as if he'd been hit. He
shook his head and wiped cold sweat off his forehead with
the sleeve of his sweater. "You curse!" he whispered under
his breath, then repeated it more loudly, pressing once
more against the window. Then, in a wild flailing swing, he
smashed his fist through one of the panes and shouted
through into the foggy morning, shards of glass clattering
and tinkling against the floor of the porch below. But the
Dwarf was almost lost to sight in the mist, and the tap tap
tap of his stick was fading with him, out toward the river
road.

Chapter 23

What Was in the Wardrobe

❧

THE brandy bottle rose into the air and hovered there momentarily. Then it dipped over Gosset's glass and an amber stream of the stuff trickled out. A glass floated up and was similarly treated, then floated higher to a position an inch or so below the brim of Escargot's cap which was once again hovering about. Escargot must have been peering through the brandy, studying its color.

There was a good bit of silence for a time, but it was broken when Escargot's glass was drained. "Aaah!" he said, as if the brandy were entirely satisfactory. Then he put the glass down onto the table. "Conceited bloke, ain't he?" Escargot asked. "Pretty confident, parading up and down."

"He is that," said Jonathan, who couldn't remember having seen anyone more confident.

"He'll sing another tune tomorrow," said Escargot. "It couldn't be more perfect. He'll go along and find the raft, but it won't tell him a thing. He'll know you're here, but he won't know why. Won't he throw a fit when we play the trump card, when he finds out."

"The Dwarf isn't the only one who's confident," the Pro-

273

fessor observed. "We <u>hope</u> we have a trump card. I'm beginning to wonder just what he knows and what he doesn't."

"I'm in," said Gosset, pressing a pillowcase against a long shallow cut on the top of his wrist.

"Pardon me?" asked Escargot.

"I'm in. I'll do my part. I've made my last goblin cap. I'm a-going to get some pay for them."

"Not a chance," said Escargot abruptly. "It's not in the plan."

"What plan?" asked Jonathan, who didn't relish the idea of having Gosset along, but thought it was time that all of them shared in the plan-making. He was tired of being coerced, and he didn't altogether like the idea of being a diversion.

Escargot didn't reply to Jonathan's question, possibly because there wasn't any plan. He whirled his glass in a small circle near his head, perhaps intending to indicate that he hadn't much faith in poor Gosset and that Jonathan should admit to the plan if only in pretense.

"Secrecy," said Escargot, "that's the word. If we haven't got secrecy, we haven't got a thing."

"Secret it is," said Gosset agreeably. "Secret as a mole, that's Lonny Gosset. Not a word about it from me."

"The point, mates," Escargot said, "is that the more of us who go pushing in up at Hightower, the less chance there is we'll get out again. No, sir. We can't risk it. Mr. Gosset and Dooly and the dog will stay here. There'll be plenty for them to do. There's liable to be monkeyshines played on that raft, especially after nightfall. And we might need it bad later on. We might have to push off and run for it with who knows what behind us, and so we don't want a bunch of goblins having a barbeque on board. There'll be three that go and three that stay."

Jonathan thought about it for a moment. The Professor lit his pipe and smoked over the idea. Gosset wasn't upset in the least. He nodded, in fact. "Mum's the word. Lonny Mum Gosset they used to call me. Just let me have a go at those goblins. I'll take that tower down stone by stone." And he clutched at the air once or twice as if taking apart an imaginary tower stone by stone.

"I agree with the plan," said Jonathan. "It couldn't be better except that it won't take two of us to make a diversion. I'll do for that. The Professor can stay here and see to things on this end. If we aren't back in twenty-four hours, they spring full sail for Twombly Town and raise an army."

Professor Wurzle took his pipe out of his mouth and grinned at Jonathan. "Not at all likely," he said. "Not within a half mile of being near the target. If anyone goes," he said, "it'll be me. I'm going to see the inside of that tower if I have to get inside posing as a brush salesman. But I agree with Jonathan otherwise. It's a good plan. We'll entrust the safety of the raft to Mr. Gosset here. What do you say to that, sir?"

Gosset had a foolish grin on his face and was staring away in some undiscoverable direction. He snapped out of it for a moment, then turned to the Professor. "Huh? What? No. It was what?" He paused in expectation as if awaiting an answer. The Professor didn't press the issue. He said, "Quite, quite," and nodded his head. Gosset nodded his head too. Escargot filled Gosset's empty glass.

"I don't know if I want to stay here or not," said Dooly, watching Gosset out of the corner of his eye. "I think maybe we should all go. I've got my whack-um stick and all. If we get back to the raft and there's goblins aboard we'll just thrash 'em. We done it before."

Jonathan didn't altogether like the idea of hauling Dooly along into any enchanted towers. But he didn't like going without old Ahab just as much. And leaving Dooly with Gosset to watch the raft was about as good an idea as leaving Dooly alone, perhaps worse. Dooly would likely have to spend most of his time watching Gosset rather than the raft. Perhaps they should tie Gosset to the main mast and use him as a sort of human scarecrow. Put a great long club in his hand. So Jonathan tipped Dooly a wink, and Dooly caught on and nodded happily.

Gosset seemed to be growing fuzzier and fuzzier, as if his mind were wandering off down some dim pathway that only he could see. A glazed look came over him and he stood up all in a rush like a man who has heard a robber slinking through the front room in the night. He put a foot out slowly and softly, and set out toward the big wardrobe against the wall. Dooly's eyes were open about a half mile, but he didn't say a word and neither did anyone else. It seemed fairly certain to Jonathan that Gosset had gone round the bend, as they say—that the morning's doings had served to add to the horrors of past months to set him off across the borderland. But there was just the ghost of a chance that he had heard something off in the direction of the wardrobe that none of the rest of them had. Gosset paced slowly and purposefully across the floor, reached one trembling hand out toward the crank handle on the wardrobe door, and swung the thing open so wildly as to nearly tear it off its hinges. He staggered back hooting and collapsed all of a heap in a dead faint.

Everyone dashed to the wardrobe in time to see a tiny pink mouse scuttling through a hole gnawed through the back panel. After Gosset's tale of the fork wielding moths, Jonathan wouldn't have been half surprised to see that the mouse wore an overcoat and carried a whangee. But of course it didn't. It was just an ordinary mouse, not at all unlike the mice that frequented the bookstore in Seaside. Since he'd discovered that mice are so terribly fond of books, Jonathan had developed a curious liking for the beasts. Ahab apparently had similar feelings, for when the mouse poked a tentative snout out from behind the wardrobe and twitched his nose and whiskers about, Ahab sniffed at him a bit and wagged his tail as a sign of friendship. Like all universal signs and symbols, tail-wagging is apparently well understood by mice, for this one squeaked out a mouse hello and dashed away through a hole in the baseboard.

They rooted through the wardrobe, suspecting that something other than the obviously friendly mouse must have caused Gosset to take such fits. He was still unconscious, laying there in a pile, breathing heavily. There was nothing else, however, in the wardrobe save a few pairs of tolerably well-worn shoes, and a tweed coat.

The Professor loosened Gosset's shirt, and the four of them dragged him up onto the bed where he began snoring in a healthy way. The rafters retired to the library, slumping about on the couch and easy chairs. Escargot pointed out the fact that it was past noon and high time to eat. So they broke into the knapsacks and lunched on bread and cheese and jerky. After lunch the Professor dozed off lying on his back on the floor with his hand clasped on his chest. It wasn't more than a moment before he began to snore. It seemed to Jonathan that if a man wants to snore when he sleeps, he would do well to lie on his back—somehow that seemed to promote snoring. He no sooner considered that he, under normal circumstances, couldn't fall asleep while someone in the room snored, when he began to get drowsy and do just that. They had, after all, had a restless night, so it wasn't at all strange that an afternoon nap would seem so irresistible.

In fact they spent the entire afternoon dozing and poking through Gosset's books. Along near nightfall, though, all of them began to grow restless. Escargot's step could be heard first in one corner of the room and then in another. Several times Jonathan could hear him clumping into the bedroom to have a peek at Gosset, who still snored away. By mutual, unspoken agreement none of them made much noise. When they spoke, they did so in whispers, for they all hoped that Gosset would remain asleep until darkness fell so that they could slip away without him.

In low voices they boiled up a plan or two, or at least Escargot did. Jonathan and the Professor, never having been within shouting distance of the tower on the ridge much less inside it, found it difficult to offer either a plan of their own or reasons why Escargot's plan wouldn't work. In the end they resigned themselves to the fact that Escargot was the general of the campaign. It was his idea that he lay low, as he put it, in the woods until the other rafters had made their presence known. They would lead Selznak to believe that Jonathan and the Professor were the usurpers, as it were, and when the Dwarf was confident that he had them in his power, Escargot would spring his trap. He didn't elaborate on the trap idea, even though the Professor pressed him for details. Escargot said finally that the less they knew about his own plans, the less likely they'd be to upset them. If Jonathan and the Professor knew about this secret plan, then they'd have to act as if they didn't, which, of course, would be a dangerous thing. Jonathan rather suspected that there wasn't any plan. But he had a certain trust in Escargot, who, after all, could have turned round and sailed across the seas anytime he chose over the past weeks. All things considered, it seemed likely that Escargot had more motive than merely ridding the valley of goblins and such.

The sun seemed intolerably slow in setting. At about seven o'clock it hung in the western sky as if regretting having to settle down for the night. But when it finally touched the tops of the White Mountains, it sank like an agate marble in a bucket of water. The rafters stood in Gosset's high window and watched it slip away. The fog that had sprung up around the Dwarf had crept away just as mysteriously, and it was a fine evening. Or at least it would have been a fine evening to do something sensible or do nothing at all.

Twilight hung about for a half hour or so, the sky darkening by degrees. When the first star appeared away down toward Seaside, the rafters decided it was time to go. They were dismayed to see, after the sunset held so much promise, that wisping tendrils of fog seemed to be creeping in off the swamps, shuffling along close to the ground. The Professor pointed out that swamps could often be counted on to contribute that sort of thing. But aside from the fact that the night would be a bit shadier and more frightening for the fog, it would, after all, serve to hide them somewhat.

So they set out.

Gosset showed no signs of stirring. He seemed to be making up for lost time in the sleep category. The rafters tiptoed off down the stairs, Ahab leading the way, and passed through his open front door into the night. The air was wet with the promise of fog and the night roundabout was silent as if already muted by it. There was no moon yet, and wouldn't be for another hour, so the forest encircling Gosset's house was a black wall, broken by nothing but an occasional pair of yellow eyes.

As they had agreed, Escargot carried nothing and had left Gosset's hat behind in the library. He was to walk along behind Jonathan, Dooly, and the Professor and whisper directions if it became necessary. Otherwise he would speak only in an emergency and then as little as possible. None of the rafters were to speak to Escargot at all.

There was little choice but to sneak into the town of Hightower by simply slipping along up the river road. The chance of meeting anyone else out on the road after dark was unlikely, unless, of course, they happened upon a band of goblins. But bands of goblins almost always caper along amid a flurry of cackle and uproar, so they determined to hide themselves in the edge of the forest at the slightest hint of trouble.

Dooly tripped over a root before he had gotten beyond the perimeter of Gosset's front yard, and he went tumbling with a shout into the bushes, snapping branches and making a grand row. There was no use arguing about it or warning him to be careful; they simply picked Dooly up, dusted him off and listened for a moment for changes in the night sounds surrounding them. There were none, so they popped out of the brush onto the river road and snaked away toward town in the darkness. They'd gotten about one hundred yards when, from behind them, they heard a bang and a shout, and then silence. It seemed certain that either Lonny Gosset had awakened and set out to search for them, or that goblins were having a go at his house again. Given the mysterious visit of Selznak the Dwarf that afternoon, it wasn't at all unlikely that the latter were the case. One way or another, there was nothing to do but go on, the quicker the better.

Chapter 24

Hobbs' Shorts

❧

I<small>T</small> wasn't such a long way into town; in fact before they had traveled more than a hundred yards or so they spied the eaves of a house through the trees. The house—more of a cottage actually—was dark and silent and overgrown with ivy, the huge trefoil leaves as big around as plates. More cottages appeared, and a little path wandered off to their left in between two rows of them. The river road slanted away right toward the Oriel.

They followed the path on instructions from Escargot, and found themselves creeping along a dim avenue between shuttered houses. There was no ruin, as there had been in Willowood or Stooton, but here and there a shutter had been pried from a window and the pane of glass broken. Either marauding goblins had idly vandalized the homes and pitched rocks through the windows, or something was living within, creeping in and out of the window for some odd reason rather than using the door.

There were no signs of any human inhabitants. The little winding street of cottages led, finally, to the center of the village and a cluster of shops and pubs and the Hightower Hotel. Most were boarded up. The same signs hung in the windows of some of the shops that Jonathan and the Professor had remarked on weeks earlier. The pub with the wire-gummed proprietor was locked securely and on the door hung one square sign that read simply "Out." They slid past Gosset's Millinery and angled across the road to Hobbs' General Merchandise, one of the few stores along the road that seemed still in business. A light glowed in the rear of the store, and through an open doorway within Jonathan could just make out the top of Hobbs' head, sort of bobbing there as if he were nodding over a book. Despite what the Moon Man had said about the townspeople having run mad, Jonathan was happy to see Old Hobbs going about his business. No good, after all, could come from giving up and running off.

"There's Hobbs," Jonathan told the Professor. "Do you see him there in back?"

"Yes," said the Professor. "He looks as if he's fairly active. Engaged in some business pursuits I don't doubt. Working on his ledger book. Perhaps we should approach him."

"What for?" asked Escargot. "If he's as much help as that bloody Gosset we'll have to throttle him and lock him in a closet. We don't need anymore help from crazy men."

"You'll find that Mr. Hobbs is of sterner stuff than Lonny Gosset," said the Professor. "We might need an ally yet. At least we should alert him to the fact that we have a plan afoot. We needn't reveal its nature."

Escargot grunted, but didn't argue. The four of them went creeping back along the side of the building, Ahab brushing along beside them. Lamplight glowed through a rear window, and the rafters edged up to it, not wanting to reveal their presence until they'd had a good look inside. They were doubly cautious as they approached, for from within they heard the sound of voices—two voices it seemed, or perhaps three.

When he peered up over the sill, Jonathan half expected to see a band of gophers dressed up in bits of Hobbs' clothing. But much to his relief, old Hobbs sat placidly before a burned-down fire counting little piles of copper coin. The Professor smiled as if to say, "I told you so," and they all watched for a moment.

Hobbs seemed to count out about ten copper coins and stack them in a neat pile an inch or so high. He counted ten more and stacked them alongside. Then he added up another pile and another and finally, when he had a dozen neat inch-high stacks of coin he layed a straight-edge across the top, bent down, and eyeballed the whole thing as if checking to see whether all were level and true. All in all he had about a hundred of the stacks balanced about the table, and he nodded and smiled at the things as if they were school children all waiting at attention to file out onto a playground. It might have been evidence of Hobbs' "bearing up" or it might have been something else altogether. They decided to watch for a moment before beating on the window to get Hobbs' attention—and it was a good thing they did. For as he measured away at the piles, he began to speak to himself, and then to answer himself, and then to break in and interrupt his own conversation. Finally he shouted at himself to be quiet, stopped speaking abruptly, and exclaimed, "So there!" very loud.

He piled up a last tower of copper coins then began sorting through a mess of small white buttons and dried lima beans. When he'd fingered out fifty or sixty of each, he took his ruler and hashed about in the pile, scrambling everything, buttons, beans, and coins, into an odd salad. He picked up a double-handful of the mix and poured it over his head in a slow stream, shouting to himself all the while. The only words of the bunch that Jonathan could plainly make out were the words "Wealth! Wealth!" which were run together with who knows what all sorts of other sounds. It was a sad pass. Hobbs rose from his chair and scooped the remains of his wealth into a flour sack, at which point Dooly pointed involuntarily toward him, clattering against the closed window. To everyone's amazement, Hobbs wore an enormous pair of checked shorts, cinched at the waist with a length of red ribbon. Below that were pale bare legs ending in mukluk clad feet. The rafters dropped as one when Dooly's hand hit the window, but a few moments later when they dared to look in once again, Hobbs was going about his business in an industrious but inexplicable way.

The rafters sought the road once again and hastened on

through town out toward the swamp and the ridge. It wasn't until they passed along above Hightower harbor that they stopped to rest for a moment. Escargot observed that he was glad to see that Hobbs was indeed at work at his ledger book, then laughed in a low down way, indicating that he'd likely seen funnier things in his time. Dooly wanted to know why Hobbs wore those incredible shorts, and the Professor said that it was doubtless some goblin prank—that he was put up to it and forced to wear them. Jonathan hoped so. He liked to think that Hobbs wasn't wearing them by choice.

There above the harbor, Hightower could be seen atop the ridge, all in all about a mile or so away as the crow flies. Its walls rose dark and solid against the night sky. Between lay the swampy lowlands, dotted with stilted shanties and bulbous moss-covered trees. Occasional lights glowed in the swamp huts through windows that, in the distance, seemed to be the eyes of wild beasts in the swamp. The night was full of noises. The screech of bats could be heard off among the trees, and away above in the rocks of the ridge, the baying of wolves rose on the dark air. Fog lay over the swamp, eerily hovering a foot or two above the ground like a misty gray blanket. The path lay, finally, straight away into the swamp, and there was nothing to do but push along. According to Escargot there was but one trail across the swamp and up the ridge. If they wandered from the path they'd end, likely, in a quicksand bog or in the lair of some swamp devil or viper. There was little hope of secrecy for any of them other than Escargot, but then that seemed to be part of the general plan. When the moon was tilting up over the trees and peeping out from among scattered clouds, the four of them and Ahab plunged off, the great hulking trees roundabout completing the evening gloom. It was likely coming on toward midnight.

Along the path beneath the trees it was monstrously dark and overcast with shadow. On occasion they could see patches of vaguely moonlit clouds through the gaps in the foliage overhead. The trees were scattered and clumped and rimmed with dark morass and marsh grass and pools of dim water, but their limbs bent out so alarmingly that there seemed to be an almost unbroken canopy of leaves overhead. More than once Jonathan fancied having seen a snake—once several snakes—winding away into the swamp beside the path. They were long and very thin and seemed to be in no apparent hurry to be off. Ahab caught sight of the first one but paid it little mind, for there in the shadows of the swamp the snakes were forbidding in an undefinable but deeply felt way.

Long clumps of moss hung from the branches, and occasional droplets of water plunked onto Jonathan's head or down the back of his coat. They had to trust Escargot when they came to forks in the path, for with the exception of a few scattered orange lights away out among the trees, there was no sign that they were within a hundred miles of habitation. The tower on the ridge had disappeared entirely from view.

As they crept along, wary of meeting a party of goblins or of coming upon a gray-skinned troll looming up out of the shadows, the fog kept rising to envelop them, then sinking away again to hover in the forest. Most of the time the mists rose about their knees, and it seemed as if they were gliding along like spirits through some shadowy night-lit underworld. It was impossible for Jonathan to know how far they'd gone. They climbed across fallen trees, mossy and wet, that lay broken on the path. Jonathan could have sworn that it was the same tree each time—that they were circling around, stumbling randomly along through the murk. He determined to watch for the tree again, but for a long silent time they didn't clamber over any more fallen trees, so he began to think that his imagination was acting up.

Muted noises reached their ears finally after what seemed hours of creeping through the gloomy forest. There could be little doubt they were goblin noises—the hollow gonging of a mallet on an iron kettle and the weird toneless howl of willow flutes and the chaotic cackling laughter and gobbling of the little men, capering away somewhere close by.

The rafters went along carefully, staying out of the occasional patches of moonlight and crouching for long moments in shadow to peer into the dark recesses of the swamp around them. Through the trees, finally, glowing orange and yellow through the misty night, lantern-light could be seen through a window. It shone from within a stilted swamp hut with slat sides and a shingle roof, falling to bits from age and disrepair.

The lamplight reminded Jonathan a bit too much of the cabin in the forest near Stooton Slough, and he had a strong urge to ignore the whole business and be on his way. But the deviltry here was obvious. This was no odd goblin trap. A dozen or so of the things were cavorting within this ruined shanty. It occurred to Jonathan that they were "goblinizing" it—a word the Professor would surely approve. All of the rafters watched silently from the shadow of an alder as goblins lurched out onto the porch of the cabin, hooted and gobbled and whacked at the railing and lurched back inside. They seemed to be holding some sort of a meeting, for twice in the space of five minutes small parties of goblins tramped in out of the shadows of the woods in a businesslike way. Once, with much hooting and blathering, a half dozen or so reeled out and down the wooden stairs and away through the swamp, one massive gnarled goblin hurling a tin of some nature after them.

A figure appeared shortly thereafter, outlined in the lamplit window. Jonathan could see that it sported one of Lonny Gosset's caps, sidewise on its head. The thing cackled with laughter and dumped what must have been the contents of a silverware drawer out onto the roadway, for there was the clatter and clang of cutlery as the contents of the drawer fell together below. The sound, apparently, pleased the marauding goblins somehow, for something like a cheer rose from a number of goblins within the cabin. One of them stumbled out and down and retrieved the spilled silverware, then clambered back into the cabin and dumped the boxful out the window again.

There was the sound of breaking glass and a wild screech shortly after the cutlery had been dumped and hooted over for the third time, and then the sound of scuffling and wild gobbling. The lamplight wavered and swung for a moment, then crashed out as the lantern very obviously fell from wherever it stood, and broke. The darkness lasted a moment before a new orange and red light flickered up and began to climb up the walls inside. A rush of goblins stormed out onto the porch, down the stairs, and away into the swamp. Two goblins hurtled out in their wake, scratching and biting and both afire from head to foot. They rolled sizzling into a pool across the path, leaped up, and followed along behind their friends. The flames spread through the abandoned shanty as the rafters advanced along the path.

All in all it would have been an odd display had it not been goblins who were involved. Jonathan thought of stopping to attempt to put out the fire, but on close inspection the ramshackle structure was such a ruin that it would be no worse off burned to a heap of cinder than it was whole. So they let it smolder and burn and passed along out of the firelight back into the darkness of the swamp.

Soon after they had resumed their trek they began again to hear the baying of wolves, now before them, now behind, now up and away ahead of them as if from the rocky slopes of Hightower Ridge. Once or twice Jonathan caught a glimpse of red eyes off in the swamp and heard the stealthy pad of feet somewhere near. And once, not long before the end of the path through the swamp, the whole lot of them stopped in a bunch to stare at what seemed to be about a thousand tiny yellow eyes peering weirdly at them through the misty moonlight that covered a dark pool. It turned out they *were* eyes—the eyes of innumerable frogs, all heaped about in the crowded pool and silently watching in the darkness.

They only paused for a moment, then hurried along for another two or three minutes before the overhanging branches of the trees fell away behind and they found themselves beneath the cloud-dimmed sky looking up toward the rocky fastness of Hightower Ridge, the tower itself a monolithic pile of shadows beyond the crags above. They began to pick their way along the path that rose upward out of the misty air of the swamp, clinging to the shadows of the rocks and listening in slowly growing dread to the grim howling of wolves above and around them.

The moon seemed to Jonathan to be their one ally. He attempted to lighten his spirits by thinking that above them in the starry sky, elf galleons, if rumors were true, might well be casting wonderful nets into the seas of clouds and fishing for who-knew-what sorts of celestial jewels. He had an inkling, although it may have been nothing more than a rather deep hope, that from somewhere far above their movements were observed, that they weren't as alone in the dark night as it seemed they were. He had an urge to shake the magical fish coins out of his bag and lay them out in the proper pattern just to be able to nod once or twice to the Moon Man. But the tower loomed above, and there was no time for magical coins or for wishing he were someplace else. Escargot grunted out the suggestion that they stop and reconnoiter, so they did. They slumped finally in the shadows of a little grove of trees where they had a reasonably clear view of the back and side of the castle.

It was built of great blocks of gray-black stone that had worn smooth over the centuries. Blue lichen and green and brown mosses splotched the walls, making for darker, shadowed patches against the dim surface. The tower itself pushed up out of the rocks of the ridge and thrust some four or five stories into the sky; light glowed through scattered windows. Somehow the dark height of the thing was chilling. It had such a somber, dismal look about it that even on the warmest spring days it would still be sunless and bleak. Chunks of stone appeared to have been broken away here and there as if the tower had been struck by lightning or shaken by an earthquake. Heavy vines twisted up the sides, but most of the vines were bare of leaves.

While they crouched in the trees, they listened to rustlings roundabout in the woods and to the baying of the wolves away up the ridge. Twice in the few long minutes they were there, gray wolves padded out of the forest and skulked along the edge of the castle, disappearing once again into the trees.

To the rear of the castle was a great window of dusty, leaded glass. Flickering light shone through onto the trees behind, and the light jumped and waved and glowed and dimmed—clearly firelight. From within came the sounds of gobbling and cackling and hooting and gonging, as if there were some sort of goblin revel in progress.

The rafters crept off through the shadows, pushing along toward the firelit window to have a look within.

Pouring from a stone chimney along one rear wall was a mass of thick smoke accompanied by huge sparks and dark, shadowy forms and unsettling shapes. The smoke dissipated into the night air like steam, but the dim shadows that accompanied it fluttered and tumbled and seemed, finally, to fly off into the distances, some on what appeared to be great, slowly flapping wings, silhouetted against the night sky. The rafters found themselves, finally, behind the castle and on the steep edge of the rocky slope of the ridge. Below, the tops of the swamp trees thrust up through a blanket of fog that seemed to be rolling languorously up toward them from the morass below.

After lying still for a few moments and listening to the wolves, and then the silence, the company crept along toward the lighted window, flattening themselves against the stones of the tower. Through the dirty window they could see an immense hall with a high, trestle ceiling and with great carved pillars holding the whole thing up. Away to the right was a wide stairway, spiraling off toward the upper levels. Before them was a fireplace built of the same gigantic blocks of stone as the tower itself. The fire within glowed as if it had been burning for years on end.

There before the fire, stoking it with a long, dark poker, stood Selznak the Dwarf, his pipe in his mouth and his stick in his hand. His broad cap hung on a peg near a massive, barred door.

Jonathan was vaguely surprised to see that the Dwarf was bald on top, that he had sort of a ring of hair. It seemed to buck Jonathan up a bit actually, because he immediately wondered whether Selznak was self-conscious about his bald spot and whether, like Mayor Bastable, Selznak drank vinegar and rubbed snake oil onto his scalp in an effort to restore his hair. It was probably unlikely that he did, and it was astonishing that even magic and enchantment couldn't restore hair.

Shouting and gibbering around him were a dozen goblins of varying shapes and sizes who waved vessels of drink—intoxicating drink from the look of it. Selznak put his poker down and fanned the flames by squeezing away at a great, suspended bellows until the fire leaped and roared. He bent down and grasped an armful of fuel from a pile of pale wood against the wall. He seemed to inspect each log before tossing it into the fire, and, as he did, Jonathan was horrified to see that what the Dwarf held was not wood at all, but long, bleached dry bones. Selznak stepped back and fanned the flames once again. Then he reached inside his cloak and produced a stoppered vial which he uncorked, sprinkling lime-colored powder into the fire. A greenish *whoosh* of flame arose like a cloud, disappearing up the chimney, and the fire abruptly died down to a mass of glowing embers. There, clacking and chattering in the midst of the fire was a hellish and jerking skeleton, dangling above the flames like a marionette. The thing danced and waved, and the goblins in the room became quiet and stood in wide wonder, seeming frightened of the thing themselves. Selznak pounded his stick three times on the stone floor, and the bobbing skeleton clattered out onto the hearth and jerked around in a little circle, its bottom jaw working spasmodically. It stopped, finally, when Selznak pounded once again on the stones, and it put its hands to its face and began to weep. It turned to face the window then peered out from between bony fingers and grinned.

Skeletons, to Jonathan, pretty much all looked alike, but he didn't have to think long before he knew that he'd seen this one before, or at least that he'd seen one with similar emotions. He and the others watched in frozen horror as, step by slow step, the thing clattered toward them across the wide hall, now weeping, now chattering, now bursting into wild laughter as the goblins fell away before it.

A wild, piercing scream tore through the night not two feet from Jonathan's ear. He leaped back, heart soaring, and fell over a long wooden bench, punching out once or twice at the empty air around him, hoping vainly to strike whatever demon it was that had shrieked into his ear at such a ghastly moment. But it had been no demon; it had been Dooly. And it was Dooly, who could be seen disappearing at a dead run back down the road toward the swamp.

Chapter 25

Dancing Skeletons

❦

THE Professor pulled Jonathan upright, and they heard Escargot shout as his feet scrunched away down the road after Dooly, "It's up to you, mates! I have to stop the lad!"

There wasn't time to be mad or frightened or anything else, for the grisly skeleton clacked away at them through the window; and behind, stepping from the fire, was another. Selznak laughed like a demon and pounded his staff against the flags as he dusted the fire again with the contents of the vial. Jonathan, fighting an impulse to follow Escargot and leave the Professor to work things out for himself, grabbed hold of the bench he'd fallen over instead. The Professor, as if reading his mind, hoisted the other end, and they swung it once, twice, three times together and sent it smashing through the window, shattering the bony horror capering there.

There was the crash of breaking glass and wood and the clatter of white bones on the stone floor, followed by the wild ululations of mad goblins. The second skeleton wandered aimlessly, and *whooshes* of green flame from the fire heralded the issuance of others. Jonathan hefted his club and threatened the first goblin that hopped across to the shattered window toward him. The thing had no fear, however, and waving taloned claws and gnashing its teeth, it raced at him. So Jonathan smashed it across the side of its silly head and sent the thing sprawling through the rubble. The rest of the goblins went wild at the sight and raced about, working themselves up. Selznak seemed to think the whole thing monstrously funny, for he looked on gleefully, whacking away with his staff. The second skeleton completed one last turn about the hall, stopped, seemed to see Jonathan for the first time, and stepped jerkily along toward him.

The Professor, meanwhile, cranked away at the seeker. The whirl-gatherers twirled and the thing shook as if in the grip of some great force. As the Professor struggled to hold it, it burst from his hands and buzzed off through the open window, into the hall. Goblins fled shrieking in every direction, and even the grim skeleton hesitated and took a step back. Another bony image, wavering above the fire, rattled together and fell in a heap in the embers, the fire roaring up about it. It was as if everything within the hall had sensed that some nature of elf magic had penetrated the mist of evil and gloom.

Selznak stopped his thumping as the thing tore out of the Professor's hands, more because of the change of atmosphere than because he knew what thing it was that was flying toward him like some squid-spawned bird. The seeker shot straight across the hall as if it had been called home at last and slammed smack into the forehead of the odious Selznak, pitching him over backward onto the ground. The seeker spun away, not played out by half, and angled off across the hall in the general direction of the skeleton which reached out with one halting arm and clutched at it. The seeker sailed right on along, instigating a rain of finger bones, and left the skeleton waving a bony stump.

Selznak clambered to his feet, tangled in his robes and furious as the devil. He was reaching for his staff when the seeker buzzed down on him again, bonking him on the nose. He was astonished, no doubt, that such a marvelous and persistent weapon was, overall, so ineffectual, and when the seeker raced his way the third time he beat it to bits with his staff and kicked it against the wall. Two goblins rushed for the weapon, but when they grabbed it they fell back as if burned and let it lie there in a heap.

The Dwarf shook out a fold in his robe and when he did, the vial of powder he'd been sprinkling into the fire fell out and broke on the floor, the fine dust within blowing on the breeze that came through the open window into the heart of the flames. *Whooshes* of green sparks burst up the chimney, and first one, then another skull appeared, bobbing in the flames. Selznak tried, at first, to save some of the dust, but left off the effort, slammed his staff onto the floor, and shouted gobbled orders at the goblins standing roundabout and setting the whole lot of them into an uproar.

As he swung his club for the second time, it occurred to Jonathan that Selznak hadn't much of a sense of humor when it was he who was appearing ridiculous. But Jonathan hadn't time to think about it much, because before he could recover from his second, very effective swing, he was borne down by slavering, scratching goblins.

He fought and kicked and tossed goblins to and fro, but the things seemed to be made of rubber. Each time one would spin away against a wall or rebound from a *thwack* on the head, it simply sprung to its former wild state and sailed back in. It went well, all in all, for Jonathan and the Professor at first. Once the struggle was underway, it began to seem that about twice as many goblins as there were would be needed to accomplish the job. But just when Jonathan was taking heart, he heard a violent floor thumping. The struggling mass of them was quickly overshadowed by a tremendous hulking, hairy beast—nearly the size of a troll—a stooped thing, with arms half again as long as they should be; its knuckles nearly scraped along the ground. Aside from its tremendous size, it was a foolish-looking thing—a monster that looked as if it weren't altogether sure it was one. As it stood there looking down at them, Jonathan heard the Professor whisper, as if in amazement, "The Beddlington Ape!"

It reached down and wrenched Jonathan's club from his hand, scattering goblins in the process, and after a bit of hasty thought, Jonathan decided it best to just relax and play along. There seemed to be little use in struggling with the thing. A batch of goblins swarmed round again, and Jonathan and the Professor soon found themselves lifted bodily and borne among goblins into the interior of the hall.

Jonathan hoped that they'd created the diversion Escargot needed, because they'd accomplished little else beside mayhem. When he thought about it, he hoped Escargot was still involved in the caper. But the more he considered it, the less sure he was that Escargot hadn't given the venture up and slid away toward the river, expecting that he and the Professor, once involved, would have no choice but attempt to finish the job. Who could say?

After subduing Jonathan and Professor Wurzle, the goblins turned their attention on Ahab, who proved to be no easy beast to capture. He raced about the hall barking and nipping and managed to latch onto the pants of one goblin and drag him off bodily. Having no fear of bones of any sort, he bowled through the handless skeleton and knocked the befuddled thing into scrap, its grinning skull bouncing with a hollow thud to the floor. The goblin managed finally to pull himself loose and roll away shrieking.

Ahab, no doubt feeling outnumbered and finding himself pursued by the ape thing, dashed away up the stairway toward the upper reaches of the tower. A half dozen goblins set out after him, but Selznak whacked away at the floor with his stick, shouted strangely. Instead of pursuing Ahab, the goblins then dashed in a clump through the smashed window and set out around the tower toward the swamp. The Beddlington Ape watched them race away, poked a long finger into its ear for a moment, then shambled off after them. There was no way to say for sure, but it looked as if they were after Dooly. Following the skeleton incident, there was little doubt that Selznak knew all along of their approach to the castle, and so would, of course, want to account for Dooly. Jonathan hoped, when the goblins disappeared through the window, that it was only Dooly they went out after.

The Professor, Jonathan could see, was in a state. He was glaring roundabout himself as if itching to run mad and teach these filthy goblins a lesson. He was probably at an advantage over Jonathan, for he had a smaller regard for magic, evil or otherwise, than Jonathan, and so hadn't quite as much fear of the Dwarf and his staff.

Perhaps the goblins made the error of supposing the Professor old and tired, for although six of the things held onto Jonathan, only three guarded him. He seemed to relax and grow cooperative for a moment—right before thrashing out with his right foot and kicking the leg-clutching goblin across the floor. He pitched the other two to the stones before the first could scramble back into the fray, and leaped across to clout one of the mob that was holding onto Jonathan. The lot of them seemed surprised and rather more anxious to race off howling than to hang onto Jonathan and let Professor Wurzle knock on their heads.

Selznak still stood by the fire watching the fray. He hadn't said a word. After his first effort to save the green powder, he gave up doing anything at all save pounding on the flags of the floor and shouting cryptic orders. He seemed strangely unperturbed, as if he were watching a stage play and were getting ready to call down the curtain. Behind him, roaring up in the great fireplace, orange flames raged and heaved and green sparking flashes erupted about every other minute. Twitching and dangling above the flames were a chorus line of dancing skeletons, a new one bobbing up each time the green dust set off another uproar. Now and then, when Selznak pounded his staff, one or another of them would lurch out onto the hearth and clatter away into the hall. Some of the skeletons danced briefly over the flames, only to collapse in a heap when the poof of green set another one afloat. Once a yellow skull shot out of the fire like popcorn and rolled off across the floor. The skeletons in mounting numbers traipsed back and forth in a dazed state. Selznak paid them little heed once it was clear that he could do nothing to stop the green flame, and a half dozen or so lurched finally toward the open window and made off into the night.

By the time the Professor kicked his way loose and set upon the six goblins, the hall was a roaring tumult of green and orange spark and flame and of stumbling skeletons and wild goblins all surging to and fro in a frenzy of activity. Through it all Selznak stood placidly. He watched as Jonathan tore himself free from the last and most stalwart of his goblins and, along with the Professor, turned to face him. It seemed as if it were time for a showdown.

Jonathan wasn't at all sure what to do, but he *was* sure he'd better do it before the Beddlington Ape got back or before Selznak decided to activate a few of the skeletons that were still creeping out of the fire.

If Snood's device was, as Twickenham had insisted, in perfect order, then Selznak had it somewhere in his cloak; perhaps around his neck on a chain. Just as Jonathan and the Professor turned and set their sights on him—just as Jonathan thought about Snood's device and that the watch might well be on a chain around Selznak's neck, he found out that, in part, he was mistaken. The watch wasn't on a chain around his neck; it was on the end of a chain and shoved into a vest pocket—a vest that the Dwarf wore beneath his cloak.

Selznak, in fact, held the watch in his hand. Jonathan couldn't get much of a glimpse of it. He could just see that it shined gold in the Dwarf's palm. Whether it had any hands on it and whether they pointed toward the correct time, he couldn't say, but he intended to find out. He lunged toward the Dwarf only to see, out of the corner of his eye, a befuddled skeleton emerge from the green flame and stumble toward him. Jonathan realized as soon as he went for the watch the skeleton would trip him up. He was right. The two of them collided, the skeleton shivered into bits, and Jonathan shot head-foremost into the pile of bones against the wall, rolling up into a sitting position before coming to a stop.

He continued to sit there. The Professor stood half poised to spring on Selznak himself, but he didn't spring. He just stood ready like a piece of odd statuary with a very determined look on its face. Jonathan wondered what the Professor's problem was. Then he wondered what his own problem was—why he sat there in a heap of bones while the Dwarf walked about leering at them. The answer, of course, was the watch in the Dwarf's hand, now on its way back to his vest pocket. Jonathan commanded himself to stand up. He focused all of his attention on his legs and, with all the mental energy he could muster, he thought, "Arise, legs," but they didn't. Hopeless! After pondering for a bit he found it curious that he could still see and think and hear, and he wondered whether that phenomenon was due to the Dwarf's control, or to the Dwarf's lack of control of the watch. He wondered, too, whether being able to see and hear and think was an advantage of any sort. Given the nature of his captor, it might not be.

Around the hall stood random, frozen skeletons, and over at the foot of the stairs were two frozen goblins, one leg in the air as if they'd been stopped in the midst of a good lively run. Across the windowsill was the hunched form of a skeleton that had been attempting to drag itself out over the casement and escape. The room was glowing with firelight, but the fire in the hearth seemed to Jonathan to be suspended, waiting there as if expecting orders of some nature. The topmost flames licking up toward the chimney were tinged with the emerald glow of the magical powder. Waiting and hovering in the green flame was the last of the grinning skeletons, fully formed, but seemingly condemned to linger there, buoyed up by the flame.

All around Jonathan was silence, and he was conscious only of the sound of the blood in his veins and of the grim laughter that filtered into his mind and sounded as if it were an echo that had traveled a great distance to find him. It was Selznak, who was laughing; an evil grin crept across his face. He stopped grinning for a moment and reached up to pull his hat off its peg, clapping the thing down on top of his head.

Outside all was still dark, and in the frozen fire the skeleton still waited. Jonathan sat like a pudding there on the bones. He hoped, among other things, that he wouldn't start to drool and that his hair, which had been tousled in the collision with the skeleton, wasn't pushed up into any ludicrous tangle. It was bad enough being sprawled out helplessly in the midst of a bone pile without adding further indignities.

Two goblins appeared briefly at the window, one of them wearing one of Lonny Gosset's hats. They peered in momentarily then dashed off again in a flurry of gobbling and gesticulating. Close on their heels came a third goblin, and running like Billy-O; behind him, surprisingly, was the wild and unlikely Lonny Gosset, an upraised cudgel in his right hand and a shout on his lips. Gosset didn't even bother to look into the hall; he was after goblins, and, from the look of him, he was meeting with a certain amount of success. Jonathan wondered just how extensive the Dwarf's power was—whether there were frozen goblins, maybe even a frozen Theophile Escargot outside in the night. Clearly there were limits, inasmuch as Gosset was anything but slowed down. There was little Jonathan could do, however, but sit and think about it.

Selznak disappeared for a time, then appeared once again. The Professor stood staring about himself with the same look of determination, poised to spring. Lonny Gosset appeared at the window once more, himself pursued this time by the Beddlington Ape. But of all the activity that transpired roundabout him, the oddest occurrence by far concerned a coil of rope that very mysteriously floated down the stairway along the wide wooden banister. It descended about halfway, then paused there. Then it began to float upward into the complication of trestle beams that spanned and supported the ceiling of the great hall. It inched its way up a rough pillar and out across a wide hand-hewn joist, black and smooth with age.

Jonathan watched the progress of that coil of rope, understanding as he did that Escargot hadn't run off at all but was up to some trick. What it was, Jonathan couldn't say. Perhaps he intended to lasso the watch—snatch it out of the Dwarf's pocket on the end of a rope. But that seemed, all in all, fairly unlikely. After all, it really didn't much matter to Jonathan. He couldn't shove in and lend a hand if he wanted to.

Chapter 26

A Vast Surprise

It occurred to Jonathan, as the coil of rope disappeared from his sight, why Escargot had rushed off so hurriedly. Although it was true he'd gone off in search of Dooly, he no doubt also rushed away so as to be beyond the power of Selznak and his pocketwatch. The diversion he wanted Jonathan and the Professor to create was intended to compel Selznak to use the watch. Escargot had somehow managed to slip in upstairs and creep back down again, carrying his coil of rope. If the coil had been about half its size he could have simply shoved it in under his cloak and walked smack in through the open window. That would have been more his style, or so it seemed to Jonathan. But then perhaps Escargot was taking no chances. His fear of the Dwarf and his enchantment and of the powers of the watch had likely made him wary. And Escargot, after all, had an air of confidence about him, but never an air of recklessness.

Jonathan pondered all these things with a certain amount of satisfaction and took heart in the fact that everything was becoming considerably clearer. He hoped Professor Wurzle was alerted to the floating coil of line, but there was no way to tell. It was certain, however, that

Selznak was unaware of the phenomenon. He had returned and was busy working some sort of magic over a pair of crossed bones, a toothy-looking skull, and what appeared to Jonathan to be one of those rubbery Halloween snakes. More likely it was a stuffed snake of some vile persuasion. Just what Selznak was cooking up no one but he could know. He seemed to be happiest when playing one of his magical pranks—blowing billows of fog and great undulating smoke rings out of his pipe or creating dancing skeletons from fire and green dust and bones.

The Dwarf reached into the fire and plucked out a flaming coal which he thrust into the mouth of the skull, setting the thing aglow like a jack-'o-lantern. Then he began to drop bits of dried leaves into the thing's mouth, and the leaves smoked away like incense, sending dark shadows up into the hall, seeming to be winged like great wavering ghosts of bats that fluttered roundabout, some of them sailing out through the window into the night.

What bothered Jonathan was the thought that the Dwarf's incantations and snake-wavings and bat shadows were likely intended for something other than show—that they had something unpleasant to do with him and the Professor. And he could only wait and watch and wonder what it was that Escargot with his coil of line was up to.

But he didn't have to wait for too long. For as Selznak whacked at the floor with his staff and sprinkled his powders and leaves bit by bit into the glowing mouth of the skull, a very neatly and expertly tied noose came dangling along out of the ceiling beams—painfully slowly it seemed to Jonathan—and settled smoothly around Selznak's neck.

The Dwarf, aware of the noose only after it was already about his neck, threw his right hand out and swept the glowing skull and the snake and the crossed bones off the table where he'd been dealing with them and onto the stone floor. Jonathan watched as a look of rage mingled with amazement came onto the Dwarf's face. He cast his staff to the ground and clutched with both hands at the tightening noose that threatened to pluck him from the floor and strangle him. Selznak's mumblings and chantings were replaced by an echoing shriek, and he seemed to be doing a light little dance on tiptoe. His face grew red through his beard, and his eyes seemed likely to shoot out like meteors at any moment. He gasped and danced and danced and gasped, but hadn't enough wind left in him to do anymore shrieking or cursing.

He quit clutching, finally, at the noose around his neck and groped beneath his cloak to find his vest pocket and the pocketwatch within. When he pulled his hand from his cloak, he held the thing at arm's length, the chain torn away from the button it was clipped to as if Selznak were wildly attempting to show it off. The rope loosened, the Dwarf dropped down onto his feet, and his eyes seemed to settle back into his head. There was a long moment while he stood thus, waiting.

Escargot gave the rope another tug just to make his point, and Selznak jumped up onto his toes again and made his pop-eyed expression. The rope slackened and Selznak settled again, but he didn't relax much. He looked to Jonathan, in fact, as if he suspected that whoever was up in the rafters somewhere might well give him a third tug, just for sport. Escargot's voice, very businesslike, shouted down from overhead:

"Move and you're hung!"

The Dwarf made a bit of an attempt to look up toward the ceiling, but that, apparently, took his head farther along in the wrong direction—a rather uncomfortable direction at that. Selznak eyed his staff lying there not three feet from him. He slowly stuck out a tentative foot to try to pull it in, but his foot hadn't traveled more than two or three inches before the rope tightened and he was jerked upright.

When the rope slackened he made no further effort toward the staff. He stood there as slow minutes passed, contemplating the whole affair. Finally, when it seemed certain that whoever was above him was tolerably able to wait him out, the Dwarf spoke.

"Do I have the pleasure," he asked in a gentlemanly way, "of speaking to my old associate, Theophile Escargot?"

"Aye," came the reply from above.

"I thought as much," said Selznak. "Your skills haven't diminished any over the years."

"Not a bit," agreed Escargot.

"And the lad? How is the lad?"

"Tolerably well," Escargot replied. "Pounding the daylights out of your goblins from the sound of it."

"Is he now?" Selznak winked at Jonathan as if the two of them were in on some privileged information about that very subject. "My goblins seem to enjoy that sort of thing. Odd lot, goblins. The more trouble they can stir up, the happier they are. It doesn't seem to matter if it's they or somebody else who suffers for it. But how is the lad, really? Happy to see the old place again?"

"As a lark," said Escargot.

"He'd have been happier, I'm sure, if he'd stayed on a few months longer the first time he was here. I could have taught him quite a bit. Perhaps I will yet."

"Seems unlikely," said Escargot, giving the rope a twitch or two. "I'll be doing most of the teaching around here. All you're likely to do is dance."

Selznak shrugged. It seemed possible that Escargot knew what he was talking about. "Don't mind if I have a smoke?" the Dwarf asked.

"Not at all," said Escargot. "I suppose it's traditional."

Selznak let out a little, unconvincing chuckle. He returned the watch to his vest pocket, pulled out his pipe and tobacco, and proceeded to have a smoke. Jonathan half-expected to see billows of fog come rolling up out of nowhere, but they didn't. And after all, all the fog in the world wouldn't remove the rope from around his neck. Finally, after tamping away for a bit and puffing and relighting and tamping some more, he shoved the tobacco and matches and tamper back into a pocket and once again removed the watch, holding it up in front of himself as if checking the time. "What is it, exactly, that you want from me?" asked the Dwarf, removing the pipe from his mouth. "I was led to believe that our score was settled. We made an agreement, after all. Or have you forgotten it? The lad for the watch. Then you saw fit to toss the pig-bird into the bargain without a bit of discussion. And what did I do? Did I turn you into a toad or set the lizards on you? No. I said to myself, it's just old Theophile up to his pranks. And I turned the other cheek, as they say. I knew you were cowering in the underbrush at Hinkle Creek. But did I light it afire? Not a bit. I'm a philosopher, as you know, and not one to set about revenge or to take umbrage. Not Dr. Selznak. And yet, here you come creeping into my home and looping rope about my neck as I go about minding my business. Insufferable, I call it. Quite insufferable.

"But I'm a philosopher. I've pointed that out. And I'm willing to forget this entire matter. However, I'll expect recompense from these brigands here who found it a good idea to beat out my window. Perhaps we can come to an agreement. They, unfortunately, aren't in the mood to discuss it right now, so you can act as their counsel. What do you say?"

Escargot remained silent.

"It's the sad case," said Selznak, "that I'm in need of parts. Nothing vital, mind you, no hearts or brains or arms or legs. I need only a liver and a spleen and twenty-odd feet of good vein. They wouldn't miss it." And he winked at Jonathan again, although it wasn't the friendliest wink.

"Wake them up," said Escargot, in no mood for jolliness. "Wake them up and give the watch to the old man. Any hint of a trick and it's you who'll be needing a new neck."

Selznak laughed, puffed on his pipe, pulled it out of his mouth and looked into the bowl as if expecting to see something wonderful in there. "You're always amusing. I've always said that when it's larks that are required, Theophile Escargot is the man to see. You haven't failed me yet, sir, and apparently you're still in good form. You've traded me this very interesting watch in good faith, and now you expect me to hand it back to you. Are you willing to give me the lad too? And these two nitwits. Can I have them?"

"You can have this," said Escargot, and he gave the rope an incredible tug, sending Selznak's pipe catapulting out of his mouth onto the floor, a burning wad of tobacco popping out of the bowl. After kicking for a few seconds, the Dwarf's feet found the floor once again and he recovered a bit. He managed, through it all, to clutch the watch. He had a fierce look about him when the rope slackened, and the air *whooshed* in and out of his lungs. When he recovered he said in a hideously calm voice, "If you do that again, Mr. Escargot, I'll make further use of this watch, and you'll likely join your friends down here on the floor. It would be best, in such a case, that you rather curl into a ball so that when you hit you'll preserve your vital organs. I can't tolerate wastefulness."

"That would be interestin', mate," said Escargot in his seaworthy way, "but I wouldn't hit the floor. Not hard anyway. This rope is tied around my waist and looped over a beam. If I fall, you'll be up among the rafters, choked blind."

"And you'll suffer great internal disruption," said Selznak. "That wouldn't serve."

Outside in the darkness was a tumult of activity. On more than one occasion goblins looked in at the window, saw the scatter of skeletons and rafters and fellow goblins, cast a quick look at their trussed master, and dashed away into the night once more. Now and then the howling receded down toward the swamp; then it seemed to work its way back up the road toward the tower. Wolves bayed, goblins shrieked, bats flew in through the window and out again—and, every now and then, a spindle-legged skeleton jerked past, head swiveling this way and that, hollow eye sockets seeming to peer about as if searching in earnest for something to frighten.

It was altogether odd that Dooly and Lonny Gosset were able to keep such a lunatic horde of grim beasts and goblins busy by themselves. Jonathan waited in expectation for the Beddlington Ape to come clambering in with Dooly under one arm and Gosset under the other. Escargot's plan would run into an undeniable snag in such an event.

The Dwarf appeared to be thinking the same thing. He seemed to be at a loss as to what to do with his hands and looked as if he wished he could reach his pipe. But aside from that he was tolerably calm—waiting about, it seemed, to be rescued by his minions.

The howling and gobbling raged even louder outside, as if a pitched battle were being fought directly in front of the tower. After a few minutes of silence within the hall, Escargot spoke. "If the lad comes to harm," he warned, "it'll go bad for you. Very bad."

"My friend," said the Dwarf in a sort of tired way, "it's going to go very badly for a number of people—one of them a celebrated thief. You've made a mistake throwing your lot in with these scalawags. We could have accomplished great things, you and I. We still can. You haven't any idea of the treasures I have, sir. Not an inkling."

"I'll have more than an inkling before the night is through," said Escargot.

And so it went for another hour or so until it seemed to Jonathan that he could barely remember a time when he wasn't sitting there among the bones listening to Selznak and Escargot strike bargains. Finally, through the window, the night turned from black to deep blue to gray. The tumult outside faded and returned and there was a deal of shouting and stomping around the side of the tower.

A wild voice, deep and strangely off key as if it were produced by something trying to imitate a human's voice, sounded from out of the misty morning air, mouthing the following strange words: "Woe unto drunkards!" came the voice, pronouncing the *kard* in drun*kard* like a person would pronounce *card* in playing *card*. "Woe unto drun-*kards!*" it shouted. "Woe! woe! woe!" Then after a pause, "Bloated with ale!" And after that a long, drawn out *"Wooooo!"* and the Beddlington Ape, torn and deranged, staggered into view outside the window. It had a look of wild fury on its face. When it saw its master there, head in a noose, it growled low in its throat, reached into what it no doubt imagined to be a shirt, and pulled forth nothing less than one of Lonny Gosset's caps which it jammed down over its squatty head.

Selznak shouted at the thing in an odd language, then turned toward Escargot up in the rafters. "This has grown tiresome. We'll play a different game now." He shouted again at the Beddlington Ape and it bent over to climb in through the window, anxious to do its master's bidding.

Jonathan wondered why Escargot didn't simply hoist the Dwarf into the air. But then that likely was easier said than done. Besides, even if Escargot hung the Dwarf, things would go badly for him and the Professor. Then a grim thought struck him. If the Dwarf died, he and Professor Wurzle would remain puddings until the Moon Man could be summoned to set them free. All in all, there wasn't much hope as the Beddlington Ape, shouting his grim lament, hunched toward them through the shattered casement.

There was a shout outside. Not a frightened or abrupt shout, but a deep, thought-out sort of a shout that seemed to shake the foundation of the tower. Even Selznak looked up in wonder, as did his beast, who paused midway through the window, turned to see about this new commotion, and was clubbed from behind with a three-foot length of wood shaped like a ball bat. The thing was staggered. It fell back outside. Then with a hollow thud as the club smashed down onto its head a second time and it fell in a heap there, atop the skeleton that had almost made it out into the night three hours before.

Dead silence. The ape twitched once and groaned. "Woe!" It wailed convincingly, then gave up and lay there, breathing heavily. From out of the shadows lumbered one of the finest things Jonathan could remember having seen. If a unicorn had stepped out, the sight of it wouldn't have been half so rare as was the sight of Squire Myrkle, laughing in that slow way of his and dressed for mayhem. He had a squint-eyed look on his wide face as if searching for someone else to poleaxe. When his eyes lighted on the Dwarf, he seemed to perk up, and he set about climbing over the sill and into the hall—no light task for the Squire.

Most amazing of all, however, was what seemed to Jonathan to prove the old adage: "Once lost, twice recovered." For there atop the Squire's head was perched nothing less than Mayor Bastable's hat, battered but recognizable. It wouldn't have come close to fitting the Squire except for the odd fact that the Squire's head rather narrowed on top. All in all, Jonathan didn't know what was the greater marvel, the appearance of the Squire or of Mayor Bastable's hat.

Bufo and Yellow Hat stormed up about then shouting something about wild men, but they paused long enough to help the Squire in through the window before nodding to Jonathan and the Professor and dashing off. They were back in a trice, though, along with Dooly and Stick-a-bush. Among the four of them, they carried an inert Lonny Gosset. Dooly had a wide slash on his forehead, and his face and hair were matted with dried blood. Somehow, though, he looked as if he'd never been happier—as if the wounded and bloody head was about ten times as valuable as a head without such decorations. Dooly and the linkmen piled in, bumping Gosset across the back of the collapsed Beddlington Ape. The combined weight of Gosset and the ape served to smash the skeleton beneath into a pile of ribs and backbones. The skull popped loose and rolled into the hall, stopping near the loose skull that had, hours before, shot out of the fire.

The Squire poked at it with his club, then poked at the other one. Then he chivied one about the floor, lining it up with the open mouth of the fireplace, and whacked it with the end of the club as if he were playing golf. The skull sailed upward like a comet, square into the still hovering flame, and smashed into the chest of the skeleton that was waiting there. The thing just broke apart and the pieces fell back into the coals. The Squire shook with laughter. He picked up the second skull, lifted Mayor Bastable's cap off his head, and shoved the skull into it before putting the hat back on. He turned to Selznak and said with a convincing air about him, "The Squire has a skullcap now," then laughed again.

Selznak looked to Jonathan as if he were about to go blind. As if he'd seen a few wonders in his time, but was faced here with something outside his ken.

The Squire bent over and peered into Jonathan's face, poking him on the tip of his nose with a pudgy finger. "The Cheeseman is asleep," he said. "But he has his eyes open. That's an odd thing. The Squire hasn't seen such a thing before. And this dwarf seems to be hanging himself. He's a sad dwarf, living among goblins."

"Hello, Squire!" Escargot shouted. The Squire looked up into the ceiling beams but, of course, saw nothing but the dangling rope.

"It's Grandpa!" shouted Dooly. "He's up there in his invisible coat!"

"Can he fly?" asked the Squire.

"I don't know," said Dooly, not quite sure how to respond. "I don't think so."

"Take the watch from the Dwarf," said Escargot. The Squire hulked across and plucked the watch from Selznak's hand. Selznak was fuming. It seemed to Jonathan that steam would soon start pouring out of the Dwarf's ears if he didn't simmer down some. He could picture Selznak tapping up the cobbles of Gosset's drive with fog issuing from his ears rather than from his pipe.

The Squire, holding the watch in his right hand, bent over and picked up the stuffed snake that lay on the floor. He looked it over for a moment, laughed, and wiggled it in Selznak's face. He shoved the snake away into his coat for later use.

"So now you must have the blasted watch," said Selznak darkly. "And what will you do with it?"

"I don't want it," replied Escargot. "But you'll break the spell or you'll die when the sun comes up over the forest."

"Don't get theatrical with me," said Selznak. "What do I care for your threats? It's me who breaks the spell or no one at all. You know that as well as I do."

"Squire," said Escargot, "send your lads upstairs to find the dog. He's sleeping in the long corridor on the third level. On the fourth they'll find a room full of cages of beasts. Have them carry the beasts down, take them outdoors, and release them. On the fifth floor is a laboratory. Let them smash it to bits. But make sure they stay away from the sixth floor if they value their lives and their sanity."

Bufo, Yellow Hat, and Stick-a-bush dashed off up the stairs to do his bidding. In a few moments Bufo clumped back down carrying Ahab, who was in much the same condition as Jonathan and the Professor. He laid the dog next to Jonathan, who was, all in all, relieved to see Ahab, enchanted or otherwise. Shortly thereafter the three of them began to file down the stairs carrying cages of strange animals. Some of the cages held identifiable rabbits and raccoons and opossums and such, but many of the cages held beasts that no one beside Selznak the Dwarf had seen before. There must have been many cages of such things, for the three linkmen kept about their business industriously— up and down and up and down the stairs, then up and down some more. The Squire took a grave interest in the beasts, acquiring an instant fancy in one—another winged pig but with the nose of an opossum and the tail of a beaver. He instructed Stick-a-bush, who carried the cage, to lay it in the corner.

Dr. Selznak watched the proceedings, seemingly without interest. Finally he said, "Breaking my laboratory apart won't serve, you know."

Escargot remained silent. The Squire walked over and looked the Dwarf in the eye, pulling the snake out of his pocket and waving it in his face. Selznak pretended to pay him little mind. "You can reduce the tower to rubble, but your friends won't be any better off. I'll propose an option. If you'll give me your word that there'll be no chicanery, I'll start them back up. We'll revive my ape and he and I will leave. You'll not see us again."

"And the watch?" asked Escargot.

"The watch is mine," Selznak stated flatly.

"You haven't got any sense," said Escargot. The Squire apparently assumed that it would be a good time to tickle the Dwarf's ear with the tail of the snake. "There's another man," said Escargot, "who can start that watch up again. You know who I mean."

"And how," asked the Dwarf, "will you summon him? Send up a kite? A pigeon?"

Escargot was silent.

"The Squire will fly a kite," said the Squire helpfully, thrusting the ridiculous snake once again toward Selznak's ear and giggling. "The Squire must have a kite to fly."

Dooly, watching the proceedings but wary of coming within ten feet of Selznak, edged around past him and untied the bag on Jonathan's belt.

Jonathan felt like cheering when he realized what Dooly was up to and was powerfully glad that Dooly knew about the four coins. He was immediately deflated, however, when he considered that Dooly couldn't possibly know how to arrange the things.

"By golly, lad!" shouted Escargot. "You're the only one among us with an ounce of brain matter."

"Yes, sir," said Dooly. "I have a powerful lot of it. Mr. Bing said these coins was eyeballs—his eyeballs. But now I don't hardly see how they can be."

Selznak watched contemptuously, not knowing, of course, what it was Dooly was after in the bag. He seemed tired and had a new look of nervousness about him. Dooly found two of the coins and laid them on the hearth. He scrambled them this way and turned them over that way, and seemed amazed at the weird fishes that appeared then disappeared as the coins were flipped. Squire Myrkle watched the process nodding sagely, then turned the two coins over once or twice, marveling at a couple of particularly strange specimens.

"What ho?" shouted Escargot.

"Not much ho," said Dooly. "I don't get no eyeballs. I only get fish."

"Do you know the order?" asked Escargot.

"What order? I just heard there was eyeballs involved. I didn't hear about no order."

"Of course there's order, lad," Escargot replied. "There always is. Nothin' works without it except maybe goblins. Lay out one of the coins with the fish swimming east."

"Where's east?" Dooly sounded puzzled.

"Toward the broken window," said Escargot. "Turn it so it looks like he's swimming toward the window. Then take the next and make him swim toward the fireplace." Dooly carried out the orders down below. "Now put one next to that, but make sure it's faced west, out toward the big door."

"One next to that?" asked Dooly. "There ain't but two."

"There's four," Escargot said. "There's got to be two more in the pouch."

Dooly rummaged in the pouch once again, pulling out a red bean and a horse chestnut and a little round ivory ball with an elf rune on it before coming up with a third coin.

"Here it is," said Dooly, laying it next to the other two so that the fish on it faced the door.

"Now the fourth," said Escargot.

"Fourth?" said Dooly stubbornly. "A man ain't got but two eyes. Who needs four of 'em?"

"It won't work without four," said Escargot. "I know about these coins. Find the fourth and put it down facing the hall. Then take all four and turn them around clockwise so that they all face each other. So that their noses almost touch."

Dooly fumbled in the pouch, shaking out several odd

items. "I have it!" he shouted finally. "It was lost down in the corner."

Then a very strange thing happened. The coins, all at once, were not on the hearth at all; they were, apparently, back in Jonathan's pouch, or at least they weren't apparently any place else.

Escargot spoke from above: "Well, what are you all goggling at? Did *he* come?"

"He came," said Dooly, "but he went away again."

"Capital," said Escargot. "Absolutely first rate. We'll see some results now, by golly. Let's see if he can out-trump us now!"

Selznak didn't appear to be in the mood to out-trump anyone. He seemed, in fact, a bit haggard, as if the evening had worn him thin. Bufo, Yellow Hat, and Stick-a-bush dashed off upstairs for another load of cages, taking them, as instructed, outside and opening the cage doors.

"Fish!" said the Squire abruptly. "Fish and chips! Fish and vinegar! Clams and oysters! Squid and crab!" He confronted Selznak, who was clearly pondering his next move. "I'll eat now," said the Squire. The Dwarf said nothing. Once the idea of eating sprang into existence, it seemed to overwhelm Squire Myrkle. When Bufo strode up to report the laboratory smashed up and the strange animals outside, the Squire didn't seem to hear him. "The Squire will eat now," he said to Bufo.

"I could do with a spot myself," Bufo replied. "Let's have a look around for the pantry."

"The Squire will eat the pantry," said the Squire, who quite possibly was capable of such a feat. Bufo, knowing it was useless to argue, set off toward a likely looking alcove near the stairs in front of which stood the two inert goblins, one of them still holding in his hand a cup which contained whatever it was the goblins were drinking when Jonathan and the Professor first put the bench through the window. The Squire pushed at one of the goblins and the thing went over like a tree but landed in the same position he was in when he stood. Squire Myrkle shook his head as if in wonder over the goblin's stupidity. "Here we have it!" Bufo shouted from within the alcove, and the Squire, anxious to see what it was they had, lumbered in after him.

"I'm tired of this," Escargot called from his perch overhead. "My legs are beginning to cramp up and my foot's asleep. What do you have to say for yourself, mate?"

Selznak at first apparently had little to say for himself, but it looked as if he were thinking hard. He really hadn't many options. It likely seemed a poor idea all the way around to hang around and wait for the arrival of an airship full of unsympathetic elves.

"Perhaps we can come to an agreement," he said slowly.

"Of course we can," Escargot stated. "As quick as you please. Any number of them. They all begin with your waking up the Professor and Mr. Bing."

"I'll need the watch. The fat man took the watch. He's probably eaten it by now."

"Squire!" shouted Escargot. Not a moment passed before the Squire, squeezing through the arched stone doorway of the alcove, hulked back into the hall. He held what appeared to be a turkey leg in one hand and a tankard of ale in the other. There was a long, crusty loaf of bread shoved in under his arm. His cheeks puffed out like balloons, as if he were storing food against the winter.

"Give Doctor Selznak his watch, Squire. There's a good fellow," said Escargot.

The Squire lumbered over to where Selznak stood with his head in the noose and peered into his face. He broke off a lump of bread as big as his fist and offered it to him. The Dwarf seemed inclined neither to accept the piece of bread or to refuse it. He just stood there with his mouth clamped shut looking at the Squire evilly. The Squire waved it in front of his nose for a moment, shrugged, tore a great bite out of the turkey leg, and headed back toward the kitchen.

"The watch, Squire," shouted Escargot.

The Squire stopped, set his mug of ale down, and rummaged in his pockets. He brought out the stuffed snake, a rubber lizard, a handful of big marbles, and a glass globe about five inches in diameter, but no pocketwatch. "What do you have there, Squire?" asked Escargot. "What's that big glass ball?"

"It's not a watch," the Squire said, shaking his head. "It's a marble. A tremendous marble. It's the Squire's marble now." He held the thing up so that the rays of the rising sun shone through it. The globe seemed to be alive inside, as if an entire universe revolved within. Squire Myrkle stared into the globe, transfixed. The turkey leg in his free hand dropped from his fingers and *thwacked* against the stone floor, falling into the mug of ale and knocking it over.

"Squire!" shouted Escargot. "The watch, Squire!" But the Squire couldn't seem to hear a thing. Bufo, however, dashed out of the kitchen to see what the fuss was. "Is it this watch you want?" Bufo asked, holding the pocket-watch by its chain. "The Squire left it on the sink. He doesn't care much about watches—can't tell time actually. He says he doesn't need to."

"Give the watch to Doctor Selznak," said Escargot, "and take that globe away from the Squire."

Bufo did what he was told. When he plucked the globe from the Squire's hand, the Squire looked about him, searching for his turkey leg and ale, and was chagrined to see them spread about on the floor. "Who's been at these?" he asked, casting a suspicious eye around.

"That fellow over there," said Bufo quickly, pointing toward a skeleton. "Poor beggar was starving."

The Squire picked up the turkey leg, pulled a few bits of dust and floor scrap from it, and stuffed it into the grinning mouth of the skeleton which collapsed over backward, the turkey leg protruding from its mouth. "Chap's too thin," said the Squire, bending over and pinching at its bony wrist. "That can't be good."

"Not a bit," said Bufo. "Let's find something more to eat." He and the Squire disappeared once again in toward what must have been the pantry.

Selznak stood there fingering the watch as if contemplating some new deviltry. He was obviously loathe to simply give in, but he was undeniably in a tight spot. Escargot decided to have done with the contest.

"I'm going to hang by my hands from this beam," he said. "If you make a move toward the rope I'll drop, and you'll break my fall when you shoot up into the rafters. If you try to freeze me with the watch, I'll probably drop anyway and the result will be the same. Do you understand?"

"Frightfully clever of you," said the Dwarf.

"When I'm all arranged," said Escargot, "I'll let you know. You can wake these blokes up and hand the watch over to the Professor. You have nothing to gain by playing me false."

"What do I gain by cooperating?" asked Selznak.

"You can leave here with your idiotic ape."

"I want the globe," said Selznak.

"You'll have to talk to the Squire about that," said Escargot. "He seems to like it. It's just a toy anyhow. Get old Lumbog to make another one. Together you could probably figure out how to do it."

"Fine," said Selznak. "I agree. Shall we get on with it? I have work left undone."

"And it never will be done, most of it," said Escargot. "Ready on this end. No pranks now, or you won't be a dwarf any longer."

Selznak, with a cold look in his eye, poked the button atop the watch with his thumb, and Jonathan found himself scrambling up off of his pile of bones with such energy that he nearly piled head on into the Professor who leaped forward, finishing the lunge that had been cut short and dashing across to snatch the watch from the Dwarf's hand.

The task was obviously easier than the Professor supposed. There was no struggling or fighting involved. Selznak was trussed up and very clearly didn't need to be grappled with. The Professor pulled himself up short once he had the watch, a look of amazement on his face. "What the—" he said, seeing Yellow Hat and Stick-a-bush there and seeming to observe the noose around Selznak's neck for the first time. But he hadn't time to say much more.

Chapter 27

When Squire Myrkle Came

THERE was wild activity all through the hall. The goblin lying near the stair sprang up and, with its fellow, rushed about in circles as if having run mad. The skeletons all woke with a jerky start, and one rose unsteadily to its feet, astonished by the turkey leg in its mouth. It pulled the thing free, losing a couple of teeth in the process, and dropped it to the floor.

The Squire and Bufo wandered in out of the kitchen and watched in amazement as, one by one, the odd collection of goblins and skeletons found the open window and door and made off into the morning. From outside could be heard a cacophony of wild squawks and screes as the animals in the cages celebrated their freedom, following the goblins into the woods. The pig-bird in the corner yowled once, then looked about to gauge its effect. The Squire went over and poked several lumps of bread through the cage bars, and the thing was immediately satisfied, apparently liking the look of the Squire. It seemed to be a pleasant enough mutant.

The Professor held the watch at arm's length, handling the thing as if it were an infernal device. "It was the watch!" said Professor Wurzle. "It must have been the watch!"

"It is that," said Escargot. "Every bit of it."

"I can see that," said the Professor. "But I mean for the past who knows how long. Where have I been? I was here all along, right?"

"That's right. All along. Frozen," Escargot explained.

"Astonishing!" the Professor looked the watch over with new interest. "Absolutely astonishing."

"Hold him now," said Escargot, "while I get down from the ceiling." He appeared a few moments later on the stairs, the cloak of invisibility under his arm.

"Where did you think you were?" Jonathan asked the Professor.

"Why I don't know," said the Professor. "Right here, I suppose. But one moment you were diving into the bones and I was set to lunge for the watch, and the next, here we all are."

"You didn't see any of it?" asked Jonathan, perplexed.

"Any of what?"

"Of the Squire and the ape and Lonny Gosset and everything?"

"I can't say that I did, did you?"

"Every bit," said Jonathan. Then, after thinking for a moment he said, "Almost every bit. There was one point there I'm not sure of."

"This is odd," said the Professor. "Dreadfully odd. What are we going to do with the good doctor?"

"He goes free," Escargot stated flatly.

"I don't at all agree with that," the Professor objected. "We should hold him until the elves arrive."

"You hold him. But first he goes free; then you can catch him again. I stick to my bargains."

"What bloody bargain?" asked the Professor. "I don't know anything about any such bargain."

"The bargain I made when you were stiff down here," said Escargot.

Jonathan and Dooly bent over Lonny Gosset, who was showing signs of stirring. "I agree with Mr. Escargot," said Jonathan. "This has been ghastly enough already. Let's have done with it. Give him his hat and stick and ape and send him on his way. Without the watch he doesn't amount to such an incredible lot anyway."

"Why did you make such a wild bargain in the first place?" asked the Professor. "You had him. All you had to do was truss him up and wait it out."

"Because," said Escargot, "I have no intention of waiting anything out. You gentlemen will have to give Twickenham my best. Tell him I've taken his coat to have it cleaned and that it worked admirably. Tell him that if he has any other villains to subdue he can look me up. It's been pleasant working with you lads. I don't regret it a bit."

"Are you leaving, Grandpa?" Dooly asked, abandoning Lonny Gosset. "When are you coming back?"

"Come spring, Dooly lad. In April you and I will take a bit of a cruise. How does that sound?"

"It sounds fine," said Dooly proudly. "Don't take no nickels, Grandpa."

"I never mess with them, Dooly. Not Theophile Escargot." And with that revelation Escargot pulled his cloak on and disappeared. Jonathan heard his feet scrunch across toward the door and down the stone steps. All was silent when he reached the grass outside.

Selznak picked up his pipe and staff and went over and prodded the Beddlington Ape. Like Lonny Gosset, the ape revived and stood up shakily, looking about as if lost. With the ape in tow, Selznak followed after Escargot, not looking at any of the rafters or linkmen, but making good his escape before any of them changed his mind and decided to make an issue of his departure. Outside he stood for a moment on the drive. Then he whacked his staff against the stones savagely. A blast of cold wind swirled roundabout him, blowing his cloak in a rush of sailing autumn oak leaves. When the wind died away the Dwarf and his ape were gone.

"We shouldn't have allowed him to leave," the Professor said.

"We were probably lucky that we didn't force the issue," replied Jonathan. "Who knows what capers he was likely to cut?"

Lonny Gosset moaned and held his head in his hand.

The Squire offered him half a loaf of bread, but he didn't take it. He looked at the Squire in amazement and sat on the bench that the Professor and Jonathan had tossed in through the window.

Jonathan rummaged in his bag and hauled out the four coins once again. He laid them on the hearth, each facing a different direction, then turned each to face the other. The fish on the coins shimmered and seemed to wiggle a bit and fade. Tiny beams of rainbow shot out and revolved about like the little rainbows thrown by a prism dangling in a sunlit window. The fish blinked away, the coins seemed smooth and empty as glass, and then, on each of them, a puffy-cheeked face appeared wearing a pair of enormous fishbowl spectacles. There could be no doubt as to who it was, looking about the hall there from the vantage point of the four coins.

There was the noose, dangling empty. There were Jonathan and the Professor, awake and healthy. There, in the Professor's hand was the pocketwatch, no longer, obviously, in the possession of the Dwarf. The Moon Man smiled, winked, and vanished.

"Let's go," said Jonathan. "Our job's not done until we get those cakes home."

Lonny Gosset was in no shape to walk through the swamp, so they put him on one of the linkmen's ponies. They shut the oaken door of the tower, not bothering to put out the fire in the fireplace or to investigate the upper reaches. Jonathan had had enough of Hightower Ridge. Professor Wurzle gathered up his ruined oboe device and, as they left, said that come spring he intended to return and poke around in the tower a bit more extensively.

And so off they went toward town, winding along through the swamp which wasn't half so forbidding by day as it had been by night. Hobbs sat in a chair on the board-walk in town, drinking a morning cup of coffee. He seemed amiable—far more so, in fact, than he had on their trip downriver. Upon being informed of the defeat of the Dwarf and his goblins, however, he smiled and nodded and said only that Dr. Selznak was one of his best customers —his only customer, actually. Jonathan told him that with any luck trade would pick up noticeably in the next few weeks, and Hobbs was happy to hear it. They left Lonny Gosset in Hobbs' care and hastened away toward Hinkle Creek, but not until the Squire had bought up Hobbs' supply of pecan twirls and a couple dozen eggs. Besieging towers, apparently, had a stimulating effect on the Squire's appetite.

The raft was untouched. The bushes were still heaped about the deck and twined through the mast, and there were no signs of goblins—no fishbones or bits of scrap and trash. Jonathan, the Professor, and Dooly all encouraged the linkmen to come along upriver with them to Twombly Town for the Christmas holidays, but the linkmen very graciously declined. They had, after all, their own families and celebrations to attend to at home, and they'd be several days still on the river road before they crossed over into linkman territory. And perhaps more importantly yet, they had sent word on from Snopes' Ferry that a linkman army must be raised and marched to Stooton, and that they'd meet that same army along the road after they'd dealt with the party of goblins who had stolen the Squire's marbles bag. That was the first mention of the lost marbles bag, and it gave Jonathan a tolerably good idea. Anyway, Bufo pointed out that with the flight of the Dwarf and the recovery of the watch, the evil in Stooton could no doubt be overcome without the aid of the Squire's army. In fact, no longer being held in thrall by the Dwarf's enchantment, the goblins at Stooton were likely already on their way back upriver to the Goblin Wood. Bufo pointed out that armies are well and good when a menace is abroad in the land, but when it's not, then no one with any sense would want to pretend it is. The sooner the army could be disbanded and sent home, the better off everyone would be.

It all made a great deal of sense to Jonathan, and to the other rafters as well, although all of them were sad to part company with the jolly linkmen for the third time in as many weeks. But part they did, after two very important things were accomplished, one of which concerned the bright idea Jonathan had come up with at the mention of the Squire's marble bag.

Although Mayor Bastable's hat looked dapper, or something like that, on the Squire, it was, after all, Mayor Bastable's hat. Jonathan, therefore, decided to effect a trade. So after the invitation to winter in Twombly Town was extended and politely refused, he hauled out the marbles bag recovered from the goblin at Stooton Slough and traded Squire Myrkle straight across for the hat.

"Marbles!" shouted the Squire, overwhelmed.

"The very same," said Jonathan, "that Mr. Blump gave you in Seaside."

"Good old Blump," said the Squire kindly. "Blump, Blump, Blump. He gave the Squire a bag of marbles once, much like this. Very like it."

"This very bag," said Bufo helpfully.

"But it was stolen by rascals," said the Squire, "after we crossed at Snopes' Ferry. I thrashed the little goblins from one side of the river to another. Beat them silly. Took this hat from them too."

"So you did, Squire!" shouted Bufo approvingly. "It was an astonishing sight, gentlemen: the Squire with his truncheon defending the ferry. They set fire to Snopes' farm and ran off his pigs, but they were a sorry-looking crowd when the Squire reined in on Behemoth there." He pointed to the Squire's pony—a pony considerably larger than its fellows and so deserving, likely, to be called Behemoth. "There were forty of 'em," Bufo continued, "but four hundred wouldn't have slowed down the Squire."

"Well it might have *slowed him down*," put in Stick-a-bush, who had a look on his face which seemed to imply that Bufo were laying it on thick.

"Not a bit," said Bufo. "The filthy things were on him in a trice, yowling and making their ridiculous noises, but the Squire laid about him and scattered the whole pack from there atop Behemoth. Smote the things—that's what he did. Smote them mightily, right down the river road, past Snopes' farm and off the end of the dock onto the ferry. Then he smote 'em into the river!"

"Hooray!" cried Dooly, overwhelmed.

"Smote, smote, smote from the boat!" said the Squire, a poet himself in a sense.

"But they stole his marbles bag, the blighters," said Yellow Hat.

"And we found it again down toward Stooton," said Dooly. "I smote a few myself with a frying pan."

"The Cheeseman gives me a new bag," said the Squire, still not having fully understood the complicated turn of events. "When the Squire calls for a cheese, Mr. Bing has it. When it's marbles he wants, why there's Mr. Bing." The Squire stuck out his hand so Jonathan could shake it. When Jonathan took it, the Squire waved their clasped hands around thrice in a circle and said, cryptically, "Windmill, windmill, windmill," before letting go.

"That's one of Blump's gags," explained Yellow Hat.

"I thought so," said Jonathan.

The Squire peeked into the bag, then closed it up quick, not wanting to engender any marble rivers. He squinted up at the rafters. "Why, Mr. Bing, did the elf put a couch on his front stoop?"

Jonathan guessed that the answer had to do with certain scientific principles, quite possibly with rigor mortis, but he couldn't for the life of him see how. "I haven't any idea," he said.

"So the Squire can sit about on spring evenings," said the Squire, laughing heartily thereafter. The rest of the party laughed too, Dooly most of all. It seemed to be a far more sensible gag to Dooly than the rigor mortis joke had seemed. Stick-a-bush, on the other hand, didn't laugh quite so heartily but seemed puzzled by the thing, or else not given over quite so much to politeness as the others.

Bufo, after they'd all had ample time to appreciate the Squire's anecdote, cleared his throat and was overcome by a look of inspiration and poetics. "Gump and I have a bit of a poem," he said, "which, given the occasion, you might find suitable."

"Here, here!" cried the Professor with enthusiasm.

"By all means," said Jonathan, learning for the first time Yellow Hat's actual name.

And so Bufo and Yellow Hat, or Gump as it were, launched into their poem, each of them reciting every other verse:

> *Oh goblins laughed at Snopes' farm*
> *Til Squire Myrkle came.*

> Then goblins up and down the road
> Cried out, in fear, his name.
>
> About them raged the barn afire;
> They strutted round and pranced,
> And forced poor Snopes, incredibly,
> To perform a foolish dance.
>
> A tragic sight it was that eve
> When the Squire came along,
> But goblins paused and quaked in fear
> And sang a different song.
>
> When through the smoke they spied him,
> Wide as half the sea,
> They fled into the waters there,
> And he laughed to see them flee.
>
> Oh the goblins fled from Snopes' farm
> When Squire Myrkle came,
> A-marching through the mig-weed
> A-shouting out his name!

"You've gone and boggered up the last verse," said Gump. "You've tossed your filthy mig-weed into it and ruined it!"

"Nonsense!" cried the Professor before Bufo had a chance to protest. "It was capital—beginning to end. Couldn't have been better." Following the Professor's enthusiastic response, there was relatively thunderous applause. The Professor repeated that he thought that the poem was astonishingly good and said that he and Jonathan and Dooly would carry it back to Twombly Town to spread the tale of the Squire's heroics.

They shook hands, finally, and said a few goodbyes, and the three rafters promised to come downriver on a visit fairly soon. With that, the linkmen were off, down along the river road toward the Elfin Highlands and linkman territory.

Jonathan, Dooly, and the Professor set about pitching brush off the deck, and Ahab did his part too, wandering about and looking things over as if glad to be on the river once more. By ten o'clock or so they were poling the raft out of the mouth of Hinkle Creek, and Jonathan and Dooly set to pedaling while the Professor manned the tiller. None of them had had satisfactory sleep over the past forty hours or so, but the promise of home and the excitement of victory served to overcome any tiredness and to rather buoy them up and push them along.

They pedaled off and on all that day and most of the next until, in the afternoon, a good wind blew up, cold as a smelt, and they dropped the sails and made good time in the direction of home. They were all, by that time, bundled in jackets and blankets, and they had the coffee pot going out on deck along with a number of hot potatoes to take the chill off a person.

"I wish I'd been a bit more help there at the tower," said Jonathan when all of them were gathered below the tiller canopy, munching steaming potatoes.

"You and I both," said the Professor. "But Escargot's plan, if it was a plan, worked surprisingly well, and you and I played our part in it."

"I suppose so," said Jonathan. "When he rushed off after Dooly, though, I thought we were in for it. I thought we'd end up with fins and beaks and traded to a bunjo man for string beans or something."

"That was a powerful mean looking skelington," said Dooly, mispronouncing the word. "I thought he meant to eat me."

"He ate the Squire's turkey leg," said Jonathan. "Or at least one of them did. I don't think it agreed with him. Seemed to be hard on his teeth."

"Well I just ran for it," Dooly continued. "I didn't even think. Grandpa said it was a reaction. I lit out down the road and ran into a bunch of goblins coming up out of the swamp. There was a mess of 'em, all coming along like sixty. And mean! Let me say. And behind 'em waving this big club was old Mr. Gosset, just wild! It was a sight. Strike me for a lubber if it weren't."

"Strike me for a lubber?" asked Jonathan.

"That's what Grandpa would have said, him going for a pirate and all. Anyway, I sat in the bush, shaking like crazy, and here comes Grandpa, whispering my name. I, of course, cries out, and he says that I'm to stay in the bush and leave the fighting alone—that it weren't safe up at the tower. He said you'd fetch me after it was over.

"Well I hung around for a few minutes and there was a powerful lot of shouting and all. It seemed like Mr. Gosset was giving them goblins a lesson. Then who comes up the path but the Squire and Stick-a-bush and all, and my don't the Squire look grand. He was ready! So I jump out and nearly scare the daylights out of 'em, and the five of us and Mr. Gosset, we cleaned them goblins up. Then that ape come up out of nowhere and whacked Mr. Gosset, and the Squire said he'd get the ape, and he did. That's what happened to me. That's it in a nut."

"Well we were all glad to see you," said Jonathan. "I was never so happy to see anyone as I was to see you and the Squire and all. It would have gone bad for us otherwise."

The Professor agreed and said it must have been a close one. Then they all agreed that the Squire was a continual amazement and was "one of the lads."

"I'm dashed if I can understand why you could see and hear the whole affair and I couldn't, though, Jonathan," said the Professor. "It could quite possibly have something to do with atmospheric pressures. The fog, you know, presses in at the lobes of the ear and roundabout the forebrain and has a direct effect on sound and vision."

"I didn't know that, actually," said Jonathan. "That's fascinating."

"It's my theory," the Professor continued, "that due to my slightly advanced age, such pressures had the effect of closing off certain vital humors and that such stoppage resulted in my total incapacitation."

"You're probably right, Professor," said Jonathan, "although I don't know anything about humors and pressures and such. It could be, though, that I was the exception to the rule. I'm certain, in fact, that when Dooly pulled the last of the four coins out of my pouch, I missed a good bit, and then came back around when the coins were returned. If I had to guess I'd say it was elf magic that got in the way."

"Magic again," said the Professor. "That's too easy. A

man of science doesn't trot out magic to explain odd phenomena."

"But you can't deny the coins work," said Jonathan, "or that the watch stops things short."

"Not at all," said the Professor. "But I firmly believe that if we pried the back off this watch, we'd see a thing or two that made admirable sense." The Professor opened his pocketknife as if to have a go at the back of the watch.

"Professor!" Jonathan shouted, flabbergasted at the very idea of such meddling.

The Professor laughed and put the knife away. "As you say, Jonathan," he said. "You're the captain of this vessel. If it's magic that makes things go round, then that's fine with me." He studied the watch for a few moments, turning it over in his hand. "I wonder if there's any reference to this sort of thing in *Limpus*?" he said finally, and ducked into the cabin for a minute before emerging with one of the ponderous *Tomes of Limpus* in which he was quickly lost.

After that, they sailed upriver until long after dark, and moored the raft well out into the river to take no chance of shenanigans. After all, the Dwarf had fled but there was no telling what sort of pranks he was still capable of playing. Jonathan was fairly sure they could deal with his fog and his dancing skeletons and such. If worse came to worst, the Professor had the pocketwatch and could take a turn at freezing the Dwarf or his ape or any of his other odd minions. Still, they decided they'd all sleep more soundly with a hundred feet of river water stretching away to either side of the raft.

And sleep soundly they did. None of them, including Ahab, awoke before ten the following morning. Jonathan started to hop out of his bunk when it struck him that it was what you might call desperately cold. His breath was as visible in that morning air as steam from the smokestack of a train, and the warmth developed sleeping under a feather comforter all night evaporated almost immediately. He pulled on two pairs of socks which, wisely, he'd left under the covers all night, and a sweater and a jacket, both of which seemed frightfully cold. As soon as he abandoned his bunk and set about building a fire in the stove, Ahab climbed in and buried himself beneath the blankets, peering out at Jonathan with a relatively satisfied look in his eye.

After coffee and breakfast had geared them up a bit and given them heart, they went out into the crisp morning. There was a gray sky overhead and it seemed a safe bet that it was working itself into the mood for a good snow.

An inch of ice crusted the low spots on the deck, and the seats in front of the paddlewheel were covered with frost. The idea of sitting there on the cold seat and pedaling the raft upriver wasn't too attractive, but there wasn't much choice—there was no wind to speak of, only a little ear-numbing breeze from up the valley.

So Jonathan and Dooly put canvas cushions down on the seats, and although they were still cold as codfish, it was better than sitting on frosted wood. It turned out that pedaling was just the ticket, however. After ten minutes or so Jonathan peeled off his jacket and pushed up the sleeves on his sweater and began to feel bad for the Professor huddled there shivering at the tiller.

So it went for about three hours, and after lunch it went along so again. The shoreline was beginning to look a bit more familiar, the closer they got to home. The alders were, for the most part, bare of leaves and the forest on either side of the Oriel was dark and quiet. Few animals seemed to be venturing out for any reason at all. Most, likely, were digging an extra room or so in an underground home and counting the acorns and pinion nuts to decide whether to make one last topside trip. Only the shore grasses and the water weeds were green and moving. An occasional batch of ducks landed on the river to rest up, and they quacked around and shoved their heads under the surface to see what was doing down in the river world below. But they didn't wait around long before they were off south, on their way to winter in some sunny clime.

It was no time to be out adventuring—no time to be tramping in the woods or sailing on the river. It was a time to be piling logs in the fireplace and putting up storm windows and starting up the wood stove out in the shop a half hour or so before setting in to work. It was a time to sit in front of the fire in the evening and be happy you *weren't* out sailing on the river or tramping in the woods.

Jonathan wondered what direction Escargot would take, whether he would live out the winter in his submarine at Thrush Haven, or sail away south down the coast in the wake of those flocks of ducks. He was probably on his way at that very moment, invisible beneath his cloak, striding along the twisted paths of the Goblin Wood and making plans.

Chapter 28

Three Men and a Dog

❈

LATE that afternoon they ran up onto a sandbar, but before they were stuck they quit pedaling, and the current pushed them off and back into deeper water. Dooly was the first to point out that they'd had problems with that sandbar once before. Sure enough, it was the very spot at which they'd run up against the trolls. But there were no trolls to be seen now. Aside from a rare snow troll, most of the beasts had dozed off in the deep recesses of a cavern somewhere and wouldn't awaken until March or April. Even trolls can be depended on for that.

As they swung out around the bar, Jonathan caught a brief glimpse of something moving along within the trees—walking along the river road on his way up the valley. At first Jonathan feared it was Selznak, and he started to whisper to the Professor to push the tiller over and angle the raft across to the far shore. But as he watched, he saw that the figure moving through the trees was clearly no dwarf. It was someone tall and thin—strangely tall, in fact—and wearing fairly colorful robes.

"I know who that is," said Dooly in a loud whisper.

"So do I," said Jonathan. "Let's see if he wants a lift."

Both of them shouted and waved. The robed figure paused, pushed his way through the branches of the shore trees, and clambered down onto the riverbank, knocking his hat off as he did so. It was Miles the Magician, wearing, or attempting to wear, the necessary props. He seemed happy to see them and waved his arms, so they steered the raft in around the bar and held it steady with poles while Miles climbed aboard.

"There might be trouble brewing up toward Twombly Town," said he. "I don't doubt it a bit. I'm on my way up there now to see what I can do."

The rafters clambered for an explanation as they poled back out into the Oriel and pedaled furiously to get the paddlewheel going. So Miles continued, setting his cap on the deck, tousling his hair, and collapsing onto a deck chair. "I saw him last night," he said, "the Dwarf with the ape, going along in a little fog up the river road. They had some purpose, mind you, there was no mistaking it. They were intent on mayhem upriver, and they were traveling fast, on some sort of enchantment. And there's been movements in the forest—parties of goblins heading south toward the Wood and trolls out of their caves and following along in the same direction. I saw two skeletons late last night, but they didn't seem to know *where* they were going; it was more like they were just out for a stroll. Something's afoot. Something happened to put Selznak and his brood out of joint."

The Professor, not normally given over to theatrical behavior, couldn't pass up the opportunity to pull the pocketwatch out of his coat and dangle it by its chain. Miles, startled, jumped up and peered closely at it, turning it over so as to have a look at the face, puffy-cheeked and wearing spectacles, that smiled there, etched into the elf silver.

"Do you know what this is?" Miles asked, clapping his hat back onto his head.

"Sure!" Dooly almost shouted. "We just stole it, or at least old Grandpa did. We whacked the daylights out of the ape, too."

"Well I'll be!" said Miles, mystified. "That's what the story is, is it? No wonder there's an uproar. You've taken half his power away. All of it, really."

The three of them then told Miles the Magician about the siege at Hightower Ridge and about the Squire's heroics at Snopes' Ferry and then again, when he and Bufo and Gump and Stick-a-bush arrived in the nick of time. Finally all the stories were told and they sat about into the late afternoon, puffing on pipes and taking turns at the pedaling, making as good a time, all in all, as they had at any point on the voyage.

"What I don't follow about this whole affair," said the Professor, "is why Theophile Escargot sold the watch to that fiend in the first place. I've never gotten an answer to that question, and by golly I want one. Now I'll admit that I didn't have much faith in the man at first—I beg your pardon, Dooly, for saying it—but I see him in a new light now. He didn't have to do what he did, but he did it."

The Professor paused and tamped his pipe. "Have you heard of the Lumbog Globe, sir?" he asked Miles.

"Oh, indeed," said Miles, his eyes lighting up. "I saw it once, long ago. It does what they say it does. I can vouch for it. It's one of the seven elf wonders, actually. As valuable, in its way, as anything there is."

"And were you aware," said the Professor, "that the Lumbog Globe was in Hightower, that the Dwarf owned it?"

"Seems I heard such a rumor," said Miles. "But then all sorts of things were said about Selznak the Dwarf."

"Well, that rumor was true," said Professor Wurzle. "I saw it myself. Squire Myrkle came upon it during the siege. Found it near the kitchen apparently. Now I could have sworn that Escargot's interest in Hightower centered around that globe, that he wanted it for himself. But he let the Squire have it. Didn't bat an eye. Acted as if the Squire was welcome to it. No, gentlemen, I pegged the man wrong, and I'm sorry for it. And that makes it all the more strange. Why in the devil did he sell that watch to Selznak? He would have done better to have thrown it into the river."

"The answer is simple, really," said Miles, as if astonished at the Professor's curiosity. "He ransomed the lad here. He hadn't much choice."

"Ransom?" said Jonathan.

"Kidnap money. Blackmail. What ever it is you'd like to call it."

"What lad?" asked Dooly, looking about. He was the only lad around that he could think of.

"Why you!" said Miles looking shrewdly at him. "But you don't remember it. I had a hand in that—something in the way of a spell. Mesmerized you, actually."

"To what purpose?" asked the Professor, puzzled and interested.

"Well," said Miles, "I can't vouch for it, because I've never been there. But I've heard, and I'm pretty sure it's true, that some awful things go on inside that tower— things that a chap wouldn't care to remember, if you follow me."

Jonathan and the Professor nodded agreement. They followed him pretty well.

"So when Escargot was forced to make the trade he brought the lad to me, and I wiped it out of his mind. Swept it away like sawdust off a pub floor, so to speak."

"Well, I'll be a herring," said the Professor, shaking his head over the affair. "Mesmerization is it? And very effective too, clearly." He looked at Dooly for a moment as if he were a specimen.

"Well I don't know nothing of it," said Dooly. "And I don't care to. If a person doesn't know about nothing, he don't care about it."

"That's certainly the truth," Jonathan agreed. "That was well put." But he'd barely said it when all of them, almost as one, became aware of a buzzing sound somewhere up in the dim skies. There was no wondering this time about the nature of the sound. It could only be one thing. And sure enough, there it was, a dark speck in the distance, zooming along just below the clouds, following the swerve of the shore, east along the Oriel. In a minute or two the airship drew near, dropped almost to the treetops, and sailed past overhead, Twickenham and his merry elf friends waving out at the four on the raft. The airship circled once then shot along upriver in the direction of Twombly Town.

On the following day, when the raft passed the first outlying farm and sailed within view of the top of the widow's windmill, the elves were still there. The airship lay upon the grass below the windmill, and a crowd of towns-people—likely everyone in the village—gathered there on the docks.

Gilroy Bastable, wearing an immense and ridiculous fur cap, stood arm in arm with Twickenham. The band struck up "The Jolly Huntsman" and squawked along wonderfully well when the raft came sailing around the last bend. Hats flew, people huzzahed, and there was more or less general revelry all up and down the banks and across the dock.

Jonathan knew Mayor Bastable too well to suppose there was any chance of his not having a speech prepared against the day of the rafter's return. Professor Wurzle himself was scribbling away furiously on a note pad, a sure indication that yet another speech was going to be tried out on the afternoon crowd. And there, beside the mayor and Twick-enham, was old Beezle. There was never an occasion about which Beezle could think of nothing to say. Perhaps, thought Jonathan, it would be possible to pretend to be ill and so oil out of any ceremony. But on the other hand, if the people wanted ceremony, it was the least he could do to oblige them good-naturedly. It was just as well that he felt that way, because there was ceremony aplenty that after-noon.

Everyone, as he predicted, made a speech. Beezle's was by far the most astonishing, being supplemented by charts and such, and ending with his suggestion that, in view of chicanery along the river, the town be fortified according to a sixteen-point plan over the following ten years. The plan itself was phenomenal and was such an engineering marvel that no one but Professor Wurzle understood even the first of the sixteen points. The Professor, after very patiently listening to Beezle's plan, whispered to Jonathan that the whole idea was tripe. Everyone clapped, to Beezle's joy, and then, as usual, forgot entirely about any mention of a sixteen-point plan.

The kegs, finally, were unloaded and hauled on a cart to the Guildhall where the cakes and elfin gifts were to be passed out among the townspeople. Many of the gifts were wrapped, and many were not. Children piled around and shouted when the lid was pried off one of the gift kegs. Inside were all the sorts of things they'd hoped for: brass kaleidoscopes with real jewels inside and yo-yos that threw rainbows of colored sparks when twirled and collapsible sleds that avoided rocks and trees and cliffs without being made to and jack-in-the-boxes that sprang open and released a shower of lavender butterflies and bags and bags and bags of tin soldiers and marbles and other toys less magical, but every bit as wonderful.

Mayor Bastable, overwhelmed, was perhaps as interested in the elfin gifts as were the children. Finally the Professor insisted that the lid of the keg be hammered down, since the mayor seemed intent upon digging down into its depths just to see what else might be there. Mrs. Bastable and little baby Gilroy rolled in at about then with a wagon on which sat a monumental tub of mulled cider and enough chocolate chip cookies so that no one had to worry about taking a third or fourth.

The townspeople clambered, finally, for a speech from Jonathan. He gave it a good bit of thought and said, finally, that he was happy to be home. Then he gave Mayor Bastable his hat back. For a moment the mayor didn't recognize the thing, battered and weedy as it was, but after turning it over and examining the hatband, he said, "By gum!" in a thoroughly pleased sort of way, handed his fur cap to Mrs. Bastable, and put the old river cap atop his head. "How in the world?" he began, then paused, took off the cap, and shook his head over it.

"I haven't any idea," said Jonathan. "All I can say is that your hat has had a few owners over the past weeks—trees and rivers and oceans and linkmen and goblins—and here it is back home."

"Amazing!" said Gilroy. Everyone else agreed that it was pretty amazing, and then insisted on riding the rafters up and down in front of the Guildhall, hip-hip-hooraying the whole time. That was just the sort of thing elves approve of, so they joined in and hoorayed right along until everyone had hoorayed as much as they cared to.

Twickenham and Thrimp, after all the speeches and cavorting were done, climbed into the airship and climbed back out again toting a great long clock, taller than both of them, and stout as a tree.

Twickenham presented it to Mayor Bastable, who made

another speech involving wonderful elves who give away wonderful clocks. The mayor started the thing up and moved the hands around to the top of the hour. The clock chimed in a deep, resonant way, as if it were a clock the size of a mountain, chiming from the far end of the valley. On the face of the clock was a grinning moon wearing a pair of immense, fishbowl spectacles and looking down over a twilit countryside of cottages, all made, oddly enough, of cheese. When the clock chimed, a caped, pipe-smoking mechanical dwarf issued from the recesses of the clock, pursued close on by a pitching raft. On the deck of the raft sat three men and a dog.

It was an astonishing clock altogether, and the mayor decided that it should sit in the Guildhall until a gazebo could be built for it in the center of the square. The townspeople cheered at the thought of it.

Jonathan made a final brief speech, insisting that the depiction on the clock was rather a glorification of the whole adventure, since he and Dooly and the Professor and Ahab had set out after cakes and gifts and not evil dwarfs. He told the story of how Theophile Escargot had been the "ace in the hole" and of how Squire Myrkle had appeared at the window to poleaxe the Beddlington Ape and save the day. He ended the speech by reciting Bufo's poem, "When Squire Myrkle Came," and the saga so enlivened the crowd that they insisted on riding the rafters up and down on their shoulders again, all of them cheering mightily.

It was the fall of night and the cold north wind, finally, that sent everyone home. The next day but one would be Christmas Day, and it was a good season to be indoors. Jonathan was feeling that way himself. As far as he was concerned, he could pretty much do without all the back-slapping and the riding up and down. He invited Twickenham and his company as well as Miles the Magician to spend a few days at his home, but they all politely refused—understanding, likely, that they would put rather a strain on the accommodations. Miles said that he was on his way upriver to the City of the Five Monoliths, that Selznak and his ape were quite possibly headed *that* way, since they clearly had bypassed Twombly Town. It was in the City of the Five Monoliths that Selznak had operated his sideshow. Even though the watch had been recovered and given to Twickenham, the Dwarf would bear close observation. Or at least that's what Miles told Jonathan.

So the elves departed and Miles departed and Dooly went off to his sister's house. The Professor shook Jonathan's hand and he too took off, saying that he had a few score pages of notes he wanted to scribble down yet.

In the end, Mayor Bastable went along with Jonathan to make sure, as he put it, that everything was shipshape. They hauled a cartload of Jonathan's things, Ahab riding along asleep on top. Jonathan lit the lantern he kept on the porch, wiggled the key in the lock, and swung the door open. Inside, smack in the center of the room, was a great, fresh Christmas tree, glittering with glass baubles and tinsel and smelling like a pine forest after an autumn rain. "Why—" said Jonathan. "How in the world?"

"We all knew you'd be back," said Gilroy Bastable, smiling and winking and happy as a cherub over his surprise. "There was never any doubt. Not for a moment. And tomorrow, being Christmas Eve day, we're all coming round as usual, I suppose, for cakes and cheese and port. And how in the world could you be expected to set up such a feast as that if you had to worry at the same time about decorating a tree?"

Jonathan nodded. How indeed? The mayor stuck around long enough to empty the cart. In the crates of books were a few Christmas gifts that Jonathan had carried along from Seaside. There were gifts for Mr. and Mrs. Bastable that the mayor insisted upon shaking and listening to and gifts for Dooly and the Professor and for Jonathan himself. And there were even a few gifts with no name at all on them so that droppers-in might not feel left out. As each gift was added to the growing pile under the tree, the tree itself seemed to grow a bit brighter and gayer. Jonathan hauled out two old oak bookcases from his attic and he and Gilroy Bastable loaded them full of the books he'd found at the mouse bookstore in Seaside. The mayor nodded in appreciation and carried armfuls over so that Jonathan could arrange them just so.

Finally, the cart empty, Jonathan started a good fire in

the hearth. It would have been a fine thing, he thought, to have swept up and brought along some of the green skeleton dust, just to see if he could conjure a skeleton from the flames and give the mayor an odd thrill. But likely he'd have to burn bones instead of oak logs to pull it off, and that seemed like an altogether bad idea, so it was just as well that he didn't save any of the dust. Best not to mess around with that sort of thing anyway, he supposed.

When the fire was popping, he dug around until he found a likely bottle of brandy and a can of Bledsoes Red Mixture, the mayor's favorite tobacco, and he and Gilroy Bastable filled a pipe, dribbled a spot of brandy into a glass, and slid into easy chairs where they sat puffing contentedly. Everything looked good—just as Jonathan was sure it should look. The books, the tree glowing in the firelight, the pipe and the drink and the fire in the fireplace and Ahab stretched out on the rug before the hearth—all of it couldn't be better.

"It's good to be home," Jonathan said, nodding in general agreement with himself. Mayor Bastable gave Jonathan a profound look. Then he mussed about in his hair with his fingers and said, "Indeed it is," giving the brandy bottle a profound look. Jonathan asked him what he'd think of another dash of brandy and a bit of cheese. Gilroy Bastable, putting his feet onto a stool and tamping away at the bowl of his pipe, said that as far as he could tell at the moment, all things considered, a ball of cheese and another spot of brandy would suit him down to the ground.

ABOUT THE AUTHOR

Jim Blaylock was born in Long Beach, California, in 1950. At present he lives in Southern California with his wife, Viki, and his son, John. He graduated from California State University at Fullerton in 1974 with an M.A. in English. Now he writes and teaches and, in his spare time, works at learning to build cabinets. His favorite author is Robert Louis Stevenson: his favorite book is *Tristram Shandy*. His life has been very placid, though in 1976 he and his wife were rushed at late one night by a Surinam toad while they slept. The author wrestled it to the floor and dumped it into an aquarium on the service porch. His fears that it was Cthulhu were unfounded. Nothing like that ever happened to him again.